Dear Goddess

Sophie Parkin

HEADLINE

First published in 2000
by HEADLINE BOOK PUBLISHING

10 9 8 7 6 5 4 3 2 1

ISBN 0 7472 6406 6

Typeset by Letterpart Ltd
Reigate, Surrey

Printed and bound in Great Britain by
Mackays of Chatham plc, Chatham, Kent

HEADLINE BOOK PUBLISHING
A division of the Hodder Headline Group
338 Euston Road
London NW1 3BH

www.headline.co.uk
www.hodderheadline.com

For Paris and his kind judgement,
love Mum.

Acknowledgements

Thank you and God bless for your inspiration and friendship.

Bruce Lloyd, Shaun de Warren, Ramana, Clare Foss, Lisa Eveleigh, Michael McCarthy, Tania Martin, Sarah Baron, Dominic Berning, Matthew Glendinning, Josephine Grenleigh White, Timna Woolard, Mr Crowe, Posh Charles, Sue Dalgleish, Claudia Vispi, Dean Bright, Pamina, Ian 'Pussycat' Crawshaw, Dick Bradsell, Rebecca du Pont de Bie, Tertia Goodwin, the Bennetts. My mum, Alastair, Dave, Jo and Craig, the Liebersons, Carson and Matt Baylis.

Chapter 1

AN INTRODUCTION

I had decided on this place, foolishly in retrospect. I had thought it to be informal and convivial, a good place to meet. I didn't for a minute think about crowds.

I walked into the bar and all I could see was men. For a moment I even thought I'd walked into the men's room, the lavatory of a posh football match. I hadn't; it was just another Friday night. I stood at the front of the bar and let my gaze slowly do the rounds. We had arranged over the phone that I was the one to be sought out from my costume, not a pink carnation, but I said I'd be wearing a shiny red mac, with my hair in a chignon and a beret upon my head.

There were so many gorgeous men before me I got quite giddy just looking. It seemed as though the Handsome Convention had got into town and put on this feast for my delight. I couldn't stop the smile sticking to my face, imagining which was my date, why the rest of them were there.

'Any one of these, I don't mind. I'll take whichever is going. On second thoughts, give me a selection if you like,' I thought of saying to a passing waiter. Then I looked at the waiter, who seemed as delicious as the customers, a perfect fit. He was a delightful serving mannequin, all trussed up in a long white apron, shirt, matching black tie, hair, trousers – La Coupole-style. 'And you, you can be the cherry on the top!' I could've added, but I didn't say a thing. I stood and stuffed my eyes. I was utterly perplexed at what was going on.

I am not exaggerating. I don't think I have ever before or since seen so much male beauty in one room. Maybe the moon was at a strange angle never to be repeated in my lifetime. I know I was walking around wearing rose-tinted spectacles, but it had gone beyond a joke. This was the grand selection, and I can be choosy. Perhaps I had died and gone to the angel gates and would have to be redirected. 'Your entrance is over *there*, modom.' None of them even seemed gay. This was ridiculous. I could've decked out the whole of my college class of '85 – there was a man for every occasion: blond, brown-haired, red-headed, low brows, high brows, full lips, wide lips, chiselled chins, Roman noses . . . Dressed in jeans, in suits, looking cool. I started to hunt around for the cameras, wondering if I'd walked on to a set, a shoot for a commercial, but there was nothing.

I singled out my date. He was tall and rugged with a crew-cut, and wore a brown leather trench coat, jeans and a V-necked jumper; his slice of green-eyed stare ran in my direction. Beam me up, Scotty! My, wasn't this dating fun! Why hadn't I done it before, when all the time it had been waiting there? Why hadn't I allowed myself this entertainment? Maybe I hadn't been ready for it then, but now was a different matter.

The room was wide and buzzy, and had high ceilings and white columns. Small tables were dotted along one side and a long bar ran from ear to ear, with that continental 'wish you were in France? No need' look. It was the kind of bar that never worked in London before the government decided that we were grown-up enough to allot our own drinking regulations, as long as they kept between 11 a.m. and 11 p.m. Now that we have the Eurotunnel we no longer need it. We have all you ever wanted from a day trip to Calais right here. Gitanes, *café au lait*, croissants, baguettes, Crozes-Hermitage, Dijon mustard. Now they've finally finished building it. *C'est La Vie*.

I'm not complaining at all. I think it's brilliant. All mixed up makes for a better life, gives us another chance to practise our decision-making. I had to decide whether to go up to the bar and get a drink first, or approach/leap upon what's-his-name. I felt like a poacher waiting to stun dinner to carry home; a child in a free sweetshop – slightly conspicuous. But the occasion itself overbore any self-consciousness. Some days you must accept that things will determinedly go right, no matter what you try to do to fuck up. Perhaps it was all in my mind. Some days, that drag to months, I can walk down the street and see not one damn thing as I scour crowds with my swollen eyes. Now this.

It was the end of 1998 and I was a self-sufficient girl. A painter, an idealist, a revivalist, which means I could often be found trawling my way through junk shops. That year I sported a cunning mixture of tight hipster flares in electric stripes, a seventies black suede trench coat (the belt tied, not buckled), cowboy boots and anything with a wide collar. It was a look. I was a single girl. I hadn't started on the nest, I was just looking for the peacock.

In those days I didn't care a whole lot about anyone or anything, and who should say I should have? I had a stuffed cat (low maintenance), and my work, and my head was full of decisive dreams that I would crawl the shaky staircase to when the reality of my overcrowded paint-palace studio got too much, with one too many bills to consider.

It was on one of those shaky days that the cliché had sprung to my mind, 'a trouble shared is a trouble halved', or some such rot. I inwardly clung to it and added an old standby to achieve my ends: 'she who travels alone travels furthest'. I was willing to go the extra mile to achieve that fairy tale in my head. Oh, you know, the one with the happy ending, where nobody dies but the villain, and everybody trusts and loves and supports their commitments even on the bad days. Even when you're old with pusy damp boils sprouting from your groin – something about 'til death do us part.

But why? It hadn't worked the first time! What did I think would happen?

May is an indecisive name. I've never really felt comfortable in it, neither one thing nor another in the end; quite unlike me. And when May is teamed with Knott as your surname, you know your parents have a sense of humour; at least I wasn't called

Double Sheath. You have to count your blessings in life, accentuate the positive, 'Eliminate the negative, and don't mess with Mr In-between', as Johnny Mercer was so fond of singing. Get things moving in the best direction possible.

I always think you can't wait around for things to happen, for somebody to talk to you first – you could end up waiting for ever. Anyway, what makes you so damned special? We're all the same in the end, bodies filled with souls, mixed good and bad; all divine human beings wanting to be loved. By a certain age, if you don't grab the initiative, somebody else will. Who can you blame when you're left sitting there like some donkey, braying in all directions to an empty field?

I'm a woman who can speak from experience. I've been married, I've had affairs, I've played the field. I've sat through dinners with men until I'm bored to tears, listening to them plot and plan some section of life they aspire to conquer. All because I gave my phone number to the wrong man at some party, or I've been set up by a best friend on a 'date made in heaven' for me. Escaping to the loo and sighing with relief to be alone, I've thought, If this is heaven, what on earth's hell going to be like?

As I've said, I'm not afraid of stepping forward and making my own choices these days, but how a pretty face and the right costume can mislead you. I've often felt like the hero in Whit Stillman's film *Barcelona*, bewitched by beauty and unable to get past the eyes, when assailed by so much physical perfection. That's not to say it's any easier connecting with the souls of the ugly, but there have got to be some advantages.

I can't complain or compare: God's been good to me and given me first-class packaging, which I know I've always knocked holes in. Criticising my legs as too short, though I've always had two that ran when I asked; a bum too big and sticky-out though that's always worked, a mouth that has maybe functioned too well at times; all in all, nothing to be ashamed of or even having any need of a talented plastic surgeon. I take it for granted, always have, that I won't need a colostomy bag to empty in the morning. Strange what we moan about.

Having all my faculties in place, I've decided enthusiastically upon my latest plan, today's project that has gripped my mind like a crazed thing: the lonely hearts column in the back of *Town Beat* magazine. I've always been addicted to reading those columns, them and the jobs sections. When you read those things, it's like juggling with destiny, giving a chance to the obscure. I read them and think, Today, I could change my life and become a neurosurgeon next week. The fact that I don't is another choice made. I sit in this office, typing five afternoons a week. I'm Assistant Head of Projects to Mr Jim Blackett in the Finance section. This is just a title than enables me to make coffee, organise his affairs, buy his wife's presents, type a few letters and read the back of *Town Beat* magazine, the lonely hearts column – I wouldn't be applying for anything in the jobs section, it's all too similar to what I've already got, or worse. Lonely hearts is good, though. When you start to identify with the adverts, you know you've either got to put one in or stop reading the damned things.

I had a similar obsession with problem pages when I was young. As a child I would read Dear Katie in the back of the *TV Times*. The wife who suspects her husband of having an affair – That could be me, I'd think, aged ten. Immediate identification, not as the victim, but as the husband. Or the old man whose dog had died – That will be me, except I have a cat, but if Tom Tom was a dog she would die one day, and then I'd know how to feel. Thanks to Auntie Katie's guidance, I'd know how to deal with it all. In the end I was making up the most hideously contrived problems for myself, and if the social services had ever got hold of my letters, there would have been year-long court cases and my parents and brothers jailed for certain.

My parents (being my mum and stepdad) only started to get worried when all mealtime conversation became immersed in other people's problems – my obsessions. My brothers found the letters I had signed from Barbie, about the physical and mental abuse that Ken had been putting me (Barbie) through, by trying on my dresses, ever since we were released from our boxes. For a while my parents tugged around the idea of sending me to a child psychiatrist, before deciding it would be cheaper just to cancel the *TV Times*. For five years we only ever knew what was on the BBC channels.

The point of placing an advert is that it gives me the opportunity to choose, rather than having to wait and be someone else's predilection. It gives me the control, or the feeling of it; the pretence. Is there any chance of two people electing each other simultaneously, identical-twin emotions, photocopy love? Nothing can be identical, the master forgers of the world have discovered that; no line can ever be the same as another. One of you must look first before the other's gaze follows, surely? Or is there a bingo chance that We (the couple I'll shortly be part of) could choose Each Other? Yeah, give it a shot. I've seen Rebecca Horn's sculpture and the electronic rhino tusks that, inevitably drawn together, fizz with electric current, both moving at the same speed.

I've been fantasising about these dates for years, and what it would be like. Like a lot of things you think about that rest in your mind, challenges unmade until you make that great grab. I never had the courage to go through with it before; wouldn't have even dared to answer an ad for the total fear of rejection. A pointless way to live! That was in the days when all I ever did was sit and watch the projections of my teenage mind, hardly ever daring to live for fear of what might happen, of what people might say or think of me and my moral code. I lived in self-imposed righteous rigidity, like a steel corset of conduct with the inscription, 'love from Auntie' inside. I became, it goes without saying, very dull, and worse, I did to others what I presumed they did to me – judged.

They were only ever my presumptions, there was no proof. Yet I'd speak to others about others with the authority of Miss Marple, Margaret Rutherford-style, armed to the gills. Who said, 'Assumptions are for fools and horses'? I forget, but it is my favourite sackcloth for when I feel myself slipping into the heinous behaviour of my past. I slap myself around with that quote a bit, and I'm soon free of it. Nobody likes to be thought a total fool, not even me!

Presumptions are a dangerous pastime. They lead you to live all your life in your head, to believe things about yourself and others that career away from the truth faster than Donald Campbell's *Blue Bird*, and usually end with the same result, smash-splashglugglugglug. I say 'they', but they're all mine, born of me. Fixing my beliefs about The World firmly in place, and when things become beliefs, watch out! They become set, as rigid as Excalibur moulded to the core of your brain. You need a real King Arthur to come and pull them out. I shan't tell you about my therapist, that's between him, me and my bank manager, and the four walls of his consulting room. What stories they could tell! More scary than the comic I used to read before bed, *Tales from the Crypt*. They could be called 'Wall Secrets – Psychological Nightmares of the Living Dead'. Not quite the same catchy title, but they make Bret Easton Ellis read like bedtime fairy tales.

Enough of that: just believe that I've been cleaned and purified of the vitriol of my blackened thoughts, though some of the superstitions still exist; that my aura now sparkles and innocently protects me from any dangers that there might be. I won't even notice them or draw them to me any longer; I've been demagnetised of violence.

People tell tales for all sorts of reasons, but mostly

to illustrate the way they are feeling, tales that can alarm and disarm you; don't take them personally. If you are willing to listen, I expect you could find among friends and acquaintances the two sides of a story, each and every story that's ever been thought of or read. Some try to pull at the rug you're standing on by telling you the one that starts, 'You're not going to do that, are you? I had a friend who did that once and . . .' But others can be more encouraging. 'That's a brilliant idea, I've always wanted to do that. I had a friend who did that once, and had the most . . .'

Which to choose, what to believe. Like other people's advice, we take and believe in the one that suits us best at the time of going to press.

I spoke to my friend Jules, and she told me one of the former horror tales. I only put it in so that there is a balance to the rest of the stories. A friend of a friend's sister (who's mother had danced with the Prince of Wales) put an ad in the back of *The Times*. She went out on a date with a man who, it turned out, was related to Hannibal Lecter. Not exactly dream date material, or a boy you'd want to take home to Mother, but for reasons best known to herself she accepted his offer of coffee back at his place. She drove with him to his house in Maidenhead. Once inside the door, he tried intriguingly to convince her, with a collection of little tortures, that date rape was in her best interests. She didn't agree, and jumped from the balcony for a quick escape, *splash*, into the river; a soggy withdrawal.

This kind of story feeds us women our worst fears about men, and substantiates what we've always been told by maiden aunts and in a different language Valerie ('I shot Andy Warhol') Solanas's *SCUM Manifesto*. I feel saddened by the story, not only for the plight of the girl, but because I'd always liked boating down the river at Maidenhead, and now I shall never see that G&T province swathed in the same green light again. What it teaches me in my new venture is, there's always an unexpected escape route; stick to the right side of the river; coffee late at night isn't good for anyone; and, most importantly, trust and be aware of your early-warning system. It knows best.

I might have changed a lot, but I'm still not prepared to answer somebody else's advert. The thought of composing a letter that's witty and alluring enough to be chosen by a person you've not met, and can't properly imagine from a twenty-word description, seems impossible.

'Tall, GSOH, prime nineties male seeks young blonde to share the good things in life.' Thank God that one lets me off the hook. For that, I'd describe myself as mousy. But there are others for which you don't need a psychology degree to know where they're at.

'Very attractive, Porsche-driving, successful banker looking for under-thirties, long-legged distraction for social evenings.'

No comment. Not even a laugh.

For a long time I was trying to work out what GSOH meant – Good Sex On Heat, perhaps. Great Sex On Holiday. Giggling Saucy Outrageous Heir(ess). Got Some Odd Habits. Get Some Old Herpes. Gargantuan Sexuality Over-stimulated Hormones. Guaranteed Sex On Hovercrafts.

Also, I had thought, when I saw adverts for whipping/massage/escorts, How strange that they've mentioned how many languages they can speak; it must be for tourists, but I never could figure out why they mentioned facilities such as having a TV, but not a spin-drier or a teasmade. If they were really boasting about how well they were doing in their particular line, why not mention the en-suite bidet?

I'd had to ask girlfriends in both cases, who'd looked back at me in stunned disbelief at my stupidity, for I am not a known naïve.

Good Sense Of Humour! Who would have thought it! And NS doesn't mean Non-Scene, it means No Smoking!

I've noticed the women don't use it – GSOH, that is – they either display it anyway and/or put down what they want.

'Bubbly blonde wants to be spoiled.' Concise and to the point.

'Gymnast Barbie lookalike seeks high-ranking Action Man with realistic gripping hands and voice box. No fatigues.' They might be the same girl but they won't get the same man, that's for sure.

I could be any of the things asked for in these ads, give or take a stretching machine and a bottle of bleach, but replying to one of them would feel like I was sending off a cheque to a mail-order catalogue without including my size or choice number. You can always send it back when it doesn't fit properly, but why play blind man's bluff with life? You're just asking to be picked, because you're unwilling to pay and make the decisions yourself and, horror of hor- rors, choose. Of course, I expect the many hopefuls to apply for this once-in-a-lifetime offer with no knowledge of what is awaiting them. That is why it is so important to get my emblem right.

I've studied the form, patiently waiting for the right adjectives to insert themselves. I'd like to think that when describing myself money would be no object, but with each new word another pound gets added to the initial cost of £25. I understood that it was an investment, but being all the things I was started to get mighty expensive after a while. I began to sympathise with the twenty-word: 'what does that say about any one applicant'. Worse, I was beginning to sound ordinary, too. Using everyday words to describe someone as incredible, dynamic, beautiful, witty, intelligent, energetic, GSOH . . . (see what I mean?) as me. I knew that somewhere there was a word that summed me up, and called into the psyche of applicable males.

Goddess. The word was goddess. I quote the great and good *Oxford English Dictionary*: 'female deity; the woman one adores'.

It gets around the problems of physical descriptions and invokes the power of the reader's imagination that taps into the 'inherited structure of the psyche' in the archaic depths of the unconscious. Perfect, simple and succinct.

Some might think I'm setting myself up as a patsy, but I know I'm a human-form goddess, of a type. I never mentioned from what culture. For all the reader might guess, I could be the original Egyptian Nut.

Nut – Earth Mother represented as a cow, who stood above the world, her belly scarred with stars.

Or the multi-breasted Asiatic fertility goddess,

Artemis. That would shock the *Sun* readers and *Euro-trash* Lolo-fanciers. Imagine, on page three, hundreds of breasts on one woman!

Or the Indian goddess of war, Kali. Commonly portrayed with four arms, demon earrings, a skull necklace and a blood-red tongue hanging down her chin, having just finished the dance of death. Corrr! Fancy that!

What does it matter which goddess I align myself to? There is one to represent every archetype imaginable if you scour the board. There's got to be one that's me.

Besides, we are all gods and goddesses in mortal form, it's just that some of us haven't got around to realising it, and fall to idolising iconic pop stars like Madonna, real-life model Sindy dolls and their younger sisters, babes. Emaciated goddesses who make us feel guilty for our fatty Western transgressions. We pray to their images, held high above us on billboards, and measure our arm widths to theirs in satin-paged magazines. We starve in the ritualised religious abstinence that is dieting. Abhorring our flaccid flesh, we'll punish our bodies in gyms for our evil excesses after sitting in an office all day, and that way we'll look as though we do real work. If we work long enough, our bodies will become how we want them, taut, hard, ungiving. We strive to look like lean, mean, fighting machines, not the soft malleable toys of lovemaking. We'll be granted forgiveness for that chocolate bar only by the tape measure and weighing machine. How unloving we are to ourselves.

I know that when I feel depressed, there's nothing quite like making myself feel really sick with a box of chocs crammed into the mouth watching the afternoon movie. Next comes the tub of Belgian chocolate ice cream that I bought with some flimsy excuse: 'It'll last until so and so's children come round for tea next week.' Within moments of getting through the door, shopping left as if to unpack itself, I've pulled the top from the carton to have just one spoonful. The next thing I know it's empty, and I'm complaining. I'm certain they're not as big as they used to be. I'm certain I never used to be able to eat the whole carton in one sitting, did I? Who am I kidding! These trousers don't fit me like they did. And then there's the hangover, worse than from a packet of fags and a bottle of wine, worse than being stood up at the Odeon to see *Jaws*, aged fourteen. Maybe not quite that bad.

I'm not advocating a replacement of chocolate with alcohol, but with love, since chocolate stimulates the same parts of the brain. Chocolate manufacturers would have us believe it's easier and gives us the same results. I know that's not true – I get fat when I eat chocolate and feel sick and poor, however much research is done to tell me that eating it three times a month will make me live longer. I don't want to live longer like this.

When I have a lover I feel gorgeously voluptuous, adored and abundant. In fact, just like a goddess. Often we can treat lovers and chocolate ice cream in the same way. Arousing similar greed, they can pull the pig from our hearts. One spoonful is never enough. We complain once it is finished. We argue with the contents, shout at what they have made us become. Feel guilty afterwards.

I am determined not to become the human god, demanding far more than an immortal. I shall be pleased at offerings, not requisition them as contractual. Rabindranath Tagore noticed the danger of making human gods, for when we fall short in our praise to humans, 'they swoop red-eyed with fury not at all godlike to look at'. The contradiction of perception.

I shall be a goddess to be adored, and if I'm not adored by one, I shall be by another.

What do goddesses like to do? What does May like to do? I like laughing, I love laughing – it releases the utmost pleasure beams through my body. A really good gut-holding, belly-wobbling laugh, and you can feel the cells in your body, through to your fingertips, shake. The best thing of all about it is that it's contagious. It's hard to leave a person laughing alone at a joke – no matter how unfunny it is, you have to join in. It is the ultimate in attraction. If I had all the money in the world and never had to work again at a job, I would spend my time laughing, being with people who made me laugh, making others laugh. I would be a queen surrounded by court jesters. Laughter crosses all barriers, languages, walls, religions. Imagine if policemen and soldiers were rigorously trained in the open-armed combat of laughing and lovemaking, everybody would want to join up and go to war. Armies would invade countries with laughing gas and tapes of Morecambe and Wise, while showering a country with condoms, to an easy submission.

Love and laughter fall so easily together.

I had to decide what I wanted, not just what I was. I knew what I didn't want – that list could go on for ever. It's sitting down and pinpointing what you actually do want: what is it that makes you jump up and down, in a man, on a man? I started to write a list cautiously at first, but once I got the hang of it I couldn't write fast enough, when I discovered that there was nothing in the rules about crossing out. After fifteen copies I came out with a first draft of what I call My Essential Man List. But the qualities I wanted in a man, even in a date, went on for pages.

It took a week to come up with my final entry. I'd drafted a hundred variations that sat scrunched in and overflowing my waste-paper baskets, none of them quite right, but this one seemed to hit the nail, pitch the note.

GODDESS WHO LOVES TO LAUGH IN BED
SEEKS DELICIOUS MALE COMPANION.
Photo Essential.

I did a word count and a sum, wrote out my cheque and sent it off to the magazine with a kiss for good luck. It would be printed in the Christmas edition, my intention being to start the new year in the right way.

Before I got a single reply, I had to do one thing. I had to change my name. May just wouldn't do: it wasn't decisive enough. It was the only thing that fiddled my resolve rather than matched it. Now I had the chance of having the kind of fantastic, dramatic name I'd always wanted, that would suit the brilliant girl in the advert, the woman I am. Goddess.

I toyed with Sitwellian-style names: Edith, Allanah, Hortensia, Sacheverell. I looked through the Russians for inspiration: Grushenka, Masha, Anna, Olga. I turned repetitive and French with Nana, Gigi, Lulu. In my heart of hearts, I knew I wasn't American and didn't even bother with the Mary Lous. I got inanely Italian with Raffaella, Artemesia, Sophia, but none of them quite suited. I even went through the Jane, Mary and Susan section, but knew it was desperation. To call myself Aphrodite seemed too corny.

Then I hit upon Faith, Hope, Charity and Grace. I could not be described as a Grace in any way; Faith seemed too dogmatic; I definitely didn't want to be seen or known as a Charity, sweet or otherwise. But Hope – I was full of it, I was more than it. It reflected my measure of optimism in this new venture, saying it, made me feel excited and blessed. I was Hope. And, not quite ever losing the sense of humour my parents had poured down into my cells, engendered in my genes, I was: Yours ever, gratefully, sincerely, Ms HOPE KNOTT.

All the friends I know who've had cosmetic surgery emerge to no gasps. Nobody ever wants to change themselves as drastically as Fay Weldon's heroine in *The Life and Loves of a She-Devil*. They might be dogged by what they see as the most hideous nose in the world, without which they might be queen, with it, only ever a wretch. When it's done, who even notices that anything has changed? Perhaps nobody will notice any modifications in my name. I can see it's no revolution, but it makes all the difference to me. It alters the way I feel about myself, and that's what matters. I've done it the other way. I married my way to a new name, and I can see that that was extreme now, but it seemed the right thing to do at the time. There are always myriad reasons why you marry; why shouldn't one of them be for a change of name? It was just unfortunate that the man to ask me was Thom Aberwraythwaite. I wasn't dragging that crocodile tail around the back of me for the rest of my days, and when the whole affair crash-landed, it was back to Knott.

Names can dominate your life when you're overly attentive. A long time ago we were so superstitious that people would never reveal their real names to anyone but those closest to them. A nickname would suffice for the others, in case they chose to use it in unholy ceremonies. To know someone's full name was as powerful as having a nail clipping of theirs, or a lock of hair. Maybe I'm afraid, too? I don't think so, but the subconscious can do strange things. Now I've made my decision, I shan't mention it again. From now on I'm Hope incarnate.

Each day was full of the turmoil of anticipation. Putting in for change is one thing, but the physical demands can be stressful. I started to recognise palpitations thumping my form each time I passed a newsagent; I began blushing at the tube adverts, boldly telling strangers on the platform to buy the latest issue of *Town Beat* magazine – and this was all before it came out. Could they tell that I had penned part of the copy? I wondered which of them would answer, and what their letters would be like.

On the morning of the publication date I rushed down the road to the corner shop and bought the first copy, on the top of the pile, mangled by string. I rolled it up and put it under my arm, and, like Harry Lime, walked only in the street's shadows until I ducked into the front door of my block. Once home, I cleared a place for *Town Beat* on my work table, and pretended to ignore it by whistling and washing a cup until the kettle boiled and my tea was made. I pulled a stool over and put my cup down. I wanted to draw out the delicious excitement, slowly flicking the pages, reading the articles and looking at the coming week's TV, all the things I never usually read before it got put in the bin on the movie/art pages, virgin in most of its other sections. Then I would reach the lonely hearts. But I couldn't do it, I couldn't wait. I tore straight to the back and searched the columns and there it was. All neon-lit to me, it positively tinselled out of the page, dazzling with its witty attraction. Would anyone else get a reply to their meagre ads? I felt sorry for them. I'd stolen their thunder. It might as well have been the only one on a blank page. Who'd bother writing this week to any of the 'Rescue me, Brunette needing mouth-to-mouth'? Sad, all that effort and outlay for a snog.

I didn't tell anyone, not even when the copy was in, not even the newsagent. I didn't need the GSOH that some of my friends would have undoubtedly employed. I wasn't sure I'd tell any of them that I'd actually gone through with it and done it. London's big, but sometimes not big enough when you're trying to avoid friends in the search for a little privacy.

Each day when I wasn't in the office at paid employment, the dreaded Toad work, as Larkin so beautifully termed it, I was sitting in my studio painting, for that is what I am if the truth be told – a painter. I would sit and think about the people I knew and the chances of them answering a message like mine. If I did, others I knew must have, but whether they were brave enough to admit it was another question. There's still a stigma stuck to advertising for partners, as though there's something common about not being formally introduced, like being in 'trade' in an Edith Wharton or E. M. Forster novel. We don't know where it's been, but then how well do we truly know anyone? We can pretend to be anything we like and stick with it, sell it to our nearest and dearest as our identity. If you tell it right, your list of lies, lovers will believe as well as employers that you went to Eton, and not Holland Park Comprehensive. Expect the lies to mesh to your central nervous system and make you as jumpy as a rubber ball. How do you enjoy the house in the Boltons, next door to the Sultan of Brunei, when one day your schooling shows up in casual conversation, ruins a select dinner party with cross-examination and pours acid on your ulcer? Your children despise you, your wife leaves for an elongated holiday with her ski instructor, just like my aunt, and suddenly nobody much cares to be seen talking to you at the club. Bad form, old boy. Tell lies that can't get found out.

I walked along the street and wondered if the road sweeper had sent off an application, looked at *Today in Parliament* and figured the odds of a political request. Enough of them do strange things in their own time, why shouldn't they . . .? People on buses, my boss at work – nobody was safe from my scrutiny until the morning my mailbox was filled.

Six days of dismal disappointment went by until, on the seventh day, the word appeared, and like God, changed the world. Mine. You've never seen such a rush back up the stairs to my fourth-floor retreat. To watch me, I must have looked as though I'd had a double shot up the bum of steroids and amphetamines. I jumped back into bed with a cup of coffee, still in my jeans, and sat there, a Father Christmas with his post sack.

'Yum, yum, yum,' I said. This is more delicious than having a birthday on Christmas Day, I thought.

The milk had boiled to a slight froth and sat on top of my coffee like icing on a cake, a steaming pungent vanilla scent into the cosy warmth of my one-room habitat. It is my one extravagance, my coffee. The expensive paints and pigments that I save up for from the Ye Olde Sweet Shoppe-style shop Cornelissen's, are necessities, they are my life blood. Coffee, from the Algerian Coffee Stores in Old Compton Street, is my treat and reward. Buying it, drinking it, sniffing it in the bean-brimming, druggy surrounds, heart palpitating with the first cup of Italian espresso drawn down. Giddy, I reach for my purse and pay for my quarter, all I can afford this week. I can smell it all the way home, and so can everyone else. I see them sniffing ecstatically in my direction, catching the aroma of freshly ground vanilla coffee. It's like walking along the road with an incredibly handsome boyfriend.

Behind me, I've stacked my pillows. The massive mound on my duvet-covered lap is full of single requests. I'm too excited. I don't even notice my side table, with its toppling book tower, that looks at me each night and morning and says, 'When are you going to do something about me?'

Just as I'm about to rip the brown-paper envelope apart and let its contents fall out in a broken snowstorm mess, I realise something is wrong. The jeans. The jeans I put on to run down and collect the post in, feel too cold and hard against the warmth of my duck down. I take them off in the way I used to as a child, not wanting my brothers to see and mock the plumpness of my girlish thighs, so different from their lean-strung, football-kicking machines. Covertly I'd undress under the sheets, or wriggling impossibly in my sleeping bag on camping holidays. 'I don't want to get cold!' I'd scream back at their mockery.

Flinging my jeans out on to the floor, I'm jumpered, knickered and socked in bed, as though going for a snooze, typically English, unable to yield completely to the resting conditions of the siesta. Feels strange at nine on a Tuesday morning; I can't possibly go to bed, I'm not tired. It reminds me of being eight, face streaming with tears: 'I'm not tired, I won't sleep, I'm not tired, I'm not t—' Even when fast asleep, I'd mumble objections to the last. I could never give up gracefully.

Somewhere I have found the courage, and I take hold of the envelope. I can't find any excuse to put it off. I rip it open and pour the oversized confetti over my head, bathing in my secret delight of adulation. There were envelopes of every colour, size and condition. This is what it must feel like to appear at the Royal Albert Hall and have a standing ovation. Decisions, decisions, mind-blowing decisions. Which to open first, once I had counted them – a staggering sixty-nine replies. How did it come to be 69 of all numbers, not 68 or 70, but 69? I laughed an appropriately dirty laugh and swigged on my coffee before getting down to the real pleasurable work – the reading. Snobbishly, I divided the envelopes between brown and the others. I admit I put the environmentally caring, reused, gas-bill window envelopes to the bottom of the pile: it conjured up too many connotations for the future. The gift on Valentine's Day, an already picked-through box of Milk Tray, full of half-eaten soft fruit centres.

I ordered the coloured envelopes methodically with the posh, thick paper at the top, but then if I had the choice at dinner, I'd always eat my pudding first and be too full up for the lump of meat. I ummed and ahead about how many to open, revealing the disappointments or excitements that lurked within. Whether to draw it out, take some to read on the way to work for the afternoon; take some to read at work; save them for the evening. Read them all straight away.

I had a commission, a boring old bestial portrait to finish that could wait. Both dog and master stared accusingly at me from the easel at the other side of the room, indecipherably different. Some people choose their pets to look like them right from the beginning – why wait? They must think it's like buying matching shoes and bags. Sometimes I wish I'd never got into painting animals, I'm sick of painting fur. 'This is my last one,' I say back to the dog's recriminatory stare. I've decided I shall make a leap of faith this new year, and go forward with my funny mythological paintings (funny to me, strange to others). I am in a Diana the Huntress frame of mind, always painted with dogs. Perhaps the males in my postbag will be so delicious I shall go back to male figure painting.

I used to think there was a sure-fire market among the gays I knew for paintings of naked men. When I had my show the year before last, called *Nude*, my gay friends were all so closet they'd never even told their mothers, let alone a father, between them. Their guilt drove them to buy all the naked women, rather than adorn their walls with anything remotely suspicious. I had one patron, definitely gay, who had a harem of Knotts in his living room to rival the Ingres in the Louvre, just to prove to his dad he was straight. A man's naked head and shoulders was 'too much', he said, wrinkling his nose. Naked genitals had him heaving. 'I wouldn't put those in the freezer,' he shuddered, disapproving of their blatant vividness. It was true, they looked just like men's genitals. In the end all the male nude paintings were bought by women.

Since then, I've thought that perhaps it takes away the magical excitement, makes it all too ordinary, frightens the frisson and its illicit sexiness, once you can have it painted and hanging on the wall. How often do you see men hiding their erections along the corridor rooms of the National Gallery, embarrassed by their bodily reactions to the Rubens? The nation encourages them to look, even gives them free entry. It advertises, billboard-style, Bronzino's raunchy 'Allegory of love and time', now showing! The painting that got Victorians sticking on fig leaves, now sits on the side of a red double-decker bus, showing its all as it winds its way on the route number 22 from Hackney to Piccadilly. Up the road and in the darkened side alleys of Berwick Street, the same men stare in pink-faced lust at the glossy, ripe, coloured photos in strip-parlour windows. The same girls from a different time stare back, that much ruder for the lace that hides and ties, the make-up that covers their faces in all colours and shades, hair fluffed to obscure shoulders and ears, falling beguilingly towards ordinary tinselled breasts. Porno-queen goddesses.

'Dear Goddess,' the first letter started, and I was thrilled. It was written in gold ink on white vellum.

Dear Goddess,

I don't know your tastes or what is delicious to you, but friends have told me I am delicious, so perhaps I am?!

I have no idea what is expected in this kind of thing, but perhaps a description of myself is called for. I am just over six foot, 32 years old, went to Cambridge University and run my own company.

I like lots of different things, I believe in creative diversity in all things.

I like laughing in bed.

I've been out of a relationship for over a year,

and I'm looking for an independently minded woman with her own life and friends. I aspire to equality and interdependence in relationships and friendships.

I'm not looking to rescue anyone or to be rescued. I love romance, but not the mythical epics of silver knights on white chargers, except between book covers and in the front row of the Empire, Leicester Square.

I enjoy socialising and having fun.

If any of this grabs your attention, call me and I can find out who and what you are, after being a goddess.

I do hope you call. My name is Tim.

My heart was beating faster than as if I'd chewed at a Nicorette, but just one, as is so often the case, was not enough. I glanced at the photo of a handsome blond man dressed in all the right clothes. I found myself quickly writing 'poss.', and putting it to one side, even though he hadn't even said what he did. His own company? Could be an offal importer for all I knew. He wasn't a scriptwriter.

The next envelope was thick and pale blue, with an American stamp that made me overlook the too-tight, neat, small handwriting. My eyes were bright with excitement when I saw that the letterhead ended in

New Orleans; I could already see myself at the coming year's Mardi Gras.

'Dear "Goddess".' How dare he put inverted commas around my title, who does he think he is! I thought, making myself laugh before I read on.

'I was in London over Christmas and saw your ad. I'm writing back to you on the plane home because I'm returning in a month. I'm an American artist, teacher, tennis pro, nineteenth-century romantic, film freak and all-round great guy!' I stopped to look at the photo of an all-American, blue-polo-shirted, clean-cut dimple-faced guy with the weirdest quirky expression. Bad face day he'd written over it and I had to agree, but wondered why he should send me a photo of it.

'I have eclectic tastes and am fond of the avant-garde. Some of my favourites are Vermeer, John Irving, Joni Mitchell, Kate Bush . . . But I'd like to know your favourite fairy tale, film, character, city, etc.'

I could see us on a date, politely smiling at each other, waiting for the mime show to start at the Riverside Hammersmith. I'm sure he was a very nice guy, but I didn't want that kind of avant-garde. I didn't wish to be so cruel that it was his bad face day that was making me laugh in bed. Even his reassurances at the bottom of the letter didn't convince me to put him on the A-list. 'You won't be disappointed!!' Was he trying to tell me something about his size?

I did a lucky dip for the third and came out with plain white WHSmith writing-pack paper. Inside, spellings had been scribbled out and the hand was erratic, but he hadn't included a photo to back up his claims of gorgeousness.

Dear Goddess,

I have just seen your ad, so I thought I'd reply as I'm delicious and like to laugh in bed too. (There hasn't been much to laugh about lately – isn't that heartbreaking?) I'm not going to waffle on about myself for pages, coz you'll have to contact me to find out more. BUT I will say that I'm a palaeontologist, 25, tall, dark and handsome, looking for a stunningly gorgeous companion to go through old times with! And whatever hedonistically else happens . . .

If this is you, please reply with photo.

Yours

Hector

Cheeky git! Did he think he was interviewing me for a job? It momentarily unsettled me until I realised I didn't have to answer any of the ones I didn't fancy.

Besides, he didn't have a phone number. Throw *that* to one side. Youth! Back to the smart, heavyweight paper.

The next envelope to catch my eye was a smart, rich, red dust. I held it to my nose before sliding my fingers inside its luxury depths. Luxury indeed: it was from the Jamaica Hilton, stamped through with its insignia. How nice, I thought: if it's the manager perhaps free hols could be in order while he upgraded his guest list with goddesses – a man who thought to his future. I liked that. Or maybe a guest wanting a little help with the sun oil and rum punches around the pool.

Dear Goddess,

God here (only kidding!). No doubt you will have received dozens of witty, erudite letters from trendy leftist millionaires. Obviously this is not one of them.

Basically I'm Irish, 6 foot, 40 years old but don't look, feel or act it, single (recently separated) and I love my work as a designer. I'm into new experiences, travel (I'm on a hotel consultancy business trip), reading, sports, art, food, movies, etc. As a caring, honest, passionate guy, I think I've got a heck of a lot to offer the right woman. To lessen my chances with you I enclose a fax photo.

Good luck in your quest, Happy New Year and
be very careful out there!
Ewan Healey

I was quite taken, especially with the photo that
showed a sophisticated and handsome man – definitely a man, not a boy – in western hunk style:
cowboy boots, jeans and a chequered lumberjack
jacket and a cap with doggy ear flaps. He was laughing, and underneath was written: 'Very important
businessman in serious meeting.' 'Def. poss,' I wrote.
But there was something that worried me about the
letter, the menace of having written, 'be very careful
out there'.

I couldn't make up my mind if he was being
threatening or kind. I'd call, and find out from his
voice.

The next of Basildon Bond's best was covered
mostly with a wonderful photo of a naked boy with a
grin from ear to ear, a bucket covering his salient
features. The simple message scrawled beneath said,
'If you're interested I could visit your box! Love Roger
(22, met. policeman).' The phone number was from
some distant province. I was already achieving my
aims, laughing in bed with all the delicious male
companions I could undress.

Others I opened that morning had me near to tears: tales from cabbies of deceased wives, lonely tax inspectors, friendless foreign students, divorced lawyers, aggressive graphic designers, regressive estate agents; the list was endless. Here were sad men tricked by life, dreamers slapped by reality, boys incapable of becoming men angry at their years, men disappointed in themselves. I was pleased, though, that so many saw themselves as delicious. It's no good thinking you're ugly even if you are. Someone somewhere would answer their pleas; not me.

They were not all doom and gloom, and being an optimist, my 'possible' pile had risen to a ridiculous mound. So many seemed truly delicious, and funny with their enthusiasm. The problem I had was to be selective, but I had to do it – I couldn't possibly date all fifty of them, and wouldn't it be unfair on the ones at the end of the queue? Call it psychic energy, vibes or chance. Would the ones I'd choose to date be any better or worse than the ones I didn't meet? I shouldn't imagine so, but I had to use my instincts. I took fifty to work with me, feeling dizzied by the adulation, having spent all morning seeped in men who asked only for my gaze and gave me their best wishes. I was in a privileged position, yet I could commiserate with pop stars who woke up with it each day and went to bed drowning in it each night.

As I got on the tube, and all the way down the street at the other end, I couldn't stop the Cheshire-cat grin that engulfed my face. I hugged my bounty bag in my arms close to my chest, like an unopened present of gold bars or Tiffany trinkets, the one that hadn't been given to me at Christmas. The present I was giving myself this year.

Chapter 2

WRONG BY A MILE

What was his name? I'd almost forgotten his name. I looked into my bag, fumbling for the letter between old chewing-gum wrappers, a minimum of five lipsticks, a sadly unused Durex (it certainly would not have been in my bag if it had been!), some pens, my notebook (always carry a notebook, one day it might carry you) and a scuzzy, once beautiful fuchsia suede wallet. A letter.

His name was Bill. Bill's a fine name. It has integrity naturally built in. Wasn't one of the men in *Seven Brides for Seven Brothers* called Bill, or was it one of the sailors in *South Pacific*? Whichever, Bill sounded, and now looked, good.

I walked towards Bill and his welcoming smile; he

put his drink down and seemed to come towards me. We were going to get on well, I could tell. Someone was tapping on my arm.

'Hope? You must be Hope,' said a voice I recognised from the telephone.

I shifted my gaze and turned to smile up to my left and then, seeing nothing, looked down to focus on the nervous, ticking smile that crossed the plump, bearded George Michael face before me. Did this man need hope, I thought. But how did he know it was me? 'Yes? I'm Hope, that's me.'

'I'm Bill.'

'Of course. Of course you are, Bill. How nice to meet you,' I said rather too enthusiastically, to cover myself from the avalanche of my disappointment and stop it crashing upon my head and breaking it open. Distractedly I noticed a body trying to push past me, a beautiful blonde girl with the smooth, unsullied skin of pampered youth squeezing into seventeen. She went straight into the arms of my hunk. I shook my head in disbelief at the taste of the man I had thought the moment before was to be my date. Coping well, indeed! He was laughing delightedly at her youthful enthusiasm as she filled his face with kisses. They were clearly not big brother and little sister. If they were, I was calling the social services.

I was grateful for the small mercy of being saved

from total humiliation on my first approach. I couldn't have stood the embarrassment of flinging myself in slow motion towards the wrong man, his arms held out for another behind me. That would be as unpalatable as a weak *Goodies* sketch; in fact I was sure I'd seen something like it enacted by the other Bill, Bill Oddie. Did all Bills come from the same mould? At least I had been saved that sadness. Small mercies, very small mercies, and I'm grateful for every one.

'Can I get you a drink, Hope? What would you like?' said the Danny DeVito at my shoulder. I took my hat off and wished I was wearing my flat trainers, apart from other things. I've never been good at talking down to people; I've spent so much of my life trying to stand erect. The high, strappy wedges I was wearing would have been the right height for the treacherous, canoodling Arnie in the corner. Why had I begun to doubt my luck and scuppered my chances?

I turned back to my companion and tried to summon charm and a smile and not to keep twisting my head to view what wasn't available. I felt like a child being made to leave the funfair without any candyfloss. Wretched.

'I'll have a glass of red wine, thanks, Bill.'

I watched him turn to the bar and heave himself back on to the high stool from which he'd descended to catch me. He'd held a stool next to him vacant for me, bagsied by a copy of the *Daily Telegraph*, I couldn't help noticing. My uncle Philip had always read the *Daily Telegraph*, 'best murder and sordid trial coverage', he used to say, scandalising my auntie Charlotte, a staunch Labour supporter and *Guardian* reader.

Bill had his back to me now; so I had a better chance to view his balding patch that was rapidly being deserted by the strands of hair pulled and greased over it from one side. It was gathered neatly into a little ponytail at the nape of his neck, a short stumpy thing, a Jack-Charlton-of-the-nineties look. His jacket was loud, double-breasted and brilliant green; his shirt sat uncomfortably beneath it in a confusion of intense purple and mustard Paisley, the collar uncomfortably buckling to cross the jacket's neckline. His trousers were tight black faded jeans and his feet were encased in neat little Chelsea boots.

I'm not a fetishist, but I do have a thing about shoes. I'm always buying them as treats instead of the much-needed necessities of clothing which will be falling in rags off my shoulders before they're replaced. While my boots and shoes sit lovingly polished, horned into shape, my clothes lie in dishevelled unironed heaps on the floor. I suppose I'd call myself 'shoe-conscious'.

I have found myself judging a person by their shoes. If the wrong shoes are on the right man, they become a stumbling block to my feelings, a harridan's scream to my sensitive ears. Good shoes and bad shoes cloud my sensibilities. I cannot continue a conversation with a man in grey lace-ups or white Italian slip-ons, yet beige corduroys are fine. I'll be obsessively drawn back to stare at ugly shoes again and again, to study the minutiae of their detail, like a Hieronymus Bosch painting or a gruesome horror film. You might stick your hands to your face for the duration because you can neither bear to watch nor miss it, but your fingers slide to and fro, working like skin-pink venetian blinds across your eyes. I notice each crease in the leather or plastic, the wear at the heel, the scuff at the toe, the bulge from the feet within, every buckle, every style. I have made judgements because of shoes that make me ashamed. I am seriously trying to stop my shoe-crazy decisions, but it's like keeping flies out of the larder in the summer, or ants from a picnic.

I am not a great fan of Chelsea, the football club or the boots, but with the rest of Bill's attire they were utterly appropriate. It meant that I was able to forget about his packaging and try to concentrate on the man within. I had liked his letter; that was why I was there, I had to remind myself, though he hadn't included a photograph as requested, so what did I expect? I had chatted to him briefly on the phone, and thought he had sounded interesting, and interested about the rest of the world. I like a man with a nice wide interest and I know it's nothing to do with size, but what you do with it that really counts. The interests I mean.

I felt sorry about his obvious nervousness, there at the bar, and the amount of effort he'd put into his grooming for the evening and his drive into London from Oxford. I felt sorry . . .

'No trouble,' he'd assured me. 'I do it all the time.'

I'd suggested the bar in West London, not too far from the motorway, not so groovy as to be intimidatingly Shoreditch, but not a pub. How was I to know the Handsome Convention would have just got in? I wondered if he'd noticed, and hoped he hadn't. Do academics notice human beauty, as an archaeologist did he only value the old? More at home at the bingo than the disco?

Pity kept rearing its ugly head, and I had to keep on reminding myself that I hadn't signed up for the engagement party, that I was a free agent and that I didn't owe Bill a thing, other than the fruits of human kindness and respect that all people deserve. He wasn't putting himself up as a charity case, it was only I that was cruelly assessing him as such.

Over the phone I had agreed to dinner, because I'd thought it was the least I could offer if someone was coming all the way to London. I wouldn't have gone to Oxford on the promise of a fifteen-minute cup of tea, so why should he? But I was beginning to wonder why I had tied myself to some unknown anchor for an entire evening. I was learning.

Bill turned towards me with his ticking smile, handing me a drink, and I returned a wide and uncomplicated volley, not as honest as I would have liked, but my senses were engulfed by his heavy musk-based aftershave. I tried to stop the twitching alarm of my nose. I had to cut off from the rest of the room, try to cut out the handsome devils that had assailed my sight on arrival. It wasn't easy.

I am ashamed to say that I could feel myself trying to hide. First behind the wide white column to the right of my seat, then by pulling my beret back on my head and across my face and registering my back to the rest of the room. At the same time I wanted to challenge my crass judgement and snotty style view. I wanted to be proved wrong about appearances and personalities. I was determined to discover that this was a really nice man, that it would be possible to fall in love with a man like this who didn't care about, or was just confused by, the flood of fashion choices in today's market; that appearances don't matter, it's the person beneath that counts. That there is no right or wrong to taste, no good or bad, that you cannot be tastefully challenged. I wanted to think the best of him, give him ten out of ten for trying, but whenever I say that, my schoolgirl mind returns with – Very Trying! I couldn't kid myself to the same degree; I couldn't find this man attractive. Any other man in the room . . . But with Bill I didn't even want to take my coat off with him, let alone my boots, or to leap gyrating and uncontrolled on to a giant waterbed. I didn't want to sit in the seat next to him, let alone in the cinema, with his aftershave, and I could never, ever have sat in the cosy double Pullman seats of the Chelsea Cinema with this man. I didn't want to dance naked with him into the Pacific Ocean, never to be seen again. What I am trying to say is, he didn't send my hormones bubbling, heart racing or, Me. Friendship seemed the only thing up for grabs; I couldn't even think of one girlfriend he'd do for. And all this before we'd even had a conversation. How quickly I jumped to judge.

'Cheers! Here's to.' I saluted my glass to his and started down the road. 'How was your journey? I hope you didn't have too much trouble finding this place?'

'No, it was easy. Good choice; I like it here, it's got a friendly vibe, a good atmosphere. Salut!'

He raised his glass to mine, and downed half his drink in one.

'I was needing that,' he explained. 'I've had one hell of a lousy week. I thought things were getting better. Anyway, enough about me. How's your week been? Tell me a bit more about your paintings. Did you bring any slides?'

'No. I'm always being told I should carry slides about, as selling opportunities and self-publicity, but I hate the idea of being an American granny abroad.' He looked perplexed, so I elaborated. 'You know, one of those women who corner you on holiday and at every opportunity regale all with stories of their families and the never-ending collapsible pack of photographs.'

Explaining the quip made me feel as boring as the grannies themselves, but without the heart. 'But you're right, I should give more people the chance to be charmed and delighted by my extraordinary talent,' I added with a laugh.

Bill raised his eyebrows and nodded his head seriously.

'I'd like to see them. I'm rather a good judge of paintings. I'm a creative kind of guy, good eye. I know a little about art.'

I felt as though he was saying, 'I'll be the judge of that, young lady!' but he iced the remark with, 'But

I'm sure if you think they're terrific they must be. Especially if they're anything like you!'

I wasn't convinced he meant the last part, I didn't have the heart to tell him how dangerous a little knowledge can be.

'So you said you liked jazz. I thought we'd go on from here up to the Jazz Harbour. There's someone really interesting playing I've been meaning to catch.'

I couldn't say no; there was something in his eyes, the effort so obviously made. We'd made all the usual Braille conversation, feeling blindly about each other's unknown corners of thought and feeling, anything to hang a hook on, but nothing seemed to catch the nail of my determination. Except the word jazz. At that point experimental would do; in fact it matched perfectly. I knew I was being condescending, agreeing to go with him, even though I couldn't bear to watch him struggle off the stool. I'd had to look away at the beads of sweat that had been hill-racing before careering into his eyebrows and an over-large mopping handkerchief. To have him seen as my diminutive escort out . . . Nothing is any big deal, I had to remind myself (and don't start thinking and neither is he!). Maybe I said yes as an excuse to get out of the body-beautiful bar, feeling that people were watching me, thinking, What's a gorgeous girl doing with a man like that? Must be rich, powerful, stupendously generous and clever! I had listened to my laugh jump out of my mouth, way too loud, every time he said – well, anything. Time to go somewhere dark, smoky and loud, for all the most obvious camouflage reasons.

We walked out of the bar. Nobody looked at us; it must have been because I was projecting *cousin*. I never notice what my cousins wear; I'm just glad to see them, or my brothers, and they have captured the market in hideous shoes.

We travelled in a taxi, for the strange reason that he thought his car might have been damaged, parked as it was in a rough area – West London was rough to Bill.

People broke and stole in London. There was no respect for the beauty of other's possessions. In England there was no admiration for earning things, like in America; just jealousy and destruction, because you could have and they couldn't, he explained to me all the way there.

'So what kind of jazz are we going to see?'

'Well, I've already told you it's modern, experimental. It'll be interesting; this group have been working towards a new sound. As an artist I'm sure you'll appreciate it.'

I smiled back, unable to answer, 'Don't bet on it.'

I hate experimental jazz. I hate it; that's all there is

to say. A few noises along the lines of *eyherrgh, yuchh, umph*, might explain my gut reactions. Was I the very same girl on the phone who had laid claim to loving all things new and modern? 'I'm always ready to listen and learn; I like a change.' At that moment I had thought I did. Now I looked longingly out of the automatically locked windows and watched parts of beautiful London, dark and bright, suspended from my grasp. I was even beginning to feel resentful towards the new modern taxi with its seat belts and electric-microphone talking system.

I wasn't a prisoner; I could ask the cab to stop for me to get out at any time. I could do that, and yet I couldn't. Frightened of confrontation, fearful of hurting this man's feelings, I sat on and got out when the journey ended, when he said, 'Oh, good, I think we're here.'

He paid for the cab in a studied and proficient way, as I slid out, bumping my head. The slit of my skirt pulled away to reveal my stocking tops. I felt racy and embarrassed by all the connotations. Saucy Underwear Girl Craves Hot Sex On First Date. Bill tried to pretend he hadn't noticed a thing. I wished in that moment I'd been wearing navy-blue gym knickers, covered by thick Lyle tights and a heavy pair of corduroy trousers belted with a hefty brass buckle – oh, and a 'no entry' sign.

Maybe there would be somebody I knew inside. I would blend into the crowd and bump into them and have a jolly good time. That thought brought a smile of optimism to my lips, only to be wiped by that damned mind of mine bringing up the rear guard of, 'And how would you introduce Bill?'

'Hi, Jonathan, I don't think you know Bill. Actually, I've just met him myself. Yes, through a lonely hearts column.'

There was a crowd at the door, and as we pushed through to the front, there was little or no conversation between us. I thought of starting a 'so do you come here often' conversation that would lead us on to the finer discussions of jazz technique and history, but I had reckoned on needing that line as soon as we got in the door. Was I arrogant or wrong to assume that this dating business was the financial burden of the male? Rightly or wrongly, I assumed it anyway, and had no trouble walking in through the entrance leaving my liege to pay our way. To be seen with a girl wearing this much red lipstick gets pricey; anyway, the place had been his suggestion, I thought defensively.

The place was thronging with atmosphere. Some of it should have been redistributed to Sunday nights elsewhere. It was full of a good-looking, well-fed, jazz-beat crowd. None of this starving-artist, existentially broke, needle-infected Chet Baker look. There was no one here whose first and last penny would be spent on dope; blown in a subconscious haze. Hell, these were probably lawyers on their night out, and happy ones too, who could afford the prices, the look. Any white powder that fell from their noses was pocket money spent on sweeties, not the meaning of life. At home they probably had fresh sheets, and wine undrunk in the fridge. It sounded nice, abominably civilised.

'So, Bill, do you come here often? I mean, to see many gigs.'

'Yeah, when I get up to London, it's a good scene.' He nodded his head, surveying the scene; and obviously felt part of it. 'But I think it's time you bought me a drink. I've just paid a whacking eight quid each for us to get in here.' He raised his eyebrows in disbelief at the charge; or was it at my leaving him to pay?

'Shall we go and sit upstairs at a table?' I asked, rather sweetly, I thought.

'No. I'm not hungry, and I think you have to eat if you want a table, or you get charged extra. These places are a rip-off all round. Let's get to the bar. I'll have a double vodka and Coke.'

'Fine. Oh, thank you for paying my entrance. I'll go

and get the drinks, and maybe you can find some-where we can sit,' I said amiably, while thinking, He doesn't ask if I'm hungry, mean git! But I was glad to get away to be at the bar by myself.

I stood happily watching everyone else getting served, listening to the support, until I had to put my request in, in case he got suspicious and came to find me.

'A double vodka and Coke, and a red wine spritzer please, plenty of ice, thanks.'

This wasn't so bad: the music was a lot better than I could have suspected, with a lead singer whose voice glided into the sky before sliding to the floor.

I went to find Bill, who managed to get a space in the corner farthest away from the stage, cosy on a banquette. I didn't think I'd manage to squash in, until he moved a little and said, 'I thought it would be better to be at the back while this stuff's going on, then we can talk.' That was what we were there for, in the end, and unless I'd left then, there would be no getting away from it.

'So, Hope, is this your kind of scene? I like it when you know that you can come to these kind of small, offbeat places. I find it stops me getting into a fixed mindset on life. You know, I've had it pretty hard since splitting up with my last girlfriend; it's easy to isolate yourself. Sure, you go to work, but eventually you have to come home. I hate to quote Burt Bacharach, but the lyrics seem appropriate: "A house is not a home when the two of us are far apart." You know what I mean; artists are sensitive to those sorts of things. I mean, you may be . . . What I mean is, you still have feelings.'

He looked earnestly at me through the dark smoke of a stinking cheroot he'd set light to. I ducked a cloud that was ballooning towards my face.

'I try,' was all I could think to say, seemed to cover all sides.

The couple next to us around the table were arguing about which flat they should move into together, his or hers; who would give up the power, their past.

'. . . But at least I've got a garden, and it makes all the difference in the summer.'

'What's the point in having a garden that faces on to a main road in Brixton with all the juggernauts going by? All it means is that you're easier to burgle. Come on! When was the last time you did any weeding, let alone planted anything? A garden doesn't make any difference.'

'It does! I planted the Christmas tree last year. It didn't take, but at least I tried.'

'Anyway, I've got a better kitchen,' he said, thinking he'd won, a contented, full-stop smirk on his face, when she came in with the whammy.

'Of *course* you do, darling. You're a brilliant cook, that's why you should have the best kitchen possible. Then you'll be able to do all the cooking!'

'Yes, but I work.'

'So do I. But as you're the better cook, I think even you'll agree that if we're in your flat, you should take over the cooking.'

When such snatches of conversation seem more interesting than your own, you know you're in trouble. I wanted to join in, ask for one of their cigarettes and suggest that they give up the idea and live separately. Mind you, at that point I would have gladly accepted a job behind the bar.

'So were you with your girlfriend for long?'

It seemed a lame enough question, one to pass the time while the experimental music set up shop on stage and the tape took over.

I was feeling hot and uncomfortable. My red mac was too close to my skin, and pulled under my arms making them tender, but the choice of taking it off and showing Bill what I was wearing underneath didn't seem right. I could feel the eighty per cent of my body heat unable to escape because of my pure wool beret dampening my hair, and a trickle of sweat ran a curve around my ear. I was overdressed, yet underdressed. I took a swig from my drink, rudely crunching the ice and holding the glass to my temple while I tried to listen to Bill.

'What's time? The thing is, it was perfect, and that is timeless,' he said glumly, and swigged his drink back to get drunk before looking at me with a grimace of a smile. He reminded me of Pat's stepson in *EastEnders*, the bear who runs the video shop in the Walford soap.

'Was she an archaeologist, too?'

'No, actually, she was a dental assistant, a very good one. But more than that, she was just an incredibly beautiful person. She had an understanding of animals . . . She was rare.'

There were retorts going through my brain, making me want to snigger while I nodded my head understandingly. I thought it best to keep my glass raised to my mouth, taking little sips, but this only served to make me splutter – something along the lines of rare breeds and animal husbandry. It was seconds before I started to wonder whether Bill was a rare species, and whether his dong was donkey- or pig-style, like a corkscrew.

I once had sex with a man whose dick was shaped like a corkscrew. He couldn't have sex missionary-style without turning around. That was the night I discovered the true meaning of the word screw. I also discovered that you're not meant to laugh at a man's equipment; apparently they can be very sensitive.

'So, Bill, what are you working on at the moment? I love the thought of archaeological digs.'

'Have you been on many?'

'Well, no, but they must be fun, all that team spirit of discovery,' I added hopefully, to a man who was looking at me as though I'd ordered a Tampax for my main course.

'Exactly my point. People have no idea. I suppose you think it's like *Indiana Jones* or *Romancing the Stone*. Digs just aren't like that. They're dull, and aggressive, thankless tasks. I'm actually resurrecting a stately home in Kent at the moment, fascinating fourteenth-century architecture, which we're having to reassemble after the Victorians got at it.'

'Oh, so you are a builder?'

'Of course I'm not a builder. Not in so many words. That's what my company does, but we're very choosy about the work we take on. Oh, look, I think the band are starting up. Shall we move closer?' Bill got up and started towards the stage.

'I'm just off to the loo – I'll find you in a minute.'

I almost tripped, sliding down the stairs, what with the lean of the wall, and closing my eyes with relief and meteoric disappointment. I stumbled into a stainless-steel *pissoir*, the height of modern in conveniences, ladies. I thanked God I wasn't wearing espadrilles: the plumbing hadn't caught up with the design, and the drains' tidal effects crept up the toes of my stacked sandals. Probably the reason why stacks were invented in the first place – nothing to do with vanity and height, just common sense and hygiene.

I opened my mouth and screamed silently at my reflection as I sat on my hands and peed into the seatless bowl, my drink balancing on the sanitary disposal lid, my sanity balancing on my tongue.

Date from hell, date from hell, date from hell.

For some inexplicable reason, I couldn't keep that phrase from going through my head. At the washstand I washed my hands and dried them off on the only thing available – my mac. The drier wasn't working. Hopeless. I fished around in my pocket for a lipstick and re-primed my mouth-mask with its vermilion varnish. I looked about the windowless room for an exit, but there was only one way out – the way I'd come in.

'S'cuse!' A girl walked in, sheathed in a plastic catsuit with big blonde hair.

'Is there another way out of here, apart from the stairs?' I asked in desperation.

'No. Don't you like the music? 'Cos that's my bloke's band!' she replied aggressively, her puggish face suddenly close to mine. What was going wrong with tonight? Please God, take me home.

'No, God no, the music I love. Just a case of bad date.' I pulled a hideous grimace.

'Oh, never mind, love. Tell him to fuck off from me.'

'Thanks for the advice. I'll try it.' I glumly opened the door to face the rest of the evening.

If I could walk back up those stairs and keep on going all the way home, I would. At the top of the stairs I was greeted by a suddenly eager Bill.

'I was coming to find you. This is so good, this music, I didn't want you to miss any.'

'No?' I answered weakly.

On stage sat a band playing free-fall plinky-plonk music, Harrison Birtwhistle with an electronic jazz ensemble, all with matching ponytails. Looking at them brought out the Delilah in me, but I stood there powerless; freeze-framed, plus I didn't have any scissors handy.

I climbed up the well-worn stairs into my head, and on the way thought, I must remember to have these re-carpeted, to practise envisioning what I want. I didn't want to work in an office any more. I wanted to paint, and to be with people who perceived the world with extraordinary ideas – just not the kind that were playing on this stage. A different kind of extraordinary. I wanted to be surrounded by friends and lovers who held the same enthusiasm for life as I did, that burns at your toes and ignites your brain.

Rude, funny, warm, clever thoughts. I wanted to be home, snuggled up in my duvet with Clark Gable, watching the late-night movie together. I'd even settle for being with Cary Grant, as long as Clark was in the movie.

Perhaps the advert should've read: 'Clark Gable wanted'; I'd reckoned that if he was about, he'd only be interested in goddess material. I looked to my left at the Danny DeVito who thought that maybe he was Clark Gable, and my heart went out to him, my mouth automatically turned down at the corners, slightly pouting, and my forehead wrinkled. Poor thing, I thought.

'Are you all right, Hope?' Bill asked, puzzled, and touched my arm. 'Don't worry; I find this kind of music very emotional too,' he went on, and patted my shoulder.

What music? Where *was* I? What the fuck was I doing there? My body responded with involuntary shudders. I was surrounded by heaving bodies, close-packed and glowing like pilchards in the red light. Smoke caught in the air, weaving through the beams of light to end up in everyone's lungs, along with the smell of spilled pints and sweat, both fresh and old. A different perfume called Contradiction. The next day you could call it Contrition.

I thought an academic archaeologist would be a different kind of mate. His enthusiasm for modern jazz intrigued me. I only ever liked ancient, mournful, Billie Holiday, Charlie Mingus stuff, a tune to hang yourself by. I'm always ready to learn and listen to others; I like to think; I'm always ready to change. I have to say, I loved the sound of his eighteenth-century folly that rose out of a working watermill, that held undoubted attractions.

Bill had written in his letter about his passion for old things, treasures of the past, for the beauty they still possessed, like his Bentley that he was restoring, and the tortoise he still kept, given to him by his godfather on the day he was born. These touches to me seemed novel, interesting instead of indicative of somebody super-glued to the past. I was busy imagining an English eccentric mixed with Steven Spielberg's hero, Indiana Jones. Ruggedly handsome, dedicated to the adventures that lay in and out of books. Bill was right, I knew nothing about archaeology, I had only a few sad, faded movie images.

'Come on, Hope,' I could almost hear him saying. 'We're going on a dig in Inca territory tonight! Get your backpack on, we're off!'

In seconds, I'd be hard-hatted and sporting khaki shorts, a camera my only necklace, a portable painting kit left permanently by the front door like an expectant mother's overnight case. 'I'm ready when you are, Bill,' I'd breezily reply, casually flinging on a matching safari jacket.

My mind had built him into an irregular, ego-less hunk who wouldn't have had a single photograph of himself lying around. Why, the only recent picture he'd have would be the one he had given to his parents of him shaking hands with the chief of a primitive society, on finding the hidden treasures of his country and handing them back to him.

He was to be the package, the whole package and nothing but . . .

Kind, Caring, Successful, Passionate, Intimate, Curious, Exciting and Endlessly Humorous. Not a hint of Surly Brutishness in sight.

Some might say all of this is the stuff of fantasy, that it is *Romancing the Stone* out of all proportion, but I have met some extraordinary men in my life – somebody's husband, brother, son, father or lover.

Why shouldn't I have one, if I chose?

Why shouldn't Bill be all of this? Because he wasn't. He was to somebody else. A perfect match for Eileen, he had said, his last girlfriend he mourned and moaned for throughout our evening.

In retrospect, it wasn't the wrong bar or the wrong music. It was just the wrong date.

Though I like to believe that there is no right or

wrong about these things, that people's perspectives on the world are all different. We were too different. The clothes and the instant disappointment I had felt were trying to tell me something, butting my instinct into working, kindly informing me to be strong, to save face at the onset and say no after the first drink. Pity my mind, my justifying mind, had got in the way. *Pity* had got in the way. Such a terrible emotion.

The bar full of handsomes had shown me what else was waiting for me out there, in the wide yonder. I didn't have to stick with the uncomfortable, but I'd chosen it for that night. Obviously I was meant to sit through the whole dire evening just to have the last conversation, to learn a lesson.

'I'm so sorry – this has been a bit of a desperate evening, hasn't it? The music was good, though,' he ventured bravely to me, as we sat in the intimate enclosure of a joggy, black cab ride home through the emptying night-time streets.

'No, it was lovely,' I lied blatantly, crossing my treacherous fingers inside my deep, dark mac pockets.

'Well, I'm glad one of us enjoyed it. You might have been able to tell that I haven't quite got over Eileen yet. I'm not sure I'm really ready for a new relationship straight away. It's difficult. Eileen was perfect; she dressed so beautifully, is so pretty. It was unfair of me even to put you to the test; you could never've measured up. Not that you haven't got a certain something, but you look too weird for me, if you want the truth. It's hard when you've been used to the best, you can't settle for halfway. I end up making comparisons all the time.'

I most certainly did not want to hear the truth! Not from his point of view. His lime-green-jacket, sick-print-shirt, balding, Chelsea-booted, ponytailed truth. No wonder Eileen had dumped him!

I was stuck, struck dumb, as though my tonsils were being pursued by a large raw cooking apple prizing my jaws apart. Not a state I'm often to be found in. I like a chat, but now the chat was over. Even in the dark my face must have registered surprise. I could feel my eyelids peeling back to reveal one hundred and twenty degrees of white. I don't know if I said anything, but I suppose I must have muttered goodbye to the man who replied that he was sorry, but he wouldn't be calling me again.

Fine.

I saw him get into his Suzuki Tonka-Toy Jeep, glad to be speeding back to Oxford. Call me a bitch, but I hoped he'd be stopped by the motorway police for drink-driving. Real tough toys, for real tough boys – Wonka!

Thoroughly bewildered, I walked home, going over the evening in my mind with a nit comb until I reached the comforting sight of my own front door. I emptied the night's rubbish of experimental experience upon the steps, refusing it entry into my cosy flat. I hoped the dustman would recognise my mind's detritus, pick it up and squash it flat. I hoped they didn't take it to the recycling department and give it back to someone else as their date.

Tomorrow would be different. Tomorrow was a new day.

Rather obviously, in fact, every day would be different, and I never had to repeat this one again, I remember thinking as I climbed into bed and dropped the hundred-odd miles necessary for the descent into the chasm of sleep. Tomorrow I would go shopping, and I would never have to spend a Friday night like that one again, ever, I promised myself. For spending nights like that, treats are the necessary rewards. That, and the knowledge that it's now the past, history.

Some things you just have to accept as wrong.

Chapter 3

THE GEIGER COUNTING, RICHTER SLIDING SCALE

I wish I had a Geiger counter. I can't remember what a Geiger counter does, but I assume it measures, or detects and measures. What I want it to do is to measure energy. You could wave it over somebody's name and it would come up with quantifiable information: low, high, medium, a 1–10 for each section.

The lowest of the low would read dead, the highest of the high, certifiable. Maybe a sliding Richter scale would be better; but I know that's for earthquakes. It would be attached to your person, as obvious as your clothes size. Sometimes you could hide it with a large flowing garment of words, but people would know what was underneath: if they listened carefully, they could see through it.

When you filled in forms for dating agencies and job applications, everyone would know instantly if you were suitable because of your energy levels, but it would be particularly useful for dating. You just wouldn't date a low-energy on purpose. Well, I wouldn't, being in the upper bracket. It's just not a useful situation to get into, tying yourself to a tugboat, being the donkey in the relationship, getting married only to become a Pushmepullyou (the two-headed animal in *Doctor Doolittle*). Pointlessly uncomfortable. A waste of time and energy.

Apparently, if you can read people's auras (as an innate ability, without carrying any machine around), you can see their energy levels without acupuncture and reflexology, palmistry, or telepathy. There is no need for the Geiger counter. Must practise exercising my inner talents, and then I might stop getting into the eternal energy crisis of feeling as though I am the one riding a bike, while the other person is on a slow walk to China, and every five minutes I have to stop and wait for them to catch up. It gets very boring for both the walker and the rider.

The walker thinks, Why must you keep dashing off! Come on, leave the bike at the side of the road. You'll never see the minutiae of detail in each blade of grass, if you're always dashing to get nowhere.

The rider thinks, Why are you so fucking yeah,

yeah, yeah? I saw the blade of grass, but you've just missed a baboon giving birth and the flight of flamingos overhead . . .

With some people I feel as though I'm in a Ferrari, and they're barely on foot.

Now if I had a Geiger counter, I would train it on each person I spent time with, and then act accordingly. If it read low, I would walk away, no matter the sexual magnetism. It would not be swayed by alcohol or Guarana (false energy boost), or the magic herbs of aromatherapy placed on pulse points (rosemary, lavender, grapefruit, lemon, geranium), or the external packaging of the person. It would become as obvious to me as reading, 'This product contains nuts', if I was allergic to nuts. It would read, 'Energy vampire at work', and I would leave the building.

You might argue that being high-energy, being with a low-energy person gives a natural balance. *Phooey*, you know in your heart of hearts. You might argue that two high-energy people together lead to high-explosive, volatile relationships? No, they're just not suited to each other, or they've been drinking, or they've watched *Who's Afraid of Virginia Woolf?* too many times, or they're depressingly into coke. In which case, they're not high-energy, because high-energies can't take that stuff; indeed. It hardly produces an effect worth the toilet trouble, except to slur the speech, and you can do that by burning your tongue on a cup of hot coffee or visiting the dentist.

If I'd had a Geiger counter, I wouldn't have got into the past things with Dougal, Stanley, Giles, Jeremy, Joe, or Thom, my husband. But Stanley was the one that had me fooled. Stanley had blond hair and black eyes, he had a job; strange but true. He was wealthy by his own endeavours (and he wasn't a drug dealer), he was single, he was clever, he was American, quietly witty in a Bostonian way and he lived across the road. I met him in the road. Things like that don't happen, do they? Yes, they do. I met him in the road (I saw him) and followed him into the bookshop on Westbourne Grove and did a Hugh Grant on him; he played the unsuspecting Julia Roberts bit. Of course, I didn't own the bookshop, so I slightly blackened my reputation with them (no more credit, I fear), but I did get him to buy a book in the end. A large book on the female Renaissance artist Sofonisba Anguissola (1536–1625). Whereupon he was so grateful for my showing him the road to righteousness, or so I thought, that he offered to buy me a coffee. I thought it was so I could explain her portraits to him and give him a potted history of art lecture concerning thumb-screws, seventeenth-century Artemisia Gentileschi, rape, and why Gwen Johns wasn't the first female artist just because she screwed Rodin, and they said so on *Woman's Hour*, once. Later he told me it was because he had an hour to kill, and that was why he was in the bookshop, but then he got so embarrassed he had to buy the book and leave. Apparently, he didn't ask me for coffee, I just asked myself. I didn't throw orange juice over him, just a mess of shy, lustful glances. He was gorgeous and tall, with shoulders broad enough to lean on. However, I might have assumed he was slightly cleverer, funnier than was the case, because he nodded and I listened to myself more than to him, or more than was polite. He was asking the questions. Actually I think the only thing he really asked was, did I want a cup of coffee, once I was sitting down with him – oh, dear. I think I was projecting a little that month. I also thought he was gay and I was wrong there, but then I assume all men are, that way I don't get disappointed. Anyway they are, aren't they? Put any man into a prison or a public school and they end up fucking each other; put a bunch of women in the same situation and they use a candle instead. I guess it's just a dick problem – they have to stick it into something. If there's a hole, fill it; they're a race of plasterers. Maybe that's why all men think they can do DIY?

Gem, my friend, shrieked at me down the phone – you can't date anyone called Stanley! It's not allowed. I should have listened. She always speaks sense about stuff like that. I couldn't take him out in public and introduce him to my friends with a name like Stanley, she said.

'But why not,' I argued. 'Stan Lee was the genius who invented *Spiderman*. How could anyone be ashamed of that?'

'But that's his first and second name, and your Stanley hasn't invented duck-shit, except how to get money out of libellous behaviour. Give up lawyers, if not for yourself, for me.'

'Oh, so you're trying to put me off him so you can have him, is that the ruse? Well you can't – he's mine!' I answered, triumphant.

'I don't need a lawyer, and neither do you, Miss Knott. Read Dickens on Lawyers.'

'Sshkebab! That's old stuff – the past. They aren't like that no more.'

'You'll see.'

And her silence said she'd closed her eyes on the matter and the conversation was over until she was proved right. There was nothing left to discuss. I could hear her doing her sit-ups on the other end of the line.

In fact, I didn't see. I couldn't leave it at that either with him or with regaling Gem with the details, regardless of her silence. There was something in my middle-class, deeply middle-ground perspective (thank God it doesn't come out in my paintings, I'd never be able to do landscapes) that made me want Stanley. When I looked at him, I could see what the kitchen in our home would look like. That's a very bad sign. Looking at your loved one and imagining a Smallbone of Devizes kitchen is not a way forward. I could see the Principles for Children range on our kids, and I know Gem could see it in me. I could see the way Stanley and I would amass our fortune Tortoise-and-Hare style – I was the hare, he was the tortoise. Painting would become more and more 'what I did before I was married'. My paintings would begin by being hung over the mantelpiece and end up in the hall, the guest room of our second home in Sussex, the loo.

Yet sex with Stanley was great. Curious, because Thom had been everything to me, but the sex was lousy bad, actually worse than that. There was no bit of us that fitted anywhere in the equation. It's funny how very different each relationship can be. I suppose that was why I was willing to see the kitchen when I looked at Stanley. The reflection of shining taps and an American fridge in his eyes didn't disturb me, because I could see us making passionate love all over the tiled, oak and marble surfaces. Is that how normal visions of futures together are tied up?

I can't trust Gem on normal either, and if I asked

DB, I'd have to be in a serious crisis. Maybe I should research into a decent set of matching friends for a wedding present first? I'm sure my brothers would offer to chip in for the final cost, but where would they buy them from? Joe would say, I will pay seventeen per cent on my John Lewis store card; Dick would do the same (he calls himself Richard because obviously being called Dick Knott is worse than being called May Knott. How did Joe get off the ridiculous name-call? He's the youngest child, and my mother claims they just didn't think with Dick and I. I hate thoughtless parents. When I have kids . . .), but would want to get them from Marks & Spencer. Even with its sliding reputation for homogenisation, they still have one very loyal customer in Tunbridge Wells, two if you count his wife Patsy, five if you count their kids Passion, Jasmine and Ivy. My brother is breeding a disco full of wallflowers.

I haven't softened enough to have children. I can't see my nieces as humans, in that babysitting for me would be a chore rather than a pleasure. I do not coo each time I walk past a pram, in fact I look at the size of the woman pushing it and decry the dehumanisation of motherhood. As Augustus John or someone with a famous moustache once said, when the pram enters the artist's hall, the artist leaves. Meaning that you can't quantify art (mad, bad and dangerous to know) with breastfeeding bliss; that people often find it more revolting than the extremes of modern art. I'm thinking Chapman Brothers here rather than Emin. Actually I'm thinking of Stanley. I could cope with the hideous practicals of child-rearing. I know I wouldn't mind wiping bums and snotty noses, cleaning up sick. It's the time you'd spend never alone that would drive me round the bend, and as soon as you put the kids to bed you'd have the husband to talk to, asking questions and getting answers of mind-bending, drivelling unimportance. I have heard Richard/Dick and Patsy discuss traffic routes for half an hour at dinner. I have listened to my mum discuss one piece of fish for the same length of time, with Geoffrey, my stepfather and even Joe, who is gay and should be a little more interesting with it, discusses car maintenance details such as brands of shammy leather with his boyfriend Graham. Where are the discussions of world importance? Why do we pair up with someone and marinate ourselves in trivia? Is discussing war any more important or revealing to the uninformed than discussing J-Cloths, or the colour of bluest-blue cornflowers?

I knew that if I stuck with Stanley in our Smallbone of Devizes kitchen, I too would be discussing picture hooks and curtain rails, and own a Phillipe Starck lemon squeezer before long. Never to be used but always admired. 'Hmm, that's interesting. What's it for?' Neighbours called Felicity would ask, as she and the brood came round for another Sunday barbecue before getting drunk and admitting she'd slept with her music teacher's wife, when she was fourteen. Hilariously funny at the time, but deeply destructive to neighbourly friendships afterwards. She'd be so embarrassed she'd have to duck and hide every time she passed you. Until the next time she's pissed, and comes to help you with the gravy in the kitchen and puts her hand on your arse by mistake. Or admires your necklace that Stanley gave you as a wedding present, remarking on its loveliness, and lets her fingers slip into the cleavage of your bra. Mortified with terror, you do nothing to stop her as she strokes your breast more gently than a man and reaches for a nipple with her mouth (whereupon you become more mortified in case you might enjoy it), at which point your child walks in and asks what you and Felicity are doing.

So you see how it got with Stanley. It didn't stop at the kitchen; I even had the history of the neighbours mapped out in my mind – I was having lesbian affairs with them to relieve the boredom. I knew the shape of the street the kitchen would live in, and the Peugeot he'd leave outside while cycling to work.

Meanwhile we were having sex. In train stations,

on trains, in aeroplanes, airports, tubes, taxis, car, office, kitchen, hallway, living room, on the dining table, sofa, hotel broom cupboards and the occasional bed. Staying with Stanley for a weekend meant I had enough orgasms and garage-shop pre-cooked meals to last a year. Instead of walking away elated and enthused for my office work and painting, I became unbelievably depressed. I'd have to eat pesto on spaghetti, toast and crackers while stripping a basil plant whole into my mouth for its anti-depressant properties. I began to think that it was lovesickness, it was of a kind. I thought the symptoms meant that I loved him. All I wanted was some part of him inside me at all times. Was this unreasonable? Was it love?

The problem was, when we weren't engaged in stuffing our mouths with each other's flesh, arguments started. Stanley began to irritate me. He talked about his job a lot, past cases and precedences, but not in a real way – more doctored by Ally McBeal, as if I had to have them gone over by the *National Enquirer* to make them digestible. He was condescending in a TV doctor manner.

I suppose I wouldn't have minded that so much, but what I appreciated in bed, and what made him a success at work – his slow thoroughness – infuriated me, and I despised it in conversation. Going over the same point in five different aspects when you'd got the point halfway through the first telling. No wonder I looked at him and thought about home furnishings. I had to think of something while my mind raced and my head did a slow nod of involvement over dinner in a low-lit restaurant, which always had to serve steak to satiate his blood-lust craving. I'm not being melodramatic or judgemental, but in my books anyone who smiles at the first show of blood oozing on to a white plate while sticking the meat with his serrated knife, and says, 'Look at that!' every time, as though it was the first, has a blood lust.

There is a moral to the Stanley tale, and I think it's something along the lines of pretty faces and good sex don't a relationship make. But what else can you possibly want? some might cry with exasperation. For some that's plenty – good looks, brilliant sex, decent conversation, a good provider. I will point you back to the beginning of the chapter and the Geiger counter, for if the energy isn't right, the rest goes by the wayside.

Unfortunately I still hadn't learned the energy thing by the end of Stanley, and I rebounded straight on to my future husband, who was pretty ugly (I had mistakenly started to compare ugly:interesting ratio studies in the backwaters of my mind) and much poorer. I held some mistaken notion that creativity, even in a scriptwriter, was nobler than a lawyer. I pretended to make do and mend – that's what they did in the war, wasn't it? No matter, don't think about yourself, there was a war effort to pull for, the greater good, the country. Well, what country was I doing it for – my family and related animals? I do love Dick, really, I just wish he wouldn't make his own wine, and serve it. Joe I love too, as long as he holds off showing me the tattooed, pierced fashion statements hidden beneath the pinstriped façade, on parts of his body I didn't even see as a child. And my mum! I think I got married to give my mum something to do other than my stepfather. How kind of me.

My mum would have loved Stanley but I never introduced them; there was always a reason not to. I did take him to parties, but he and friends were not a success. Whether it was the exclusivity of our relationship, the constant delving into each other like an ongoing nine-month meal of obsessive physical gluttony, or that he didn't like them and vice versa, I don't know. Not just Gem and DB but Rachel, China, Tippi, Lily, Dan, Ian, Dominic, Oliver . . . All said more or less the same thing – pleasant. A pretty damning indictment of my choice, but they weren't having sex with him. I limited our time, cut out my friends and had a lot of *dîners à deux*. We saw his friends, but he only had a few, so that made it easy.

Mostly it was us two against the world, our great fight to dive into each other's bodies and become one, a sport we never tired of – until one day.

One day I said to Stanley, after a three-hour marathon of orgasmic sex, that this couldn't go on. I think I wanted to revisit my old life. I think I wanted to get back on my bicycle alone. Go shopping in the King's Road, stop and have a lasagne and spinach for one at Picasso, or an iced coffee. Get back on my bike and freewheel through the cutesy little Battenberg-coloured houses that line the streets of Chelsea and are plagued with the blue plaques of Jerome K. Jerome, George Gissing; the site of Edith Sitwell's first recital of *Façades* with William Walton, now a toyshop; Peter Ustinov's Gothic mansion, Chelsea College of Art on Manresa Road and Holman Hunt's house. Past the Chelsea Arts Club, founded by James McNeil Whistler, Augustus John et al. in the old Latin Quarter, and down towards the Embankment, where Turner, Rossetti and Steer lived on Cheyne Walk. Slowly pedal past the houseboats, as pretty as toytown replicas, and across Battersea Bridge to the park, perfect on the river, and crowned with its gold Buddha.

In the nine months Stanley and I had been seeing each other I think we walked in a park once, to go to the Serpentine Gallery. The exhibition I can't even remember, except that he decried it as total crap! And we got back into his convertible without even browsing through the bookshop, for him to say, 'Where next, my flower?' How can you explain to someone like that, that you were at the destination required for the afternoon? 'How about my place? Or we could go to a movie – there's a great new Arnie out. Your choice.' Apparently a lot of people spend their Sundays like that. I don't suppose Stanley ever saw the sailing boats gliding across Kensington Park Gardens pond, or the vainglorious peacocks strutting to the opera in Holland Park. Or listened to the jazz in the evening in Battersea Park, while rowing on the lake watching the fake waterfall on the mock tropical island that waves at the café? Or been to Clapham Common and the hippie abstract restaurant? Or sleighed down a snow-covered Primrose Hill on a black bin liner? Or swum in the weed-filled, women-only pond on Hampstead Heath? He certainly wouldn't do that, being a man, being Stanley.

I wanted to be an artist again, get drenched in the rain and not worry about the consequences to my dry-clean-only designer jacket Stanley had bought me. I wanted to go and get drunk and dance on tables and wake up with a modern-day Dylan Thomas, who couldn't get it up the night before but had lulled me to sleep with poetry. I wanted to laugh till I wet myself. I wanted to land in a foreign country and not be booked into a hotel, or know what would happen next. I wanted never to have dinner unless I was starving, always to be inappropriately dressed and un-politically correct. To laugh in the sad, cruel bits of movies without accompanying stares and cross-examination. Not to care at all, but care too much. I wanted my old self back.

'This can't go on,' I said, squeezing a large sponge of water over my face so that I didn't have to look him in the eye even though we were sharing a bath. I thought that one sentence would do it, but no.

'Sure, we won't be so frantic when we're married with four kids, and sometimes living with a nanny takes the edge off it. Hey, for the first few months of just us, living together might take some give and take, but it'll still be great, hon-bun.' And he kissed me in a smug, smudged way, dolloping some of the bath foam on to my nose as though it was the final cherry on the cake. 'I can't wait to come home from work every night and find you there waiting for me.'

'I'm sorry, Stanley. What I mean is, I can't go on seeing you.'

He was silent for a minute, the smile still engraved on his face from what he had been saying, his thoughts and words. Slowly his brow grew vexed and his mouth became a rigid line. His eyes stopped being an entrance to mystery. With their darkness, they were scary tunnels. 'My God, May, why? What is it? You're not joking, right? Don't you like the sex?'

This was harder than I had anticipated. Maybe a shared bath wasn't the right place to do it. 'Like it! I'm addicted to it, but it doesn't make me feel good.' I stumbled along, words falling from my mouth.

'Well, you're certainly doing a good job faking,' he said, removing his arm from under my back and sloshing the now cold bathwater on to the floor as he climbed out. I looked over the rim and thought of the downstairs neighbours' buckling ceiling.

'No, you know I don't mean that. Stanley, I love our sex, it's just that I feel as though every time I see you I pig out. I'm an overeater. It's not your problem, it's mine, and I don't know if I could ever do anything other than that. Us, it just doesn't feel healthy.'

'Fine! Any way you want it. I saw us living together, and now you say I make you feel sick.' He was talking and towelling his back dry but stopped to look at me, scrutinising me with narrowed eyes. 'I really haven't been understanding stuff, have I?'

'Oh, Stanley, I don't know how to explain it.'

'Try painting a picture,' he said sarcastically, and sneered in quite an ugly way. Altogether he was starting to look remarkably ugly, which rather cheered me up, in the circumstances.

'I might.'

'Can't we see each other just for sex? I'll go crazy not fucking you,' he said, leaving the bathroom, dry, naked and beautiful.

Suddenly I saw it. I'd been trying to make love, and all the time he'd been fucking. The problem had been a total lack of connection, but I hadn't known why. I got out of the bath once he'd left the room. A storm was beginning outside the window, and I remember thinking how perfect it was that the weather could so accurately mirror what was going on inside my flat.

'No, I don't want to fuck any more. I'm sorry, Stanley,' I said to his dressed figure.

'You will be. Anyway, you've got my number. Want a last coffee across the road?'

'Thanks, but no.' I went to him and gave him a hug, wrapped in my towelling robe, and as he put one arm about me the other delved into the robe.

Immediately he was hands and mouth all over me. I wished I could have given him a pity fuck, but I was too mean, too set, determined to save my butt before the drug took me with it. I pulled away sharply, removing myself from the needle, stamping down my desire. It took will-power. I knew at that point that I was never going to be addict material.

'No. Goodbye, Stanley.' I turned and walked back

into the bathroom. I stood there biting my lower lip. I heard the lock go click as he opened the door and then pulled it closed behind him. I continued doing my make-up, not moving until I knew he must be out of the building and halfway home, and then I began to cry, and outside the window, the spring thunderstorm raged, and some of the rain was even hail.

I know you're meant to face your worst fears in order to overcome them, but surely that doesn't include a lifetime in suburbia, I thought, and blew my nose and wiped my eyes. I dressed in very bright colours that day, like a gypsy from a 1920s painting, with enough kohl around my eyes to start a fire, then I went to the corner shop and bought a packet of Gauloise French cigarettes that Stanley loathed the smell of. Even buying them gave me a frisson of excitement, as though I was under age. Smoking them gave me a heady hit. I made myself a large, very strong black coffee and began a painting on the largest piece of canvas I could find, and every tube of paint I used was a different shade of red.

That night I hit the town to celebrate with DB, Lily, Dominic and Gem. I got roaring drunk. We crawled pubs like we were students again, swigging down

Blackcurrant Nasties and Red Stripes with rum.

'C'mon, honestly, what did you think of Stanley? Tell me. I'm never calling him again.'

They all looked at each other, raising their eyebrows in unison, as we sat crowded into a grotty corner upstairs at the Cambridge Arms.

'We can't say, because you'll be back with him next week and won't speak to us again,' said Gem.

'Sex is stronger than friendship,' said DB.

'Who needs friends when you've got sex?' said Dominic.

'I've always fancied celibacy,' I said. 'I've had enough sex. Friends are more fun.'

'Yeah, yeah, yeah! Until the next one comes around,' said Gem.

'Whose round is it?' said DB.

'I'll get the next one at the Spanish place. It's open till two. But you've got to tell me the truth before we go,' I demanded.

'Ooh, you're a hard bargainer for the truth. You should be a Minister of Justice, May.'

'Well?' I was standing up at this point, swaying slightly in the aftermath of my last swig.

Lily spoke first, while redoing her lipstick in the mirror of a typically ornate 1950s powder compact. Lily always looked like the last days of the Empire, but then she was a costume designer. The problem was, when Lily opened her mouth, like the star in *Singin' in the Rain* when they started to make talkies, this high-pitched screeching cockney accent silenced a room in moments. 'I always thought he was quite pleasant. No, honestly. What?'

'No, that's wrong. He was better than quite, he was very pleasant,' said Gem, smiling at me.

I looked to DB in desperation. 'Pleasant is about it,' he reiterated.

'Well I thought he was a boring shit,' boomed Dominic. 'I never knew what you were doing with him. Bet he had a big wadge, didn't he?'

'Pardon?'

'Cock,' said DB. 'He means Stanley's knife. Who's called Stanley, anyway? Stanley Big Dick.'

'No, I meant moolah-spondula, dripping lolly, big dollar, crass cash,' Dominic reiterated.

'Both,' I said bleakly into the remains of my drink. Why had I given him up?

'Ooh, can I have him, May?' said Lily, seriously excited.

'Yeah, can I have his number? He said he quite liked that sculpture of mine.'

'Fuck off, DB and Lily. You didn't want to know him when I went out with him, and now that it's over you're scrabbling for his number. Well, you can have it. Good luck and good riddance.'

And I threw them a handful of his lawyer's business cards he'd once given me, 'Just in case any of your friends might need a good . . .' I'd brought them with me to do a burning ritual with outside of *Les Misérables* opposite, but throwing them across the pub and seeing Lily scrabbling for them seemed more appropriate in the circumstances.

'Ah, poor old May,' said Gem, putting a comforting arm about my shoulder and not mentioning any sign of a told-you-so. True friendship.

'Less of the poor, I'm a richer person for it,' I sniffed, beginning to feel a little weak and weepy. I still held on to one of his cards, tight in my pocket.

The second-to-last thing I remember doing is singing with them all, 'Je Ne Regrette Rien', with little respect to Edith Piaf, all the way up Charing Cross Road to the Spanish bar. I think there was a tango after that.

I remember. A Geiger counter measures ionizing particles – see, that's not so different from energy. Link the measure of magnitude, a Richter scale to the Geiger counter with a few wires or something, and there you would have it. Perfect. I wonder if I could patent it? I could advertise it in the back of *Town Beat* magazine as essential blind-dating equipment. Oh, fuck it, I'm not a scientist, I'll do a painting of it instead, replace the cupid figure in Bronzino's *Allegory* with a machine and hook it up to all the other figures ... Or two mannequins with an iron box between them, with hundreds of electrodes and tubes joining them up ... Hey, I've seen worse in the Tate!

Chapter 4

MORE

'Can you hold it for a minute?'

'Hold what?'

We were lying close and damply naked in his bed. We were at a point in our bodily dialogue where stopping for a chat was totally inappropriate.

'It, it. I've got to find something,' he said, disengaging himself.

'But the condoms are here.'

I was amused, then confused as he drew away from me and took with him what I'd thought he was asking me to hold. Was I holding it wrong?

'I'm looking for some shoes, would you put on some shoes?' He was slightly agitated.

'What do you mean, shoes?' I was perplexed. This

was no time to go down the shops for a pint of milk and a newspaper.

By this point he was off the bed, opening his mirrored floor-to-ceiling cupboards and trawling about naked inside; most undignified. Within moments he was out and presenting me with a pair of white stilettos, as common as a pair of laddered tights and about as elegant as eating spaghetti with a teaspoon.

We'd been in the middle of passionate throes, I'd thought. Perhaps he'd been thinking that too, and had got so excited he couldn't restrain himself from seeking the sharpest thrill of all – to make a nice middle-class girl like me into a Doreen or Sandra worthy of a totter down an Essex high street.

I couldn't help my immediate revulsion. It was as natural to me as sucking butterscotch, or putting marmalade on bacon sandwiches; call it a genetic disorder. I'm not blaming my parents, my schooling, a natural prejudice, or reading too much Evelyn Waugh too young, but I don't think it helped. It was the fault of a bit of everything, I suppose, that I didn't like those shoes.

'Yuk! You can't seriously expect me to wear those!' I said, in my best Horrified of Kensington accent.

'What's wrong with them?' he asked. He was genuinely perplexed, like some idiot wondering why you have to use a pencil to make a pencil drawing. I looked back at the poor man in total disbelief: how could he not see? Was he blind, ill-educated or diseased in the head?

'What's *wrong* with them?' I parroted back, looking just like the waiter in the Bateman cartoon of a girl ordering a glass of milk in the Café Royal. I said it with the same gusto with which Dame Edith Evans screeched, 'A handbag!' in *The Importance of Being Ernest* (1952 film version).

'They're *hideous*, that's what's wrong with them. I wouldn't be seen dead in them!' I said, feeling slightly strange at having this conversation in so naked a state.

'They're not that bad, are they?' Then he lowered and softened his voice to a husky, sex drawl. 'I find it very arousing to see women naked except for shoes.'

'How many women have you had here wearing these shoes? Don't answer – I don't want to know. But I'm not putting them on, not without foot condoms, at least. I don't want some strange disease, to find myself on the bus home with a takeaway I never ordered, double verrucas with athlete's foot on the side. Delicious!'

'Please, Hope, do it for me? You'll find it sexy, girls always do.'

'OK, OK. I don't mind wearing my own shoes, if it's

so exciting. Shall I go and slip my boots on?'

I jumped off the bed in preparation, but I could see by David's face that they didn't have the required effect. His tone was crestfallen. I'd never seen a man so particular about my footwear and I was the one who was choosy about shoes.

'No, come back here, Hope. I'll see if I can do it without.'

For a moment I felt a real meanie for spoiling his fun. Why couldn't I let go and join in for once, put on his white stilettos with their window bars for the fleshiness of my toes to squodge through? But as I said, they were contrary to my nature; my cells were allergic to them, and I couldn't do it. I couldn't even look at them without feeling a wave of revulsion covering my goose-pimples.

'Look,' I found myself saying in a moment of conciliatory weakness, wanting to prove I was as game as the next girl for a bit of harmless erotic fun. At that point my revulsion at seeming a prude was outweighing my prejudice. 'I'm not against wearing things in bed, but I'm not wearing those. You can buy me some new ones. Next weekend you can take me shoe shopping, if you like.' I'm a natural people-pleaser.

Tasting this crumb of generosity in my nature sent him panting like a dog, securing his passion, his body growing stiff with his attention. His eyes seemed to glaze over delightedly, his mind must have been on pause in a shot from Luis Buñuel's *Diary of a Chambermaid*.

Looking at David, talking to him, you'd never have imagined he'd be the kind of man to buy his sex-shoe collection from Dolcis. I couldn't even imagine him walking through the door, let alone taking those shoes off the shelf and going to the counter and saying, 'I'd like these in a size six.' (How did he decide upon the shoe size most likely to fit all? I now wonder. A lot of research, I suspect.)

You can never tell what the contents is from looking at the cover.

That's the one point none of us ever seem to remember. It doesn't matter how many times you say it, how obvious and clichéd it is, like a cork it just never seems to sink and stay. You just can't tell.

On our first proper date, David turned up in a pinstriped, single-breasted suit, a good silk tie and his shoes shining like chrome, his thick blond hair gelled into place above a clean-shaven face. I know that for some, a pinstriped suit is the uniform of the perverted, but I think they're just what you have to wear to work in the City.

He'd booked front stall tickets at the opera. Some people might be snotty and say, 'Well, what do you expect from somebody who goes to the English National Opera, instead of Covent Garden? Of course they'd shop at Dolcis,' but I'd disagree. I think the imagination and theatricality of ENO productions said more about David than most things.

He was wildly creative with his conversation, adored opera, films, Northern Soul dancing and wild, heavy, classical music. He started the day to Wagner's *Ring* cycle, while dressing in one of his designer suits, fixing his hair and cologning his face from his vast bathroom collection of perfumes.

David's bathroom, indeed the whole flat, was assiduously neat, showcase-tidy. Suspiciously tidy, it looked empty the way bachelor flats can, needing another to provide clutter. Yet the walls were covered with shelves full of read books, the most wonderful collection of videos – from foreign art films and American classics to high camp – and endless CDs. Magazines had been put away, the coffee table was polished and clear, a clean ashtray always out. On his walls hung framed and signed movie posters, both modern and old, of the films he loved best. Almodovar's *High Heels* predictably dominated the living room, with its enlarged scarlet shoes upon the feet of a Spanish femme fatale. All the elements were there, but I knew as soon as I walked in that there was something not quite right about that flat. I couldn't put my finger on what it was, apart from the general atmosphere, or the lack of focus. Maybe it was the absence of 'real' art, that's always flawed; everything was so neatly perfect. Photo-finished, un-emotive design. That was it, I'd hoped. I was used to living with the mess and imperfection of my paintings. I'd never spent much time in the Graphics department at college.

They say that opposites attract, but I don't agree. How can they? We're always more comfortable with the familiar. However much it looks like opposites from the outside, the insides must match somewhere down the crease. Otherwise it's going to be like eating the most revolting food combinations. Ever thought of chocolate profiteroles, stuffed with cold jelly beef consommé and served with a raspberry and HP sauce coulis, or carpaccio of beef filet with a dribble of Camp coffee? Would you put fried bacon bits into vanilla ice cream, or squirty cream on to Toulouse sausages (whereas sausages with marmalade has been perfectly acceptable since the days of Paddington Bear)?

Just as with food combining (nothing to do with dieting!), there has to be some recognition between the ingredients you put together, you have to recognise yourself somewhere in someone else. When you're focusing on that part of yourself, you become inextricably drawn. It was not just the shoe thing; I admit that I was scared to think there were other mirrors between us.

I was interested in sex then. I haven't always been. For years it lay buried; but I must have mummified it properly after Stanley, because when it resurfaced it was all perfectly intact. Nothing too dried or shrivelled. All the feelings and urges rose to the surface as though they'd just dived momentarily to the bottom to pick up a gold coin. Which is odd, because in reality, I suppose they'd really been hammered into submission at the bottom of my priority list. Ignored for so long they'd slunk off, run away from home. It was the day after the divorce from Thom came through that desire and its brother lust shot back into my line of sight. I remember the moment exactly; I was in a bookshop (again!), and I picked out an Anaïs Nin and started to read. By the end of the first story I could've fancied the pimply Hugh Grant-style assistant at the desk. I didn't, but I entertained the notion for thirty seconds.

I had sex in my vision and the projector on that day, the day I met David. How else do you end up on a wet winter afternoon, drinking tea and having sober sex with a stranger? Is that normal? Who am I to judge?

It's not as though he didn't offer me a gin and tonic

or a glass of wine, but I never like to drink in the day (in so far as I never say never). I hate that hangover-at-six-p.m. feeling. I hate that blurred head that allows you to sit in front of a TV screen and watch without judgement the steady stream of dross that people like David choose for you and I. That's what David does. He's a TV programme-planner. He decides what films are going to pull us back from the edge at Christmas time, ease the tensions after family scream-ing matches. 'I know, what about *The King and I*,' he suggests to a crony. Crony replies, 'Just the ticket to get the family back in the same room together.'

No matter that they'll never speak again. When we're cemented in our armchairs by chocolate brazils and mince pies, and the only form of exercise worth bothering with is working the channel controls, it is David who has thought to shake us from our dulled liqueur and sherry state by showing *It's a Wonderful Life* instead of *White Christmas* this year. Complain to David.

I knocked on his door somewhere in Wandsworth, not a place I'd ever visit voluntarily, but it's where I was drawn to that day. I drove my car, blindly navigating down unknown streets in my no-sense-of-direction way, and seemed to arrive at his place by chance. Right outside his door was my parking space.

I wish I could unselfconsciously say, 'as though by fate'; sometimes it seems the only explanation, but it makes me cringe and feel out of control. I do believe in magic, destiny, miracles – all these things. You can't set out on a road like this without that protection; faith. You've got to have a secure amount of faith that allows you to believe you are always in the right place at the right time, no matter how wrong, awkward or difficult it may seem. We learn something from every encounter. You can believe that everything is perfect, and that other people's business is not yours.

David opened the door looking like a Marlboro/ Diet Coke advert. In fact I think he even had a pack rolled up inside the sleeve of his white T-shirt, and a can in his hand. His torso stood gym-muscled to just the right degree against the tight cotton pulled and tucked into his Levi's, of course. I can't stand those over-muscled-baboon, blown-up-arm types: give me a hairless wimp to that. David was good, not pretty or ordinary – handsome, but dark-blond interesting, rather like his sense of humour.

He'd talked me over to his flat with his madcap, innuendo-flooded chat. I can't think of a time when I'd been chatted up so sexually. My plans were to go swimming, I told him.

'I've got my swimsuit on and everything. I was just

out the door, but I thought I'd give you a call and leave my number on your answerphone before I left.' I hadn't called anyone for a week after the Bill thing. I didn't need another evening of intense embarrassment shot through with boredom.

'Best idea you've had all week! You must be a smart girl. I bet you look great in a swimsuit, too. I bet you look even better with it off. By the way, what *do* you look like?' Faced with a question like that from someone you've never met before and don't ever *have* to meet, you can fuel any fantasy. The power of aural sex! You can be as dishonest or as blatant as you please. So how *do* you describe yourself?

'I'm a bit like Gina Lollobrigida without the heaving breasts, my hair's a little blonder and my skin's not so olive, and my eyes are blue behind my glasses. So I'm almost identical to Gina.'

Always start with the plus points and work your way down.

Or you can be factual.

'My legs are too short for my body; I can tell that by the way those bodysuits always cut me up the middle. My tummy and hips are covered, like my thighs, in horrendous stretch marks. I get through a stick of cover-up a month because of my spotty chocolate complexion. I'm a faddish dieter and exerciser; every time things get better I give up. My eyes are a squinty grey, my nose a mushroom snub protruding through my uncooked-pastry skin and my hair is flyaway, thin and greasy. I look best dressed in an extra-large brown-paper bag, pulled over my head and down to the ground.'

Or:

'I'm five foot nine with my stacked shoes in place. I've got light, very sharp straight hair. My eyes are like violet almonds, my stomach's as flat as an ironing board when I do my exercises three times a day. I've got perfect ears, unbitten nails and my measurements are: 36, 26, 36, give an inch or two. I wear bright orange lipstick and in the summer, my nose and shoulders freckle.'

I chose the last description, for that is how I felt about myself that day, but catch me on another day, or premenstrual, and it could've been one of the others.

'Wow! What's wrong with you? I mean, you sound fun, witty, bright, a dream. I thought anyone who put an ad in the lonely hearts column must be at least fifteen stone with halitosis, but I was prepared to put up with that because of your ad. I didn't imagine you really would be a goddess.'

'Don't judge me on my description.'

'I wouldn't dream of it, but you sound beautiful. Has anyone ever told you your voice is like liquid chocolate?'

The amount I eat, my vocal cords must have absorbed some by now, I thought, but said, 'No, but if it was true, I would've consumed it by now.'

'No, nobody has ever told me that either, but yours does. Do us a favour, skip your swim and come and get your physical exercise over here. You can show me what you look like in your swimsuit, and then we can do a few press-ups together.'

'I don't know, I'm not sure.'

'Not sure how to do a press-up! Don't worry, I'll give you personal tuition. Otherwise we're only going to have to wait a week. I don't know if I'll be able to. I'll start howling around the office, and my colleagues will be complaining until the dog-catcher's sent for and I'm either put in quarantine or doctored. Now, would you do that to me? You can't be that cruel. I'll buy you some chocolate, little girl.'

'I'll come for a cup of tea.'

'My, you're easy.'

'Easier than you can imagine,' I volleyed back.

I like to see myself as straightforward, with the looks of a mousey Louise Brooks when my hair obeys. I don't know if it is the truth, but it's what I see every time I look in the mirror. I don't like to be heavy, or life to be complicated, or to drag around the overbearing soul of a deranged Ophelia. That's not me or my style. Bring it up, and if you don't like it, let it go. That's what I say. A simple DIY therapy course. That way you don't even need the couch, let alone the psychiatrist. You get to save fifty pounds a week and spend it on your phone bill instead. I'm always telling my friends, but will they listen? About as often as I do, but keep on repeating the same story like an old India hand, and it just might sink into your pores.

I'd only rung David when I had because I was annoyed with the response I'd got from the one I'd really liked. He was called Toby, and it made me think of a cuddly teddy bear. From all the replies – all sixty-nine of them – his was the face that shone out like a sunflower and put the rest into the shade. He was yummy, delicious, gorgeous – there was no other way in my mind to describe him. I felt like I was window-shopping with all those replies, with a heavy wad of spare cash in my pocket and me saying, 'I'll have that one', pointing my finger at the most expensive, Toby.

The letter was perfect, literate, funny. He had my obsession with cosy, offbeat cinemas and cafés, a delight for the finer ice creams of life, was inquisitive about the rest of the world and had a strange way with words. Unfortunately, his answerphone message said he was away until the end of the next month, so that was that. What to do?

As a rule I never go for seconds, second-best,

second-hand. First choice, first served, first time, fresh off the rollers, brand sparkling new – that's what I like in men (clothes and paintings are different). I didn't want to compromise my first pick of the pops, but then I thought, Hey, Hope, they're all new, fresh, first-time dates for you, why not go for it? I couldn't find a good enough reason not to, so I designated myself three and a half weeks' playtime. I left my message, name and desire on Toby's answerphone, and then, faithful to the last, I tried David.

I wasn't expecting to sleep with David (always a strange euphemism) when I called him, but the electric charge down the phone pulled me to my least favourite district on that rainy Sunday.

I was on David's doorstep, and that was the important thing. His letter had been funny and unrevealing, other than that it said he had a professional job in films that he loved, a car, a house and likened himself to a cross between Boris Karloff in mad monster make-up and Christopher Jones (who he?). He included photocopies of three photographs, 'guess which is me', and the one that was him was graffitied with a blue moustache and the names were under the others. Not too hard to guess. He was better-looking than the goonish photo-booth shot, but the pivot of our attraction was humour and raw animal desire.

Animal attraction hardly ever takes aesthetic good looks into account, let alone class, personal hygiene or shag appeal. Instinct is hard to ignore. Look at *The Postman Always Rings Twice*, the one with Jack Nicholson and Jessica Lange, that old cracker, beauty and the beast. Strange how it's never portrayed the other way round – the inner, captivating appeal of the outwardly grotesque woman to the young, kind, handsome, sexy man, trapped in a loveless marriage.

When he opened the door, I was pleased to see that he didn't bear all the marks of his picture. He'd left off the blue marker across his upper lip; his sideburns weren't green and there was only the merest hint of red around his eyes.

'The gorgeous Hope, I presume?' he announced, looking down at me.

'And you must be David. I hardly recognised you without the green sideburns and no tache. I hope you didn't shave it off on my account?'

'Oh, no, I've been meaning to do it for ages. I figured it was the one thing getting between me and the Head of the BBC job. Don't stand out there getting wet. Come in, come in.'

'Thanks,' I said, brushing past him, feeling the electric charge and his growling magnetism – or was it mine? Whoever it was, something was growling.

Outside, I was leaving behind the kind of wet

Sunday afternoon that turns London into an old Hitchcock set, and unites its residents upon a common moaning theme that reaches its height of cheeriness with: 'Nice weather for ducks.'

Inside his flat I wished for a roaring log fire, a plate of freshly buttered crumpets, a rug to lie upon and a cup of tea to warm my hands around. One out of four seemed achievable. The slim, modern radiators had replaced the unnecessary mess of the old fireplace, sea-grass rush matting covered the floor and a modern, angular Japanese sofa seemed to be the thing to sit on. There were no crumpets. I'd left all that cosiness behind, at home.

While he put the kettle on for my tea request, I looked around the room, studied the book spines and the video collection and wondered what I was doing there.

When he returned with my steaming mug and a glass of wine for him, I was almost surprised and thought about leaving, but we started to talk tentatively, slightly embarrassed at the awkwardness of the hour and situation.

'Before we go any further I must ask you a question,' I said so boldly that he looked serious. 'Who is Christopher Jones?'

He looked blankly back at me, as though I'd been accusing him of an unknown crime. 'Christopher

Jones,' I repeated. 'You put a picture of him in your letter to me, and I don't think you look anything like him. You look much more like Hardy Kruger.'

'Hardy Kruger, now. I hope not, I think he's a bit dead.'

'No, Hardy Kruger in the sixties. You're lucky I didn't liken you to *Freddy* Kruger. He *is* a bit dead.'

'I am, aren't I? Is this you on a nice day, or do you change with the weather?'

'And can you get a refund on your postage? No. Yes. Who is he? *Christopher Jones* sounds like a shop in Covent Garden.'

'Ah, Christopher Jones was a star whose potential had been realised by the early seventies. His claim to fame was having Shelley Winters play his mother in a truly supreme film called *Wild in the Streets*.'

'No. Never heard of it.'

'I might have a copy here you could borrow, or I might have had to bin it on my thirty-fifth birthday because of the plot line.'

'Don't tell me you got too old to bear the word, wild?' I said, arching a just-thirty-one-year-old eyebrow.

'I'll ignore that comment and tell you the story. Christopher Jones plays the part of our hero, and an LSD pusher who becomes a rock star before becoming president of America – essential credentials, you might think.'

'Of course.'

'When he gets to the Whitehouse, he makes a law that all citizens over the age of thirty-five, including Mother Shelley, are sent to "Paradise Camps" to eke out their meaningless lives on a steady diet of acid.'

'Sounds brilliant. Where do I get this movie? The plot line's slightly reminiscent of Aldous Huxley's *Brave New World*, but he always was fond of a bit of hallucinatory help, along with Cary Grant. Did you know that when he was making all those Hitchcock films in the late fifties and sixties, he was off his head on prescribed acid? He must have seen your film, or been interned in it.'

'I thought you were a painter. How come you know so much about films? And drugs? Oh, my God, you're not one of the five million in London writing a script, are you?' And he cringed in anticipation.

'What, one of the half of London's poor sad fucks, that is? No, I'm not, I just like looking at them. Actually I'm writing a series, and it's in the post to you already, on starving nineteenth-century female artists.'

'No! No?'

'You're right, no.'

I could see the relief fall into his face and his body began to relax as I sat back into the green baize-like fabric of the sofa. He smiled at me, an off-centre, sexy

111

smile that made his eyes twinkle and my hormone levels escalate.

Sometimes I feel I have no control over my body, especially when I'm ovulating, or the moon hits full. I smiled back, and somehow our vision got knotted, and, like a needle on a stuck record, my eyes couldn't leave the groove of his face. My body pulled away to put my empty cup on the table, but my sight didn't follow and the cup fell on to the floor. The spell was broken, the tea spilled.

'I'm sorry,' I said and bent to find the cup, picking it up laughing.

'Careful, careful. That's a priceless Habitat mug you're dropping there, one of a set I wanted to have valued on *Antiques Roadshow*. You've got to look where you're going.'

'You're right. Where am I? I've been ignoring my mother saying that since I was two, and bumping into lamp-posts, too busy watching the sky.'

'What's that morbid saying? "We're all in the gutter, but some of us are looking at the stars." '

I'd put the unharmed priceless mug back on the table. 'Thank God we are. Imagine if you had to spend your whole life looking at the dog-shit-covered pavement.'

'You might not have the chance to walk in it.'

'Quite.'

We both laughed, ice cracked and we began to melt towards each other. Before I knew it, this stranger's tongue was in my mouth.

A first kiss is always a peculiar thing. It's as though you're going for an instant connection while trying to discover each other's boundaries with your lips and teeth. It is the most excellent precursor to whether or not your bodies are in any way compatible, because if your mouths don't fit, your hips are going to jar. I speak from experience, trust me. In the past, and my fitful, foolish youth, I have ended up in bed with boys whose teeth clashed against mine like a battering ram against a door. Nothing about our mouths fitted; there was no warmth or comfort or feel of velvet tongues deliciously touching. So of course I went to bed with them, with the thought that at least if we were fucking we wouldn't have to be kissing. How could I be surprised when sex with them then felt like a battering ram against a closed door? To some this may sound screwball – it does to me now – but I was a wacky teenager who did strange things in odd places, in order occasionally not to have to wake up alone in the middle of the night in my haunted squat. I know – most people would move house. That was my past, not how I am now. Believe me, I'm not anything I used to be.

David's kiss was a delectable delight of enveloping,

moist, exploring muscle, and his hands were much the same way, but dry. Experienced was the word that jumped to my blanked-out brain as I drifted into sensual mode and became a mass of vibrating cells responding to his touch, or a blob of liquid Terminator metal continually transmogrifying. Within moments, but it might have been hours, we had entered the timeless zone, we were on the floor and I was back wishing for a rug and log fire. David was finding, as he undressed me, that I wasn't as easy as I had claimed. My swimsuit and second skin enclosed my body to an annoying degree, and we had to stop while I shed it and dived back to the discomfort of rush matting.

Posh rush matting might look good, it might be practical, cheap or expensive, but I warn you, if you are in the habit of seducing on your living-room floor, think again. It is a passion killer, and gives you Chinese burns on your bum. Far better to invest in sumptuous, toe-sinking, deep-pile wool carpets. Unfortunately they stain rather more easily, and that is probably the reason why people tend to have sex in bed. The problem with sex in bed is that it makes you feel married almost instantly, and can be as much of a bucket of cold water as sex on the beach with sand in unwanted places. I think outdoor sex is an overrated pastime: in the woods it attracts ants; in meadows, hay fever and flies; in winter, colds and in cities, attention and neurosis.

Give me good old-fashioned hotel sex for heightened excitement and relaxation. It's allowed but it's not familiar, and that's why it works. I'm not sure if paying for the room adds to it, but at least you don't have to change the sheets or clean out the bath, and if you're lucky, you get to experiment with bidets, jacuzzis and a good power shower.

We moved back on to the sofa and David took off the tent of his boxer shorts. I'm not in the habit of laughing at men's dicks, because it usually has a bad effect, but the size of David's seemed to me ridiculous. Maybe I just wasn't used to them. I'd been out of currency for so long I'd forgotten they came in all sorts of shapes and sizes, but I was pretty sure I'd only seen the like of his on a donkey before.

'Where do you expect me to put that?' I laughed. 'You can't imagine it's going to fit, not between my legs. You can't be serious!'

'Ssh. Don't worry, I'll handle that side. Close your eyes and relax.'

I was worried whether the condom was going to fit, let alone me, but when he told me to close my eyes in his soft, lilting voice of passion, I did as though told by a doctor. I was to be a brave girl with the dread of a needle before the anaesthetic took effect.

Sex that first time with David was dreamy. The weather, the time, the place certainly had that effect of other-worldliness. I came with the thunderous noise of self-absorption, then I realised it had been him howling too. Those poor upstairs neighbours! How often they must have thought about ringing the police about the strange noises coming from below, and that day I had joined in.

It was a wonderful sense of release after so long. It had been years since Stanley and I did anything. When he withdrew, I felt oddly empty. We lay side by side, catching our breath once I had rolled off him in that 'just had sex with a stranger is there anything left to say' way, and then we played the waiting game. Who would open their eyes first, and what would the look hold? But I ruined the stilted atmosphere by laughing.

'What? What's so funny?'

'I can't believe what I've just done. I've never in my life leapt into sex so stone-cold sober, not with a stranger.'

'Have you forgotten my name already?'

'No, of course I haven't. You know what I mean. I don't know you, yet I'm in your house and having sex with you after forty minutes of being here.' I looked at my watch, still on my wrist. In fact a couple of hours had passed. 'What is your name, anyway?'

'How could you forget a name like Agamemnon! It was good, wasn't it, whatever my name is. The proof of positive attraction.'

'Absolutely. I can't deny that. I mean, have you ever done that before? You were cheating today because you had a glass of wine.'

'Of course I've done it before, in whorehouses. Don't worry, I've never been into anything other than safe sex.'

'Oh, so you regularly have sex with prostitutes?'

'No. But I have in the past. Does that surprise you? Most men do, otherwise there wouldn't be so many of them. Whores, I mean.'

'Yes. But, I always wonder why men want to degrade themselves so much as to pay to have sex with a stranger.'

'Is this any different?'

'Yes. We're two consenting adults who both wanted to do it without any money being involved. There might have been all sorts of other reasons why we wanted to do this, but we weren't taking anything from each other, apart from some mutual pleasure.' He kissed me on the cheek in a familiar way.

'I certainly took that. I've never seen paying for sex like that. If I did, I wouldn't do it. Perceptions.' He jumped up and stretched, flexing his muscles.

'I'm hungry. How about you, feel like something to eat? I make a wonderful spaghetti in tomato sauce, by Heinz.'

I nodded a yes back. He must be joking. I smiled, but I wasn't there. I removed myself protectively from the man who was getting dressed in front of me. Getting back into his T-shirt and jeans, picking up the used condom and hastily ripped packet to put into a bin. I slipped back into my swimsuit and shirt and lay down again on the sofa. I was thinking about men who have sex with prostitutes, about all the stories male friends had told me about their first and only (or so they say) experience of it. At least David was honest, which was probably more than Thom had ever been to me about his nebulous night-time philandering.

Thom is my ex-husband, and best friend for many years until marriage. I think Thom must have paid for sex: he never wanted it free from me, and it would have seemed mighty odd in the end if he had. Maybe he got it free from others in brief encounters or long affairs – wouldn't I have known? You'd imagine so. How easily we connect and disconnect, I thought, hugging my satiated empty self.

'Do we get hungry after sex because we want to feel full again?' I shouted to David when he announced that the food was on the go.

'No, we eat because we want to have enough energy to start all over again,' he answered, back at my side, between kissing me across my face like a hovering butterfly, very lightly and sweetly. His lips alighted upon my ear for a delicate nibble, before kissing a thunderous smack into my ear, making me shriek and turn on him, biting and tickling. We were on the floor again, and somewhere the microwave turned itself off with a *ting*. Heinz it was. David never joked about food or sex.

I got home that night, put on my nightie and got straight into bed. I didn't even have the energy to sink into a warm bath, though I wanted that warm, submerging cleanliness, but I didn't think I could have stayed awake waiting for it to run. That day I had discovered the meaning of the phrase shagged out. I could barely walk to my car on my gelatine legs. I almost thought I would have to abandon my dear sweet Mini to a lonely night in a strange street and take a taxi ride home. I couldn't do it. The idea of being sober and the added expense of a taxi to the other side of London was too much. I drove home in a more intoxicated state that night than on many nights when I had caroused around the town. Once in bed, I fell into a seaside sleep as though overdosed with ozone, oblivious to the answerphone on my bedside table that flashed waiting messages throughout the night.

When I woke in the morning, it was ten o'clock and the phone was ringing. Before I could fumble my sleepy fingers to it, the answerphone picked up. I heard David's dark brown, Sean Connery impression. 'Why, hello darling, I'm sorry you're not in too. How about a spot of opera tomorrow evening? Give me a call. It's a rare performance of *Princess Ida*, directed by Ken Russell. My office number's 450 1972, vintage year . . .'

'For what?' I picked up the phone and heard my own voice echo around my studio, and tried to turn the damn machine off.

'Hope? So you are there. What have you been up to on this fine and glorious day?'

'Sleep, glorious sleep, I'm happy to report. I think I stole the sleep of the gods last night. I'm hardly awake now. You might be able to tell.'

'The rigours of self-employment, eh? Well, I've been in the office since half past eight, I'll have you know, young lady!'

'Don't blame me. Somebody's got to do it, to keep this great British nation of ours prospering. Anyway, what's 1972 a great vintage year for?' I yawned back at him.

'Are you sure you're that interested? I was going to

say a TV series like *Randal and Hopkirk, Deceased*, before I was interrupted. Much as I'd like to spend the rest of the morning chatting, I'm afraid I've got to get off the phone and do some work. So how about the opera, baby, how are you fixed for Tuesday night, huh?'

'Nothing I can't cancel. Sounds good.'

'I'll call you back with the times later. Thanks for my best Sunday in years.'

'Yeah, it was fun, wasn't it? I'll let you know if my legs ever work again, my lawyer will let you know if they don't. I'll speak to you later. Thanks for the wake-up call.'

'Have a good day. See you tomorrow.'

Meeting at the opera, David seemed tired but delighted to see me, showering me with compliments, programmes, intermission champagne. I went unsure but excited. There was still a buzz of energy between us, the kind that seems to send voltage down the cables of your arms and legs. Afterwards, we had dinner at a restaurant close to his house, which made no sense to me since we were in town. At least it was closer to where I lived, but he had his car with him and didn't want to drink and drive. The food was all right; better than microwaved pasta in tomato sauce, local bistro food, swept along by the fads of the month. No honest delight in what was in there – the raw ingredients, if you'd been able to unearth them, drowned beneath layers of sauce.

As soon as we sat down David started to moan about the injustices of his work. I tried to change the subject, but he kept returning to it and I felt myself being sucked into a world of office politics that I didn't know and didn't want to know. I found myself advising him on where he should stand, listening to his stories of paper warfare with concern. There was hardly any talk of art or films; even the opera we'd spent two and a half hours sitting through. Odd, I thought. Had a bad day at the office, dear?

We went back to his house for what he hoped was shoe-time sex, but he was sadly disappointed. He managed to finish what he started but I didn't. He called me a cab home on his office account, and I left feeling perplexed as to what it was that had seemed so jolly and why it had fallen into this hit-and-miss evening. I had been feeling good about David. I'd said in my mind, 'Why not! Go for it, girl.' But I left that evening feeling like a waste-disposal unit fully dumped into. Fuck! Why did I have to get one of those Thoms again?

At home I made myself a cup of tea and looked through my letters, which made me feel better. Laying out the best five (besides Toby's, royally preserved up on my pin-board), I closed my eyes, shuffled them around and picked another date. David had said he was off to Berlin in a couple of days for a conference. I'd hinted first, but the message didn't get through, and so, as subtle as a mallet I asked why didn't he take me too, but he didn't leap at the offer.

I know I would have been sacked from work for bounding off, but since I was going to hand in my notice anyway I wouldn't have cared.

I knew my next date would be different.

I would follow my own advice, and let go as quickly as I'd picked up.

By the Friday, David had rung from Berlin apologising all over the place for his miserable attitude. I was out at the time, but I got it all from the answerphone in a rush of contrition, followed by pleas and orders. He'd wished I'd come with him, saying he hoped I'd not forgotten about the shopping trip. He said he'd ring me Saturday morning and pick me up in the afternoon.

Good job I didn't get lucky Friday night, because it was only five minutes between his phone call and sudden arrival on Saturday morning spouting MacNeice's poetry, Shakespeare Sonnets ('Mine eye hath play'd the painter and hath stell'd, Thy beauty's form in table of mine heart'), with Buck's Fizz to drink and croissants to dunk for breakfast, and flowers, lots of flowers.

I was still in my dressing gown. We drank the champagne, coffee and orange juice and talked. Talked and talked about Donne, Dostoevsky, McCullers, Huston, Tarantino, Perec, Louis Malle, Chekhov, Hal Hartley, Terry Frost, Dylan Thomas, King's Cross. It was friendly, funny, jolly and warm, our talk, and not a hint of sex about it. I was beginning to see the way his brain worked – fast and meticulous, high strong jumps from one idea to the next – and it suited my Woolworths pic an' mix mind. I liked David, which just goes to show you don't need formal introductions for friendships.

'I guess we should be going. Do you want to get dressed, modom, for our shopping expedition, or are you going in your dressing gown?'

The champagne was finished and I felt quite giddy, my stomach wobbly with all the liquid whooshing around inside. I got up and went to the bathroom to expel what had drained into my bladder and jump in the shower.

'Do you think I should? Perhaps my baby doll would be more appropriate.'

I didn't realise how closely I'd hit the nail on the head, and neither did I anticipate what putting a fake-fur tiger-skin trouser suit on would do to David. My clothes closet is by the bathroom; in fact it's the airing cupboard. I live and work in such a small space that everything turns into something else, and even the ceiling isn't wasted, because I've built a balcony, more like a bed on stilts, that you can only ever crawl into because it's so close to the roof. But it's cosy, how I like it.

I emerged from the bathroom, skins and make-up in place, blacked-out eyes with vermilion lips as shiny as my patent-leather boots, and David's jaw dropped. He leaped upon me with the weight and urgency of a Great Dane.

'Was it the hat that did it?' I asked him, in that quiet aftermath which followed the fast, furious action that had us both swept along on a tidal wave.

'It was the whole thing. You look fabulous. Promise me you'll always wear this. Will you put it on again, my tigress?' he growled up at me.

'For you, anything, but will it have the same effect? I'm not sure I could cope with an action replay.'

'I'll try to control myself, but I can't promise anything.'

We walked to Soho, quite separate. I kept pointing to nice shoes in shops we passed, but David wasn't interested. As long as he was picking up the bill he'd buy me the kind of shoes he liked. He made his way around the Paul Raymond district of London with quite alarming familiarity. He said it was from working in Wardour

Street a few years ago, and who was I to doubt that more than probable truth of all those lonely lunch hours, and trying to keep out of the rain? He led me into a basement shop, and I couldn't help myself looking around to see if anyone had spotted me going in.

Inside the shop was a world of fetishism – leather, zippered masks with matching handcuffs, liquid-plastic skins, rubber nappies for grown men, crotchless knickers and nippleless bras in every kind of synthetic material never normally used for underwear. I saw that look on David's face again; I now recognised it as being tied to his passion. He was so excited he'd become nervous. I feigned an interest in the dress and skirt rack, and I could feel his eyes watching me and then I could feel him, weak and breathy on my neck, 'Are there any you like?'

'This one's not too bad. This one's nice.'

'Would you like to try them on?' he asked through constricted throat muscles.

'Do you like them?' I replied, seriously teasing him. 'Which one do you prefer?'

'I like them both. A lot. But if we're going to buy shoes as well, perhaps you should just have one.'

I could have insisted, or hinted that I wanted both, and I know he would have caved into his desire, like asking an alcoholic to stick to his resolve of just the one drink when the whole bar was there for the price of an overdraft.

'Would you like to try those on?' the butch, multi-pierced assistant asked. 'The dressing room is downstairs. You can go in together but don't take too long, OK?' he finished, in a bored, resigned way, as though he'd spent the whole day evicting wankers and perverts from his shop.

I tried both of the rubberised plastic dresses on, to David's mesmerised stare, and chose the one that could vaguely be worn in real life without too much adverse comment. It had long, tight sleeves, padded shoulders, pointed breasts and a two-way zip that went from knee to neck. But its principal feature was its shiny black tightness. The only way to keep it clean was with a can of Mr Sheen.

Though I chatted away happily, there was hardly a peep out of David who had become meekly zomboid to my dominatrix appearance. I started putting shoes on and I could see him trying to keep a hold of his consciousness, but it was definitely him that chose the shoes. They were the highest, shiniest, pointiest shoes I had ever seen. To get my feet into them I had to arrange my feet with my hands to a two-in-one gradient.

If you saw a hill as steep as those shoes, you'd be fearful of walking down it barefooted. These shoes weren't made for walking. You could stand for five minutes, you could totter for three steps, but that was it. They were drawings of shoes that some crazy bastard thought somebody would actually buy; he must have met David in a bar. They were illustrations from a Frederick's of Hollywood shop catalogue, only a little less crude than the advertising cards of working women stuck up in telephone kiosks (once upon a time only around Mayfair), and that's what I looked like. Just give me a whip or a cane, and I too could be telling men off for money. I could give up the art and become rich.

I started to snigger in the mirror, but I stopped when I saw the disapproving looks from the counter girl. Fetishism is a serious business, not to be laughed at; it can't be made to look ridiculous, otherwise it takes the pleasure away from the pain. I felt like a cartoon cut-out: give me a couple of wigs and I could have been a stand-in for Modesty Blaise or Jessica Rabbit. I suddenly understood all the pain and stress involved in becoming truly two-dimensional.

For me, two dimensions just wasn't enough. I changed back into my tiger wear and wished I had on an ordinary pair of jeans instead of this loaded costume. David got out his credit cards and paid the two-hundred-pounds-plus bill, the shop took their imprint and said, 'That'll do nicely, thank you.' It was me that felt the ouch! Everyone else was happy. We walked back up the stairs and the sky seemed unrealistically light; it should be dark when you come out of places like that, like the cinema. I wanted to change the subject, since I wasn't allowed to laugh at the weirdness of our afternoon, the discomfort of my feelings about being there and part of it all. I wanted to get back to where we were earlier on that day, in the safety of words and playful, intellectual theorising, if we had to play mind games. I realised I'd only seen two sides of David's hexagon-shaped life. I didn't know him at all; here, on a stroll, was the perfect opportunity, I thought. I linked my arm through his and casually asked him about his childhood.

Never again, I swear, will I ever bring up that issue-filled subject again. Not with fetishists. Or I shall ask all applicants for the post right at the beginning, Did you have a happy childhood? If they say no, I'll say sorry, the position was filled this morning. So-called normals say you can't blame everything on your upbringing; it's the way you turn it around in your mind that affects your ideas and your thinking. I do agree with that, but how much pain can you turn around and view positively? Where is the cut-off point? Where is the division between horror and distress, annoyance and pain, pain and pleasure, where boundaries become confused and one lightly entwines the other in its hold?

For some this may be a regular, predictable tale, but I don't come from that side of town. I had parents who loved and adored me, gave me presents on my birthday, at Christmas and many times in between. I got pocket money once a week and spent it on sweets. I sat on my stepfather's lap reading books and laughing. I sang songs with my mother walking down to the shops, and had tickling competitions which I always lost. I found out about sex when I was fifteen in the back of the cinema. My parents might have had rows and probably should have divorced, like my mum and dad did when I was small, but haven't, but still they took the time and taught me that I was special and loved. My stepdad saved our family, my mum always says. I suppose she was right; he's a kind man.

David had a father who was a pillar of the community, the mayor of the town he came from, in the West Country. This father liked to drink and stay out late, and when he came home he had a fondness for using his wife as a human punchbag, both for his fists and his cock. David's mother would wake him when she heard her husband's heavy, stumbling shuffle and the confusion of finding the right key to fit into the lock. Cross and defeated, he would end up banging and shouting at the door for his wife to open up.

Meanwhile, she would be bundling young David into his dressing gown and hurrying him out of the back door before his father could do the same to him; some nights she wasn't fast enough. David would sit huddled, close to the door, winter and summer, waiting, listening for signs that his father was comatose and it was safe for him to return. I expect if that happened once, it would lodge in your memory like a stain until your therapists found the right dry-cleaning agent, but six times a week (Sunday was holy), until you ran away from home at the age of fourteen, I thought it was a miracle David was so sane. When I asked him if he'd ever talked to a therapist about it all, he looked at me as though I was mad.

'Why would I? There's nothing wrong with me,' the implication being that perhaps I was the one who was tuppence short of a shilling, a harpic agent (clean around the bend).

'You don't have to be mad. Some people go to therapists because their parents got divorced.'

'Well mine never did, so I don't need to.'

I left it at that.

Back home, I tried to liven up the proceedings and changed into my new outfit. I tried to make out it was just a bit of fun, and David seemed to enjoy it all, but it wasn't the same. David wanted to take photographs of Jessica Rabbit, all heels, stockings and tight-kneed skirt. I agreed; it seemed the least I could do for this poor boy, for that was how I now saw him. At the last minute, before the shutter went down, the thought of somebody coming up to me with a seedy mag open at 'Readers' Wives' made me jump, grab a book and cement it to my face. I'd never been so close to John Betjeman, before or since. But David I could never be close to.

The moral could be, don't have sex with someone you don't know, but I prefer the one that goes, trust your instincts. That first Sunday was perfect for absolving the loneliness of a damp, cold day for both of us; it didn't need to be anything more.

Chapter 5

BEEN THERE, SEEN IT, DONE IT

I thought that having affairs, like the one I'm involved in now, should be a fun, light-hearted thing. It could be. You drag these things down into serious, depressing conflicts when you start to analyse, compare or compartmentalise bits of relationships.

Hell, I've gone and done it again! I think, as another one hits the wall.

Mum says all these fears are personal to me. I should deal with them and then they wouldn't be appearing in my couplings. My mother, with the perfect marriage. I thought the whole business of relationships was about connecting with the other, listening to them, as well as you. Isn't that what's normal? This *normal* thing, I never did get it.

★ ★ ★

A mild flirt over the olives, and the affair had begun. I didn't really fancy him, though I liked the way his hair curled. He was tenacious, he kept following me. Each time I turned around, there he'd be. I was charming enough in return – I could afford to be, not knowing anyone there, including the host, the travel writer whose publishing party it was. I had only just met Ben, and Ben knew everyone, but then so did James. For his own and later, obvious reasons, James just didn't want to introduce me to anyone.

Ben's was the letter that began:

Dear Goddess,

Let me raise you to Dionysus' level of Olympian heights. Be my equal, and we can have Rome for dinner (Greece really isn't good enough). Send me a flight of golden-winged messengers with your telephone number, or it might be easier to call me so that I can summon forth mortals to make the necessary arrangements.

I await your reply with breathless desire,
Benjamin Jones

The photograph was taken on a summer holiday, and I suppose my suspicions should have been aroused, on seeing that something had been cut off the side and a slice of somebody else's flesh still remained in the picture. It wasn't a nipple or a lipsticked mouth, nothing obvious, but it was a different kind of a tan, slightly more golden; I noticed the light blonde hairs once I got the magnifying glass out.

It was probably his better-looking mate that he'd cut off, some gorgeous blond hunk. Signs like these are worth looking at.

The letter I read as a charmingly academic kind of challenge, and what girl doesn't like dinner in Rome; perhaps I should have seen it as simply pretentious, which, looking back, is what it seems. At the same time I read all the letters, I laughed at them all, I took hardly any of them seriously. I thought they all must be writing with a sense of humour, a bit of their tongue in my cheek; but I was mixing my correspondents up with me.

Benjamin was long and lean and dark, with chocolate-brown eyes. He had an Italian or Jewish look to him, with his curving, sensuous mouth that looked as though it was capable of a good laugh, amongst other things.

I picked up the phone and called.

'Jenkle, Jones and Pride,' an officious receptionist answered. Slightly thrown, I decided not to tell her that the goddess was calling – poor girl, it might be her first day at work.

'Yes, hello. Could you tell me what kind of company this is?'

'Architects, of course.'

'Of course, thank you. Do you think you could put me through to Mr Benjamin Jones?'

Better, I thought, to ask for his full name, in case it was his father picking up the phone.

'I'm afraid Mr Jones is in a meeting. Can I get him to call you?'

'No, that's all right. I'll call back this afternoon.'

I should have picked this up as another sign; not that I've got anything against architects, though they can be retentive control freaks, but who can't be? Just the fact that he wasn't there on first calling, that it wasn't an easy connection. All these things can act as little signals, but I always choose to ignore them when it suits me, and regret it at some future date, when keeping a stiff upper lip and trying to sing, 'Je Ne Regrette Rien', with a suitably wobbly voice. The way you do at the end of an affair, with tears of vitriol racing acid lanes down your cheeks and scorching your heart.

The next time I rang I got through to Benjamin, architect, partner of a small firm with big intentions, I gathered from his plummy, understated manner. Half of me had expected, and longed for, the sing-song, valley, boyo voice that a Jones should have, but he'd come from the wrong side of the tracks and had that slightly clipped, Cardiff, sent-away-to-school accent.

'Goddess, how nice to hear from you! Listen, can I call you back in say, half an hour or so? Are you free this evening? Maybe we could meet up? Oh, damn, I've got this thing to go to, but if you don't mind popping in? Sorry, I'm blathering – do you mind if I call you back?'

'Not at all. I'm in for the afternoon.'

And the next day and the next day, I could have added. I'd just given up my job at the office, and was now spending every glorious day ceremoniously anointing my old office clothes with paint, not just watercolours, but non-get-offable oils. That way I could never go back, even if I could never afford roasted vanilla coffee again.

You have to make leaps of faith, and when I'd got this new commission, I thought, Fuck it, I'm no temp! I'm a permanent painter. It's funny when you dare to jump, and you listen expectantly for the sound of a parachute opening and then it usually doesn't appear. But when you jump and expect to free-fall, the phone rings to catch you at the other end. Straight away I had another commission, a portrait of some-one's granny. It could be wonderful, all those lines – maybe I could make it into an etching later on. I also had an offer from a gallery I'd sent some slides to months ago, to be part of a three-man exhibition. I was feeling my way along Easy Street, as though any moment now I would get my sight back after all those dark years of office life.

I could meet up with Benjamin tonight and flick my hair back over my shoulders, raise my lowered eyes to meet his and say truthfully, 'Actually I'm an artist' whilst throwing away my white stick.

He had glasses on. He definitely didn't have glasses on in the photograph. How was I supposed to recognise him? I sat at the end of this bar in Soho for half an hour, and I was just starting to manufacture some fresh khaki bile in between chanting peace and good-will mantras, because stress isn't good for anyone, and everyone knows that stress is bred from anger, suppressed rage and all the little annoyances that build up in life – from things like being STOOD UP!

I'm just going to finish my drink, put on my lipstick and go to the pictures for the night, I thought, until I remembered that I didn't have any money to go anywhere but home. I was being forced to buy my own drink in this swish bin-hole.

I'd been staring at the door waiting for Mr Gorgeous to walk through it with a swing, and now I turned despondently to grab my bag and hoof off the stool on the give-up-and-go. So what? He wasn't that fabulous, and I could finish the first coat of my new painting. Besides, I had enough dates to keep me going for months. Now that *was* exciting.

I couldn't slide off the stool; it was covered in velvet and stuck to my skirt and tried to follow me to the floor. I wrestled my way out and tried to walk away but it wanted to come too, caught now on my coat. I felt someone laughing at me; I thought it must be the cheeky-chappie barman who'd tried to catch my eye on arrival, so I barked, 'Have you no control over your stools?'

When I looked round, it was a man in glasses who'd been enveloped in a newspaper the whole time I'd been sitting there. He'd kept looking at me and smiling, and now he was laughing at me and I was joining in. Real goddess material. I don't think so.

Would Rita Hayworth have behaved like this? Only after the Alzheimer's had set in. I stopped and looked closer. Was it him? It was hard to tell with his clothes on, and he'd lost both tan and hair. His glasses cut across the chocolate-brown eyes, and he looked older, but it was worth a guess.

'Now that we've got the wild animal caged' (the bar stool stood impeccably replaced by a bewildered manager, who'd come to help me out) 'you wouldn't happen to be someone I'm meant to be meeting?' I said to him, oh, so casual.

'I was hoping you were going to say that, but I don't know the name of the person I'm meant to be meeting, but you probably do. Were you meant to be meeting them at six-thirty?'

'I was, and it's now almost seven, so if you happen to be Benjamin Jones, you're late.'

'What can I say, Goddess? I'm sorry. Would you like another drink here, or do you mind if we show our faces quickly at this publishing party and move on? Then we can go somewhere quiet for dinner and talk.'

At least he wasn't indecisive like me; I was feeling quite unsure about signing up a whole evening with a stranger who'd sat and laughed at me.

'OK, I'm up for the adventure, but do you think you should introduce me by my earthly name, Hope Knott? Knott spelled with a K.'

'Wasn't that the last thing to come out of Pandora's Box?'

But not the last thing to go in, I would have replied to anyone else, but still wanting to make a good impression that didn't involve filth, I'd try to remember it for another time.

I sensibly answered, 'And save the world from War and Pestilence. I know, I have a heavy burden upon my butterfly shoulders. Do you wonder that I advertise for laughing companions?' I raised my eyebrow quizzically at him as I felt his admiring gaze glide down and then up again, stopping for a moment at my Wonderbra cleavage, before resting in my eyes.

Why do men do this? How can they so obviously do this? They have to do the physical check-over and clock your bust measurement before they can speak to a woman. Women are just as inquisitive, but maybe we're just a little more subtle, or are still held under a silent rule – it's rude to ogle the contents of a man's trousers. Girls are taught at nursery that it is not polite conversation to ask, 'How big is it, then?' or, 'Let's have a feel of your packet.' I have a Scottish friend, Rita, who says shape is all, and stands around beaches and swimming pools assessing shape and size, and won't think of going any further with a man if she gets the feeling that his dick is too thin, 'like some horrible old stick prodding around in you, and it's worse if it's too long. I hate that. You start to feel like gagging, and it's not even in your mouth! The other thing I can't stand is droopy old balls, ones that graze the pavement as they walk down the street, swinging in different directions and bangin' like sponge clackers. I can't stand that.' And who can?

This is what girls talk about, boys. When you think they're discussing your chest hair or biceps, whether we like you tall or blond or bald. We don't give a sod, as long as you don't bend over and show us your ginger bum hair. The rest we can put up with, even the eternal question that you only ever want answered in the affirmative: 'Yes, yes, yes and God, how you made the earth move.' George Segal and Glenda Jackson in *A Touch of Class*. Another movie classic shown at two in the morning. (Blame David's programming.)

Ben paid the bill and saved me my taxi fare home, and we began to walk.

'I take it I'm not the first response you've had, or answered?'

It was a peculiar conversation to be having, walking down the back of Wardour Street, too much like too many others that have been held on this street over the decades. We passed a telephone kiosk covered in cards advertising speciality talents, amazing proportions and graphically lurid illustrations, with large-print telephone numbers for the myopic or elderly. I looked at Ben's glasses. I liked the glasses, the straight broad shoulders on which hung a smart suit, the lips that covered good teeth and his large nose.

'Wishful thinking?'

'Pardon?'

'Aren't you projecting slightly?' I said, smilingly, trying to explain his own double entendre to him. He wasn't that stupid, just momentarily coy; I could tell with these men now.

'Well, of course. I quite understand if you don't want to talk about the others. I'm just curious.'

He did have a nice smile, but it wasn't a look I'd fall in love with. He was handsome, but too conventional. He dressed like a Frenchman, and not a cliché of one: I love a man in a beret and black polo neck exhaling garlic and carrying only onion-flavoured condoms. No, Ben was conservative – smart, stylish, uniform Euro-Brussels. It's a look, not one to lust after, but it is a look.

'I don't mind,' I said jauntily. 'I'll talk about anything. What did you want to know? By the way, where are we going?'

'Oh, forget it. Tell me a bit about you, but you had better be quick because we're almost there.'

'Well, you know my name. I'm thirty-two years old, single, I live in Bayswater, and I adore fresh olives and anchovies, expensive perfume and Klimt, lipstick and Bronzino; and I'm an artist.'

'Oh, really? What kind of work do you make?'

'Nothing to do with buildings. Actually, I'm a painter.'

Unfortunately he couldn't see me flick back my hair or look sincerely into his eyes – it was too dark, and he was looking for some doorway, but at least I'd got it in. Sometimes I set myself little challenges, things to include in an evening, to do or say, key words or actions that make me laugh, private jokes that I only ever share with my stuffed cat. Try getting 'transubstantiation' into a conversation with anyone other than the local priest.

'Ah, here we are,' he said, and held the door open for me in the kind of gentlemanly way you only see in old movies now.

We walked up some dirty, lino-clad, narrow stairs to the noise of a party in full chattering swing. A rugged, handsome man in a long leather trench coat came down towards us and I pressed my back to the wall to let him pass. He smiled a thank-you at me and I almost followed him out of the door. He reminded me of someone, couldn't think who; someone I'm sure I'd sighed over.

Instead I followed Ben through the door into a room full of navy-blue publishing girls, T-shirted rucksacks and journos. You could spot the journalists – all of them were crowded around the makeshift bar at one end of the room.

We shouldered our way across some kind of publishers' office common room. Too many unsold books lined the walls, and they weren't the book being promoted. That got to rest upon the mantelpiece: at least that stack was disappearing. Did it matter that it was being taken for a sister-in-law's birthday present, or sold on to a second-hand bookshop? The wine Ben handed me in a sophisticated plastic glass was the cheap red teeth-staining variety, but I was happy enough to have it. I enviously watched him light a cigarette, and wished I had something to do with my other hand, interrupt a conversation with, 'I'm sorry, do you have a light?'

I looked around, conscious of my obvious appearance in the room. I didn't match any of them; I was a physical outsider in their world. Too red with my nails, lips and floor-length velvet skirt, and certainly too shiny black with my mac, boots and bustier. I was not wearing pedal-pushers and an anorak, or a small black or grey dress.

Set up, Ben asked if I would like to meet one of his oldest friends, Harold Bones, the explorer and author of *One-way River – Adventures on the Orinoco*. I couldn't say no, or stop thinking of the Wombles. I was off, following a stranger across the room and pushing into the star circle. I wasn't just introduced to Harold but to everyone else: Simon, Peter, Josephine, Derek, Gemma, Charles and James.

Forget about the rest – James was large and polo-necked. James wasn't handsome, but there was something about him that gave him a glow, and he was clever. I'm a sucker for clever: call me an intellectual snob, but I hate always winning at Scrabble in my family. He was confident but not a peacock; older than the men I was used to, and, like Ben, not my type, but in a different way.

James had the inbred confidence of a major public school, the rock-solid, grounded leader type that the minor ones floundered against. He was politician material of the old school. I seemed to spend all my time sizing up the sexual mating possibilities of every man I saw: newsagents, motorcycle messengers, boys on the bus, in the bank. The mating game was stalking me or vice versa, or maybe it was my body wanting me to reproduce?

I started to feel guilty talking to James, and turned to look for my date, whom I still knew nothing about and who knew next to nothing about me. Maybe he didn't mind, maybe I wasn't his type either, but I was obviously James's.

James was a professor in his early to mid forties, who was passionate about Italian art and the line of philosophy that he lectured and wrote books about. Benjamin looked apologetically in my direction as though I'd been stuck with the club bore, as his friend Harold earnestly grasped his shoulder. That was my reprieve.

James was making me laugh, and then Ben came to join us. What were we talking about? Renoir's *The River*, Rabindranath Tagore, Ramana, India, Artemisia Gentileschi, Judith and Holofernes, Matisse and

Ingres. I stopped and turned my attention towards Ben, who wanted to introduce me to some other people. We drifted away, but soon James was by my side again, and so it went on all evening. I kept walking away, and he kept appearing like some magic act, handing me olives and pouring me more wine.

By ten o'clock most people were drunk, with tannin-stained stomachs, or they'd brought their own. Somebody had put on some music. Ben was dancing with a stringy blonde in beige court shoes. James was sitting on a table that I was leaning against. I was drunk. That was it. I leaned against him and could feel the light pressure of his large hand touching my hips in a cautious, only-just-beginning-to-work-his-way-around-my-body kind of way. His eyes were sparkling like he was a boy in a toy shop who's allowed to choose his own Christmas present and finds what he's always wanted: 'I'll have this one, don't bother with the wrapping!'

His hair was damp or greased and shone, one dark curl dangling seductively down his forehead in front of his eyes. I looked at him again and thought, He is kind of sexy in his black polo neck and trews.

'So this is what academics look like this season?' I teased him, manipulative woman, putting my face too close to his to talk, drawing away to laugh not noticing my winey breath or stained lips.

'What are you doing now? Would you like to have dinner?'

'With whom? Do I get to choose anyone in the world?'

'Dinner with me is the only choice, or no dinner at all, young lady,' he said, sternly mocking me.

'The problem is, I seem to remember I came with a date who was taking me out to dinner.'

I looked about in a lost, bewildered fashion for Ben, who I was certain I'd seen moments before. 'But I haven't seen him for ages. Do you think I should go and look for him?'

'My advice is no.'

'It's odd, I don't really know him.'

'Don't worry, I've known him for years. I can fill you in,' he said in an amused way.

'Promises, promises,' I replied.

Exciting mischief gleamed from his eyes, mirrored from my own.

'An even better reason not to look for him. Shall we go? I know the ideal place, just around the corner. We can talk about him all night if you like.'

'I suppose I could ring him in the morning.'

'You could. Or not bother.'

'Don't be cruel.'

'I promise to be a pussycat for the rest of the night.'

There's cats and cats, I thought.

I knew he wanted to kiss me, and I was beginning to fancy the idea of him smudging my lipstick, releasing my corseted breasts from my satin-ribboned bustier. I was wondering what he would be like to kiss. Would it be very academic, by the book?

He didn't kiss me there at the party, not in front of the others – I figured he was shy. Not so shy, though, from the licked words he then tumbled into my ear, gently massaging my corny vanity, something along the lines of, 'luscious beauty'.

That night, anyway, I felt like Ava Gardner in a Hemingway movie. Irresponsible Hollywood movie moguls giving us role models of wild coquettish drunkenness, I never did bump into Gregory Peck on any of those nights. Instead there was James: that was what I got, a James, and he looked like one too. Not the Dean type either, but maybe I got that one wrong as well. Maybe that's just what he was, more so than any Stewart, not solid and reliable and James-ish at all.

Oh, *boys*! I wouldn't mind the wolf's clothing, it's the way you dress up as men that's so confusing.

Once we were outside walking along the road, we became like shy strangers sobered by the slap of night air. Me, trotting too fast, taking quick, backward, guilty glances towards Ben, who'd probably gone home already. I prayed, 'Do unto others as you would have them do unto you', and it didn't feel too comfy.

James and I didn't touch or walk too close; if we had it might have fused the street lights, put London into a blackout. The current remained unbroken, quietly sizzling all the way through a dinner I couldn't eat, or concentrate on. I pushed some fish around a plate and watched him guzzle a meat stew, manly food. Only our feet dared to touch our flesh, though kept apart by shoe leather. The relief of dinner being over, meaning we could leave, was like being given an epidural halfway through an amputation.

As soon as we were out the door and on the pavement, he pulled me towards him with great, bear-like arms. He seemed big against a pale, full-mooned sky and I felt small, and that was nice. He kissed me with all of his mouth and tongue, and if I was drunk before, I was stumbling after him now into the taxi he had hailed, or had I hailed it dancing across the road, my long red skirt gathered up in my hands, clicking my heels like a show-off auditioning for a dance number?

I remember giving my address to the cab driver and sliding back into the ungiving seat, before returning to face James and his damp, enquiring tongue, softly, insidiously working its way between my lips. He didn't kiss like you'd imagine a professor would kiss; that's all I can say.

Upstairs in my flat, with the all-pervading smell of oils, we drank some more wine of a similar tannin quality to the publishing party's offerings. We sat on my sofa, things moving on apace with his hands, while my clothes were moving off. My sofa is too comfortable; it makes people feel too much at ease. It's blue, deep and wide, and once you sink into its upholstered depths, there is really little incentive to leave, as though you're being cradled by a warm ocean.

There was a break for oxygen and refreshments. I breathed deeply in anticipation of going back down under, but he interrupted me unexpectedly with words, and even I know you can't kiss, drink and speak at the same time. Not without mess; something gets in the way.

'I have to tell you something,' he started.

Oh-oh, you do, do you, what now? I thought. He's forgotten the condoms.

'Don't worry. I think I've got some in my bedroom.' And then out it came. No, not that.

'No, not that,' he started. 'I think you ought to know that I'm . . . (Muslim, an only child, asthmatic, celibate) . . . married.'

I was shocked.

'You're not! You haven't mentioned it once all evening. What, like married married, with children married?'

'Yes, with two children.'

'Well what on earth are you doing here? Where's your wife? Why wasn't she with you tonight? Go home, now.'

I was up from the sofa and striding purposefully towards the kitchen area of my open-plan studio flat, all of four steps. I had to put the kettle on, make tea, make time.

Tea's good for shock, they're always making tea in war films and police detective series.

'What you need is a good cuppa, plenty of sugar,' they always say. 'Put the kettle on, Constable, she'll be needing some tea after I've finished telling her about the man she thought was her husband.'

James didn't leave the sofa, but he put his head to rest in his hands and didn't look at me when he gave a tired explanation, as if he shouldn't have to.

'We go out on our own. She wanted to stay at home,' he said.

I could understand why, if he always went off to dinner with other women.

'I'm not surprised. So you've got this unhappy marriage where your wife doesn't understand you, is that it?'

I'd seen enough movies to know this plot: Jack Nicholson in *Carnal Knowledge*, Jack Nicholson in *Heartburn*; Jack Nicholson has that part sewn up.

'No. I have a happy marriage,' James said, so poker-faced I believe he meant it. 'And I want to keep it like that.'

'So what are you doing here? What were you doing following me around that excuse for a party?'

'I wanted to be with you. You're exciting, funny, clever, sexy, and it has nothing to do with my marriage.'

'And nor do any of those adjectives? Can't you wife-swap with your next-door neighbour if things are getting a bit dull around Camden? That's what they do in other suburbs of London.'

I can't be that clever, I thought. If I was, what was I doing talking to a man about his wedded bliss at one in the morning with my lipstick all over his mouth?

'I've never fancied men, I'm afraid, and I don't think the local MP on our other side is up for it. I could be wrong. Hope, dear, come here. What I mean is, you're special.'

'I know I am. People have always said that to me, mostly at school. Special. Special Needs. So thank you for saying so, but I still don't understand. Are you usually to be found at parties picking up women to have affairs with? How long have you been married?

Oh, do you want tea? Peppermint or Earl Grey?'

You see, all that money spent on my education was worth it – no academic results, but I never forget my manners in these sticky situations.

'Peppermint please. Four years. This isn't the first time; in fact it happened once before.'

I ploughed into him like a cross (and I was) examining counsel, and he replied not guilty with all the confidence of his profession. James the psychologist plus James the philosopher could twist a situation to be seen from any perception he wanted, just like any art history professor. I suppose what also made me cross was the fact that he hadn't mentioned my paintings once, even though we were surrounded by them. Maybe a comment like, 'that's nice/good/brilliant/genius!' was too much of a commitment to expect from a married man on the first night.

James didn't seem to find anything odd or strange about his predicament; in fact my coldness seemed to spur him on. I was the challenge he wanted to argue his way across, an English Channel to goose-grease his flesh for. I had thought it was me who was the manipulative one, but not at all. By the end of the night, I hadn't agreed to anything, not to sleep with him, not to have an affair with him, but we'd snogged until my face had been thoroughly exfoliated. What's in a kiss? I thought, collapsing into bed.

★ ★ ★

My first thought on waking the following day was, I was kissing a married man last night, this morning. This must be a sign that I have some morals left, waking with a guilty pang.

It was morning by the time he'd left, walking off into the sunrise in his black leather coat flapping in an early-morning wind. I'd looked out of the window at his receding figure and had a moment of regret, for his being married, for not giving him anything of myself. Thank God I didn't have to go to work any more.

For a day I wondered, would I, wouldn't I? Me, Mrs Dogmatic, wouldn't touch a married man with a broomstick. Why! You'd be cheating on your sisters with a no-good hound. I regaled my friends with tales of the outrageous behaviour of married men. I remembered my mother's stories of my father's adultery. I remembered my father's stories of my mother's adultery. All sorts of theories flew into my mind of why this was on offer to me. Perhaps I was being given this relationship to understand and forgive my father and mother more fully. Perhaps I was repeating my mother's behaviour, who'd had an affair with a married man before she'd divorced my father for his adulterous ways, before she met my stepdad and became his other half. For days I remembered all those family jokes against dowdy old nagging wives intent on keeping their husbands from having any fun. My mum was always fun, but maybe not enough for my real dad. Did it feel morally better to be the wife at home, or the 'skirt' in the restaurant, the night-time, high-flying fun?

I was right: friends were shocked by the prospect of a married man's advances; I wasn't so old-fashioned in my thinking. They were even more shocked when I started to see James, though not as much as I was. I explained to them regularly, as well as to myself, that it was to try to combat my feelings of revulsion, to go towards what I despised, to understand it better. Face the fear. 'Obviously,' I said, 'I'm not doing it because I enjoy it.' They were worried, but not for his wife's sake.

I tried not to think what The Wife must look like, pushing a pram down a nice street in Camden, a small, duffle-coated child with its mitten paw in her hand. My friends were concerned about me, sitting at home, waiting up nights for the phone to ring with easily broken promises. That I would care too much for what wasn't available. Availability was the crux in the end. I still had the others.

I was surprised at my friends' responses. I am not a sitting-at-home kind of girl. I call or I forget. All I could imagine was that it was their own worries they were voicing, for when they got into the same circumstances.

The next time I saw James, he came over to my house in his lunch break from the Courtauld where he'd been lecturing. We sat, and I kissed this stranger more for something to do, than out of any desperate passion. He was late, and that reminded me of my father, it felt familiar. His tie was a hideous expensive splodge that a wife might buy to keep mistresses away. They weren't bought by a PA. They weren't the ties I used to buy at work for my boss. As soon as he arrived, he told me he had a meeting to rush off to. This wasn't what I wanted, definitely not!

I called him a few days later to say so. I said that if this thing was going to happen at all I needed taking out, often and regularly, to smart, expensive places. I needed to be fed – I was a starving artist! I was, after all, nothing to do with his marriage, I couldn't be worrying about his family finances, couldn't hold his moral conscience for him. It wasn't good for me to be kept inside all day with the smell of turpentine, and people had died from being poisoned by the lead in oils. Besides, I wasn't some mistress to be hidden away, waiting for him to drop by, fit me in.

I told him, we should meet in public places, get to

know each other better. That was fine, he said. He felt, he said, that this was going to run for years; he was in no hurry.

Is it? I thought. Who says so?

'So where are you taking me for lunch?' he asked. I assumed he was joking, but just in case, I replied straight.

'I'm not taking you anywhere. You can take me to lunch, or we won't have lunch.'

You have to get the order right at the beginning, before the muddle in the middle gets going.

He booked a very expensive French restaurant, the kind of place that reeked of the repressed renal bourgeois. Too much cutlery, and floral trimmings; tablecloths that matched napkins and curtains and the fabric upon the walls – they probably had matching duvets and pillowcases upstairs. The maître d's skin looked as if it had been marinating in orange Bisto overnight, clashing horribly with her turquoise shirt. He wasn't on time, but I was prepared. I could have felt uncomfortable sitting in that straight-backed chair, and the way those waiters primly smile at you for taking up a table and not ordering anything. Instead I read my Walt Whitman. I suppose I wanted to impress him, in the same way that he'd imagined this restaurant would induce me. Not that I normally read *Hello!* magazine, or that I imagined James had all his meals out at a McDonald's, but we were equally matched in our snobbery.

James arrived, looking more handsome than I remembered, but maybe that was from the gleaming excitement that spread across his face, as though a feast had been laid out awaiting his arrival. I was flattered to be looked at in that way, and I liked his rush of enthusiasm. We talked politics, argued philosophy and ate ridiculously delicious, unhealthy, unhearty food that could only have sustained a snail on its way to a coronary. Having solved the world's problems, we nudged knees and caressed each other's shod feet, a provocative hand finding its way to my thigh, under cover of the table. We never talked about art, or his wife.

The end of the lunch came, he flashed his American Express gold card, signed the bill and we parted on the street corner with cousinly kisses. He was a professor with more than just university earnings.

The next few meetings all had the same feel of collusion with modesty; an impassioned snog by a taxi was the nearest we got to sex, but the erotic nature of our relationship wallpapered our meetings with a frisson that was turning to frustration. After a certain point, you forget what the magnet held.

One day when we spoke on the telephone I said, 'I

can't see the point of all this. Do you know what I mean?'

'No, I don't know what you mean,' he stoutly denied. 'I'm going to hire a tower in the country where we can run away to. I'll lie you on a hot beach in the sun and we'll let the waves engulf us. I shall make us the tenderest of traps.'

Dream on, old man. I wanted to be cruel.

'What will you tell your wife when you return with a five-day tan? "Working late at the office, dear"?'

Words, all these words. He would keep using them.

I like words too: jokes, fantasies, playful, imaginative ideas, but somewhere among them all I like a bit of practical – the mouth and the trousers.

In case he hadn't heard I said it again, to sink the plastic brick.

'I can't see the point in all of this. How can it be an affair when we haven't even made love?'

Though *fucked* was what I was talking about.

I didn't think I was rushing it after weeks of hugs and meek kisses. I couldn't understand what he wanted if it wasn't sex. That was for the stereotypical adulterous man who wasn't getting it from his wife. I wanted passionate proposals wrapped in filthy silk underwear, not decent conversation – I could get that in the paint shop.

I was beginning to wrestle with a New Man theory,

the pill's fault and the fallout of the seventies. That now, women weren't afraid of having everything that used to be the male preserve: their jobs, cars, incomes, children, homes. The one thing men could safely keep to themselves was their body. How could they be so mean, now that women were so voracious?

I started expounding my idea to James. Whether it bored or annoyed him, he interrupted with – *bingo!*

'I'm free tomorrow for the whole day. How about I come over and we can lie in bed and properly cement our relationship?'

Is it only married men who equate bed with sex?

'Lie or lie in bed?' I laughed. Somebody had to, and it didn't look like it was going to be him. 'Let's forget it. There's nothing to cement, it's not as though we're building the Great Wall of China (if anything, it was more of a semi-detached). At least if we walk away now we haven't committed anything, least of all adultery. There'll be nothing to feel bad about; it will all have been a bit of harmless fun.'

Even though I could tell the fun wasn't in my voice, and the serious nature of the thing was bringing me down. That, I didn't like. I didn't want him leaving his wife because he was in love with me; I would rather this was strictly a sex thing. I was unavailable, more unavailable than he was.

He hummed grimly on the other end, and I could

hear a bus pass by the phone box he was standing in at the end of the road from his house.

'Do you feel bad now?' he asked.

'No,' and it was true.

'I'll see you tomorrow.' And he put the phone down just as I was about to level 'control freak' at him, so I said it to the dead phone anyway.

James turned up the next day and we went to bed. It was odd. I had thought our skins would sail across each other in some silk-knit slide; they didn't. Edges caught and rubbed. But the largeness of his body and the deftness of his hands worked wonders between my legs, until I was as hard and wet as it was possible to be. I waited for a rocket penetration but I knew it was fantasy; I held in my hand his empty, softening member. He obviously disliked adultery more than I did. I let it drop and went to hold his hand, not in a moment of tenderness but one of determination – I wasn't giving up. I repositioned his fingers on my clitoris and around the entrance to my mouth, and I pushed at his head until his tongue was down there too, and I was drowning his poor face. I came with a mixture of wilful resolution and friction. That seemed to do it, and I felt him harden to attention by my toes. The Chinese used to think the foot, bound and crippled, was the most erotic part of the female body, and sex with the soft, curling, deformed flesh was as hot as you could get. I remembered that as my painted toes caressed his solid cock. He obviously didn't agree; he pushed my toes off. There was either a distinct lack of Chinese about him, or too much Camden in there.

Puffing back to consciousness, I beamed down at his pink-smudged face. 'Hey, looks like it's that condom time of day after all,' I chirped.

His face fell as he pulled himself up by my side, collapsing his head on my pillow and wiping my slime off it.

Urghh, I thought, he could have used a tissue. 'I'll have to wash that now!'

'You don't really expect me to . . .? You don't want me to wear one of *those*!?'

Had I asked him to put on a latex sex mask, fully zippered with matching pantyhose, I might have been more understanding of his reproach. I looked at him with fully uncomprehending, madman eyes as he tried to explain his way out of the sensible, natural, only way we were going to have sex.

'But they're so horrible.' His voice softened to a seductive, lilting whisper. 'I want to be with you, Hope.' His eyes joined in to plead, serious grey-hazel spirographs. Our bodies side by side, nose tips touching, slack, carelessly placed arms crossing each other's borders. 'I want to be *with* you, not separated by a layer of rubber. I want to feel you. I want to be inside you, feeling you.'

I could tell by his steady, insistent tone that he meant it. And for one second . . . Then I remembered my granny always scolding me with, 'I want never gets!'

'That would be nice, but call me old-fashioned, I just hate getting pregnant, let alone the rest. Did you know more people are getting Aids in retirement villages across Miami than anywhere else? The pre-condom generation Viagra-ed up is dangerous!'

'Can't you get some other kind of contraception? I know it's the woman's responsibility to protect her-self, but those things always do it to me.' He pointed to the condom I held between my fingers.

The woman's responsibility indeed! Remarks like that harden a girl's approach. My sympathy had gone, and now my desire was following. Who needed to have sex with men like these? I shouldn't have pushed it out of the romantic friendship league; greed made me want a good fuck and I should have looked elsewhere. Where's the professor with the body to match?

'No, I can't. I like safe sex. I like not getting diseases, I don't want Aids for Christmas or New Year. Not that I'm in any way saying I don't trust you, but I don't know who your wife is sleeping with these days.'

'She's not sleeping with anyone.' His mouth tightened on the last word, and I couldn't help myself.

'Not even you? Poor thing. Another couple of miracle virgin births.' I stopped and listened for a moment as the answerphone beeped to pick up, recording a man's voice. I continued talking so neither of us could hear the message.

'You see how all this is turning out? Don't you think this is telling us something? Let's just call it a day,' I said, stroking his cheek kindly with my hand and giving him a smile. I rose to leave the chaste sheets. 'Just think, if this was our wedding night, this could stand as grounds for divorce, if you weren't already married to someone else,' I said, laughing.

It seemed to do the trick, and he grabbed me back and wrestled me under him before doing tingly magical things with those hands and tongue and a part of his body encased in rubber.

I meant it, though, I really did this time. I meant not to see him again.

But here I am, an adult child, still trying to figure out the word 'normal', still excited at the words 'present' and 'treats'. I'm surprised they never charge me one and a half each time I go to the cinema or jump on the bus.

Surprise, surprise. James calls a few days later and asks if I'm free to go and see the great jazz man James Moody play at Ronnie Scott's. Of course I am. This is a treat. I can't bypass this treat, promising smoky jazz and red plush. Music to bully your blood faster through your veins and thrum secretly in your fingertips for days after.

Yes, I'll go and see James Moody with him, and sit too close on soft velvet seats watching him drink his double Scotches, whatever hits the spot, slams the nail. Four songs in and I'm happy, grinning like a cat – music does that to me. James leans close with the pretence of whispering something in my ear, and instead begins to nibble it. The predictability of clandestine adventures.

'I have to go home,' I reply.

Outside I'm getting into a cab, congratulating myself, and he slips in beside me.

'Can I come too? It won't be the same as the other day,' he promises. 'It'll be better.'

Promises, promises. Neither of us is being honest, and who is his wife sleeping with? I wanted to, I intended to, but I was so surprised at his gall that I didn't say no, just like that silly girl who couldn't either.

'Uh-huh, prove it!' I retaliated.

One of the things that was dogging me was excuses. I worried how one person managed to find so many that could be consistently believable. I know that faith and trust can go a long way, but at what point does a piece of string turn into elastic? What did he say when he got home? How did he feel when his wife put her arms around him as he climbed into bed at four in the morning trying not to wake her, fresh with my smell, turning sleepily to say, 'Poor James, you work so hard'? Or when he hears her on the phone to her mother, 'Poor James is working so hard at finishing his book, I don't think he'll be up for lunch. He didn't get back from the office until four last night. He has to work hard Mother, to get on in his world, that's just the way it is. Of course he doesn't want to have to work all the time.'

Or was his wife wisely greeting him like some 'Zee & Co' heroine, 'Have you been sleeping with that slut again?'

Would he squirm and make excuses? 'But honestly, Elspeth, I've told you, I must have popped out for some fresh air when you called. I was working until three. Where else did you think I'd be?'

Nice work if you can get it, and if you get it, won't you tell me how?

Terrible, fascinating dramas reeled around my mind

and made portrait-painting seem inordinately dull in comparison. I kept on wanting to resort to Jacobean tricks, painting the skulls beneath the skin, poison inside the rings, masked emissaries with hidden daggers. Endless Nosy Parker questions pinched at me. A whole list of how comes:

How come – if you're so happy with your marriage, you have to keep seeing me?

How come – you get so happy seeing me that I'm the one left bothered?

How come – you can lie so much and feel unscathed?

How come – your wife never smells my perfume, or sees my carmine lipstick ground into your pores?

I want to rub out both our egos and find out who is right, who is wrong. But there is no right or wrong; just differences, all the way along the line. You're married, I'm not.

There had come to exist between us this unspoken state about certain matters that were 'his business'. Say anything you like, just don't mention the . . . art, wife, the children, the pet rabbit or anything to do with Camden. The last two were a relief; I didn't hold an overwhelming fascination for either Camden or rabbits, but not mentioning the other subjects was like trying to forget you have a snagged nail on each hand while putting on tights. I couldn't do a Glenn Close in *Fatal Attraction*.

I began to ask questions. Curiosity gripped so tightly, the fascination of a hidden world often seemed more interesting than the time we ourselves spent together.

Q. What do you say when you get home at five in the morning?

A. I don't, she doesn't ask. She knows I have to work late.

Q. Does she think you are working all the time?

A. No, we have separate social lives. She accepts me for how I am.

Q. If you weren't seeing me, you could be doing these things with her?

A. I do, we do spend enough time together.

Q. What is enough? If you spent any more time with her, would it stop being a happy marriage?

A. Possibly. Hope, don't you understand, you get the best of me. You lift my heart to the top of my head and make me laugh. If we were married, which isn't possible, you'd get the brunt of my scowls. I'm happy with you. Let's enjoy just being together.

I could see that being married to James would not be a good deal. I could be the sustenance of his marriage for the next thirty years, and be appearing on BBC documentaries about being a long-term mistress.

Mistress in the modern sense, in which you get to keep yourself, so that at least you can die happy knowing that you broke up no families, either emotionally or financially – just cemented the damn thing together. The bright streak in a dull haircut.

'Anyway, I don't feel I'm doing anything wrong. My time is my time, and what she doesn't know can't harm her.'

Should I tell you, I thought, lying in his arms, about the time my mother found the plane ticket receipts and in whose names, the one year he wasn't there for their anniversary, in my father's jacket as she emptied the pockets, good wife, before sending it to the cleaner's? How her ignorance and disbelief welled to an anger that had her sharpening the knives for his innocent return home? How that was the end of that, whether he jumped or was pushed it didn't matter, it was the deceit in the end that did it, and had him in hospital?

If I'd told him, James would have huffed and balked at me for childishly holding on to these long-ago tales. But family histories, real or imagined, stick to you like fresh dog shit on your trainers.

I couldn't be bothered to kiss and tell. Ignorance is bliss, but it is neither definite, true nor for ever. I thought, We make our own truth, designer-fitted. 'But you wouldn't want to be the cause of a divorce, would you?' he added malevolently, and stroked my lips with his fingertip.

'Cause? Nothing to do with me, mate. It's your marriage, and it would be your divorce!'

I could see, now, that affairs were only another form of marriage-guidance counselling, but I couldn't unhook myself from the boat and clamber to the shore of self-preservation. Each time I threatened to jump, out came a present: real ones, pretend ones, pink-bowed ones and weekend-away ones.

Imagine being married to James? Trust, love, honour and obey, till death do us part? TRUST. I once saw a film by that name. The hero and heroine stood talking in a street by a wall about the meaning of love, its essence, and then the pregnant girl climbed on the tall wall and said, 'Love is trust', and fell forward, knowing that the man would catch her.

How could I be doing with a man who let lies slip so easily from his lips? Why did he bother embroiling these huge stews of lies, that cling to your hips like so many puddings? Fear of betrayal, undelivered expectations, sworn promises carelessly forgotten, tooth fairies that never came. All these things can make you lie, make you selfish with your secrets.

My father, in his blue velvet suit and purple ruffled shirt getting married for the fifth time, his smooth

hair falling beguilingly over one eye, sideburns fash-
ionably long but close-clipped to his handsome,
boyish face. His Gucci-clad feet happily used to smart
floors and walking beautiful girls to altars with
promises wrapped by Fortnum & Mason. Business
trips always insisting he go away.

Too difficult to resist, too easy to say yes, why not?

James offered me glamorous, two-night confer-
ences in Birmingham or Bristol, Leeds or Manchester,
one night in Edinburgh. Call me Mrs Greedy, see me
as selfish, but it could never be enough. Not that it
was even him I wanted to be with all the time. It
wasn't him I wanted, or was so in love with. What I
started to want was just a little proof that trust came
with love.

'Still,' as James argues, 'you might as well keep
seeing me until the real thing comes along,' and he
says it so cheerily, and then tries to comfort me as
though I didn't get the last fag end in the ashtray of
life. 'There, there. You'll make someone who's available a most perfect companion.'

I know, I know, all this is true. James as the
part-time fill-in, the snack you can eat between
boyfriends. Personally, I don't think anything else can
get into a space where half a car is still parked. Who's
going to ask you out to dinner when you've got your
face in a bag of chips? Who's going to ask to hold

your other hand? I'm not an empty space with a Reserved sign, a clamped car waiting for a joyride.

With James, I couldn't feel like a goddess. It was time to reclaim my pedestal, bring it down from the attic, polish it up and clamber back on. I didn't have to wait to be pushed; I would know when it was right to try free-falling off it.

I think I'll just give Benjamin a call; I feel a bit peckish. I wonder if he remembers that we never did have that dinner? Dring-dring, dring-dring! 'The caller knows you are ringing, and is engaged on another call. Please call back later.' I've got the message, this time! Now, where are those letters?

Chapter 6

WHAT'S WRONG WITH AN ANORAK?

What's wrong with an anorak? Nothing. Anoraks are practical. They wipe clean after a muddy day out; they keep the wind out on a windy day, especially if you put the hood up, and, best of all, if it rains you're covered; they're waterproof.

Anoraks, for all this, are now fashionable – for the moment.

They come in groovy designs and colours, are stuffed with feathers, the better to keep you warm, or they hang like ponchos and are even called by different names. The humble anorak that comes in silver and turquoise and is called Puffa to some, to me it is still an anorak. An anorak in the old sense of a worthy, dull thing, worn not by explorers of the polar regions, adventurers into the mysteries of life, but unresponsive watchers, static observers of life and trains, and the occasional skier.

For all of the above reasons, it qualifies as a loathsome object.

It would not find cupboard space, or even floor space (where most of my coats tend to live) in my home, whatever it's called. I'd rather have 'a pig's foot and a bottle of beer', as old Bessie Smith was so fond of saying.

No, anoraks have never done me any harm, but I think if I was in the psychiatrist's chair I might be talked back to revealing in my childhood that the horrible Harriet Horn-Smitth wore a particularly nasty breed. The ones that come in muck green with diamond stitching, elasticated wrists, corduroy collars and detachable hoods. You don't see them about much these days, unless you hang around the French Lycée in South Kensington (are you a Francophile paedophile?) or Wimbledon (anywhere?), or perhaps Harrogate, and then they are mostly navy blue.

When Harriet wore hers, they were uniformly green and copied for a cheaper price by Marks & Spencer with added toggles on the drawstring around the bottom. Harriet had the expensive version, and sat wrapped in it winter and summer, thrown into the playpen of our square. Each day after school, and all day in the holidays and at weekends, come wind, rain or snow, she would be slammed through the gates by her mother, Mrs Horn-Smitth, who must have liked her as much as we did.

Nowadays I'd feel sorry for a little spiteful brat of Harriet's smelly mis-demeanour. I'd probably call the social services, poor thing. Who can guess where she is now? A research scientist, a Jacobean tragedy scholar, or running a children's home in North Wales, perhaps? Who knows, but at the time the pain she felt could only surface for the rest of the world as malice and ill-intent; no nervous disposition, that girl. Harriet was the girl who, on finding a nest of bird's eggs, would stand guard over them until they hatched, whereupon she began torturing the defence-less, pink, bald babies. On days when the local animal inhabitants of the square had been used up, she turned to us child humans for her experiments in forced berry-, worm- and earth-eating. Even on the top bar of the climbing frame you weren't safe from Harriet, and some piece of tree that she'd try sticking up your bum, grazing down your leg or knocking your ankles with.

Horrible Harriet, with her pale carotene hair, fringe always too short, John Lewis clothes, a mouth like a cat's bottom and a nose like a Disney animal cartoon. Poor Peter got the worst of Harriet; most of mine and

Joe's (my younger brother's) injuries were sustained while protecting Peter.

Peter did not wear an anorak. Peter was dressed by his grandmother until he was seven in girl's frilly dresses with matching knickers and lace crochet cardigans. This was not Peter's fault, this was Peter's grandmother's fault, who looked after Peter and told him he was a girl. She wouldn't send him to school, instead, she dressed him in his dead mother's childhood clothes, growing his hair and tying it in rags each night for ringlets the next day. Peter, of course, found out that he was a boy as soon as he met Harriet – his blond curled tresses didn't fool her in the least. Anyway, she was always pulling people's knickers down, and the inevitable revealing of his gender had her screeching with laughter. Poor Peter was teased remorselessly, bullied and beaten.

One day, Peter had all his hair shorn off and was sent away to a minor public school, where he could put all he had learned from Harriet to good use. He was dressed in grey shorts and a blazer, and finally allowed to be a boy. I don't suppose he'll ever be a man.

Joe and I agreed he was a far nicer girl. Harriet would never have been nice, even given a sex change. Wired, caged and muzzled might have helped.

I have reason enough not to like anoraks.

Andrew had been nice enough on the phone, and though I had suffered some disasters in the intrigue of meeting some of the replies to my lonely hearts request, on the whole I was having fun and enjoying the learning curve that all new projects throw up. Which was better, I suppose, than throwing up over new projects.

Some only got as far as the phone call. I didn't want to meet up with Psycho, as I now call him, the Kentish Town psychoanalyst who was studying the pygmy tribes of southern Africa but wanted to know if I'd take him to a rubber club, as the last girl whose advert he'd answered had taken him to a transvestite fetish evening and had encouraged him to paddle away at her bottom. I thought of giving him David's phone number, but thought even David wouldn't appreciate it.

Mark, however, sounded sweet on the phone. He was a junior-school music teacher, but just the suggestion of meeting up at the McDonald's in Piccadilly before hitting the pubs for a Saturday night filled me with despair. Maybe I was being a Belgian snob, but I don't like burger bars that don't serve mayonnaise with their French fries. If he'd said Burger King, I might have . . .

In comparison, Andrew sounded sophisticated. When I rang him it was just after six on a Friday, and I was in a bored mood. I was wishing that Toby would hurry up and return; weeks had gone by and I was still seeing James the married-git, who didn't count and wasn't part of my project. I had a date with Lionel the lawyer for Friday lunch that I was quite looking forward to as promising, and was meeting Steve the poet in a coffee bar for a recital in the evening, which I wasn't so sure about, poets being unpredictable. But the thought of it was nice.

I had put a message on Andrew's answerphone, and had left it like that.

Andrew was obviously a man with brains, for two reasons: he dialled 1471, got my number and called me back. He had also, in his egotistically written note, not included a photo.

I am currently away on business, am intrigued by your advert but short of a photo of myself, I write anyway. As a woman of the world, a goddess no less, you will appreciate that no man worth his salt would sit in a booth, or let himself be judged on a photo alone. Enough to say that I enjoy the good things in life, am wise, witty and rich to boot! Do you like the South of France? It is made for goddesses.

It was written on Colombe d'Or paper, a particularly expensive, luxurious hotel in the South of France. I admit it: it wasn't so much his egotism but mine that worried me. The note said nothing about him, and it was quite apparent that it said more about me for calling him – it positively shouts, GREEDY! Greedy, greedy guts. It also made me feel positively Victorian. These signs are little snob ratios, he's testing to see if I know what the Colombe d'Or is, and whether I have been there, or have magazine aspirations to go. Actually my aunt goes every year with her toyboy ski-instructor boyfriend, who now, only teaches her. She made her money in biscuits, and is known as 'one hell of a smart cookie', after leaving my uncle.

I was already having second thoughts about calling Andrew, about being unfaithful to a man I hadn't even met, Toby, when the phone rang and the crackle and roar told me it was a mobile in a car.

'Is that you, Goddess?' came the voice through the interfering static, followed by a juggernaut's rumble. It shocked me: what if my old great-auntie Dilys had answered the phone? Not that she lives with me, but he didn't know that.

'Yes, for it is I, and who are you, mere mortal?' I haughtily returned.

'Andrew. Andy. Listen, sweetheart, I'm about to be in your neighbourhood in about fifteen. Can I entice you out for a glass of bubbly?'

I was briefly taken aback. Goddesses weren't supposed to be available on the off chance; goddesses had diaries and PAs, but I was undeniably thirsty, as well as so sick 'n' greedy with my Victorian attitudes I'd die of consumption soon.

'As long as it is in fifteen minutes, because I have to be somewhere later.'

This was no lie, I lied to myself, we all have to be somewhere later, even if we've been run over by a bus – then we have to be in the mortuary.

'That's fine. I imagined that a goddess would be booked; I just rang on the spur. I hope you're not offended?'

'No. Just one thing: how do you know where my neighbourhood is, where I live?'

'Just watch out for the E-type Jag. I'll be inside it,' he said abruptly, finishing the call.

He probably won't turn up. He can't, he doesn't know where I live. But still I went into the bathroom and began to paint. First the curve of my lips, with firm and delicate strokes, outlining them and then filling them in with the small golden lip brush and the ground-down remains of Potent Pink. Then the lids of my eyes, with aquamarine. I sprayed on two shots of perfume, one at the delicate dip between the collarbones at the bottom of my throat, one on to a wrist before rubbing it with the other and staining both. I changed from my jeans into a red skirt, my grubby jumper was off and thrown to the floor and replaced with a seamless, expensive-looking top, black with small cyclamen-pink buttons that looked too delicate to undo. It wouldn't appear that way after it had been through the wash half a dozen times and was showing its true high-street quality. I zipped up my black suede knee boots, brushed my hair and remembered to put some knickers on. None of those 'up your bum' types, I hate those; I refuse to believe that anybody finds them comfortable. Some advertising company has made women believe that men find them sexy, like high heels, and so automatically we try to find a way to believe that they are fine to wear. Justifying g-strings as freedom we expose a wobbly expanse of marked bum and get thrush every month from the corrosive rubbing action. I like sensible knickers that pull your tum flat, that run from thigh to belly button concealing everything in Spandex, school-gym mystery; it's a protective casing, and I'll still wear high heels. The seduction of make-up I don't have to justify in the battle for women's liberation. I'm a painter, if there's an unadorned surface I cover it, it is an advertisement of my skill or lack of it. It is an emotive, creative production, my protection, it is my mask. Behind it I can do what I like.

The doorbell in my garret goes. I pick up the intercom. 'Hello?'

'Goddess, it's Andy. I'm downstairs, double-parked, so don't be too long, darlin'.'

I had a bad feeling about this. People who call anyone darlin' before meeting them want to be closer than agreed upon, either that or they are just damned lazy and can't be bothered to alter their speech patterns between strangers and friends. It was also his tone of voice. Why do I not listen to my instincts? It's greed; I wish I could just say inquisitiveness.

I grabbed my bag, took a last look in the mirror and skipped down the stairs, all one hundred and twenty-six of them, in my rapacious hunger to get to the E-type, champagne and the good things in life.

Good things in life can be as simple as a bag of oranges, especially blood oranges, whose season lasts about two weeks each year. It's special, and that's the point. Stuff you don't do every day. Sure, I don't drink champagne every day with an accompanying plate of caviar, but you wouldn't have to do it very much for it to wear thin. Good things in life are: not to be hungry (physically or emotionally), to have a warm coat in winter and cool clothes in summer. To have a few best friends you can discuss a good or bad book/movie/man/other friends with, while walking along the Embankment to laugh at new acquisitions at the Tate Gallery. Soup and then ice cream. Electric blankets are also excellent when you don't have central heating, like me. There are lots of other things that appear to be the good things in life, until you are there experiencing them and wondering why the hell you aren't enjoying it. Andy was one of those, but I couldn't quite put my finger on it at the time.

Andy must have been a nip-and-tuck forty-nine (I wouldn't discount plastic surgery – or do we call it facial enhancement, for the vain?), so he could have been fifty-two. He dressed young: slightly sporty, designer jeans, pouched khaki anorak and his mobile phone looked like an airline pilot's talking device, or cone-breasted Madonna in concert. He was leaning on the roof of his car as I came down my steps.

'Hey, look at you!' he said. I smiled, because what do you say? Did he mean, *Look* at you! – what a dog, or Look at *you*! – what do you think you look like, or did his slight American drawl mean the even more embarrassing, Look *at* you! What a babe! From his eyes, I fear he meant the latter.

I don't want to be a babe. I am very decided on that, otherwise I would dye my hair peroxide blonde, grow it long and have it layered to go with some false breasts. I would have called myself a name that ended with a 'y' sound: Pammy, Jackie, Cindy, Annie, Penny. I could have chosen Barbie if I'd wanted to be a babe. Hope is another thing altogether.

'Hello, I'm Hope.'

'You certainly are! Nice! Get in the wagon, princess, and I'll drive you to a great watering hole I know.'

'Great car.'

'Yeah, it's a great motor. Like the best girls – it always goes when you wanna.'

Hello, *eeek*!

'No, sorry, that was a joke. OK, do you do Notting Hill?'

'Well I've been there, so I know it exists. Don't they have a market called Porto-something-or-other Road?'

If he wants to do jokes, I can do jokes, but not in this case – I was just being sarcastic. I do live in Bayswater, and it has always been next door to Notting Hill Gate like the poor relation, but a while ago some of it married a rich Arab and had a baby called Whiteleys where marriages are arranged around the shopping-mall fountain and people who suck presidents' dicks do book signings.

But it wasn't my street. In other words, for me not to know Notting Hill would be like the Queen pretending she doesn't know her daughters-in-law exist; however much you'd like to pretend otherwise, they're still going to be there.

'So you go down the old 192, or are you more a

Westbourne chick, or Old Cow?'

'Not so much of the old, thank you. The Westbourne.'

'Okey-dokey, the Westbourne it is.' He had a jocular, cheeky way of talking.

We are speeding along the park, turning down in the direction of Westbourne Park Road. I suddenly think, What if I know someone and they see me getting out of an E-type with a W-type? W as in wanker? Stop, Hope! Judging somebody else's son, I secretly slap myself into order.

'Hey, this isn't the Westbourne.' The car has stopped down a small, quiet street dotted with posh neighbourhood shops, expensive boutiques that are open for one hour a week by appointment.

'I've got a better idea – let's go to Julie's bar.' He opens his door. 'It's cosier. They know me here.'

'Do they? As what?'

'As Andrew.' He turns his head and gives me a 'are you weird?' look. I return a smile, as though that is the expression he has just given me. Which gives him the impression that maybe *he* is the one stuck in the psychodrama with *me*. Maybe he is. Be afraid, Andrew, be very afraid!

Inside the dark, antique bar soaked with seventies revivalist medievalism, Andrew relaxes slightly with a click of his manicured fingers, and so do I. I am not going to bump into anyone I know here.

'Hope: a drink? Champagne?'

'That would be lovely,' I smile, and let my eyes wander around the tapestry hangings, the Pugin-style carpet, the little nouveau lights, until they grow accustomed to the dim setting. Andy takes off his glasses and the lines around his eyes become more obvious. I stare and decide that it's his forehead and bags he's had removed. If I really loved him would I wonder these things? Would I be checking for new scar tissue? The answer is immaterial. It really doesn't matter, because I've only just met him through an advert, plus, he has found out my address and number without my giving them out. I am annoyed about that bit because it says on every page of adverts, Do not give out your address or phone number until you feel confident about your new friend. i.e. they are probably stalkers, mad rapists, or recently released care-in-the-community customers and we are not taking any responsibility for the hash you make of your life by getting involved with them. We are not sueable. Got it?

What I have got, from Andrew, is my choice taken away. What he must have is the entire telephone directory on CD-ROM.

At times like these, I wonder about myself. I had the choice to say no and I didn't use it. I will drink the first glass of champagne too quickly, to make the occasion more bearable. If I am looking through rose-tinted spectacles, then maybe I can listen to the man next to me who looks more and more like an ex-Radio One DJ put out to grass and who now works on commercial radio; not Alan Partridge, but a pop-music giant of yesteryear popping the champagne cork in front of me as though Mike Reed had just won the Grand Prix.

'So, Hope, I may call you Hope, might I? Cheers.' He bangs his glass into mine. 'Had any success yet?'

'In what way, exactly?' I am trying not to be too hostile. I am trying to remember that I can get up and leave any time I like. That sometimes I enjoy being friends with people who are quite unlike me.

'With the advert, of course,' he says, rather too loudly for my liking.

'Well, I've been on lots of dates, and that's been fun,' I say with a double dollop, as though it truly has.

'You want to try advertising in *The Times*. A better class of person reads *The Times*. You could find yourself a really rich bloke in *The Times*.'

'Is that so? It wouldn't have occurred to me. Do you work in Murdoch's advertising department?'

'No love, property. I thought about advertising, actually, but yes,' he stopped to hold his drink up to the light, to study the bubbles before gulping the contents and verifying, 'yes, I'm in property.'

'An estate agent? It must be fascinating, snooping

around other people's houses all day. Terrible what happened to Suzy Lamplugh, though.' This is my big step to connecting, I think.

'Development, actually.'

'Oh.' I'm stumped for a minute. I know nothing about development, apart from the few books I've read on the self and finding the inner child, when what I've been searching for is the inner adult. 'Knocked down any interesting buildings recently?'

'No; what we build over them is much more interesting. I work with some top-notch architects. The best.'

'Good.'

'What do you do when you're not advertising yourself around London?' he asks, wrinkling his nose unattractively.

'Do? I'm a painter,' I say smugly.

'What, like painter and decorator, or artist type?' and he sneers as though it is a dirty word.

'Yes, an artist.'

'Not one of those modern ones that do stuff and pretend it's art?'

'We all pretend it's art; that's how it comes to be real. I paint portraits, actually.'

'Oh, I like portraits, I can understand portraits because though I don't know much about art, I—'

'Know what I like?' I finished the sentence for him.

'Yes, me too. Landscapes?'

'Dogs. At the moment I'm doing a portrait of a dog.'

'Don't like dogs. The Mrs, ex-wife had a thing about dogs. Actually I think she was one' (he pauses to laugh, but sees me sneer and continues) 'small, furry, yappy things. I used to kick them when she wasn't looking. They always shat in my shoes.'

I can understand that, I thought; any moment now and I could be following their lead. Instead I do the questionnaire stuff, robbing him of his private information.

'So you've been married? Any kids?'

'Only one great kid, Georgette, very talented, doing lots of commercials. She's at a very good stage school. You've probably seen her in stuff. Car commercials, mostly.'

'Oh, she'll be able to keep you in your old age.' As soon as I said it it seemed inappropriate, but maybe he hadn't noticed that he was cruising towards his pension.

'That's the idea, if her old boot of a mother ever lets me see her again.' Suddenly he looked beaten, his skin showing grey beneath the tan, the small, unsure boy's eyes wavered for a moment and the bully became the victim he always was. I felt sorry for him, but then he made me feel better by pulling out a fat cigar and puffing away at the smelly thing like a big man.

I had to ask.

'So what went wrong with the marriage?'

'The birth did it; Georgette.'

Surely not the star wonder child! Ruining the marriage of her parents? That's a terrible thing to accuse a child of, even one that goes to stage school, I thought.

'I don't suppose she did it on purpose,' I say with a soft note of commiseration.

'Of course she didn't!' he says rather angrily. 'It's her mother I'm talking about!'

I look bewildered, and he sits me down with his eyes and handles my arms, explaining the details slowly for the backward child that I am. He is being consolatory.

It is an endearing story of blame. It is ancient and modern, man and woman, an obvious mystery, lust and life, birth and contraception; it is a bloody, contradictory conundrum. It begins with love, doves and roses. Squelchy sex and passion, months of body-diving and groin lust reserved for one, and then some old-fashioned wedding bells.

'Well, a man will agree to anything before he . . . on the verge of orgasm.' Andrew tells me something I already know, but have never fully worked to my benefit.

Suddenly the wife's up the duff, bun in the oven, preggers.

'You'd have to be a pervert to want to shag a pregnant woman.' Andrew tells me something I didn't know. So why am I under some odd illusion that to make love to the woman you love, who is carrying your child, must be the most intimate and wonderful thing in the world?

'Anyway, I don't fancy fat women.'

But I'm fat, I want to say. No you're not, I would like him to reply, in order that I can say, I am on the inside. But the probable truth, if I interrupted Andrew's flow to say but I'm fat, is that he'd more than likely answer, yeah well, and carry on. So I keep my mouth shut and listen.

'So, she wants me to watch the birth. I tell her it's a mistake, but she keeps on saying it'll be one of the most wonderful things I'll ever witness – the birth of our child. I should have listened to my instincts, but instead I go along with her thinking. Well, I was there at the creation, I might as well be there for the miracle birth.

'I have to tell you this straight, Hope. I hope you're not squeamish?' he asks me with a gleam in his eye and an irrepressible smile, like he's leading me to Never Never Land. 'It was the most disgusting thing I've ever seen in my life, worse than being in a butcher's, no, no, worse than an abattoir. Blood, shit and guts . . .'

What Andrew was trying to tell me, I think, was either that suddenly he was faced with the biggest disappointment in his life, or that the act of birth was too massive a concept for him to bow to. That his wife became his mother. When this beautiful, erotic hole had unexpectedly been turned into a screaming red gash of a mouth. All the sensuality of breasts, skin and limbs, all the hidden secrets of the body had exploded raw and coarse under his gaze. That she had stepped from the pages of a men's monthly into a feature in a medical journal.

'Well how can you ever make love to a woman again when all of that has gone on?' he had asked, seeing my glazed, bemused expression. If he had stopped to open my head up he could have clearly heard the word dinosaur, followed by, there really are still men out there who are like this! He obviously didn't do that, because he then went on to give me more details (perhaps he was doing it on purpose).

'This new man stuff is just crap! I mean, what good did it do me, having to witness the woman I loved having her eyes torn out with pain' (what about her vagina? I wanted to ask) 'covered in sweat, her hair matted to her head' (not the hairdresser-smoothed locks he was used to seeing on the pillow) 'the revolting screams' (harridan shrieks of life-giving pain) 'and the disgusting smell. I'll never forget the smell. Have you been to a pig farm? Got the picture? It's not exactly Janet Reger, is it? She could have put me off sex for life,' he said, turning glumly to his drink.

I thought how I could put him off sex for life, and not by having his baby. Unanaesthetised circumcision, perhaps? A little castration with a rusty blade? No, I'm not that cruel; I'd use a brand-new Gillette or a shiny Sabatier knife.

'No,' I agreed, 'it's not glossy catalogue sex fantasy stuff at all. It's real life and death stuff!' I added enthusiastically, because the essentials of life are so much more interesting than the nuances of fancy sauces that we dress the contents of life in.

'Death? Now don't you start getting all morbid on me! This is supposed to be a bit of a laugh. Do you advertise much?'

'What?'

'Just, you get a different type of bird depending on whether they're from the Internet or the *Observer*, bit brainy. The *Sunday Times*—'

'No.'

'You should try it. You might get dinner at Tramps.' He nudged one knee between mine and raised an eyebrow, as though that might possibly happen tonight. For a moment it made him look like Roger Moore, what with his Bisto tan. 'I've taken girls for dinner at Annabel's that I've met through the *Sunday Times*.'

'Thanks for the tip,' I say, removing his hand from my knee. 'My God, is that the time?' I say, getting up to go, pushing brusquely past his body blockade.

'We haven't finished the champagne yet. Can I give you a lift?' I ignore his pleading protestations. I am demonstrating my right to say fuck off to Peter Pan, and my, it feels good. 'Listen, what did I say?' he asks my departing back.

I courteously turn my face to him and reply, 'You don't want to know, sweetheart!'

'Cheap slapper bitch!' I almost think I can hear above the slamming of the door and the ring of its old-fashioned bell. I am striding off and away, through the streets and towards Notting Hill. I make a mental note to move flats soon, very soon, but for the moment, until Coffee Republic appears in Mayor Street, Hackney, I'm happy to use the west London facilities. I keep walking, almost seduced by a cab to escape faster, but I don't succumb. I reach Notting Hill and fall into the coffee shop and order my usual. I look out of the window over to the Gate cinema, *Life is Beautiful* – Tonight, the letters read.

'That is so true!' I say out loud, laughing to myself, like some sad, lonely person.

'Pardon me?' says the brown, blue-eyed American in polo shirt, faded Levi's and Nikes sitting next to me. Everything Andrew aspired to be; a youth god –

maybe he once was all that.

'*Life is Beautiful* – Tonight. The sign on the cinema over there, see? I was just agreeing with it.'

'Oh, yeah sure. Weirdo!' He looks at me and moves away.

Shit! Get me outta here. Dear God, please move me east, no not later, NOW!

I have the whole evening ahead of me. Should I

1   Go east on the first available tube to Liverpool Street.

2   Go home.

3   Go to the cinema and hide from the world in some cold, air-conditioned (I've never once been too warm in a cinema) darkness.

4   Call Rachel or Gem.

5   Go to late-night opening at the Hayward, National Gallery or Borders/Books Etc./ Waterstone's.

6   Read *War and Peace*.

7   Go and see Mum and Dad.

8   None of these.

9   A selection of these.

I leave my coffee, but not before toying with the idea of throwing it at Dickhead in the white teeth and matching socks. At times like these, I wish I smoked cigars for their obnoxious quality. People could ask me to leave and frown at the smell and I would tut condescendingly into their faces. At times like these I wish I still carried a ready supply of stink bombs like I did when I was ten. Forget grenades – that's the real way to make an anarchist's exit!

I cross the road, trying not to believe that someone out there will try to run me over (because that would be paranoia, and I'm not that self-indulgent yet), and walk down the street towards Waterstone's on the corner, because I know it's still open and the cutesy second-hand bookshop is closed on Kensington Church Street. I am a sucker for second-hand bookshops. The one place in the world I could never, ever live is Hay-on-Wye, because it is full of them and then my life would be made up of sidling along dark, narrow, book-lined corridors and I'd never get married, divorced, have children, affairs, go on holiday, have retrospectives at the Tate (or the Hayward), achieve incredible successes with lemon grass, exercise or *feng shui*. It could all happen for me in those bookshops, but only, you understand, in dreamtime.

I stop at a telephone box and sort through the copious caverns of my bag and eventually fish out my wallet (with change – very impressive) and my eighties hangover Filofax. I call Mum.

'Hello, Mum, it's me, May.'

'Of course it is. Darling, how are you? How's town life?' She's called London 'town' ever since we moved with Geoffrey from our Islington square to the Hog's Back in Surrey when I was eight.

'Oh, I'm fine,' I say, sounding suddenly flat.

'Really?'

'Sometimes I am.' I come clean to myself.

When she says, 'Do you want to come home?' she says it in the same way she used to when she would ask me if I wanted a hug for a hurt finger and wet eyes, when I was small. It makes my voice catch, and I grow an Adam's apple the size of a boulder, and I didn't even know I was upset when I opened the kiosk door.

'May, sweetheart? Darling, c'mon now, what is it?'

'I don't know,' I blurt out in a blub of tears. 'I didn't even think I was *yaarrreahooo . . .*' I heave and splutter and sob, with the occasional screech or yelp.

'It's all right. You come home this weekend, and you can tell me all about it. OK?'

Sniff, sniff. 'Yup, thanks Mum.' I shudder back into some sort of self-control, wiping my eyes that are full of mascara and snot on to my jacket sleeve. 'I don't know what happened. I think I'm just premenstrual. I'll come on Saturday. I love you, Mum.'

'I love you too. You know how proud we are of you. Now you look after yourself. I worry about you sometimes. Are you sure you're OK? It's just, the steak-and-kidney pie's on the table, and your dad—'

'Me too. Thanks, Mum.' I put the phone down and feel marginally better, half jealous of the pie they are about to eat, half annoyed at the life my mum's been curtailed into having.

Am I jealous that my stepdad always takes her away? It seems like she's spent the best part of her energies either making pies for him or worrying after my brothers and I, years after we've left home. Occasionally she'll take an evening class in watercolour painting, computers or a new language, to have her enthusiasm quickly redirected by my stepfather's agenda.

If I could give my mum a present, the best present in the world, the one she would treasure most, it would be a big lump of time for herself. I imagine the hand-painted satin-bowed box full of empty time vouchers and the look of – no, the thrill and excitement spread like margarine across her face, her eyes brimming. My dream, not hers. And one I can't even save up for. Secretly I'm glad, because I couldn't bear her feigned interest in a present that wasn't pretty and textile. A Bloomsbury set of something.

The truth is, she isn't one for the conceptual, art or otherwise. I tried to explain a piece by New Gideon Sherman to her, that the art was the document, that art wasn't about paintbrushes filled with colour, that art didn't stop at a Patrick Heron retrospective, and she'd answered, 'I don't know, May, about your old Gideon's work, but Patrick Heron suits me fine when it comes to modern. I pity that Damien Hirst's mum.'

'At least she'd always have a roast for Sunday lunch.'

'Why?'

'He preserves farm animals in formaldehyde.'

'You wouldn't want to eat that after all those chemicals had been on it. Genetically modified thingumajigs, yuk.'

We are all on our separate journeys. We can't live other's lives for them; we can't will their lives to be different because it makes us feel uncomfortable to watch them scurry or beg. I find it hard to accept that Mum has her life the way it is because she wants it like that.

I suppose I am too guilty of it myself to believe that she loves to be needed. Loves darning the holes in all of our laddered souls. If only things had been different for her, when she was born; if only conditions for women had been different. But maybe I am conditioned to believe that, because in fact women have done amazing things all the way through history. Women have been courageous and valiant, and pressed their hands into history's cement; taken up swords and fought battles. Is it that I can't bear to believe that my mother wasn't one of those? That staying at home was enough for her, that imprinting your name in the fame game means little, when you've made sure your name will last in the non-egotistical fashion, by bringing forth life? By assuming responsibility of caring, the bravery of commitment towards others?

Fuck, where have we women got ourselves? Apart from halfway up shit creek without a paddle, with only our hands to keep us afloat? We refuse to go back, but we're too afraid to brown-water-raft down. So we cling to the ideals of romance and happy families, marriage and babies, but we'll keep our careers going (just in case it doesn't work out), and make sure when we choose the house that our name is on the lease but not the mortgage, and that way we get to keep the house, but not the repayments when it comes to the divorce settlement (remember to keep the furniture invoices for the court case!). I don't know how women can accuse men of being ruthless when it comes to marital contracts. Certain members of our species have always been working them out, just in case! Hey! Just like some men. Men aren't from Mars, or women from Venus; just a percentage come from Uranus, regular temperature around −353°F.

★ ★ ★

I ring Gem.

Gem is a painter really, but pretends to do illustra-tion because she wants to buy her clothes from Joseph instead of the Notting Hill Housing Trust, Red Cross and Oxfam (though that's getting a little dear these days!) like me. I sometimes wonder if my commissions are just large illustrations on canvas with oils, but then I will put the dog's eyes into the owner's sockets and think otherwise. Something Gem is never allowed to do for *She* magazine.

Gem has just bought a loft in Hackney.

'Gem it's me, May. Fancy going for a drink? I'm in a phone booth in Notting Hill and I might jump if you don't say yes to The Showrooms, Barleymow, Two-floors or Vibebar in half an hour. Yes, that's the choice. No, I can't be bothered to slag up to 192, and Muthers is too depressing. OK, that other pub, yes I know where it is. I'll see you when I get there.'

I didn't care about the trawl back to Bayswater; I just wanted to escape a Thursday night's west London blues. Spilled half-pints of lager on a fag-laden wob-bling Formica table top don't make me as depressed, but an array of new-season Prada handbags lining the bar top at 192 does.

If it's not jealousy, what is it I hate about Prada handbags? Why should they make me depressed?

Surely they're a sign of success? I hate the fact that women invest all their energies in playing back into men's games. Don't give me that bullshit that women want stuff like that just for their own private pleasure, to luxuriate in. If there weren't other women to show it off to, that they've got it and therefore will be able to catch a richer class of man because of their Prada vagina, they wouldn't desire it. Did I say vagina? I meant handbag, of course I did. And then men see the Prada handbag and think that sow's vagina must be made of a silk purse, or something like that, and all the time the men at the top of these designer labels that must be printed all over our clothes with invisible signs of cut and style, are getting richer.

Some women starve, and their children go without, to afford items like these. Others buy them from Spitalfields market for a tenth of the price and laugh, passing them off as a day's shopping in Sloane Street. That I can understand, but I still wouldn't do it. No doubt there are some women who can understand buying second-hand clothes, but would never do it. Then we are equal.

I push into the delicious, smoky, beery, human den smell of the Bricklayer's, no perfect clean glass bar and designer, air-conditioned perfume to be assailed by. It is a pub, it is a pit of donkey-jacket warmth of the old school. There aren't even any beer mats, just beer in pint glasses and pork scratchings and lots of young people, not trying to be old and sophisticated – they're just old enough to order a drink.

No, I don't fit in, but I'm not turned away. The blokes look like my brothers used to; maybe that's why I like it. Nothing like a bit of incest to keep it nice and cosy in the family. If I was halfway decent I'd say they looked like my brothers' mates, all good comprehensive boys. Maybe I *am* perverted and weird.

I go to the bar and order a half of Heineken; nothing fancy here. I look about the corners of the bar and see no Gem apparent, so I go back to the bar and wait it out in my corner. A bloke comes in. There is something slightly odd about him: grey T-shirt, jeans, shaved hair with an ash growth prickling through, a silver earring. He stops at the bar and then turns to smile at me in a ghoulish, silver-toothed fashion; the earring is what must make him appear like Captain Hook, with the slogan *Pervert* across his chest. The contents of it come from somewhere else. He has breasts like Cameron Diaz, braless and with prominent nipples. Hell, am I ordinary!

I try not to stare, in case he approaches me. There is something obsessively magnetic about the oddly peculiar, like looking at two-headed babies in research hospital jars, like rows of pickled fruit suspended in thick syrup, at once beautiful and hideous.

'May!' said Gem, striding towards me. A big, gleaming, beautiful smile glossed her face, her blonde hair, newly cropped, fitted her head perfectly with the help of gel.

'Gem, your hair! It looks great.'

'Thanks. How are you, May? You look fab too.'

'Thanks. Didn't I tell you? I'm called Hope now.'

'That's nice. Deed poll?'

'No. Just decided.'

'Oh. So do you want a drink, May?'

'Nobody buys a drink at this bar tonight except me!' a voice commands, and a small, thick, black hand grasps a wad of fifties and waves it over our heads like a fan. 'Whatever you like, folks – the drinks are on me. God, I've always wanted to say that!' he laughs hoarsely. 'I sound like the Milky Bar Kid. The Milky Bars are on me! Got that wrong – the blackie bars are on me!'

Gem and I look at each other.

'So, what are you having girls? Anything you like – double voddie and tonic, what's it to be? We're having all the champagne in the house, so you can't have that. But anything else, just put your drinks order to the bar. What's your name, doll?' He comes over to Gem. The whole bar is watching. He stretches out his hand for the shaking.

'Gem.'

'Gem, that's a jewel of a name, my love, ha, ha, ha. Jewel, gem, get it? I'm, Mike. Laugh, then, that's right, lovely. Now don't you go getting lonely, I'm back to my mates now. You should be careful with a bum like yours – somebody's bound to want to put something in it.' And he laughed a dirty gutful.

Back with his group of friends, he began opening the finest champagne the house had to offer. Served beautifully warm, he sprayed it over each of them in turn like a garden hose.

'If I want to go to the loo, you're coming with me, right?' Gem said to me nervously.

'Fine.'

'I don't know what it is about blokes who take over pubs and look like Miami gangsta rappers; there's something I just don't trust there. I mean, in Chelsea it would be fine, but here we're just a little too close to Bow Bells and the Jack the Ripper guided tours.'

'Don't worry, little girl, I'll look after you. Now what are we going to have to drink on Mike? What do gangsta chicks drink? Bacardi and Coke?'

'Jim Beam and Coke's what you two want,' said the barman, overhearing.

'I think I'll stick to Heineken. 'Arf a lager, please.'

'Twice.'

'Missed opportunity,' he replied.

'He's thinking more about his till receipts than our bodily ones,' I whispered to Gem, before asking, 'How long do you think it'll take for the day to finish?'

'What do you mean? It's half past eight.'

'It's just that I'm having a slightly weird day, and I'm wondering whether to call—'

'The Samaritans? No need, hon, I'm fully trained. What's up?'

'It's that man–woman thang.'

'Why do we bother? I've given up. I'm now officially celibate,' announced Gem.

'You're always saying that. As soon as you do, there's immediately lights, camera, action. I just mean, I thought the whole thing of dating was supposed to be fun, and then men start taking it seriously and then it becomes catching, and it doesn't seem to matter how much I vow to myself, the future surrounded with bells and cribs appears in a christening card.'

'And . . .?' she slyly coaxed.

'And I refuse to get married again.'

'No matter how much your mother hints?'

'Exactly.'

'What about Mike over there? He seems a laugh.' She pointed to the man buying our drinks that was shaking the last bottle of champagne down a mate's trousers and laughing heartily – Mike, that is, not the mate.

'Yeah, yeah, the power game.'

'So been dating anything nice recently, to leave you in this sorry state?'

'Everything, and not necessarily nice. Interesting, but I'm starting to get a rather sad, hackneyed outlook on the world.'

'What do you think I've got from actually living here?'

'I thought I'd join you. My garret existence is wearing implausibly thin. Bayswater doesn't exist; it's just a hair extension attached to Notting Hill Gate, and not a nylon one at that. All the cafés are gone.'

'Don't worry, they haven't even arrived here. Apart from The Bean.'

'I'd feel at home here,' I said and meant it.

'Maybe.'

'Do you think we're getting too old?'

'Never. I'm never going to think I'm too . . . anything. Especially not old. I refuse to be an ageist; I like people too much,' Gem rallied, raising her glass.

'You're going to have to start wearing an anorak,' I teased.

'No!'

'That's just the sign I was looking for. When you

start to defend something, it's usually because you've become it. Like a Blairite. Do you remember when we all wanted to get married, when Honor and Harry did?'

'Yup.'

'That wasn't because we'd got marriageable. And now that we don't, it's because, crap, because we're all spinsters. I was trying to disprove your impregnable theory.'

'To be youth, you have to wear it. Fake it to make it. I know what I'm getting you for your birthday,' Gem teased. 'One of those really nice Daz-white poncho-cape anoraks, four ninety-nine down the market. Sorted.'

'At times like this, I wonder,' I said, and I meant it, though we kept up the meandering chat and ended up dancing with a twenty-year-old chef and a post office worker, into the early hours of a Charlie Wright's International Club morning.

On the way home on the night bus to cheery Bayswater, I wondered how Gem and I had got, from being the sneering infidels of our college days, once around the village green and out to become sneering thirty-somethings, when everyone else we knew now wanted to get married and have babies. Having done the marriage thing, I had my own reasons for not jumping back in the water. Both of our faces were

starting to scar from the richness of our life expect-
ancy – that's what crow's feet are, isn't it? Lines and
bags gathered from still being on the party circuit.

There is an age, somewhere between seventeen
and twenty-one, where if the heart hasn't turned to
stray mush with first love at fourteen, it will gently
calcify into a light crème brûlée with a hard crust.
Every affair will slide off you unless they equip
themselves with a sturdy pickaxe. I was like that. I
know Gem was, leaving in the middle of the night, as
untraceable as the Loch Ness Monster. No phone
number, hardly a name; I'd like to blame it on Erica
Jong or *Looking for Mr Goodbar*, or the contents of a
good bar. In the end, I think either you are or you're
not. Maybe it comes from the sheer, fifteen-denier
desperation, the pick, pluck and discard spoiled-brat
school of emotional development. Anyway, Picasso
was allowed to have his Blue Period, and as I got used
to surfing the crimson wave, I grew a heart as hard as
a long-term gobstopper, with a mercury filling. I don't
think we were unusual; loads of my friends followed
a similar fashion, male and female, gay, straight, or bi;
maybe it was the time. No; I think of it as a rite of
passage. A demystification of sex and relationships, as
important a ritual as going to college, where you
learn to realign your perception of your own behaviour as well as everyone else's. Then suddenly, when

twenty-two hits, and onwards . . . you marry the first proposition. Thom. I wonder where he is now?

Sometimes I slip back into old behaviour . . . And, quite frankly, my dear, when I do, I don't give a damn. It's like riding a bloody bicycle (in upper-class syllables), I say to myself.

I know there are some men (Andrew?) who are frightened of women who don't conform to Meg Ryan's cosy image. Women who refuse to chew their lower lip in self-doubt (because even if they feel it, we won't be brazen enough to show it!). Women who'll write, 'WANT TO FUCK?' with a finger full of invisible ink on the back of a new friend's shirt (that way you can find out if they're dyslexic at the same time!).

Don't be frightened – learn to deal with it. We got it from you big boys, in the humour section at the back of a second-hand bookshop. I found a book called *How to Avoid Matrimony* (strictly for rogue males, how to swallow the bait without getting caught) *and Still Get What You Want from Women* . . . I thought it might give me some tips on dating if I just cancelled out the wo— at the beginning.

Apparently, trollops are much the easier because you can treat them as equals, and you don't have to say much except, 'Well?' and they answer, 'When?' Emancipated (wo)men never want to marry either (so a good bet!) because ironing nappies would take up important debating time. The only snag is, they are almost always astonishingly ugly, so not worth the trouble. Divorced (wo)men are useless because they are just looking for a replacement.

The problem with women like Gem and I (and I wish it weren't the case) is that we are so much more discriminating than the bachelors of yesteryear. If only all we wanted was a leg-over from a trollop! But we also demand humour, beauty, intelligence, camaraderie, spirituality, a love of washing-up, someone who never moans, enjoys their work and actually has employment (nothing worse than men who hang around the house all day), loyalty and somebody who likes their mother (and all other women, including sisters), and who has a nice father. I don't care what they do with their shaving stuff, clothes, music collections and their general male habits. A car isn't even essential; the rest is. After some of these dates, I'm beginning to wonder if I ask for, expect, the moon with my wishes (Times to wish: on seeing any kind of altar, on finding one's own eyelashes dropped on one's own face, stars – the astral variety – cutting birthday cakes, Father Christmas lists, on throwing money into fountains and waterfalls. Plenty of opportunities).

'Ask and you shall receive,' Mrs Rodgers taught me in RE.

It's not much to ask, is it?

Chapter 7

FRIENDS AND OTHER LOVERS

I am an optimist, I am an optimist, I am an optimist, I am an optimist, I am an . . .

The date with the lawyer was a fucking disaster. I mean, the archaeologist was bad, but the lawyer, fuck the lawyer. Scrub that. I wouldn't, I didn't, and I have no intention to . . . ever see that man again. How does that song go? I won't give my number to that *scrub* ('an animal of inferior breed'). No, he didn't try to date-rape me, but he could be arrested for boring ('the act or process of making or enlarging a hole; repetitious and dull') me to death.

I may be an optimist, but I am a realist too.

When I say this man was dull, just believe me.

Now I feel like Rhoda, Ellen Gilchrist's heroine,

who can bear anything but boredom, and to relieve the boredom she seeks the shelter of danger, with drink, sex, bullfights, and marital violence (usually with somebody else's husband). Rhoda has not behaved well, but she always repents and believes that she can stick to her resolution and accept some good solid life, but then she goes and gets bored again.

I feel like Rhoda.

Tonight I will go and meet some tish-tosh poet in some dive in the Brompton Road, and walk out of the poetry recital halfway through while he's in the loo. I will meet up with my friend and mate DB, a sculptor, that I always get into fun and trouble with (in that order), and I will carouse my way about town until I end up with a cloying-truffle hangover for two days, beginning with the soupçon of a splitting head (not solvable with Disprin) and a fractured reality. Everything I touch will break or miss. On the third day, I will resurface with that cloud of wooziness that I am not sure will ever disperse.

How organised am I? My whole weekend and Monday is already planned, and just because I wasted my day having a boring lunch with Lionel the lawyer. See what you've made me do, Lionel? At least I have somebody to blame for my tragically reactionary behaviour.

Really, I am angry at myself. It is not Lionel's fault. How could it be his fault? He is as he is. Somebody will like him, somebody else's daughter, but not my mother's. It is my fault for enduring the mind-numbingness of the encounter, and talking too much 'me, me', because I couldn't bear to listen to what he might have to say next. I am cross because I revealed some of myself too soon to somebody I had no interest in, whom I couldn't care a sod for, and therefore I feel undeniably cheap and kind of grubby; frayed around the edges. It's that feeling you get when you wake up for breakfast with last night's make-up on, that cloying, stuck feeling of old mascara sealing you up, lipstick rivulets running from your mouth.

Some people might kid themselves that this is how they feel after a one-night stand, but I have to tell you, this is worse. One-night stands happen when you are physically drawn to somebody: there is an engineering of body chemistry, there might even be a little touch of magic dusted with serendipity, and if you are not too drunk, you might get an orgasm, too!

What I have just been through is worse, you will have to take my word for it. I sat willingly at a table and had first a drink, and then agreed to lunch with somebody in a green Belgian coat with tightly curled hair, no lips and a smug girth. I listened willingly to his tales of rugby, office politics and minor-public-schoolboy theorising about the world, and willed him to like me. I connived coquettish smiles, laughed at his jokes (which weren't even funny to him, so why was I laughing?) and generally prostituted myself in a more shameful manner to my morals than any working girl sitting in the lobby of the Ritz. Worse, there was no reason why I had to do it. Nobody was forcing me to tell him what my favourite painting is.

('Tell! Otherwise your dad gets it, kneecaps first, right!')

I am not so hungry, so why did I need to be so desperate as to seek the ordinariness of this dull man's acknowledgement? Even as I sat there I veneered myself into the girl this man wanted, but inside my head, instead of thinking what our children might look like or how well my dad might like him, and I'm sure he would, I was thinking nasty, mean, cruel thoughts.

At that moment, I thought seriously about slicing the top off his head and eating the contents of his soft, warm, grey brains, like they do with monkeys in China. While he was eating his chocolate pudding, I looked at him putting his spoon to his mouth and wondered about the texture and taste on my tongue of his warm matter. I was thinking, Get up and turn the table over on this decent, racist, white Englishman and scald him irreparably with the coffee pot, so he will never be able to have children. He will be so ashamed of his scars he will never be naked with a woman again. That bad, huh? And at the end of lunch, I kissed him goodbye on his cheek and said I'd ring him. I can never answer the phone again now, it will have to be left permanently on answerphone, because God forbid I should talk to him again – I would probably agree to marry him!

I said, 'Thank you for a lovely lunch.'

I said all this, and wouldn't have cared if he'd been run over by the next car as he stepped off the kerb, because I meant none of it. I didn't feel I was being a charlatan, not even once.

Is this good manners or very bad man-hating? This is primeval Celtic hatred from the collective unconscious of thousands of years; it is class war. I wonder if this is what Christine Keeler thought as she went down on a government, and watched nice men drenched in shame at their greedy indiscretions?

I feel such shame for the dishonesty of my behaviour, to myself, let alone to him, that there is nothing else for it but to go out and get rip-roaring drunk, let it go and absolve myself. If I am lucky, I will transmogrify into the molecules of an alien planet and wake up tomorrow morning as a Martian shower attachment; a nicer thing than the one that stands here now, both the shower attachment and me. Then I will have some purpose, some form, and no brain to haunt me.

For now, I will just have to stand under my shower and imagine what it must be like. I shall scrub ('rub hard so as to clean') myself of this encounter, before dirtying myself with others with the kind of dirt that leaves a clean, earthy taste in your mouth, compared to that left by the Lionel Experience. Other people embarrass themselves when drunk, I do it sober.

I take off my clothes. My smart little dress with the 'dry-clean only' label. I put the dress on a hanger out on my balcony, hoping some wind will blow through it with new life, blow away its past life experience. I ring DB and he says yes, that is where he was going to meet Rachel at around nine. I shall meet them there and have a great night and be my old, nice, funny, kind-person self again and never be frightened by the force and violence of my thoughts.

First, I must date Steve the poet.

One piece of comfort came to me as I took my bra and pants off and stuck them in the dirty bin. At least I never thought of strapping a leather dildo to myself and buggering Lionel into howling submission like my friend Sweetie does (by then it was too late; I'd already thought of it and it made me laugh), and the spell was broken. I scrubbed ('the use of water to remove impurities') Christmas-gift miracle reviving treatments into my skin, washed my hair, shaving my legs while I waited to rinse the conditioner off. I held the attachment between my legs and felt a frisson of excitement as I hosed myself clean. A thought appeared like a bubble in a cartoon: maybe I would meet somebody tonight without all the toshiness of letters and adverts; maybe this afternoon had salved my curiosity, in the way reading Nathaniel West's *Miss Lonelyhearts* never had. Maybe it had blocked up the pipe dreams. Or maybe not. Or maybe the poet really was a poet.

I flung a towel over my head, winding it into a neat turban, and began to rub myself dry with a big clean white towel in the way an old husband had once told me to. As soon as I remembered Thom, I stopped and wrapped the thing around me and waited to get dry in the way . . . well, in the way I had always done before men started telling me how to do things. I contemplated my nails and wondered if I could get away with plastering them over with another coat of polish. I checked my toes just in time to see a thin stream of toe-polish red blood wind its way past my ankle, heading for the floor. I scooped it up with a tissue, tracing it to its source. Which was not between my legs, I was happy to say, otherwise I would have worried all night about having dysmenorrhoea like Viv, T. S. Eliot's wife, and ending up bleeding away in a mental home. I'd just seen the video. It was just a nick from my greedy razor, slightly beneath my knee. I tore off a little tissue and stuck it there the way my dad (although he's my stepfather, he has been a dad to me in the bicycle-mending sense from the age of five) had, littering his face rushing in his morning shave to get to some very important meeting, scarring himself in the battle of daily duty. I would ring and go to see them soon; not just say it, do it.

'Hello, Mum, it's me, May. Yes, I'm fine, how are you? And Dad? Yes, I'll come down in a few weekends. Yes, on my own. No, I haven't got a boyfriend yet. Yes, I'll let you know as soon as I do. My painting's fine, just another commission at the moment. No, I'm not going to get a proper full-time job again, not yet. How was France? Good, lovely. Well done you! Give my love to Dad. Yes, I'll let you know when I'm getting married. No, I haven't seen Thom. I have to go now, Mum. No, I'm not pregnant. I'm meeting some people. No, not a date. Don't worry, I'll keep you posted. Yes, lots of love to you too. Bye, Mum, bye.'

At least she knew I wasn't dead. Sometimes my calls just sound obligatory, yet at other times I could speak with her and I wouldn't know whose voice was saying what, and our laughter performs osmosis, which is the scary part of closeness. It's like putting the phone down and reeling back out into your own identity like a drunk into daylight from the warm, closeting dark of a pub.

Remember the old seaside postcard? The mother-in-law joke adapted from Oscar Wilde's 'All women become like their mothers, that is their tragedy. No man does. That's his'. Cocky young man to beautiful sexy woman in front of frighteningly large battleaxe: 'Of course I want to marry you – unless that's your mother . . .'

It's the opposite with me. If any man met my mother, he'd want to marry me for what I would become, but there's the tragedy for both of us. There's no chance.

One night, Thom stumbled home starving, demanding his dinner as soon as he came in the door, ripe with the smell of adultery.

'Where's dinner?' I wish I could seriously have said your dinner's in the dog, but we didn't have one. So I shouted back from the comfort of the bed where I was snuggled up reading, 'Dinner's in the tin.'

My mother would have risen and whipped up a quick Elizabeth David and sat and watched him eat it.

My tragedy is that I married my father. I wouldn't have minded marrying my mother.

★ ★ ★

I went to my wardrobe. There is only one, and most of its contents lie on its wooden floor. Sometimes I wonder if inside that closet perpetual autumn reigns, forcing my branch-like hangers to shed my garments eternally. In truth I know that I throw my clothes in there because I cannot be bothered to spend time like normal people do hanging my clothes in ordered symmetry. Do normal people do that? Or does everyone hide their disorder behind smart closet doors like me, the veneer society? They probably spend a lot less time ironing than I should, though I don't, because now I have my way and don't go to work, I walk around in crumpled creases except for special occasions. Was this evening special enough? Hmmm, I thought, digging through the cupboard's bottom until I found my favourite suit, pinstriped and miraculously clean. Another dive produced a tie, polka-dotted, and a clean shirt. I made the Herculean effort of digging out the iron too, though for what I don't know. If the poet was a poet, then what were a few creases? At least the clothes were clean. Later on, at The Bin with DB, it would be too dark for anyone to see a drunk's creases on his face, let alone the clothes, and DB would only laugh at my making the effort.

I love DB. I love him unconditionally, like you would a pet cat. I love DB because he is a sculptor and has stripes of brilliance running through him like the ages of the earth on the side of the Grand Canyon; all to do with timing. He is still funny, though he spends too little of his life sculpting and too much of it in The Bin drinking, which you would imagine would make his other career untenable, that of a kept gardener to a few kept women. I wish I'd never given him *Lady Chatterley's Lover* as a career proposal. We all need our toys, especially women in Barnes and Eaton Square; he manages. Friends ask me why I haven't slept with DB, he is so funny, so good-looking, great body, fun to be with, clever, talented, flaky – he must be gay. Maybe I am flaky too, but I don't want it in sleeping companions. I have snogged him, and he's quite a good kisser, but with sex you can tell he'd just be a shagger. Besides, he's more fun as a friend, to discuss his and my humiliations, with no semblance of compassion. What we look for in bed partners is sadly not what we are drawn towards with friends. If I slept with DB, he might tell other friends, and I am too egotistical to want the insides of my thighs or the spot on my bum discussed with another, the way he discusses things with me. I know the internal details of women from him that I pray I'll never meet.

If I slept with DB I would be forced to remember the way he made love every time we went for a drink, and then would follow the problems of when and if it would ever happen again. Simpler to say no, and I have. On Margarita-soaked nights, walking through Soho Square, when the summer sky collided with the ground and one step could've taken you on to a star. And I said no. Which proves that I have greater decision-making ability than I believe I have, because faced with a coffee shop that demands you choose between black/white, skinny/fat, latte/mocha/cappuccino/with syrup/espresso/macchiato, single/double . . . I can't make a choice. I am no captain of industry in an American coffee bar. I weakly ask for a white coffee, but take it however they give it, because they don't have vanilla coffee anyway.

I sit and wait in the designated coffee bar, The Troubadour. The Troubadour is an old-fashioned beat coffee bar. It should have a notice on the door that says, 'Long hair and sandals only.' It doesn't. Anyone goes in, and can furtively read their Simone de Beauvoir, Sartre, Terry Southern, André Gide or Nabokov; it is not Will Self country. Coffee is served white or black, to go with the chessboards that litter the tables. The benches are wooden, and so were the staff, horribly surly, but now nice people have bought it, and you can have smiles too. Englishmen haunt the back rooms, picking up naïve, dispossessed refugee students who haven't even advertised.

Early for once, I reread the poet's letter, amid the
mass of coffee pots that decoratively litter the walls
and ceiling; he is number eight of my favourites. His
photo was hard to fathom, a photocopy from a
magazine in which he'd been interviewed. I suppose
he must have thought it would look like showing off
to send me the original. I wasn't sure I'd recognise
him, but I was in my designated uniform. The usual,
but with biker boots and my new-look Lauren Bacall
hairdo, falling straight and like a half-drawn curtain,
parted down the side. I had taken up smoking for the
night, to complete the look, but it was making me
feel sick.

Steve Tive was glib and fast on the phone. Slightly
practised, knowing how to push a conversation forward in a funny, sweet kind of way; but pushiness is
often the cardigan of insecurity. I wasn't sure, but I
thought, Got to give a date a chance for a cup of
coffee, a chat, it's no big deal. I had to be somewhere
else later on, and who knew what might happen?
Anything was possible when you started out under
the auspices of hope. A poet couldn't be all bad;
others might disagree, but at least a poet is a person to
have an opinion about. What can you think about a
broker, except dollar signs?

I sat and waited, drank my coffee and eaves-
dropped on the surrounding conversations. On the

next table a pale-haired woman said, 'I've been reading this book called *Making Friends*. It's got some quite good tips in it.' She was talking to her arm, but there was a man sitting opposite her. He seemed occupied with assessing the room through a stream of his own smoke, but said nothing. She lifted her head with a gigantic effort, looked straight at him and asked, 'Have you read it, I wonder?' The skin on her face was translucent and pulled against her bones; only her child eyes were softly protruding.

I wondered if they too were on a blind date. I wondered where they could've put the ad – the *Wandsworth Guardian*, or the *Chelsea and Kensington Post*, delivered free to homes in the area. The man was hefty. Which one had advertised? I wondered. He was slumped comfortably into his own fat, and could hardly bring his mouth out of his chin to reply. He put his cigarette in an ashtray and squashed it out in one; stubbing it out would have required too much effort.

'I don't think that's the answer, I really don't.' I was becoming entranced with this couple. It reminded me of:

> Jack Sprat could eat no fat,
> His wife could eat no lean,
> But between the two of them,
> They licked the platter clean.

Now modern:

> Jackie Sprat could eat no fat,
> Her bloke could eat no lean . . .

I got out my pad from my bag and began to draw them. A perfectly acceptable thing to do with a café full of book-reading, chess-playing, home philosophers. In fact, that was what was needed to complete the scene, a berated, bereated artist.

He started again. 'I really don't think that's the answer. There's got to be something deeper. Books like that are too easy. Well, it's like saying you have to go on a diet to solve your fatness. That's not dealing with the fundamental problem,' he said, getting into his stride now and almost moving his head. 'You see, it's not tapping your creativity. I mean, for instance, how can you say that? Just put some words, thank you very much, into somebody's mouth and expect them to succeed? It's all very well, but I don't think it can work! Has it worked?'

On the mournful note of his last question the woman looked up, a bit basset-hound-like, her hair like ears, with her brown eyes and the slight protuberance of her lower lip.

'It's not that sort of book, actually. It's more profound . . .'

'Oh, I didn't . . .' He seemed to run out of energy, and couldn't be bothered to finish the sentence. He left it hanging, like some half-pegged-out washing, the way brothers and sisters, husbands and wives do. The woman looked at him now, properly willing him to reply, to finish what he'd begun; we were all waiting, including him. I prayed at that point, 'Please God let me have a lovely date with Steve,' and he must have been free and listening.

Steve was easy. He had no embarrassment with the situation, me drawing or us dating, and was much better-looking than his smudgy picture, and the moment he arrived I felt a recognition. Not that I could think that I had ever met him before, but there was definitely something there. Talking to him was like a pillow conversation, one of those things that goes on for ever and after hours have passed, you're sure there was something concrete said or established, but in fact nothing was. Absolutely nothing. We started talking about writing, careered through the entire history of art and ended somewhere in the disastrous dating game of, 'I'll tell you mine, if you'll tell me yours'. Actually it was more like a competition as to who could get the worst in first. Motormouths to the ready – *go!*

There was a girl called Laura who went off with his stepfather on Christmas Day, thereby ruining not only his relationship with her but also his mother's, and making an anniversary of it! Each year they all could celebrate Christmas, as it got easier. It never did for his mother. The stepfather and Laura bought a house in the same street as the mother and had children, lots of them, so that even if she couldn't see them, she certainly heard them, every day.

I wasn't even a contender in the misery game compared to Steve or his mother; I was an amateur, with my petty stakes, never having dated my stepfather or my father's boy/girlfriends.

Steve's intense blue eyes raced backwards and forwards as he gabbled his tear-provoking tales of laughter Mancunian-style. He said he wrote poems about each and every girl he had ever dated.

'What would my one be like?' I wanted to know.

'I'm not sure, but I'll send it to you when it's done. It's difficult. Wilde wrote the best line: "Something was dead in each of us, And what was dead was Hope." *Ballad of Reading*.'

'It can't be that bad. Have you ever been there?'

'No; I think he was talking about the gaol, but you could think about having it as your gravestone epitaph.'

He started to scribble on a paper napkin.

Dream, faith, aspire,
Trust, believe, desire.

Pandora, Pandora, you just couldn't wait
To open the box to let Hope be my fate.

And then he scribbled over it.

'No, that's crap. It'll be much better. It'll come as soon as you go, as the bishop said to the actress.'

'Ah, the story of my life.'

'Your life so far . . .' He wiggled his brow cheekily.

'Story of *My Life as a Dog*.'

'Haalstrom directed?'

'Excellent!'

That clinched the deal; we were on the same wavelength, official. He knew all about one of my top ten films. The terrible thing about it all was that there was a little equation missing from our joint chemistry set. It was like getting home from Ikea with all the pieces of a bed, to discover the nuts are missing that go on the bolts. So you have to take the whole thing back and get lost again and queue and wait and weep, boo, hoo. Well, there was no going back to Ikea with Steve, because the bolts to us had never been made. I had more of a sexual attachment to the shower than I ever would with him. If our parents had arranged a marriage between us, I suppose we could have worked something out, but as it was, neither of us felt an obligation to do anything but have a good time. Where does sex come from? Has it been genetically modified yet, like tomatoes?

'Steve, it's been really great meeting you, but I'm supposed to be meeting some friends in town at nine, so I should be on a bus.'

'Another date, huh? No dinner?' he said, looking vaguely gloomy in a way that would almost make you want to run off with his father.

'No, no, not at all. I'm meeting friends, those things that you have lots of when you're not dating people, and then dump as soon as you get a boyfriend.'

'And then wish you hadn't. Oh, yes, I think I remember those things. I'm too shamefaced to call any of them up now, after the way Laura treated them all.'

'You could make some more.' I smiled cheerfully at him, and then felt sorry for him. I knew how he felt.

Those calls you have to make.

'Hello, it's me again. No, I'm not married. Yes, it all collapsed like a house made out of loo rolls with the first downpour. What are you up to? Oh, you've got a new boyfriend, great. So you don't want to come out to play? No, OK. Hey, another time.'

Another Saturday night in front of grim TV docudrama/interior decoration/family gay sitcom and programmes about holidays you can't afford to go on. Still, you can watch the presenters having a good time, and that makes you feel much better, doesn't it?

I hate TV programmers – pervy fetishists! Oh, look, she looks like she's having more than the free holiday, she looks like she's having the cameraman too! Lucky cow – how'd she get the job? Why can't I have a job like that, eh? That's how Saturday nights make you envious.

'Steve, why don't you come too? Make new friends, influence people, recite poetry, that kinda thang.'

'That's really sweet of you, Hope. You wouldn't be embarrassed?'

'About what? Hey, I won't tell if you won't.'

'Where are you going?'

'The Bin, Soho.'

'God! Are you a member? I've heard of it, but I've never been.'

'Well it's a great place, so come.'

'I'm not sure I could. Lots of famous people go there, don't they?'

'Yeah, so? Come and join. Anyway, you're set to be famous, aren't you?'

'I don't know if I'd want that. I mean, look what happened to the Spice Girls.'

'Well, everything has its downside, and not all famous people marry footballers. In fact, I can't think of one poet who has. Not even Pam Ayres married a footballer.

'Look, I have to go, so if you're coming we've got to go now. Otherwise I'll call you. Or just come later, and whistle once you get there and I'll hear.'

'Whistle!'

'Yeah, you know how to whistle, don't you, Steve? Just put your lips together and blow.' I had wanted to say that to somebody all my life, but especially today, with my new hairdo. I laughed and waved and was out the door.

I was pleased I had made a new friend; he was certainly too timid to be a lover. You've got to jump in the sea and not care about the temperature, occasionally.

'Oi, you dykey!'

I don't turn around, but keep walking and ignore the violence of the strange voice in the black of the street. 'Fuck off, wanker!' I silently mouth on my way from the tube in the direction of The Bin, artists' den of iniquity.

'Dicky dykey! What's it like with a woman, eh?'

It comes again, the voice closer, more threatening, through the darkness. I wish I hadn't worn this bloody suit, but I refuse to be scared even if there are no lights except for neon strip-joint signs. Nobody understands about dressing up any more; since Princess Diana died everything is so serious. I thought the world would take on some more peaceful resolution; it would be the tea-tree oil to our wounds, a plasma balm to our molecules, but no, everything is serious.

The pressure on my shoulders is serious. It is seriously another's hands using me as a vaulting horse. I stumble under the weight, the shock, the scream that pierces my ears. And then I see DB's face.

'Ha-bloody-ha! I suppose you thought that was funny?'

'That's because it was. You seriously thought I was an escaped squaddie come to pin my dreams upon you, little boy? Where are you going anyway, the Gateway Club? I thought you were coming to see me,' he said with an attractive sniff, grunt and throat-squall as he gathered his body's phlegm content back into his mouth to gob like an Olympic Arab into the gutter.

'I was coming to see you in Regent's Park zoo, *animal*!' I observed.

'Ah, c'mon now. Are you all huffed up from my little joke?' He lovingly put an arm about me and squeezed my shoulders.

'No, your manners. You see, DB, I love you, but sometimes I don't love your behaviour,' I explained in simple child-psychologist terms. 'You scared me, you little prick, and besides, I don't look like a dyke. Do I?'

'Nah. It's quite a sexy outfit, and you're bound to

catch any indecisive bi's in it. No, honestly, it almost makes me want to go gay.'

'So, what's new?'

'Always got to have the last word, May, haven't you? No chance for the rest of us.'

'Yes. No. Buy me a beer.'

The place was packed, Friday-night-style, but Jim and Rachel had found a table somewhere in the back, so we sat there snugly restless, like eggs breaking into smoking fat, waiting to settle.

A couple of drinks later, I started to feel the weight of someone's gaze. Why it took scientists all that time to work out that solid matter produces invisible energy, I'll never know, when everybody can feel the weight of a hidden presence in a silent house, a concentrated stare upon the breast like a mosquito's hovering descent. I looked to my left and saw my mate Sol's back; to her side was the brown owner's gaze. He had a foreign face, maybe Greek, disturbingly light hazel-green eyes set in a tanned skin, a sexy, half-slanted smile and a great dentist, but he shouldn't have let the same man do his hair.

I smiled back, out of common decency or just common behaviour, and joined in the game of catching glances and throwing them back beneath lowered, mascaraed lids for fifteen minutes. Then Sol turned around, disturbed by the noiseless racket.

'May, honey!' she called across, waving her arms as if they were banners. 'How have you been? *Where* have you been?'

I signalled back for her to come on over. I could see her talking to the others through the smoke-filled crowds, the weekend-starts-here bustle. Together they picked up their table and moved it across the room, chairs and all, next to ours, no matter the inconvenience to others. Jeremy began to shout at her about messing up his place, him being the manager. She blew him elegant kisses through her long, beige, American hands as though she were making bubbles, but the only bubble was the Afro of hair around her small, sculpted, pretty face.

I wasn't surprised.

Sol always did have a thing about DB, like most girls around us. One day she might be able to afford him, I teased her, if she saved up all her pocket money. It is a tease, because she has the money already – she's a trust-fund baba – but she won't spend unless you twist her arm. She wants to be taken for an artist just by hanging with us, but the only person she's fooling is herself.

'Oh, DB, I didn't realise you were here!' she says, as if anybody is going to listen or believe her.

He smirks at her and raises an eyebrow – all right,

he's seen her, and what does that imply? Then he says charmlessly, 'That space is going to cost you a round of drinks, but it'll probably be cheaper just to buy a bottle of champagne.'

'DB!' I say, startled. He laughs back.

'Oh,' says Sol. 'Is that a joke? It's just, I'm kinda broke.' She still doesn't sit, while some anxiety crosses her face like a small child crossing the road. The very rich can't take a joke when they haven't made the money themselves. Suddenly she redeems herself without blowing what she thinks is her cover. 'Oh, Alex, can you buy us a couple of bottles of something bubbly?' And she sits down, whispering conspiratorially to us, 'Alex is the rich cousin. He's over from Boston doing a course at the AA.'

'Should he be drinking if he's in AA?' Rachel adds stupidly.

'Not Alcoholics Anonymous! The Architectural Association. I know, it's *so* confusing.'

'No, Rachel meant the other recovery service, didn't you, darling?' says Jim at the same time, as Sol listened intently to DB.

'Not really,' says DB. 'See, they all merge, in the end, with the Automobile Association. Ah, good man, clear the decks: champagne,' he adds theatrically.

Of course. Alex. The one I've been exchanging glances with, and he's rich and he's young, but not too young. As he comes closer, I catch the shape of his expensive clothes and think, There will be no classless society while cashmere still exists, and you can tell the difference between Lynx and Chanel. Smell that. Pass the money, honey.

Once we are seated and have chatted and drunk our hind legs off, we are all grin-stamped. I sit next to Alex all evening, and have avoided the closeness of his stare. Finally I say something in an intimate, I-know-there's-something-between-us way. The only way you can when you're stewing nicely.

'So how long have you been gay?'

'Who's gay? It sure ain't me.'

'Sorry! You smell too nice to be straight. For England. I mean, if men wear perfume—'

'Aftershave.'

'Aftershave, same thing. If men wear it here, they either splash humungous amounts over themselves in place of showering, or wear battery acid.'

'Uh-huh?'

'OK, I'm just saying you smell nice. No big deal.' I turned to go; he didn't want to take the bait, dumbass. So, I'd find someone who did. Some nights you drink to shag. But wasn't I looking for a boyfriend? No, not boyfriend, life partner, regular shag. And would that mean I'd shag to eat and drink? I was confused. No, I was tired and emotional. No, I was drunk, and needed another drink.

Alex caught hold of my arm as I turned to leave.

'Hope, do you want some more champagne?'

'OK.' Don't sound too enthusiastic! 'Yeah, thanks, that's just what I need.'

On the other side of the room, DB lay on a purple chaise longue, being fed plastic grapes by Sol, who was also simultaneously massaging his temples and ego. I watched him catch her hand and put it down the front of his trousers, and listened to her shriek and him laugh and then, left to her own devices, delve there herself. They would actually make a good pair if she could get over padlocking her wallet every time she left home. He needed someone rich to continue sculpting, she needed to be needed, though she was under some illusion that what she needed was pampering. Hell, she'd been pampered all her life; what she actually needed was unpampering, some serious Pashmina neglect to wrap around her shoulders and keep her chilly at night. DB would be good at that.

'Your champagne, madam. I thought you'd need a clean glass.'

'Ah, I see I'm just in time,' DB jumped in, interrupting what I told him later he should feel guilty about. Why Alex and I could have been a beautiful thing. 'Don't worry about a clean glass, I've got this.'

He held up an empty silver tankard mug that he must have unhooked from the ceiling of a pub in Kent but which actually came out of his pocket.

'Ugh, have you washed that out? It looks like it's got cobwebs in it. Don't want to waste good champagne.'

'If it offends you, dear, of course it must go.' And he balanced it on the thick, gilded frame of an expressionist portrait, so that it sat like a hat upon the head. 'Oh, May, I only wanted a little dinky,' he added, pouting pitifully.

'Oh, Alex, I think you'd better just give him a little if there's a spare glass.'

'Yes ma'am. Surely.'

'Alex, where do you come from?'

'When I'm not being gay at Harrods' perfume counter?'

'Ah, touché!'

'Boston, Mass.'

'You don't sound at all Irish.' Why did every American I met come from Boston?

'Well, my family originally came from New Orleans. Though I doubt if Solitaire would tell you that. She was Cajun.'

'What? Sol is called Solitaire?' I sniggered.

'Hey, don't knock it, it's the only game in town!' DB pointed at me and adjusted his face to look like Andy Williams's for a moment.

' "And every road I take makes me down . . ." or something like that,' I sang along.

Poor Alex looked totally bewildered but happy. Hey, if these Americans come over here trying to steal our bohemia in exchange for a few bottles of champagne, what do they expect?

'So, you're, like, an artist, Hope?'

'She's not like an artist, in any shape or form, my good man! She *is* an artist, except that when I knew her, she was called May. Ah, those were the Mays . . .'

'. . . My friend.'

'We thought they'd . . .'

'Never end . . . We'd drink and dance for ever . . .'

'Cut the crap singing, loveys, and who the hell thinks they can come into my place and start *whistling*? I'm not having you in here. We're not doing *To Have and Have Not* auditions, dearie. Shut the fuck up and fuck off,' shouted Jeremy's voice from the other side of the bar. Somewhere he slammed the door in someone's face. It was too late, for DB and I were well into our stride, and I never heard the whistle and Steve never got into The Bin.

AARGH! I was awake, but was I alive? My eyes wouldn't open but there was breath in my mouth, bad breath, but still, better than nothing. I felt around with my hands for assurance that I hadn't fallen into the pit of hell, or that at least if I had, I had managed to scramble my way back out. I felt a leg, but it wasn't my leg. A hand was on my breast and it wasn't my hand, but at that moment I couldn't be sure it was my breast. What happened? Where was I? One eye obliged me by opening, and I turned my head to look at the body on the other side of me. One thing I was sure about. I hadn't had sex. That's always a nice reassurance when you can't remember straight away the shattered windscreen of the night before. Well it wasn't Steve, so nothing spoiled there. And it didn't look like the American, Sol's cousin, which was a pity, so it could only be . . .

'DB? What are you doing here?'

'What, honey?' he blurred in a sleep-sodden voice. 'Come here.' And he grabbed at my body and was beginning to do what two people do when they've slept together, or what a male dog does to a bitch on heat.

'DB! Please remove your erection out of my thigh! You are not permitted to gain access to this restricted area, gottit?'

'May! I didn't know you were here. I thought you were Sol.'

'Yeah, well, imagine how *I* feel! I thought you were a cashmere-covered Old Bostonian.'

'Disappointment all round, then.'

'Thanks a lot. Most men would be very happy to wake and find some naked Hope in their bed,' I said, slightly miffed. 'I know, I know, you're not most men.'

'Oh, May's a little upset I don't want to shag her? We can soon sort that out.' He grabbed me by my arse as if to . . . But I squirmed free and stole the duvet, curling myself into the corner.

'I'm not called May any more, I'm Hope.'

'Not for me. Ah, diddums gone sulky.' I growled back a reply.

'Easy, Tiger,' and he began to stroke my back in a most seductive and suggestive manner, and I was happy to lie back down and be appeased. Eyes closed, head thumping nicely into the pillow.

Little kisses followed on my shoulder and snuck up to the nape of my neck. Tiny kisses as light and soft as kitten paws stumbling across my face. Just as his lips reached my mouth, his hand landed on my bum.

'No!' Everything stopped, freeze-framed. We had said the word simultaneously.

'I'm no fun. Sorry, DB . . .'

'Sorry, Hope, I don't think we . . .'

And we both started laughing hysterically, until we were rolling around in the bed like a pair of bad hyenas.

Later, we sat in a greasy spoon round the corner from DB's council flat behind the British Museum (only DB could have a council flat by the British Museum – everybody else has to make do with Forest Hill or Hounslow!) and force-fed ourselves bacon, sausages, eggs, chips, beans, mushrooms and tomatoes. The breakfast absorption of the stomach's alcoholic remnants. Huge mugs of tea and a plate of Mother's Pride buttered white slices helped.

'You know we could have,' I said.

'Another beautiful friendship saved in the nick of time.'

'So you believe that if you shag a friend, the friend goes out the window and they end up as just another one-night stand? Do you believe that?'

'No, 'course not. I think we could still have been friends, if you'd been any good at it.'

'Well there'd be no chance of that,' I said, laughing.

'No? I'm sure I could feel a definite *je ne sais quoi*. I think if we'd done it, we would have fucked like rabbits and forgotten ever to get up and eat.'

'Died on the job.'

'Happy but hungry. And when they found us, we would have been devoured by maggots.'

'How romantic!' I said, pushing the remains of my plate to one side. 'You have an enormous propensity—'

'That's what all the girls say.'

'Ha, ha, I was going to say, to make me feel very sick.'

'You see, May, Hope, whatever you're called today, I knew something would come between us. Thank God we never married. I mean, I do want the set of matching fish kettles, don't get me wrong, but now I've discovered you're allergic to me, it could never have lasted.'

'All's well that ends well, then.'

'Except for the cheque.'

'What cheque?' and in front of me he waved a Coutts & Co. cheque for ten thousand pounds.

'This cheque.'

I grabbed it to see whose account he was drawing on. The printed name said Miss Solitaire Reece.

'Just a little Reece's Pieces.'

'How did you get that?'

'I worked for it. I had to work hard for it for ten full minutes. My nob's still red at the end, do you want to see?' He started to unzip his flies.

'No, I don't! And if you expect me to believe that Sol pays for sex, it only leads me to lament, Mr DB, John Ford's sentiments: "'Tis pity you're such a whore." You call yourself a sculptor! Can I be your agent?'

'Let's see if we can bank it or exchange it for real money, then I can pay you back for breakfast.'

'I didn't realise I was paying!'

I waited outside the bank, as nervous as a skate caught by a lonely, long-haul fisherman, so I practised my tap-dancing until DB resurfaced.

'And?' I said expectantly.

He looked grim, shaking his head in disbelief.

'I never thought. I trusted her. It's your fault, she's your friend!'

'What happened?'

'She signed her name ET. The cheque was not valid, and I gave her head and I *hate* doing that in toilets!'

'Ah, DB, I'm sorry. Next time it's cash or nothing, eh? Disappointed, like a million prostitutes before you. The path of true love never did run smooth.'

'It did for Divine Brown after Hugh Grant.'

'But where is she now?'

'I thought you were meant to be the optimist between us!'

'I *am* an optimist. I am an optimist. Repeat after me,' I insisted of DB all the way down the road. 'What do optimists eat? C'mon, play the game. What do optimists eat?'

'I don't know, what do optimists eat? I give up. OK?'

'Spanish stew. They eat Spanish stew with bits of chorizo and smoked pork, chickpeas and potatoes and peppers undulating in this delicious, spicy, tomatoey, smoky meat sauce, because . . . You want to know why?'

'Why?' He sounded really bored and unimpressed with my cheeriness and his lack of cash.

'Because it always tastes better the next day. And by sheer chance, I have a pot of it on my stove. I'll buy some bread and chocolate, and we can go to my home and watch the afternoon film and eat optimistically all day until night falls.'

'And tomorrow I'll wake to find an optimist in my bed.'

'Yes. Exactly. But tomorrow it won't be me.'

'Hmm, I wonder who it'll be . . .'

'You didn't really think she'd give you ten thousand for a shag, did you? I mean, did she say, "DB – because I'm worth it! Here's ten grand." Because presumably you are too?'

'Hey, you've missed your chance now. You'll never know,' he grimaced greedily back at me.

At that moment I could have leaped on him, grabbed his head and lunged my tongue to the back of his throat and silenced his smug smile. Perhaps he was daring me to.

'Well, hard luck to me. Would it have been? You're sure you would have been up to it?' I grabbed towards his trousers jokingly, and he ran away up the street shouting.

'Get away, madwoman.'

And I chased after him shouting, 'But I love you, Cyril, don't leave me, please. What about our ten children? They miss you, Daddy.' And everybody stared as we laughed.

Suddenly the weekend was all mapped out. Not by Lionel at all, but by my friends and my lovers.

Tomorrow I would get back on course on a solid stomach full of Spanish stew, I would pick up the letters and read them all over again. Maybe not all of them; maybe do a lucky dip, the reading hadn't seemed to work so far. Never mind, as Scarlett O'Hara is so fond of saying on my video of *Gone with the Wind*, tomorrow is another day. Kind of obvious, but it's nice to be reminded that the past has gone and the future lies ahead. All we've actually got is the present. Maybe I'll go back home and see Mum and Dad after all.

Chapter 8

EVE'S TREE

Toby was gorgeous, Toby was lovely, but there was something very hopeless there, which made it worse, because he was everything I wanted. His eyes were blue and sparked with endless, wicked-humoured twinkling, his hair was black and curled deliciously and he had the most beautiful mouth that I have ever seen on a man. His mouth said *kiss*, and you couldn't help but jump to its silent command. Later, I learned that he didn't always mean it.

Toby had been worth the three-week waiting period. Toby was worth the awkward, embarrassed phone call to find out that he hadn't answered the ad at all; it was his brother Lomax who had replied for him. But he held the whole thing together with such good humour, and agreed to meet me for a drink, for the fun of it. I liked his attitude; that's just why I was doing it.

Some people you are meant to meet in life, and I knew that as soon as I saw Toby, and after half an hour of easy chat we both knew it; we'd been separated at birth. The sex wasn't the thing. Though we were both attracted, there wasn't that buzz of raw, fractured energy that zip-codes between the genes. There wasn't that addictive, physical passion, but I couldn't think of one person who made me laugh so much, and that I looked forward to seeing with such anticipatory bliss.

The first drink led inevitably to dinner, bed and breakfast and the weekend, and neither of us wanted to let go until Monday beat its steady path to our door. Toby had to go to work. Toby was a literary agent. A young, successful, rich, high-flying, brilliant, beautiful god of an Oxford man, who was better than all that. He was nice too, with good teeth.

It seemed there was nothing wrong with Toby in those first few weeks, and I would have paid that magazine a hundred times its price for finding me him. Nothing until the morning he phoned me up and said, 'I have a confession to make.'

'Oh, yes, another one? Is it better or worse than your last?' I nudged jokingly.

'Better, I think.'

'Come on, then, what is it?'

His last confession had been that he was purely a commercial agent, and would never represent anything literary, except by chance. I had said, never mind, even when he admitted that he was in it for the money and that wit and wisdom was only useful if it could be translated into the German and American markets. Of course, he admired publishers such as Marion Boyars and John Murray, and would read their authors, but he would never have them as clients when their audiences were so limited. There was nothing he liked more than mass-market appeal, he'd said. Which was one of those peculiar, hypocritical characteristics of people who only shop at Fortnum's and don't know the meaning of the word Somerfields, let alone George at Asda. Toby was odd. Maybe it was the eighties that had done it to him.

'But I can't possibly tell you over the telephone. Do you eat lunch? Perhaps we can meet up for something before we set off. You might decide that, once I've done my confessional, you don't want to go.'

'That bad, huh? OK, lunch.' I still assumed he was joking, and was trying to find excuses to see more of me. That egotistical, huh? Yup!

'Good, I'll be round to pick you up in ten minutes, then.'

'Fine, see you then.' I was enjoying my self-employed lifestyle, good and proper.

This sounded more serious than his last confession, and there was something about the way he said 'ten minutes' that pulled the string of dread within me.

He was there just as he said he would be, punctual and dapper, still in his pinstriped suit, with handkerchief and matching Jermyn Street tie. The Hon. Toby Somerton, BA, MA. He was fond of his titles. He twitched a smile and went to kiss me on the cheek, a restrained, dry peck; strangely formal.

'Nice to see you. So glad you could make it,' he said, and off we walked, arm in arm, avoiding the confessional box until we were snugly seated at a table in a nearby restaurant.

It was one of those restaurants where you can't understand how they keep going, full of pairs of bored women fiddling with their food through the hours of lunch, waiting for husbands or children to reappear, exhausted from the rigours of modern shopping. Sitting there with this odd tension was like being in a foreign country without the currency.

'You see, it's like this,' he said, after the waitress had disappeared with our order. 'I saw Eve last night.'

'Hhmm?' What else could I say? Who was Eve?

'And I don't think I can give her up. I mean, I know I can't. She's going away for the next week, but I shall see her when she returns. So you see, our affair can only be a short one.'

'I see,' I said, but didn't in the least. 'No wonder you couldn't come to dinner last night. It might have proved rather awkward.'

Inside my stomach flipped and flopped and I could feel all my yellow-primrose enthusiasm drizzling to a snot-grey-green drip. It was like being promised a shiny red bicycle for Christmas, with glowing mirror chrome, in the toyshop window, and having all that yearning to be sitting on it but with the plate glass eternally separating you. You pass the store every day for a week, and then suddenly somebody else buys it and you see her riding around the neighbour-hood, proudly perched on the leather seat. Who the hell was Eve to come interfering into my weeks of waiting? Toby was the pudding of my advertising spectacle, and now he'd been ordered by somebody else!

'Indeed, indeed. So you see, I quite understand if you don't wish to come away for the weekend, though of course I'd love it if you did.'

With that brief conversation, Toby was designating the game rules. Still, I was Hope, wild girl and optimist, inappropriate dresser and grown-up: there were no boundaries or markings yet, I noted. If I accepted the state of play Toby was giving, I could still write in a get-out clause, but then I'm always doing that; making myself detached, or worse, becoming a semi. If I wasn't careful, I'd end up in suburbia.

'I'm not sure why you are telling me this, Toby. It's your business what you do in your spare time, but thank you for being so honest.'

I played for time, looking towards the middle distance to settle my mixed and unmatched jumble of stomach nerves. I'd been dealt an unexpected blow and I had to think positive. The other girl was quite a considerate let-out clause, but I didn't want one; I'd only just dipped my toe in the damn water, and it didn't feel like I'd had a bath yet. And another thing! He was already putting a time limit on how long I was allowed to stay in. For all he knew, I might become a mermaid and never want to leave the tub. Maybe that's what he was afraid of. How dare he assume . . . It made me sad, and for a moment I almost told him. I wished he wasn't placing such definite limitations on things so early on. As fast as a slice I asked myself, do I need this? Is this fun? Is this what I want? Is this what I paid my hard-earned cash for, to come halfway down the list to some secondary trollop? But the only consideration that seemed to outweigh everything was, 'He makes me laugh.' It's true, he made me laugh. We would lie in bed reading, cerebrally separate, then suddenly be caught by a ticklish delight.

Why?

Sometimes laughter is enough of a reason. The fingertip-touch control can be delicate and often impossible to find on another; the fact that we touched each other's simultaneously was a near miracle, when I think about it.

I sometimes wondered if I was laughing with him or at him, but he always joined in, I suspect because he was playing at being a caricature; a sartorially elegant fop in a world overtaken by baggy-jean-bummed, rollerblading urban youth.

Remembering what I'd learned in the book I'd just finished (a seriously spiritual tome called *The Path Beyond Sorrow*), I tried to be honest. It was hard, but all these feelings were mine, and as the book said, I was the only one responsible for them. It was my conditioning that made me feel jealous or sad; it was my perception that saw Eve as an adversary.

'I think the point of my coming is that we have a great time together, and make each other laugh. At the moment what you do with Eve is your concern. When it starts to impinge on me, I shall tell you. (I lied: it was clearly already impinging.) Whether we sleep together again is something else. If we don't get on, we can set pillows up between us down the middle of the bed.' As I said it, I meant it.

'Quite,' he said, but I noticed his slight wince at the mention of schoolgirl pillow divisions. I had purposefully not said top 'n' tail; there were too many erotic connotations. 'I'm so glad you're going to come.'

'So am I. Thank you for asking me.' We were still caught in this strangely formal use of language.

'I'm certain we'll have immense fun. Now, let's eat some of this delicious-looking food,' he said, more for the waitress's benefit than ours; at least she departed smiling.

The confession was over, and we silently agreed to leave it unmentioned. Now that we'd finished huffing and puffing the climb up the snowy slope, all we had to do for the rest of the weekend was sail down it on the sleigh, yippeeing all the way. Of course, we both knew we'd have to climb it again at some point; a mole in a lawn never goes away, it just burrows to a different point in the garden. It was over for now, and the first haul is always the hardest, but its dark paws would soon scratch through the surface once more.

We bantered on through lunch, an absurd, self-perpetuating kind of humour which played among words and memories and made me laugh, as though we were equally matched partners on the tennis courts of Betjeman Land: 'Pass me the fish-knives, Norman', and, 'What was Captain Haddock's phone number?'

After lunch we strolled back to my street. Toby got into his car and drove away. I went upstairs to finish packing, changing the contents of my case again. Was the yellow right? Should it be the pink or the blue? Perhaps blue. I lay down on the sofa and tried to concentrate on the church spire that I can see from my window. I tried to wait it out, contain and dissipate it with prayer, but the tiny bruising on the right side of my heart hurt each time I breathed out. Bruising disappointment. It needed care and healing, comforting and cosying. Time would do it in the end, would mend my pumping, pounding organ, but what if it wasn't my heart at all, but a chip off my ego? How to mend that? Whatever: his confession had brought me a sigh that could pierce a steel sarcophagus, something I'd almost forgotten since that red bicycle, aged seven, and now it was slowly streaking up inside of me. Why had I summoned it back now?

I couldn't wait any longer. The spire wasn't enough, and I jumped on the phone and dialled Mum.

I had told Mum about my little adventure of a project, and I could feel her raise one of her elegant blonde eyebrows on the other end of the phone. 'Do as you must,' she'd said. 'But can't you find a boyfriend out of all your other friends, if that's what you want?' At the time Mum was going through her anti-men phase (Geoffrey excluded), regaling me with tales of her best friend's last husband buggering off, as she so neatly put it, with one of the friend's gay boyfriends. But then you never knew with Mum; one week she was on them, the next off. Dad didn't know either; one week he'd be the 'Northern Git', the next week the most wonderful man in the world. 'I'm so glad I chose him to be your father.' It was nothing to do with him, it was just her Gemini nature.

'At least he didn't tell you he had Aids,' Mum said.

'True. That would've been nice after sleeping with him already. Aids, herpes, syphilis. How do I know *she* hasn't got them?' I was talking about Eve.

'He's being honest. He didn't need to be – think of it like that.'

'Oh, no, I am, but it's a no-win situation; somebody ends up being lied to. Poor Eve! Something else to add to her tree.'

'Cheeky bugger, though, imagining he's the one who'll be calling it a day! He doesn't know you, then. Say to him, thank you for your honesty and we'll play it by ear. It's not going to stop you seeing other men, is it?'

'Oh, God, no!' and at that point I meant it. I was going back through my box of letters as we spoke. I was out and looking for a male Eve – would that have to be an Adam? I can't stand that name.

This time I was different. I wasn't going to try knitting. For months I'd gone empty-handed, I was on my own jolly way, picking up the occasional bit of thread but not weaving it into me. Separate. Anyway, bodies don't drop anchor like the mind; they sail as easily out of harbour as they sail in.

'Trust and believe and stay in the day. Decide to have a nice time. Don't project. Let yourself be light, have fun.' She'd been reading those books I'd given her, I thought. Good thing too – I needed talking to like this, and a wave of daughterly affection flooded through me towards her. 'If it's not, you can always catch the train home. Think of it as going away for the weekend with new friends, not the heaviness of a complicated love affair. It's just your perspective. When you find yourself having nasty thoughts, change them and try to see the good.'

Mum gave the easy, outside view. Inside the box of my brain, the conversations in my mind are what destroy me; what wear us all down. The decisions and beliefs we stamp through our heads that separate us inexorably from others and from ourselves, to kick hope from the door and isolate us. That's when we all become Pandora, clinging to our little boxes.

I decided not to mention Eve's name, not make any jokes about apples or snakes, especially not where my name was concerned. Remember, Hope fled first out of Pandora's Box; if Toby did, it was his affair, but he couldn't get me to listen to his confessional. I was determined to be in this for the fun.

All weekend I managed it, staying light and uncomplicated, laughing and jokey, but on Saturday night we all drank too much. I suppose I must have drunk to forget; I certainly forgot to reapply the perfect bow-shaped mouth, and lipstick bled and smudged clumsy and uncontrolled about my mouth like the unintended words I found myself saying. Mean, unthinking, spiteful barbs, all the harder for being wrapped in sugared laughter. Not satisfied, I gathered Toby's friends as ammunition to spit too, and then how did I feel? Awful. Toby's public humiliation didn't sit well with me. I would have liked him to tap me on the shoulder and ask to discuss what was running my velvety quiet up the wrong way, but of course we both knew: the unmentionable that was becoming what the apple had become to the original Eve.

On the Saturday we had prepared a huge feast of a meal for that night, six courses of gluttony, if you included the crisps and peanuts as separate courses.

Melon with black pepper and Parma ham.

Guinea fowl with salad and new potatoes.

Summer pudding with crème fraiche.

Goat's cheese with Muscatel grapes.

White wine, red wine, sparkling wine with pudding, brandy with coffee, even sherry with the crisps.

The meal was the right size for the house. We were staying in a magisterial baroque hall with divided staircases and curved doors that fitted into shaped walls. The surrounding gardens were manicured and pretty, everything beautifully in its place. These were the kind of friends that Toby had made at Oxford, so even I could tell he hadn't just done a secretarial course there. On the front lawn was a line of fountains and lily-covered carp ponds; and on the back lawn all the ingredients for summer croquet. The real grandness of the place stood to the right; an ancient and magnificent cedar of Lebanon, that threw its measured shadow like a Caravaggio or Georges de La Tour painting.

As soon as I saw that tree I wanted to hold it, to lie in its branches, my skin settled next to its rough, rippled bark. It was that kind of tree; so steady, so strong, so well rooted, and its heavy permanence made you think, I want some of that. No amount of blowing could fell that tree. At that moment, what with all the Eve hoo-ha, I wanted that tree more than I wanted Toby. I wanted to lie at its feet and kiss its arms and together, pray to God. I could stay with a tree like that, and be faithful, I thought. But a tree is not a man. This man Toby wasn't this tree; even I could see that, with or without glasses. You see, I'm not entirely stupid. Toby's friends, Sebastian, Nancy, Gerry and Georgia, whom we were staying with, were nice, professional, well-dressed, worry-free singles; just like Toby. I liked them, but then I liked Toby.

Everyone changed for dinner, out of cooking aprons, but I couldn't change enough for my liking. Ideally I wanted to change into a water sprite and go and join the fairies dancing down at the bottom of the garden. I was beginning to have worries about my happiness stakes. I was not feeling sane or comfortable.

More guests arrived, one of them an old girlfriend of Toby's who lived on the county borders. Toby was honest, he told me all about Hortensia Hinde, who had decided after her second child that her husband wasn't going to make the mark and inherit the title, and she'd bravely left in search of a richer and better-bred replacement. What were her chances? I wondered.

'Zero,' said Toby, 'now she has the children.'

'You never know,' I said. 'It can be quite an asset having children, past the sleepless-night stage. Besides, it proves she's a woman. That's attractive.'

'Hmm,' said Toby.

'To a man it should be.'

Hortensia arrived in a glorious embossed velvet jacket, and I commented on its loveliness, but Hortensia had to run it down. 'Oh, this old thing, it's nothing. Fifty pence from a junk shop.' I wondered if she thought everybody would say how clever to find it for fifty pence, but I didn't really think so. It seemed more like she was deflecting attention. It was only the landed gentry these days who could afford to boast the novelty of poverty, like a new profession; nobody else in England liked the smell of it in case it caught on. I was wearing a bright green silk-satin dress and would've wallpapered perfectly into the well-kept lawns. It was also from a second-hand shop, but I was only claiming its designer-label status.

Just before dinner I crept outside the house to tree-hug myself to sanity. I stood like a stalk with an unruly creeper of rag-curled hair and nobody could see me but the night sky. Back inside, we all huddled around the roaring log fire as the dark blue, frost-filled evening crept through the French windows. We sipped our sherries, just as grown-ups do. Crisps demolished, we sat in front of our place names around the long, mahogany table and discussed current affairs, oh, so civilised – but there was one empty seat.

As soon as Stephen walked in, he was drawn to my side. He was the other dinner guest, the young lord of the manor. I wasn't interested in talking to this hearty rugger-playing surveyor; he seemed to come from another world, one I didn't like. I could imagine him at school, the one who strung the new boys up by their feet and dunked them into the flushing toilet bowl; that's the kind of dark, glossy-haired hearty Stephen was. All my niceness and sweet resolve was skidding nastily away.

Toby sat opposite us, watching, drinking, getting morose, unable to join in across the too-wide table. I wished I'd been sitting by Toby, laughing. I wished I'd been sitting by anyone laughing. I turned to my other side, to Gerry, almost through spending his trust fund with heroin's help, but was now out the other side, a thin film of sweat always breaking out across his forehead. Anything to avoid talking to Stephen, to avoid thinking about drunk Toby, not worth talking to now, unless I could quickly catch up with a couple of large brandies. Then neither of us would be worth talking to, and we could sit with each other, silently incapacitated, burbling inconsistencies in a meaning-ful manner.

'Anybody want to climb the cedar?' shouted Stephen, and it was just the thing, Hortensia, Sebastian, Gerry and Georgia agreed. Nancy declined – she and her migraine were on their way to bed. I couldn't bear to see the others with their limbs wrapped around my tree; it had suddenly become mine in that brief period, in a way Toby couldn't, their clumsy, drunk feet standing on those regal branches and making twittering fun. I stared at it, at them, and it was like finding your lover at an orgy, sure that he can't be enjoying it, before turning away. Toby and I sat alone upstairs talking drunken, philandering nonsense, a scrabble of foreign ideas, an indecipherable, unreasonable righting of the world. Just drunk talk. I walked over to the window, I couldn't bear *not* to look, and watched the full, bright moon sharpen the trees. Georges de La Tour shadows, definitely. As I looked, another set of shadows grew out of them, separate. Stephen and Hortensia's tangled branches, caught in each other's bodies, wrestled on the grass.

'Oh, do look, Toby, Hortensia's having some fun.' I couldn't stop, there was no taking it back.

'What? My God, that's a disgrace! She's a mother! He's just a boy, a pompous, beastly boy. They can't copulate on the lawn, they're having the Retired Gentlewomen's Watercolourists here tomorrow.'

'Don't be ridiculous, Toby! Are you afraid they'll leave visible semen stains on the grass, hazardous to health as octogenarians skid helplessly? Or are you afraid they'll all be impregnated through their insoles? Good on them, at least they're having a bit of fun.'

'Having sex, more like! How dare they!'

I wish I was, I thought. I knew the likelihood of Toby getting anything up tonight was as slim as his leaving a full glass on the table. The more that went down, the less went up. He'd chosen to drink too much to have decent sex; it alleviated the pressure of having to perform, I thought.

Sex was for Eve. Filthy, anonymous, separate sex with a girl he had no conversation for, only whispered obscenities. Eve was malleable and obliging, dirty and sexy.

Later on we went to bed and I said, 'Fuck me, Toby.'

'You know I can't.'

'I was only joking,' I replied, and rolled over to my side of the bed. 'Not,' I whispered to my pillow, giggling. Lying in bed, fingers crossed, schoolgirl behaviour with or without the pillows. I had a horrible thought that the conversation was reminding me of Neil Simon's *California Suite*, the bit with Maggie Smith and her gay husband Michael Caine, and how it would be if I remained in a relationship like this for another twenty years. My I was being morbid! I hoped it was the brandy. Make note, don't drink brandy – ever again. 'Disgusting stuff,' I giggled.

'What, sweet? Let me read you some Maupassant, darling,' he whispered in my ear, and covered the curves of my body with his large, limp form.

The coarser side of me wanted to say, 'Fuck Maupassant, you drunken git!'

But I settled for turning my body around to his and placed my head in the crook of his neck and listened to the lull of his perfect French accent cradle me to sleep, any annoyance seeping out of the crack of my smile.

The next morning I woke early and dressed, ordered things back into my bag, neat and ready, before gently whispering to Toby's sleeping form, 'Would you like some tea?'

'Marvellous,' was his staccato reply. A normal man would say yes or no, but if Toby could say, marvellous, wonderful, brilliant, he would fit it in.

I put the kettle on and went to the bathroom, and relieved myself of an endless stream, filled from the two litres of water I'd drunk before going to bed. I scrubbed my teeth until my gums bled and they felt once more to be rooted inside my head, instead of having been left on the pillow. Cigarette smoke still clung to my hair, so I sprayed perfume over it and pinned it to the top of my head. Moisturised and cleansed, creamed and wiped and creamed again, I lipsticked a mouth back into place and drew my eyes on. I was hung-over but now beautifully masked and ready to face the world. I would never touch brandy ever again.

I opened the window wide and sucked in the glorious country air, marvelled at the beauty of the sheep so perfectly placed in the field to the right, the cows in the field to the left, and the newly splattered rain that made everything glisten with the sun on it, like crystal. I held my arms out to the sun, the sky its bluest with cotton-wool clouds, and seeing the cedar tree praised God and prayed.

'Dear God, please let me stay in myself today, be at peace with the earth, bring joy where I can, not to take on hurt and rejection just because Toby doesn't want my body. Please God, let me stay happy. Let me give and receive fun. Thank you for all this, for all of everything.'

From now on I'm not taking on anybody else's luggage; mine is enough. I'm packed and travelling (like Holly Golightly) light. I will connect, detach and stay whole. I thought I was learning.

This was the theory I'd read and would practise, because if I didn't keep it constantly in my attention, it would slip through my fingers and fly away as easily as a helium balloon on nylon string. Keep conscious, be conscious, I reminded myself, lest the low point hit and I might be swept away on the gloom tide and pea-soup fogs of depression that settled first as lightly as dandruff upon shoulders, before consolidating into boulders.

I returned to the kitchen, re-boiled the kettle and made two cups of tea, taking one to Toby's bedside table by his slumped and snoring form. Seeing him lying there, I was glad to be escaping.

I crept to the door by the side staircase, away from the first morning voices that were congregating in the dining room, espadrilles hugging the creaking floor, as I hurried out as though being pulled to an impatient lover. The tea spilt on to my toes and I bit my tongue to keep from yelping before holding the cup more carefully and going down the staircase with the red rope banister. I had to stop from running across the gravel and lawns to get there quicker. As I approached I felt shy, and stopped before I could touch it. Would it remember me from yesterday, should I be more formal, reverential even? Not after what it had witnessed last night of Hortensia and Stephen, surely? I coyly put my fingers to a branch and softly stroked its rough skin. I put my tea down and couldn't stop from hugging this huge, old, solid thing like a dearest friend. So immovably large and rooted in the earth, as if the hand of God had planted it there fully grown, and that's who it would take to get it out.

When I finally stepped away from the tree, I felt taller, I felt I'd been given roots, had got so hardy that I could withstand winters without shedding any leaves. I could feel the power of the earth, the ground's magnetism holding firmly in place the needles of my feet. I wasn't quite sure what I was meant to do now, anything or nothing. It didn't matter: everything was in its place, no big deal, all I had to do was be, be Hope. I wouldn't be fearful any more. I would be all the good things my name evoked.

The world's noise gradually came back to me, birds singing, trees rustling, humans shouting. Through the dining room's open window came the hostility of raised voices, loud laughter, big discussions. People discussing piles that had no medical significance, just tax difficulties and death duties.

I pulled the air through my body and filled my eyes with the sky and held on to the sun's warmth in her heart and let the February cold goose-pimple my flesh before going back upstairs. In times gone by I would've run to the field at the bottom of the garden, kept on past the cows and up the hill; the sound of shouting did that. Now it was all no big deal.

The scene downstairs was an upper-class Sunday breakfast, all newspapers, eggy plates and sausages, burning toast wafting the air, and under the discussion grill was poor Hortensia and her 'totally outrageous behaviour of sleeping with young Stephen, lord of the house'.

Worse, Toby said, was Stephen's behaviour. 'Young thug! Where did he think he came from, that he could go around having sex with *my* ex?'

'From next door, I imagine. Where is Hortensia?' I said, joining the ranks.

'Sloped off with her shame, I shouldn't wonder.'

'No, I think Stephen's gone off to church.'

'She had to get back to her mother's and pick up the children.'

'The only shame is the way you men are behaving. Why shouldn't she? Nothing wrong with a fuck if you can get it,' I said, really digging my oar in, childish to the last; but I meant it, why shouldn't she?

'But she was only asked for dinner.'

'What? Not to entertain us all over breakfast with her extra petits fours special?'

'I could hear the grunting!'

'Hope and I saw them copulating on the lawn. Keep a watch out for used condoms underfoot, could be a nasty accident, slippery at this time of year. If you ended up in hospital, Hope, you wouldn't be half as generous, I suspect.'

'But what about the Retired Gentlewomen Water-colourists, they're out there today. Toby, you can tell them, maybe put up a sign. Beware Used Condoms,' Nancy teased.

'It's your brother's responsibility, Nancy. You can jolly well tell them.'

They good-humouredly bantered all through coffee and croquet on a frozen lawn, which we could hardly bang the hoops into, about Lady Hortensia's prospects.

I walked off for one last communion with the red hill, having lost again, and more interested in keeping warm. When Toby came to find me I was talking to a woman who lived in the gamekeeper's lodge on the estate.

'This is my lift approaching,' I said. 'I'm sure he's come to wrench me from the country and back to the city. It's been nice talking to you,' I said, utterly sincerely, because it had been nice to talk to someone who seemed ordinary/regular in her country clothes, and who wasn't just pretending for the weekend.

'Ah, there you are, Hope. Are you ready to leave? I've packed your bag into the car, the others have gone on to the pub. I said we'd meet them there for lunch. I see you've found a friend, how clever you are.'

'Yes, aren't I? I'm sorry, I don't know your name. This is Toby Somerton and I'm Hope.'

'Hello, I'm Anna Humphries. Toby Somerton? Aren't you the historian, Greek expert? I've heard of your books.'

I tried to cover my smirking laughter, the nasty, low side that kept hitting at Toby for Eve; no matter the tree's powers and new-found roots, it felt good to laugh. 'I'm sorry. The only book Toby's ever penned is the visitor's book, and he didn't leave a comment.'

'Yes, I'm afraid you're sadly mistaken.'

'No, I'm sorry. Then you must be an artist or a pop star.' You see, it wasn't only me who thought him so handsome.

In the pub, when Toby recounted the tale, he said the woman was obviously raving. An escapee from some high-security mental institution who had wandered into the grounds. Then he chastised me for laughing at the mention of his Greek abilities; why shouldn't he be an expert? But then he was intrigued as to which pop star he could be.

'The drummer from Sparks.' 'Ice-T on a country retreat.' 'Michael Jackson escaping imprisonment', were the possible suggestions given out by Nancy, Sebastian, Gerry and Georgia.

'We've got to be going, haven't we?' said Toby, when he wasn't hailed as a fashionable star. He stood up authoritatively. I had been told by the others that as soon as Sunday arrived, Toby was leaving, and going back to another life. But I was happy to go: everything seemed easier. I was ready to get back home, be alone for longer than half an hour, maybe go to the pictures this evening. I snuggled down in the car seat, cranked down almost flat, for a moment making me think about sex, as in 'these would be handy for', then I put a tape on and turned to Toby.

'You don't mind if I sleep on the journey back, do you?'

'Of course not, sweetheart.'

Then he smiled in a way that could almost be construed as wistful. I recognised it as real; with all the bantering that had gone on this weekend, so much had got covered up between us. It was nice to see something true.

Lying down listening to Van 'the man' Morrison sweeping over me, and having felt so fatigued, suddenly my heart was racing with energy from some hidden pocket. 'Oh, slow, slow down,' I breathed back in, to calm the excitement of life. I could feel my flickering eyelids close upon darting retinas like in some laboratory dream experiment, images rushing past, sent so fast from my brain I couldn't hold them.

Toby drove on.

The car rushed down the motorway and rocked me into a mindless, empty sleep. I awoke as seamlessly as I'd gone under, feeling something warm, soft and solid upon my curled knee. Slyly I opened one eye and saw that it was Toby's hand, both intimate and protective upon me.

Strange boy, I thought. Sweet man, and, closing my eyes again, slipped back to the warm comfort within.

★ ★ ★

'What will you do now?' Toby asked. And I knew it wasn't just a question of how I intended to spend that evening, but I chose to take it like that anyway.

'Once you've dropped me outside my garret, I have a choice. I could finish a painting off that has to be dry by the weekend for delivery, or I could slope off to the Gate and see *The Last Seduction*. In fact, I think it's just what I deserve.'

'Sounds intriguing. What's it about?'

'It's a thriller where the girl gets the money and leaves the men stumbling around with their trousers around their ankles. It's funny, if you like them black.'

'Very droll! So that's your final decision?'

'Yes. Yes, it is.' I felt as strong as an ox.

'Would you mind if I accompanied you?'

I thought about saying, But what about Eve? and then I thought about that movie *All about Eve* with George Sanders and Bette Davis, whose immortal mouth drawled as Eve (Anne Baxter) approached, 'Fasten your seat-belts, it's going to be a bumpy night.' And how George Sanders's last words before committing suicide were, 'I'm bored!' And that the stuffed carcass of Toto the dog in *The Wizard of Oz*, the Judy Garland version, had been sold at auction a couple of years ago for £2,300. All of these things I could have said to Toby, and he would have been delighted and amused, but instead it led me to think how cheap and fast life can be.

'No, not at all.' And I smiled back at him, and we turned left through the Sunday evening traffic at Earl's Court towards the Gate cinema. 'Do you think we should have popcorn, or ice cream?'

'Both,' he said, and patted my knee, and I squeezed his hand back and then we went and watched Linda Fiorentino emasculate some cute guys and Toby cringed, and I laughed.

Oh, Lomax, what did you do, answering that advert? What made you do it?

Chapter 9

IT'S ONLY ROCK 'N' ROLL

'Do you want a line? It's your go.'

Did the room stop, or was I just functioning under a child's slow time? Drugs do that, change time, even the mention of them. I felt that everything had gone quiet, that everybody was waiting expectantly for my answer. When I turned to look, the others were doing different things, picking up a paper, lighting a cigarette, chatting, watching another video. I still felt like I was on stage. Not quite the stage we'd been watching among the thousands out there at the festival in front of the hotel, more Upstairs at the Royal Court. Small and select, but still a stage.

The straw was held out to me by Joe, standing by the Formica-topped, wood-grain desk. On top of its brown-black smoothness lay the last three messy, white powder lines.

Did I want a line? Not really. We'd been drinking slowly since the afternoon, and now it was two in the morning.

Did I want a line? No, I wanted to curl up in bed with a pillow under my head and feel clean cotton sheets across my naked skin that stank of smoke and go to sleep. Aahh, sleep, I remembered it as fondly as if it were an old teddy. I glanced covetously at both of the double beds that other bodies lounged across. That wasn't what he was offering me.

'Yes, all right, thanks.' I took the straw, holding it to one nostril, blocking the other with a finger, and took a short sniff and then did the same with the other nostril. It was just like riding a bicycle. Easy when you knew how. I didn't sneeze or anything. I didn't even think of Woody Allen films.

I took only half of what was allocated to me. Why? Courtesy (did I want to be asked back for more?), expense – the stuff wasn't cheap, and I wasn't pulling out my empty wad. I felt like the uninitiated guest, visiting gang member. There were others who needed it more than I did. I wiped my nostrils with a finger and stuck it in my mouth, rubbing my gum with some half-recalled etiquette. I waited for my bodily reactions to make themselves felt, remembering the last time I did this, ten, twelve years ago in some far-off teenage land, but people do it now more than when I once did. I have a Groucho mentality towards drugs: I wouldn't want to be part of any club that wanted me.

I tried to recall the rush, or was that speed? Amyl nitrate blew the top of your head off; no, speed burned out the passages of your nose and made your eyes water. This wasn't so mad, I thought, taking a cigarette and puffing. I don't smoke.

Did I want a line? I wanted to cross a line, fly through a hoop and jump across to the other side, maybe swim the Channel while I was about it.

The dreary, low-lit identikit hotel room looked even more depressing now. Bags spilling dirty clothes edged the walls; the contents of pockets covered the spare surfaces between the used glasses and empty bottles.

I turned and moved towards the glow of the neon-lit mirrors inside the bathroom. I was curious to see if my face had changed faster than my innards. I half expected to see Nancy Spungen or Courtney Love, some dead old peroxide blonde bleeding lipstick across a white-powdered, blotched face; fresh tracks to cover the old ones. Shockingly, it was my face that was still there, my hair auburn, my nose freckled and my eyes around my saucer-sized pupils green, not red, purple or pink. Just green. Hang on, aren't they meant to be violet? I wasn't a Martian from another planet. I was still Hope playing the rock 'n' roll game. I was away with Rachel for the weekend with some free backstage passes and a handbag full of clean knickers, roll-on deodorant, a couple of shirts and a lipstick, and everything my pockets could hold.

I sat on the loo and peed a long, low cow's stream that went on for ever into the sea. The loo paper had disappeared; I thought about disentangling the hard cardboard to wipe myself against. Why do English hotels never have bidets? Straining under the sink, I saw some tissues and used the last of their pastel softness for my purposes. Someone else could use the cardboard out of desperation.

I pulled out a lipstick from my pocket and slid it meltingly around the hole of my mouth, pressed my lips together and blotted them on an old petrol receipt lying by the sink. Another trawl through my jeans, and I found a black eyebrow pencil to darken my brows and scribble a smudge about my eyes. 'Hhmm, looking good!' One last rummage brought out a phial of perfume, which I spilled across my chest and tried awkwardly to rub into my wrists as though my hands had been chopped off.

I was beginning to feel excited. I was up for the party and all of the adventure. Hadn't I been here before?

★ ★ ★

Rachel had rung me just a couple of days ago from work and offered me, in her casual way, the chance to hang from a passing macramé chandelier. That's how I saw music festivals – hippie hangouts full of time-warp travellers, where everyone lay about eulogising over electronic guitar solos, swallowing tabs and puffing on bongs like the caterpillar out of *Alice in Wonderland*. Glastonbury, Reading or Womad, singularly lacking in soul. The kind of soul I liked, anyway. Without voicing my judgements, I agreed to go. It was neither a lifestyle I was used to or aspired towards, and I still said yes in my commitment to try anything – once.

Afterwards, I had wondered who had had that conversation – was it me or someone else? What justification could there be in signing up for a weekend of rock music, beer-drinking, mud-shoe wrestling, inedible food and druggies?

Fuck it, had been my reasoning (my, what complex philosophy!). If you never try it you'll never know, and the whole of last year I'd been chancing it with life. Bungee-jumping into conversations, getting too intimate with people I'd never see again, meeting monsters and divinities, basket cases and boffins. Why stop now? Every opportunity was a new adventure, getting to collide with the exciting and the extraordinary. Amazing things can happen all the time. It was a perception, I had those years with Thom to make up for.

We might just go for a day, me staying sober and keeping tabs on the car keys for home as I watched Rachel diving straight in at the deep end. With Rachel, unstoppable, wonderful Rachel, we'd be in with adventure, and the stars, in some cheesy hotel in a dead-end town. Every girl needs a friend like Rachel.

'Hurry up, Hope, you've been at this for hours! It'll be over by the time you get out of the loo. Everybody will have gone home,' I could hear my voice saying.

I clicked the door open, expecting to see some Mardi Gras scene, a reflection of my inner state. The brown, dimly lit hotel room was static. Somebody lay on the bed, and all my jealousy had gone. I never wanted to sleep again. Joe sat at a round, smoked-glass table and rolled a joint. Two others were laughing at a magazine, everybody stared at MTV. Nothing had changed in those hours, or was it minutes, seconds, that I was away.

'Anybody want some more drinks?' Rupert offered. 'Who wants to ring room service?'

'The hotel's cancelled all room service,' said one of the twins, either Peter or Simon.

'Anything left in the minibar?' asked Rupert from the bed, his long body sprawled carelessly large.

'Who's for the last slimline tonic? Hahaha!' said Simon or Peter callously, after pulling open the sad excuse for hospitality and waving above his head a bottle that wasn't even full.

'Somebody'll have to go down to the bar. Who wants to get the champagne? Anybody want champagne? Joe, go get the champagne. Here's my room card, put it on my bill,' said Rupert.

'I'll go,' I offered. I couldn't keep still. I couldn't stay in the zombie room. Had we taken different drugs? How could they lie there, hardly breathing? Was that talking? I wanted to meet brand-new people, cartwheel down corridors, break into the pool, get married. Not watch MTV. I never wanted to watch MTV ever again.

'Are you sure?' said Rachel. 'Are you absolutely certain about that?' She was eyeing me strangely, as though I had suggested a little light skydiving from the hotel roof. 'Will you be OK? Do you want me to come with you?'

'Of course. Don't be silly, Rachel, I'm fine. Champagne and what else, anything?' While I waited for their slow response, I took to casual teeth-grinding mixed with some gentle lip-chewing.

'More coke and a couple of ready-rolled joints and I'll be fine,' said Rachel, madly cackling. Rachel had a reputation to keep up; no one blinked.

'Two double vodka and tonics.'

'I'll have a beer and some fags. Marlboro Lights if they've got them. Here, I'll come with you,' said Joe.

My new friend Joe. Cartwheeling cohort. Elevator allegiance. Parading pal. We practised handstands in the corridor, did we?

This was the exciting adventure, down to a bar full of pop stars and music biz. This was the hot date, bucket of champagne, nothing to eat all day, half a dozen cigarettes to coat my stainless lungs with.

Bing-bing. The lift door opened on to the ground floor, reception and a bar that heaved with under-aged drinkers and over-age teenagers trying to sign, trying to get, deals, deals, deals. I was in, muffling through a crowd towards the bar, mission in mind. Joe disappeared; who cared? Not me. We were all among friends, one big family party. I smiled, and people smiled back understandingly.

'If you keep on smiling at everyone, Hope,' Rachel had said earlier on, 'everyone will think you're on E. There could be no other reason, in the music biz.'

'Hi, how are you? My name's Hope,' I said cheerily to a man standing next to me.

'Hi, Hope, didn't we meet already? You're a friend of Johnnie's. This is Clive.' I have never seen these people before.

'Hi.'

'Hi, how you doin'? You look like you're havin' a pretty good time, do you want a drink? Just arrived, or have you been on site all day?'

'Thanks, I'll have a beer. Yeah, we were down there.'

'See anything good? I just got here. My band isn't playing till tomorrow.'

'Oh, what band?' I can do this talk, the lingo-bingo stuff, californese. I didn't know whether he was in one or owned one or managed one, but it seemed to be the same conversation you had with everyone. Keep on asking questions, and they presumed that you were chief gang member of some big-deal record company.

I hadn't actually met any of them before, but I was one in a million sperm swimming in the same direction. Intimate pond life. Green-algaed up to our eyebrows. Maybe this was an experiment for them too, a first time, and they were all ordering champagne as well.

'Excuse me, I'd like some service,' I say to a packed bar in the manner of a very important person with very important people on a very important mission. 'I want some champagne.'

Yeah, yeah, doll, we can see that, coked out of your tiny skull.

'What would you like, madam?' I'd finally got

through a conversation and made it to the bar.

'A bottle of champagne, six glasses, two double vodka and tonics, a San Mig and a packet of Marlboro Lights on room . . . (the worst that could happen now is that I forget the room number) 235,' I say confidently, posed can-I-help-you smile. I should say!

'Can you sign for it, madam?' Sign for it? Double flip backwards!

'Yes, of course,' I say blindly. I've forgotten how to sign my name. Do I sign mine or Rupert Denbigh, and how would you spell that, anyway? My mind is crowded out with worries. I scrawl a signature and flash a card; it could mean anything. It's accepted. I've run the one-mile minute! 'Hold on, I can't take this tray up like this. This is outrageous!' Whole conversations whiz by in my head like asteroids.

'Excuse me, I think you've forgotten to give me an ice bucket . . . for the champagne? Thank you. I'm sorry, I know you're awfully busy.'

Somewhere along the line that's affecting my brain, I have climbed into a perspex tube, clear mercury has been poured over me but it sticks. I am coated, protected and distanced from the world. I can carry this tray no trouble, and walk across water. A strange, indifferent confidence. 'Mere mortals beware: the goddess approaches from a far and exotic land (to a

Pinky and Perky voice-over). Do not be frightened.'

'Oh, there you are, you got everything? Thanks for the fags. Shall I take the tray?' My friend Joe pockets the cigarettes and begins to lift the tray from the bar. 'Eh, it's a bit bloody heavy, you take the champagne, Hope,' he says in his heavy Northern Irish accent, and I wait for him to say more because I think he must be a politician, but he walks off towards the lift.

'Bye Clive, see you later,' I say to my new friends.

'Yeah, sure, have fun,' says the smooth-skinned American who's in a band or runs a band or scouts for bands, or something.

I follow Joe obediently, feeling the ice-cold slops upon my feet and look down to see that they are naked. How did that happen?

Surreptitious three-knock tap. No answer. Whispered, 'It's us, Joe and Hope.' The door slides open.

'Shut the door behind you,' a voice commands. I oblige with a mule kick.

'Shall I open the champagne?' Nobody answers.

I concentrate on this job. I know how to do this. I did once. The cork pops off to a corner of the room, swinging a lampshade on the way. One of the twins is pulling the curtains against any light that dare encroach into our darkness, brown curtains with purple flowers that match the bedspreads that are slipping off the beds towards the grey-carpeted floor.

Everything's grey and brown and beige except for another MTV video that stripes the screen and superimposes a crying baby's face on an endless noise of guitar solos. The champagne tastes different, strangely unexciting. I hand it out and collapse on the bed, waitressing duties done, thirst for adventure satiated.

'How are you doin', Hope?' Rupert asks beside me. We've been talking oddly all evening, or oddly talking, ever since Rachel introduced me and announced that we would be taking up floor space in his hotel room for at least one night during the festival.

'I feel like I'm stuck in a lift with only two choices, up or down, and there's no getting out until I crawl through the basement crack.' He looks at me and puffs at a joint that crackles towards his fingertips. He drops it into a convenient cup of coffee.

'Who just put a fag out in my coffee?' one of the twins screams from his corduroy coma, and everyone laughs.

'Sorry,' says Rupert, lighting another cigarette. I take it to mean he wants me to continue but I would anyway, I'm stuck on the track.

'I want to get out but I don't want to crawl through the crack. I mean, who would, when there's a sign pointing to the exit on the roof . . .'

'What crap are you going on about? Rachel, I think your friend needs help. Pass us the champagne.'

'I was just meaning, oh, I don't know . . .' I slide back into the video, watching with the same blank stare that I had so scorned earlier on in everyone else. Janet Jackson jumps off aeroplane wings and I'm in with her. Everyone else is up and snorting another line. Even I can tell I don't need that. Now everyone wants to go and see what's happening in the bar downstairs. Rachel's trying for room service, Rupert wants a CD player, Joe needs a spliff to calm down after all the coke. Rupert wants another vodka. Everybody goes quiet whenever anyone else knocks on the door. Let's pretend we're not here. We're playing a waiting game. That way everybody assumes something exciting is going on in a room where they are not allowed.

'I'm not bloody having anyone else in here,' says Rupert. 'They can fuck off and find someone else's floor to sleep on.'

I drink my champagne, and then another.

Downstairs we all troop. For the third time Rupert wants to see who's left in the bar, wants to go visit the casualty leftover list. I don't care, I'll talk to anyone. I swig down someone else's beer left on a table and go at it. Court jester – prime fool.

'Have you got a CD player we can borrow, by any chance?'

NO. NO. NO. NO.

'But you could come up to my room and check if you like.'

'Oh, I'm quite happy to take your word for it; you've got an honest face,' I say to this weasel-eyed, coke-sex puppy.

'I like your lips, how about I slide my tongue between them?' he says.

'Because I don't think you want it bitten by my teeth,' I reply.

'Don't count on it.' He gives me such a lascivious smile that I scamper back to be by my gang. Paranoia, who mentioned paranoia? Not me, must have been you.

'Hey Rupert, how you doin' man?' says one tight T-shirted, plimsolled, jeaned youth touching forty and refusing to let go.

'Fucking fuck-faced! I'm going upstairs.' At that, he staggers up, lurching with all his height. And we all follow. It's as simple as that. A twitching, sniffing entourage.

Upstairs I take off my jeans, lie down on the bed, don't notice the other five in the room, get up, drink some water. I still have some rules. Always drink water before bed. I borrow some stray toothbrush without toothpaste lying around the sink. Use the cardboard out of the loo roll to wipe myself with after another pee hardly worth the effort, before discovering the new roll. Borrow a T-shirt from Rupert and take off the rest of my clothes except for my knickers, in a strange nod to civilisation. He is the only one in the room with clean clothes. I climb between the cool, clean sheets and MTV drones on obliviously in the corner. The boys are rolling and smoking round the table in a desperate bid to climb down off the lines that took them up. My eyelids become heavy magnets to the iron filings of my lower lashes, and I forget to look for Rachel.

Who turned the lights off? The swill of the cistern must have woken me. I try to turn over, but I'm a jam filling between two bodies.

Sleep.

Who turned the lights on? The swill of the cistern must have woken me. Can nobody just piss and leave it, are we all such prudish middle-class brats that we have to flush away anything our bodies spill out? I turn over. One body gone; ahh, luxury. Too late: Peter or one of the twins slips back into bed, and I lie pushed back into the discomfort of foreign smell and heat between a pair of twenty-year-old twin backs. Some would hold this to be an erotic fantasy, mirrored back and front by smooth-skinned, supple-muscled youth. Some pay for this. I can't even bear to sleep between them. I feel nauseous.

I don't know who's asleep or who's awake in the room; some are pretending, like me, but not the one who's snoring great rhinoceros grunts, snuffles and gasps. Hey, it's rock 'n' roll. I thought six in a room, drugs and champagne meant a motion picture of orgy sex. Where do these screen writers get it from? There is not one molecule of sex happening in this dung-brown room, not one atom of sensuality between these sheets. Not one filled condom staining the floor. Unless something's going on in the next bed.

All I want to do is sleep. If I sleep, I can grab back my brain, stop it orbiting and reinsert it inside my body. I don't know what good I expect that to do; anything to help.

Water, I need water.

If I drink gallons now I can go back to sleep and I'll wake up normal and everything will be as it should, as I was. My Herculean strength coordinates my limbs and clumsily trampolines me over the bed, lurching me on to the floor. I stub my toe. I switch to automatic pilot and make it to the loo and a tooth glass to transfer the contents of the cement-dust-flavoured water from the tap into my system. Five glasses in quick succession and I feel sicker and the whirring noise that came on with the neon strip light in the windowless box bathroom is now tunnelling through my head like a Black & Decker. Involuntarily

I sit on the loo, get up quickly to pull down my white silk boxer shorts and sit back down to wade through the nausea of pints of water sloshing around my colostomy bag of a belly. If I close my eyes I might never get up again. I sniff down my nose; too late, I get the taste of pharmaceutical snot sliding down the back of my throat and gliding into my stomach. 'Oh, God . . .' my face says to my hand as a light, twenty-pound mallet taps into the nape of my neck. My throat creases up like a sun-dried tomato. At least I find some loo paper. Some to blow my nose with, some to wipe myself dry and some to rub away with the soap at the black stuff beneath my eyes after washing my face. I look through a wash kit and find no aspirins but some moisturiser. I use that instead but it doesn't get rid of the mallet. Turning off the light and flushing the loo, I notice somebody else in the mirror; it couldn't be me, even I've never looked that bad.

I pull off a bedcover already half on the floor and wrap myself in its rough grain, a chair leg now my nearest sleeping companion. I can't cope with the nubile twins. Everyone else in the room is swallowed up, comatose. I lie on the floor, eyes closed, waiting for the same fate, as the sun has a stab at breaking through the curtains. Get away, you bastard, nobody asked you in.

★ ★ ★

Who turned the light on, flushed the loo, began talking on the phone?

'Hope, are you alive?'

'No,' I groan through a corner of my limed-up mouth. I have died, been buried and the gravedigger is patting the top of my head with a two-hundred-pound shovel.

'OK hon, but do you want any breakfast from room service?'

'Panadol, aspirin, vitamins C and B, Advil . . . Coffee, OJ and hot croissants with strawberry jam. Forget the rest – I just need arsenic.'

From under my shroud I can hear other voices, staccato, corpse-like and muddied, putting in breakfast orders to Miss Efficient Rachel – or maybe it was just the way I was hearing them. Perception is all. I have none at this moment.

'So I'm just checking you've got that. We want four orange juices, one grapefruit . . . No grapefruit juice?' I peeked my head from under the covers to see Rachel raising her eyebrows to the ceiling in exclamation. 'Then three teas and three coffees.'

The twins shout across at her that they both wanted coffee. 'No, sorry, that's two teas and four coffees and loads of hot croissants and jam and hot milk for the coffee. And a cooked breakfast with, hold

on, what did you want, Rupert? Scrambled eggs . . .
lots of sausages . . . bacon . . . tomatoes and mushrooms.' I wasn't going to let her get off the phone
before the aspirin order got put in, so I mouthed the
word at her before resorting to volume and shouting
ASPIRIN. 'Oh, and before I forget, some aspirin or
panadol. Got that? What do you mean, of course you
can't give us aspirin? You mean it's against company
policy to serve drugs in the hotel? I'm talking about
aspirin, not heroin. Can't you just find some and
bring them up anyway? Oh, you can't. What do you
mean, we can't have hot milk, this is a hotel, isn't it?
Well bring the rest of the stuff up as quick as you
can,' she snapped, put down the phone and slid back
under the sheets between Rupert and Joe, a lazily
curved eel resting for the moment between two solid
rocks.

Rachel looked like that: a willowy, curving, prepos-
sessing beauty with eyes from another century that
were too heavy and dark for the slightness of her
form. Whenever her eyes languorously closed, something suggested the rest of her would too; when they
opened, the circus was coming to town, but not the
kind for kiddies. Her mouth was this small neat thing
that expanded when she smiled to break her face and
men's hearts with it – you had to join in. Her slim,
elegant fingers held the covers to her chin as though

she was hiding, naked, beneath.

'Can you believe that!' an outraged Rachel exclaimed. 'They won't serve us any aspirin because it's against their policy to have drugs in the room. Have you ever heard anything so hysterical in all your life!'

'That's all right,' Joe said heavily from under the covers by Rachel's side. 'I finished all of mine before I went to bed.'

'And mine,' said the pillow with Rupert's face in it.

'What?' said the others, in unison.

'I said, and mine. You finished all of mine too before you went to bed, you greedy bugger.'

Somebody sniffed.

'Who was snoring last night?'

'Rupert was,' I said, and I didn't know why, perhaps I remembered it happening in some dream.

'I didn't. You were the one snoring for England, Hope!' he countered.

'But your snoring woke me up.'

'And your snoring sent us to sleep.' And the twins duelled imitations of my snorting, snoring wheezes, and everyone laughed.

'I'm sorry, but what do you expect if you lead me into temptation and fuel my nose? It's gone into rebellion.' I made it, but only just, to the end of the sentence.

A million words tumbled around my brain in free fall, all trying to find sentences, triggered by the smells, light, darkness and sounds invading the silent noise of a cyberspace between my ears, each feathered thought clanking like styrofoam in a wind tunnel. I reached under the desk in front of my head to find a book in my bag. If I could digest the first sentence in front of my retina and glue it to the beginnings of my conscious mind, something might stick. Conversations floated above my head as I held the book purposefully. Somebody climbed over my body and left the room, then another, and the door closed.

'Hope, what are you doing on the floor?'

'Reading.'

'How? The book's upside down.'

The book's upside down?

'So?' I said. 'That's not the point. It's Raymond Chandler.'

'Your bed's empty, the twins are gone, y'know.'

'Can you get that, hon, it's the breakfast at the door.'

I got up to get back into an empty bed, to spread-eagle myself in glorious confinement. That was the idea, but I went and answered the door to room service instead.

Opening the door didn't stop the knocking in my head or help me clear a space for the tray. I pushed the clothes and stuff on the floor and moved the bottles and ashtrays, and transferred the fag packets and giant Rizla on to the top of a crowded TV, which was on again with the chart show.

The Malaysian waiter stood patiently watching me move the full glasses of flat champagne to another table that was littered with a T-shirted knicker mess in a room full of waste. I took the tray from the silent white-jacketed judge and edged its bulging contents on to the table.

'Thank you,' I managed as the door closed behind God's evangelical messenger.

'Will you pass me some tea?'

'OK, OK, what does everyone want?' Suddenly I was up and moving, and though my head had a loose, swimming brick in it that loped against my cranium from one side to the other each time I moved, at least I was moving. I waitressed breakfast to the others before I served myself, clearing the bedside table of ashtrays, vodka and the full coffee cup with the floating joint butt.

I arranged the pillows and climbed neatly between the sheets. I finished my coffee, emptying it into a stomach whose lining was shrivelling with regret and felt my bowels' knee-jerk reaction, the push-button behaviour of a rumbling funnel. But it didn't spoil my laughing collapse at the luxury of a bed to myself.

Something I had regular use of every day at home, deprived of it for one night and I felt like a refugee sent to Siberia. I was being stupid; too loud and boastful. Before long, Rupert was climbing in the other side with his sausages and smells of egg and mushrooms. I couldn't complain; it was his room, and I had handsome, long-limbed, grown-up company.

Breakfast was finished, cisterns were flushed, the TV turned off and tummys were full. Above the sheets Rachel, Joe, Rupert and I mocked sleep. Beneath the sheets I could feel Rupert's knee nuzzling the back of mine; his body in a dozy pretence with tentative mole-like scuffles became spooned to my back and bottom. I felt the warm tingle of response in my skin. I arched my back to fit more snugly; I rolled my shoulders, encouraging his hand to fall upon my breast and I didn't resist moving beneath his soft-fleshed caresses. I was languorous with heightened sensuality. This was the only thing to do. Each stroke from his fingers over the hairs of my skin hummed deliciously through to my clitoris and signalled my toes to point and flex. The warmth of his breath on my neck did it too; and the push of his erection on to my thigh, the squeeze of fingers upon my hardened nipple.

Who was this man? Forget it. It didn't matter. I could forget anything with this touch. We didn't kiss for a long time. We were too shy to turn and face the other, leave behind the erotic blindfold, but it seemed enough once we were naked and giggling, whispering beneath our hidey-hole canopy. Silly, teenage sex fumbling, frightening fidgets of deliciousness. Once we kissed we didn't want to do anything else; it was like finding another piece of my body I never knew I had, and I wanted to explore every particle of tongue, lip and gum, each tooth. A flawless fit. I'll take it like that. No, no alterations needed, don't bother with the wrapping, I'll wear it out.

Rarely are mouths so tailored, made-to-measure, plaster-cast kisses of perfection. I should know: I've tried the full range of high-street to couture snogs that didn't make the grade. With tongues too large to fit, too short to reach, too thin to matter. What's just right for one is just wrong for the other. Like penises. Some fit and some don't, some are too large to contemplate but others love them well enough; some too small to notice might angle perfectly in the direction of another G-spot, or be lost like a thread in a tunnel. Yes, it does exist. You've just got to find the right loofah to scratch the itch with.

Does the perfect kiss mean true love, multiple orgasmic sex, the adoring father, the consummate lover and a fit with every atom of your existence?

No. It means you've found the perfect snogging

companion, but it doesn't exclude the other attributes, and you've got to test for them. Why? Someone has to: who else's recommendations would you trust? Your mother's, your sister's, a girlfriend's?

We dived into a scurried search for condoms and each other, some kind of relief filled by foreign body parts, but it wasn't like the kissing and it should have been. Trying to keep everything inside a mockery of sheet-tent propriety. No noise, ssshh, quiet, stop breathing, no panting. Rachel and Joe might . . . might what, be shocked? I don't think so. Might see? So?

What were Rachel and Joe doing, anyway?

Whether Rupert slept or not, as I lay there, in post-coital head clearance, didn't matter. I got up and struggled back into his T-shirt to tiptoe across the room until I reached my safe haven of privacy. I emptied my bowels, turned on the bath taps and watched the hot rush fill up to the overflow before I turned it off and climbed in, awkward-limbed. Yummy. A deep, hot bath where I could submerge my head, toes and feelings, but mostly calm the boom, boom enquiries to my brain with nobody there to take the call. The receptionist must have gone AWOL. I needed the hot water so that I could slowly simmer without the marrow leaking from my bones.

I lay floating, a red-faced double for the Lady of

Shallot processing the night, the people, the images, reconstructing my thoughts and deconstructing ideas. What I had said to Rupert didn't seem so silly once I was alone and gaining clearance. This cocaine thing did feel like being stuck in a lift.

It felt like there were only ever two options, up or down. And there's no getting out until you crawl through the basement crack, and who wants to do that when there's some dupe thinking going on that says there's an exit on the roof?

Take another line, take another line, going up, up, up.

You know it makes sense. NOT. Have another drink; the last one didn't work, couldn't quite find the spot to hit. What spot? Hit the roof, and what happens when you reach it? You get to step out of the lift and walk about a bit, stretch your legs, talk to the other roof people and try shouting down conversations to the people on the sidewalk, wildly gesticulating, and they still don't get it.

This is not communication, this is the mad raving to the sane. This is levels and plains, and there is no understanding on either side about the other. Oh, drugs, they're a great way to divide. Squash into the elevator, gang. Be part of the party. Be different, but exactly the same as the rest – alone.

I wondered, as my skin sponged in the water, how

many other rooms in the hotel were occupied by the paranoid, snorting, MTV-watching, music fest rock 'n' roll gang. How many requests for panadol was the hotel turning down per hour? What kind of profit margin could I rake in per aspirin if I was to start dealing them round the rooms? No good – nobody would answer the knocks. Just as we weren't, at two in the afternoon. A whole morning, left unattended, the phone off the hook.

Was I the only one that had noticed that the hotel lifts were all called Otis, and not after the soul singer Redding? Otis lifts are called Otis after the Greek Mount Olympus stable gopher who trudged up and down the mountain carrying the other gods' shopping. Put like that, would anybody's highest aim be to pay all your money to get stuck in a gopher for the rest of your life?

Sometimes, I can see it, a drugged state can get kind of cosy, like any confined space once you get used to it. Plus points appear as easily as dirty fingerprints; it seems safe inside the definite features of four walls, a roof and a floor. You get to decorate it in whichever way you like; for Cancerians, home-makers par excellence, it can look pretty nice. But in the end, you're still locked in because it's too frightening a prospect to choose which floor to get out on. Too scary for an agoraphobic and the creatively sensitive, when somebody else has chosen the décor and suddenly you've lost what little control you thought you once had of putting something inside you and hitting the buttons the way you get to like.

I could get myself a job and a pension as the Betty Ford Clinic's chief counsellor and evangelist to the pop industry. I'd tell them all to jump, and then push them anyway. Thoughts like these drive you mad in a cold bath; no wonder the model died of pneumonia obsessing over Ford Madox Brown. I was lying there for God knows how many hours with wet, cold, dirty hair and as goose-pimpled as a newly plucked chicken, when Rupert knocked on the door and I hadn't even got to thinking about the 'fucking a stranger' part of the equation. After David, maybe it was beginning to feel normal?

'I'm almost out,' I lied, shouting, standing up, turning on the hot shower and scalding my head. At least it proved that I had some feeling left in my body. I scrappily washed my hair, wrapped a towel around me and it.

'Let me in, I only want a piss,' he was saying through the door and as I opened it. 'I'll have the shower too, now you're out.'

Before I was out the door, he was peeing and naked.

I know that we had just had sex, and reached the

closest point of bodily intimacy in orgasm, but suddenly in the mirror I was watching a naked stranger pee as I brushed my teeth at the sink. Why did I care? He was totally unconcerned, getting in the shower. Did he sense me watching him, or feel my strangeness, that prompted him to pull back the shower curtain, stick his wet head out and ask, 'Are you all right? See you've found my toothbrush.'

'Yes, fine. You don't mind, do you?'

"Course not. Just don't use my razor on your armpits.'

'Don't worry . . .'

'Don't be silly, I've got more important things to worry about than that.'

'I only . . .'

'What?'

'Forget it. Nothing.' I couldn't even handle a joke, let alone a conversation. He turned off the shower, pulled back the curtain and stood there, wet, dripping, smiling and naked, his broad, strong shoulders and long, full body tapering to his black cropped hair. Yum, yummy, delicious.

The weekend stretched ahead. Sometimes I found my brain before it began playing hide-and-seek again. Jacuzzis were found and jumped into, CD players turned up, room service ordered and rejected, restaurants visited and giggled in. The crazy, rock 'n' roll life, where days are a disturbance to get through back to night, to down another vodka and snort another line. By morning and bedtime, getting cold, I would wrap my body in Rupert's limbs and make slow love until the afternoon, when we slept. Nobody was supposed to know, least of all us; nothing was discussed, and on Monday I was getting into the car with Rachel and driving along the motorway home.

It must have been the drug-spawned, mercury-coated emotional removal.

Rupert was off to another gig, music-biz life. I left him sleeping with his soft, warm snore. I know this time it wasn't me. I was up and silently dressing, busy retrieving knickers and shoes from under beds and off trays of half-eaten club sandwiches bloodily congealed with ketchup and mayonnaise like some old, festering wound. Hotel glamour. Nobody had been in to clean the room for days, and it was starting to resemble my soul. Maybe that's why pop stars deliberately wreck hotel rooms, not because they know they can but because they'd feel uncomfortable surrounded by anything else. I had to change my surroundings; I wanted my bed, my toothbrush, myself.

Another tiptoe mission for my last pee and make-up overhaul. I was meeting Rachel in the hall in five minutes. She had to go home too; sick pay only ever extended to one day of belief in her office, a radio station.

All done, I turned off the light and too late had flushed the cistern, and Rupert was growling awake like some bear hibernation unit from Yellowstone.

'Where are you goin'? Have you left your number? I'll give you a ring when I get back.' All a girl wants to hear, whether it's true or not; at least you were asked and given the choice.

'I'm sorry, I didn't mean to wake you. Sure, I'll leave it up here.' I gesticulated to the top of the TV and the balance of crockery and searched around for a scrap of paper and a pencil. Being a painter, I never seemed to carry any around for when I really needed it. Do photographers always forget their cameras, continually missing the perfect shot, the never-to-be-repeated opportunity?

I didn't ask for his number. Strategic, huh? Just closed the door behind me and walked the familiar route to the Otis lift.

At certain moments I started to feel bad, worried that he'd ring, half wanting him to, half not. Must have been my body jolting through its chemical imbalance. Rattling my brain in the car for nasty thoughts of Rupert to ice my toasted-marshmallow feelings with.

In the end I had to stop looking at the cows abstracting the green fields with their black and white puzzles – train pictures, stop needing him, let him go, soar with the swallows and not box and file him with a pretty ribbon covering the mortise lock. Then I could start thinking about home, work, my friends and whom I could ring up as soon as I got in to divulge my adventures to. DB? I don't think I'd tell Toby, Lionel or Steve. My other life as a goddess.

The weekend, the drink, the drugs and the secret sex was all just part of some scenery I'd driven through in the rock 'n' roll jungle full of rubber snakes and pussycats – it was as wild as that. I didn't have to stop or stay, take the doggy bag or buy the T-shirt. I was as free to jump out of the jacuzzi as I was to have got in.

As Rachel said, 'At least he saw you at your worst and still wanted to sleep with you! I bet he'll ring.'

By that point it didn't matter. Didn't I see him at his worst, and still want to sleep with him? My choice, his choice, our choice. Everything was an experiment. What did Jack the therapist say to me, commitment is about committing to yourself? Ah, yes, I remember. I walk about the studio pondering the word commitment until I arrive at the dictionary. Commitment – an obligation that restricts freedom of action. A pledge or undertaking. And I'd always thought it was something nice, but it began to sound a bit like taking drugs, with the words *restriction* and *undertaking*, which of course made me think of funerals and that movie *Harold and Maude*, where a couple fall in love because they both have the same obsession, funerals. The woman, Maude, is in her seventies, and lives in an old train compartment, while Harold is just a young rich kid who likes pretending to commit suicide in his parents' mansion. It is a very cheery film, because you come away thinking there's someone for every one of us, however weird, normal, or disfigured we are by life.

I begin a new painting of Artemis, the huntress and fertility goddess, benefactor and castigator, protector of the young, her feet immersed in flowering arnica.

Chapter 10

STANDING UP AND LYING DOWN

It's not like I can't get a date.

It's not like I don't know that there are a million men out there, swimming around like silverfish across a damp bathroom floor, rushing between Green Park and Kensal Rise. I know all that.

I mean, I have been married successfully for two years (it was just the last couple of years that made it end in divorce), and I have had dates, plenty of them. I know how to make myself likeable, I am not unattractive.

Did he come in and see me and bolt through the window in the men's room? Possibly. Maybe he's just late? I am not paranoid; there is nothing wrong with being a single girl sitting in a café-bar-club on a

Thursday night alone, is there? No. Friday, and I might be getting a little nervous; Saturday, and I would have already left.

'Meeting someone?'

I have got to the point, reading my book of Brian Patten poems, where I am almost crying. They are moving anyway, don't get me wrong, but sentimentality and a deep feeling of self-pity makes me take every word literally and bury it next to my tear ducts.

'What?' I say, bad-tempered and dewy-eyed. Must remember to go home this weekend and cry on Mum's salt-corroded shoulders.

'Are you meeting someone? I just wondered . . .'

'Yes, you can take the chair, I've no use for it!'

There is something familiar about this man's face, but I can't quite see it. He's got amazing, light sky-blue eyes which give him an other-wordly look, and unreasonably pink lips. He has no need for lipstick. His face is very angular; he looks as if he has been hewn out of rock – old-fashioned, chiselled features and a solid form of thick, dark blond hair. I have time to notice all of this, because it soon becomes apparent that he is not taking the chair anywhere; he is sitting in it.

He beckons a waitress over. I notice the lights are dimming, I've been waiting here so long for that sod.

'Would you like another drink? Or aren't you imbibing anything but poetry?' he asks me in a polite, charming voice.

'Misery.'

'That bad, huh? I thought you'd a reputation.'

'I've definitely got one of those,' I return, as though I'm having this conversation with myself.

'I'd heard your twin town was fun.'

He turned to the waitress and pointed out a drink on the menu of cocktails. 'Two of those, please.'

'You've been earwigging the wrong grapevine. Who's your source?' I say like a detective.

'I don't think so. Would you like a cigar?'

'Yes, definitely,' I say, having never smoked one before in my life, but I was set upon being obnoxious in some way or other, just because I was angry. I can't believe that I've really been stood up!

I lit up, sucked, choked and coughed my guts up. Bad experiment in anger stress relief, but I was a sticker. I tried again and this time rather enjoyed its rough largeness entering my mouth, and the weird angle of holding it.

'Suits you, sir,' he suddenly came out with.

'Thank you, modom,' I retorted.

'I hope you don't mind, I ordered you an absinthe cocktail.'

'Why, had they run out of green chartreuse?' I

know that absinthe and green chartreuse have a similar reputation of making you go blind or mad, a bit like wanking.

'Yes, and horse anaesthetic. Here's to Hope.'

'How did you know?'

'What, that that was what you needed? Or that that is your name?'

'Both.' I was feeling very perplexed now. He wasn't a total stranger making me laugh, he was in the know and I wasn't. I didn't like it. There was an unequal balance of power that in my vulnerable stood-up state was hardening me into the discomfort of a leaning Pisa.

'I'm so sorry, we haven't been formally introduced.' I held out my hand, but he rudely interrupted me.

'We still could be.' He grabbed the passing mauve-uniformed waitress and whispered to her.

'Hi, Hope, I'd like to formally introduce you to Mr Lomax Somerton, Esquire,' the waitress helpfully obliged and Lomax smiled smugly back at me from the blue plush chair.

'So you're Toby's brother! How did you know it was me?'

'Toby showed me some photos of the dirty week-end you had at Longleat or wherever it was. There is a particularly fetching one of you doing some tree-hugging hippie crap. The rest, as they say, is coincidence.'

Hippie indeed! That was me and my tree he was talking about! That tree was more of a man than he was. I almost said so, but wisely thought again. You have to measure people and pepper humour carefully when you first meet. That was one thing I'd learned on the rocky path to here. 'Ah-ha. Coincidence, you say.'

'In so far as I didn't organise the child who stood you up. You were stood up, weren't you? Plus I didn't know you were going to be here. I just happen to be a member.'

'So you're Lomax, not Edward.'

'Do I look like an Edward to you? Heavens, woman, you couldn't even call me a Ted!'

'No, true, but I could think of a few other words for you . . .'

'You could, huh?'

He chewed on his cigar and took his turn to eagle-eye me in a way I'd only ever seen Clark Gable do before. It was in *Gone with the Wind*, except that it wasn't to me; my stand-in that day was Vivien Leigh, and Clark was sitting in a Yankee jail, not the plush sophistication of the New Player Club.

'Anyway, who said I'd been stood up?'

'I can't think of any other reason why you'd be sitting in this dark velvet basement alone, reading, good heavens! Brian Patten, the sound of the Mersey.'

'Well, that's how much you know me, and indeed

Mr Patten, who's more like the sound of Holland Park, these days,' I said, protective of my choice of reading.

People can be snotty and ignorant of current artistic achievement, when reputations exist from the past. We are not all the sum of what we hit the headlines for. Freddie Starr and his hamster care, Cleopatra and her asp, Guy de Maupassant and his syphilis, Nell and her oranges, Van Gogh and his ear, Martin Amis and his teeth, Bob Geldof and Live Aid, Hillary Clinton and her husband . . . I could go on, ad nauseam.

'I wondered when they were going to get a resident poet in. I've been petitioning the council for months,' Lomax said pompously, as though he was rather clever, which he probably was, but I pretended otherwise.

'Haven't you anything better to do with your life?'

'Quite frankly, no. I'm writing a fearfully dull book at the moment and my godfather's just left me nothing in his will. So what else have I to do but harass the personal column on behalf of my brother, to get rid of the hideous Eve? Have you met her?'

With that one line I was beginning to warm to him, as much as you can to a handsome, judgemental stranger with his shirt open enough for you to see a glint of hair and a slight bronze sheen covering a six-pack. I was beginning to wonder if I was any worse than a sexist male.

'No, but can I ask you a question? It's quite personal, but I have to know the answer or leave immediately.'

'That's a little drastic, but I quite understand.'

'Are you gay?' I said straight into his seductive smile as his glass reached his mouth. He spluttered into his cocktail.

'If you mean am I full of a bon viveur's excitement for life and laughter, the answer is absolutely . . . yes. If, on the other hand, you were wondering if I was a turd burglar or a sausage-jockey mattress-muncher who hangs out at the Bournville Cottage in common Clapham? The answer is definitely no.'

Through my laughter – trust me, it was the way he said it – as he regained his composure and became totally serious, I lied back, 'If I wanted to know if you were a friend of Dorothy's I would have asked.'

'Is that true, or are you making it up?'

'It's true,' I lied, and he knew it because of the smile on my face and my wide, unconvincing eyes with their shrinking pupils. 'OK, you talk like a poof.'

'What! Just because I'm showing off with a few preliminary language skills that anyone could use? I'm outraged! It's the lazy society we live in; we're too tired to talk narrative structures into our lives.'

'Undoubtedly, but what are you talking about?'

'Would you prefer me to talk like a this, or this or

this . . . Nice! Organically prepared water – Volvic!' And he stretched his accents from one side of a dim connection to another and put assorted faces with them.

'Did you want another drink?' I asked, feeling quite cheered up by all his clowning. I'd almost forgotten being stood up, until he mentioned it again.

'So who was this Edward standing you up? He's the one who should be buying the drinks, before I give him a sound flogging.'

'Lomax,' I said seriously to him, and to show my intent I took his hand in both of mine and looked into his eyes. I was feeling extremely light, yet sober – the absinthe effect. You believe yourself sober, yet that you are capable of doing remarkable things. 'I know we haven't known each other long, but if we are going to be friends, you must know . . .'

'Yes, what must I know, Princess?' he interrupted. He had a habit of doing that (was I talking too slowly?), I must correct him, I thought. He was holding my hand back and straining to look deeply and very insincerely into the depths of my eyeballs.

'Don't call me Princess, ever! And never mention my failures, especially in front of . . . royalty – except Fergie, she doesn't count.'

'You probably discuss them together all the time. Do you?'

'If you come closer to me, you horrid, horrid little boy, you'll probably feel a swipe of pain across the back of your head.'

'And discover you're an organ stealer, and I'll wake up to find my kidneys and brains have gone.'

'But I'd leave you with a fair exchange.'

'A computer?'

'No, a black eye.'

'Husband-basher!'

'You'd be laughed out of court. A little woman like me hurting a great big man like you.'

'I don't think so. I sleep with most of the judges at the Old Bailey; I reckon they'd listen. You'd get what was coming to you!'

'So you *are*! I knew there was a reason why I liked you.'

'Excuse me,' the waitress said, and leaned down to whisper in my ear. 'The gentleman whom you said you wanted to be told about when he arrived, he's here, and he's asking for you. Do you want me to tell him who you are?'

Good waitresses with this much intuition are hard to find. This was one I'd employ, but I didn't have a dining room, let alone a restaurant. She was dark with a full mouth, oyster-grey eyes with a look as open as the prairies; plus she was small, petite, so she would be Hollywood Napoleon successful. I thought about kissing the girl for the effect it would have on Lomax, but the moment passed.

I looked at Lomax looking intrigued, quiet for a minute and puffing at the foul brown thing between his teeth, and I looked at the suited City man at the front of the room standing by the gleaming black and silver bar. Smart mac, I thought, home-made-custard colour.

I knew I would see Lomax again. There was no doubt about that, but if I didn't see Edward now, I'd never see him again. I was here to see Edward after all, even if Lomax had chanced to rescue me.

'What's new, pussycat?' he sweetly enquired. The waitress waited.

'Can you pretend I've gone to the loo, and I'll be out in a minute?'

'I've said already that's where I thought you were.'

'Thanks. OK, tell him I'll be over in two minutes.'

'What is all this whispering about? Do you work here or something?'

'No. I'm sorry, Lomax, but the time has come to take down your details.'

'Not right here, now? My, you are a brazen vixen!'

'Vixen hussy moll. Have you a pen?'

'Of course, I'm a writer!' he said, as if that was one step up from my job description. He handed over a beautiful Mont Blanc fountain pen, and I wrote my name and phone number on a handy Ingres portrait that looked stunningly like me, before I opened my little black book. 'Well, what is it? Come, don't be coy.'

'I can't just ejaculate on demand, no matter how much I like a girl on first meeting.'

'You really aren't gay? Telephone number, or should I just call Gay Chatline!'

'0800 *50 50 50*! Sorry, it's 720 8889.'

'Where's that, then?'

'Battersea, the nice end. Are you about to leave me? I have a distinct feeling this is adieu.'

'You are distinctly right. I have to go and meet my date, if only to prove that I haven't been stood up.' I stood up, gave him the card and half kissed the message, 'Use it', into his ear.

As quick as a hare he turned his face and smudged his lips into mine. 'Maybe, harlot.'

'My name's Hope. I think you're mixing me up with someone else you know. It was a pleasure meeting you, Lomax, thanks for the drink. I'll see you later?' He shook my hand and held on to it a little longer as he looked at my face as if to fathom something from it, but all I'd give him was a raised eyebrow.

'Yes, I'm pretty sure about that.'

And I walked away from Lomax with his eyes upon

my arse, thinking, What are you doing, girl? Why are you always leaving the comfortable for the unknown? Shock of the new? No other answer showed up.

'Hi, excuse me,' I said, sitting myself down on the high velvet stool, still imagining myself supremely sober. Edward turned towards me as conventionally handsome as a Calvin Klein advert. The white mac had to be from Cording's of Piccadilly. I know this because I have studied all the macs in that shop assiduously. I love their macs, and there is nothing that would make me happier than to have one, but I have also studied the price tags and I can't quite justify spending four hundred pounds on a mackintosh to my bank. Edward obviously has no trouble with that. Meanwhile I hunt the charity-shop rows of macs waiting for the miracle, while I turn down dozens of Gucci, Pucci, Fiorucci . . . I doubt Edward has ever been inside a charity shop; by the look of him I don't imagine he even knows what they are.

'Yes,' he says with the smallest-sounding 's' I've yet to hear on an affirmative. What was this man doing reading, let alone answering the ad I had put in to raise myself to goddess status?

'Edward?'

'No, and please don't try to pick me up, I'm gay to women like you.' He turned his back on me so fast he didn't have a chance to catch my falling jaw. With that reply I wasn't going to say sorry, case of mistaken identity, you didn't look like the photo anyway, and stick my tongue out! Instead I looked to my other side. I was sure the waitress had pointed at that bloke. She tapped me on the shoulder.

'I think I'll have to introduce Edward to you as well,' she giggled. 'I feel like I'm in that old movie, *The Go-Between*,' and she winked at me from under her short purple fringe. Later, she came up and slipped a card into my pocket with her phone number and name. It said, 'Hope, call Mandra, the go-between, on . . .'

I was certainly collecting tonight, but what? Learning.

1 Never trust a man by his coat.
2 Always insist on meeting a bloke's brothers before you spend the weekend with him, they might be more suitable!
3 Consider the waiting staff too.

Edward was wearing grey from head to foot, different shades, but it was all grey and he didn't look like his photo. I was starting to wonder whether including a photo was worth anything. He had put on weight, and grown a few more inches since the youthful sun-drenched beach photo had been taken. I think his six-pack had probably moved house when he had moved into his late thirties.

'Hello,' he said, slightly nervously. 'I'm Ed.'

'Hello, I'm Hope.'

'Yes, it's nice to meet you, finally. Can I get you a drink?'

He had a slight northern lilt to his accent that I hadn't picked up on the telephone. If I'd realised he was from Rochdale I would never have agreed. My grandpa would be turning in his grave.

Grandpa was a stout, proud Lancashire man, and had made me promise one thing: that I'd never date a Yorkshireman. 'You can't tell them from the colour of their skin, but their coloured thoughts and perverted perceptions are loud enough. You hear me, gal?' he would shout deafly into my ear.

'Yes, Grandpa,' I'd obliquely reply.

He loved the rest of the world. Would welcome everyone from the united nations and even the ones that weren't, into his home and not let them leave till they were full of hotpot and a good strong brew. It was just Yorkshiremen. By his book, that didn't make him racist, just a discerning man. He'd go anywhere in the world as long as he didn't have to go through Yorkshire to get there. He believed Yorkshiremen capable of all the world's ills. None of them were to be trusted: they were mean, dirty, rude, Neanderthal stupid, and, of course, interbred, which meant they weren't worth breeding with as they had a poor gene pool. That ensured you couldn't date them, mate with them or bring them home – not his home, anyway. The same old rotten beliefs any racist had.

I almost felt a sense of betrayal just talking to this Yorkshireman. Edward was a human being and deserved to be treated like one, but the stereotypes that my grandpa had systematically instilled in me ran deep, however much I ridiculed them.

I was wondering why I had left Lomax. He wasn't from Yorkshire. He was still sitting on the other side of the room sniggering at me over his newspaper, and making lewd and suggestive faces. He wasn't helping, but I could help myself. I turned around in my seat, excluding him from view, and focused purposefully upon Ed.

Ed was sweet, kind, and he had a glint of humour shining in his eyes, plus he also had very good teeth, better than Toby or Lomax. He couldn't look at me without stuttering, however. His hair was cut close to his head and dark, so that you noticed his rather large ears. I like large ears and good teeth, nice shoes and clear eyes and a mix of Jil Sander and Paul Smith clothes. Ed had all of these, but when you said something funny to him, it didn't strike him to the bone; you couldn't itch him between his ribs with a line and watch him crack. He smiled, and didn't even wrinkle his eyes much. Maybe I just wasn't very funny any more.

Impossible. Perfectly possible.

'I'm sorry I was so la-late, but I had a me-meeting I couldn't just get up and le-le-leave. Did they give you the me-message?'

'No,' I said. He looked alarmed and appalled. 'Don't worry, it was fine. I bumped into an old friend, actually, so it was perfect.'

I soothed his fears until I saw his shoulders begin to relax and he leaned his elbow on the bar. He had ordered two large glasses of good wine. That was the kind of man he was; he'd go to the bottom of the page and choose the most expensive but one. Expense dictated quality, almost. To order the most expensive would have appeared ignorant, nouveau riche, the isms of the middle classes.

The peculiar thing about Ed was that he seemed so obviously middle class, but wasn't. He had picked all this up from being an assistant to an upper-class director/producer in advertising. He had studied and absorbed; he obviously thought these were the mannerisms of the London race, not a county class affectation. He'd tried living in his late father's country of origin first, but with no living relatives left in the Emerald Isles, he'd come to London. There were a lot of people from both Galway and Rochdale in London, he told me. Back home in Rochdale he still had a huge family, and each year – Christmas, of course – he went back for the regulation homecoming. He wanted to secure his career and life here, not in Rochdale, but he was no bright lights, big city boy. That was the gist of everything I got from him in an entire evening over a drink and dinner at L'Aubergine, where he wanted to show off his Yorkshireman's French and a gold Amex card. I found it very endearing, when I wasn't too busy laughing at my own jokes. We ate sublimely, something to do with fish, and I think I slurped a soup? Vegetables? Pudding? I wish I'd been there.

I talked incessantly. Why I must have been the most fascinating person on earth at that moment (remember *not* to touch that stuff absinthe ever again), because the smallest thing I said seemed to be just incredibly witty. Even if Ed wasn't capable of a good gutful of laughter, I made up for it. I think I was laughing for an entire audience the way my jaw hurt the next day (or had I given him a blow job in the cab on the way home? I hope it wasn't in the restaurant). I tried to remember, then tried to forget. I told him fascinating things about my first cat's burial, pet names I was called as a kid, intimate secrets about the whereabouts of household objects I had broken at the age of eight and hidden, and the cruellest way I'd ever split up with a boyfriend. (I sent him the obituaries page of *The Times*. The problem was, it was a little too esoteric for him and he rang up to ask if it was a member of my family that had died. Then I just had to tell him straight on the phone, you're chucked. So why had I sent him the newspaper clipping? he wanted to know. The whole thing became too messy and teenage for words, and too many of those were said as well.)

All in all I told Ed secrets, too soon. Things you don't tell strangers. Stuff I hadn't even told my mum or even my best girlfriends. I must have thought I'd gone and paid a therapist at the door of the restaurant. I knew I was doing it at the time, but I felt it keenly the next day as I went for my eye ice pack, that a dear, sweet understanding friend had given me to cure the bags that reside on either side of my nose.

The whole way through dinner he looked at me with fascinated eyes. Maybe it was just that he couldn't believe the tosh that was pouring out; it might have been that. Or he was giving me that 'I've just fallen into the waterfall of love and every time you look at me, why, it's another cascading rush' look, which was curious, because at the same time he was so quiet, but he didn't seem quiet, just reserved and hassle-free. He seemed to give the air that the world could do whatever it wanted but it wouldn't affect his pace. He was thinking, cogs were turning in the windmills of his mind, I romanticised. Well, he had to be doing something in those three hours of hilarious gabbling. He looked at his watch a few times during the evening, about the same amount of times I looked at Lomax when we were still in the bar, before he slouched out.

I didn't feel guilty, why should I? I had insisted inside my head. I was with the date I was meant to be with, Ed. Whatever the instant connection with Lomax had felt like, the electric current of his touch zooming through the channels of my skin, heading for the PlayStation of my imagination. Imagine what the children would look like . . . Imagine how witty they'd be . . . I was almost there, weeping with joy at their Master's degree ceremonies at Oxford, Magdalen College, naturally (my stepfather's)!

Ed didn't make me think of children or kitchens, his or mine, before or after sex, but he did make me think that he was the kind of man you'd never have to worry about paying the rent with: he was a provider.

Ladies! Forget the carnivores, they may seem exciting for two minutes of rough, dirt-filled, adrenaline-rushing action, but with a gatherer there's always dinner on the table and some more planned for the following season. His advert could read:

> **You can always weep on an Ed shoulder!**
> He'd comfort you and be on your side; he's good
> father material.

Problem: Not sure how much I want another father at the moment. Still got two (though never see original one).
Solution: Think I'd prefer the idea of play-fellow, rug-rat penfriend, sexing buddy. That kind of thing.

I was ambling round and round my flat, pretending to be making tea, putting a bra on, adding the finishing touches to a pug's nose and the final hairs to his protruding, salivating pet's tongue. I had given in to another dog in between finishing my painting of Artemis. I was brushing my hair, trying to make some sense, but in truth I was only pretending, because I was being eaten alive by the dreaminess – or was it nightmarishness? – of my thoughts, snippets of last night's conversation, and whether or not Ed had tried to kiss me in the back of the cab as I tried to get out.

If he hadn't, why not? Very affronted at this thought!

If he had, why hadn't I noticed? Ineffectual kisser

with no tongue? And did I vomit into his mouth? In which case, would he be calling again, and if he did, was he a masochist? I think he just about caught the short end of my cheek, and a bit of ear with his mouthful of hair. He was nowhere near my mouth. Strange expletives punctuated the air from the realms of my lips: 'Eeek', 'Help!', 'Oh, God!' and the ever helpful, 'No!' I knew I shouldn't be feeling like this after a blind date; something had gone badly wrong with it and I had a horrid suspicion that, that I could be to – Yippee! Blame it all on Lomax and his absinthe poison!

Magically, the phone rang. A repetitive vibrating musical drill entering my right temple told me some-one wanted to interrupt my thoughts.

'Hello, Gormenghast Castle,' I answered, because at that moment I had entered into Gormenghast brain territory.

'Can I speak to Igor, that's Transylvania 666?' the voice answered back.

'Sign of the beast.'

'Hope, don't be so cruel, or at the very least, be my beauty?'

'I was wondering how long it would take you to call.'

'You were, were you? Well I was wondering the same thing myself!' said Lomax.

'About me?'

'No, about me! But I never call after eleven or before eleven. Dinner tonight? Oh, and how was your date, or is that slightly *insouciant* of me to ask?'

'I don't know, is it? I better go and read my French to English dictionary or my Monopoly rules – go straight to jail, do not pass go, do not collect two hundred pounds. Dinner? Doesn't say anything about dining with Lomax. I think I require breakfast first. Oh, yes, and by the way, while I've got you on the phone, what on earth did you think you were doing, giving me that despicable cocktail last night? My head feels like the night of a thousand knives, all of them slashing away at each other. And I don't even want to *think* about last night.'

'Yeah, rubbish movie. Oh, dear, poor Hope. Poor, poor Hope feels baby sweets sorry for herself?'

'Yes,' I said babyishly, feeling slightly comforted by his false sympathy.

'It couldn't have had anything to do with what you drank later, with the Grim Reaper?'

'Who?'

'Your date.'

'Don't be so nasty. Ed? No.'

'Ed Wood. Worst film-maker in the world. Made into a film by Tim Burton, liked dressing up in women's clothes – watch out for your angora sweater.'

'He wouldn't, not Ed.'

'For sure?'

'George Bernard Shaw?'

'No! Lomax Somerton, beaming Hope to earth. Hello, anyone there?'

'Hope Knott.'

'Why not?'

'No, stop it, that's my name – Hope Knott, K-N-O-T-T. Except it's not, it's really May.'

'Hope May Knott what?'

'OK, I give up. Dinner – I shall explain all,' I said, exhausted and confused, and replaced the receiver before it began to ring again. I picked it up again.

'You want my address?' I said, automatically realising that I hadn't, we hadn't, arranged where we would meet.

'Yes,' said a dull, Scottish and distinctly un-Lomax tone. 'I got your card from a booth in Queensway. Are you—'

He was kidding me again. 'Yeah, yeah, yeah, do you want my address or not? Or we could meet somewhere.'

'No, I want to come to your place. You are the big, busty, strict seventeen-year-old?'

'You know me so well. OK, let's get it over with before all your hair falls out. Flat 9, 18 Bayswater Square.'

'There is nothing wrong with my hair! And how much are you charging for this behaviour?'

'Top whack.'

'I can't afford it. Anyway, you're only a prostitute, you're probably not worth it.' And he slammed the phone down.

It rang again before I'd even put my knickers on properly. Well, it could ring until I was dressed. I did up my trousers and answered.

'House of Sin.'

'I thought it was Gormenghast last time? You'll confuse people. Hey, I forgot to ask you for your address, or shall we meet at the restaurant?'

'Lomax, you're a funny man.'

'Why thanks.'

'I've given you my address already.'

'I don't think so. It's not on this Ingres card that looks remarkably like you.'

'When you were just talking on the phone.'

'No?'

'Just now. The sex phone-booth call. Lomax, it was you, wasn't it?' I said, trailing off insecurely. There was a horrible silence going on to nowhere on the other end of the phone. I realised that I must have given out my address to a total stranger who was indeed seeking sex! And then I thought, how different was that from Lomax, or me?

'Oh, my God, I thought it was you joking. I've just given my address to some Scottish nutter who thinks I advertise in telephone kiosks.'

'You don't? I mean, you did in a magazine. I just thought . . . God, you're so prudish!'

'This is no time to joke. This is not funny, Lomax. He'll be coming round here to murder me any minute, and you won't have anyone to eat dinner with!'

'Put like that, what do you want me to do? Say the last rites? Any preferences on burial versus cremation?'

'Stop it!' I shouted, teenage-style. I was getting cross in a frightened way, and I wasn't finding Lomax to be particularly reassuring or funny.

'I'm sorry, Hope,' he said in a Scottish accent that was remarkably similar to the last caller's. 'Shall I be round at eight-thirty to take you to a . . .' and his accent began to peter out, while I shouted back at him.

'You little shit!'

'I'm sorry, Hope. Will you ever forgive me?' Thank God he'd called me Hope, I was beginning to feel superstitious about revealing my real name, as though it was tantamount to giving him a lock of my hair or a nail clipping – stuff you can do voodoo on.

'You will remain the unforgiven. I'll tell you one thing for nothing, dinner had better be good.'

'Do you like Portuguese?'

'Yes, it's just Yorkshiremen I don't li— Oh, you mean the food, yes, sardines, delicious.'

The dinner had been grand. Lomax was warm, witty and charming, and the restaurant looked like a boat. I made sure he knew that one meal didn't make everything all right, but I don't think the goofy expression on my face said that. The soup and the wine were green, and chorizo sizzled on charcoal spits in pottery pigs as the fat ran into the flames.

That evening, I liked the food and I liked him and I told him so. More, I really fancied him, but I didn't tell him that, which was just as well. I didn't hear from him again for another two weeks. When he did call me it was from New York, where, he explained, he'd had to go to sort out his godfather's estate, and that he'd be another week. Could we see each other when he got back? I naturally agreed, but in the meantime I dated Ed, mostly, except that there was also Ryan.

Ryan was an earnest Irishman who showed me his portable photo album during our first and only dinner, and spent the rest of the evening saying how much his mother would like me. Me? Yes. And that, as a family of doctors, lawyers and accountants, they'd always wanted an artist in there to make a complementary balance.

Retrospectively, I think my major mistake was saying how much I needed my tax returns done, would love having a home birth and how knowing a good lawyer was always useful. His face had lit up like Blackpool as his hand reached for his mobile to call his mother and arrange a suitable lunch date, while we sat in a pub with straw on the floor (his choice). The passing trade of Shepherd Market paraded outside.

I can only imagine it must have been something to do with marrying before he got past his sell-by date, to collect a stash. This dating game had made me more cynical than I deserved to be.

I missed Lomax: all that Angel Delight-light humour.

I painted a lot. Good.

I moaned too much to my friends. Bad.

I went for the weekend to Mum's – good and bad.

I went there for a pale lambswool-shoulder comfort-cry, and ended up being taken to the next-door neighbour's to show me off because one of my paintings had made it into the BP portrait competition at the National Portrait Gallery and was reproduced in the Metro section of *The Times*. Which proved I was doing something dimly related to art and now it could be acknowledged, instead of giving me the 'proper job' line, as in when are you going to get a . . . or a husband.

I almost felt like giving my painting up on the spot and going to sell advertising in *Butterfly* magazine or the *Times Literary Supplement*. The good thing was the food, though possibly I didn't need any more feeding. I was getting quite big enough with Ed dining me, every date a different dinner in a posher restaurant; I think he was taking me through a restaurant guide. We'd been to the Angelsea Arms, Bibendum, the Caprice, Dakota's, the Electricity Showrooms; only four more letters till the Ivy!

I wondered if he had more money than sense. He certainly had a bigger wallet than penis, the hard twig he laid my hand upon in a moment of daring after a prolonged wet kiss in the front of his car. I watched, fascinated, his face grasped tight with the concentration of agony or ecstasy, his fingers rummaging through the drawer of my bra for a nipple to flick. There was the bungled rubbing of my hand against his dark blue jeans until the ease of relief passed over his face and a child's sigh whimpered from his throat. Regaining consciousness, he quickly turned a pinky-puce and cleared his throat.

'Goodnight, then, thanks for a lovely dinner, again. You're very sweet,' was all I could think to do or say to fill the silence. Even though I know men want to be thought of as sexy, not sweet, until they're eighty-six and have all the wrinkles of a limp penis on their faces. I stroked one cheek with my hand and kissed him on the other, before I got out of the car.

'I'll call you, Hope,' he'd leaned out of the window and shouted, and I'd waved back fondly as if to a teddy bear left on the back ledge of my parents' car when returning to college.

That had been the night before I'd gone to see Mum. I hadn't left the home number on the answerphone, I'd just disappeared, escaping any passionate follow-up call.

I prodded myself on the train. I was swelling so much I could've gone to market, and the slaughterhouse the following week. The wolf wouldn't need to blow my little house down; my stomach had forced the walls out so far the roof would fall in. I was having to let my waistbands out. Always an unhappy moment. For a second I wondered if I was pregnant. I fantasised about a baby, about living in the country, about what being married to Ed would be like, while the countryside slipped past my British Rail window all the way to Guildford and the beautiful belly of the Hog's Back.

The Dream: I was dressed in drawstring calico, my hair plaited, wandering around a walled garden with fruit racing up canes, flowers falling out of beds and the summer grass tickling my bare toes. Bees buzzed. Then I imagined Ed away on a trip, me and baby alone but for the neighbours, who looked distinctly like Mia Farrow's neighbours in the film *Rosemary's Baby*. And a cold cloud shadowed the scene and I was shoved rudely back into the dirty carriage.

That's the problem with the country, I thought, the neighbours and the superstitions! I solemnly vowed that I wasn't going to get married to Ed or live in the country, no matter how much he begged. So I kind of made up my mind about my dilemma, Ed or Lomax. Of course it wasn't a dilemma at all: since Lomax hadn't called, I had a choice of Ed or a bunch of brown envelopes from people who probably wouldn't even remember having written to me by then.

Yet all this didn't spoil the flavour of Mum's steak-and-kidney pie with buttery flaky pastry, rich, thick gravy and thin slices of mushroom with a huge splodge of creamy garlic mash. Or the next day's Lancashire hotpot, a leftover from my father's day. Endless slices of potato, and carrots with parsley, rosemary and lamb shanks melting together in her Aga's slow heat and followed by Rumble Bumble Pudding, Geoffrey's favourite, a kind of whisky/rum fool with almonds.

When I arrived, I sat at the well-scrubbed kitchen table with a pot of tea and watched my mum make the fish pie for our lunch. I listened to her rattle on about hers and Geoffrey's concerns and local obsessions, and about the lives of my brothers. I listened and watched. Slabs of cod, a pile of grey-shell shrimps and some pale smoked haddock were slumped on a handcrafted pottery dish all glossy with fleshy secretions. She took the shrimps off and put them on a plate in front of me and said, 'You can peel those if you like.' I did, but wondered about the time and bother of making one dish after another, twice a day, when there would be nothing left to show for it but . . . happiness? An expanding gut and a way to fill the days in the way she filled her pastry cases.

'Can I have some shortbread?'

'More? You and your comfort. Don't worry, this pie won't take long. Nothing like a good fish pie to mend a fraying soul.' And she rubbed my hair with a spare hand as if I was a little boy fresh in from a scrap. I stared at the oven, knowing it would take longer than she said.

Mum had always treated me like a boy, along with my brothers. If ever I'd wanted to wear pink and frills it had been teased out of me until my knees bled and I was shinning up a tree for a moment's peace. There was only space in my family for boys, and I was Tom, the honorary boy (strange that I should have married a man called Thom – or not). My mother was the girl. The cook. The nurse. The nurturing provider of all natural wisdom. My father, so long gone to a world of bonfire vanity in New York, was cast as the scoundrel. My stepfather, Geoffrey, was the rescuer, the princely provider, who had taken the burden of our family upon his wide shoulders. Me, I was the tearaway tomboy, whose life was shattered at the arrival of breasts, blood between my legs and whenever I had to wear a skirt. My brothers were sporting heroes, mathematical geniuses, and now university graduates, a breeder and providers themselves, where once only insects had been their main concern. I was the sandwich filling between the two of them. Those were our ordained roles amongst our shared wardrobe.

My mother might have wanted me to get married, but she didn't want to know about the ins and outs. She generalised all my information as if it was predictable. Lives were like recipes to her; of course they would go wrong if you kept worrying over them with the oven door ajar to see if they were going to rise. You had to give it a chance, and if you over-seasoned them, naturally the other parts would be hidden and disappear. I would cry and she would mop. Our roles.

Sometimes I wanted to hit back. I didn't know if my tears were ones of frustration towards her and the perfection of her well-defined existence compared to the chaos of mine, or just my frustrations. But I loved my life. Sometimes I wondered just how much she did hers. I had to let go. That territory, her life, was firmly out of bounds. Private stuff, in the same way mine had been when I was married to Thom and wasting away to six and a half stone. Then I'd met any enquiries with a frigidaire silence, as my granny would have said. My brothers knew to leave me alone, like the police with 'domestics'. I guess it was too much for my mum, to see that the soufflé dream she had expanded into my horizon had deflated so badly in my hands. I had no delicacy, with my muddied paws, never could make pastry, but I was always a dab hand at hash, corned beef, brilliant at instinctive, delicious messes. There is no recipe where you just feel your way through the fresh-chopped, boiled mass of mush, mix the lot up with your hands and spread it into the hot oiled pan, to singe like a proper sauté potato and serve with a large dollop of French's turmeric-yellow mustard, Heinz's blood ketchup and Hellman's, mix to colour taste, and no brand substitutes will do.

'I leaned on the fish counter and got fish juice on my jeans,' Thom explained to me one day. I had put my head on his lap as he was reading on the sofa. I hadn't even asked.

'Oh, I didn't know you'd bought fish. What fish?' We spoke of food more than feelings at that point. We would eulogise over herbs and grilled vegetables, the skills of marinating, anything to avoid talking about us. Our separateness.

'Some haddock for Mother, from Steve Hatt's. I dropped in to see her this afternoon, she asked me to go shopping for her.'

'Oh.' I turned my head to sniff at his leg. He pushed my head away, off his lap.

'I wish you wouldn't loll all over me. Sometimes you can be really irritating, May.'

I got up and left the room, but didn't know where to go. I had the choice of the bathroom or bedroom, as the living room was part of the kitchen. I went into the bathroom, looked in the mirror, looked at the window and thought, I could see myself jumping out and landing splat on the Islington kerb, just like the rain. I sat on the loo, sick with vertigo, and thought I could understand why you have to buy larger and larger houses the longer you're married. It's to get away from your spouse without being impolite, or causing offence.

It wasn't that Thom hated all women, he wasn't gay; it was just me. He never said that, but I could read it all over his face, left to right, south to north.

There comes a point, a horrible point, when you have to learn all the myriad ways in which you can be disliked. All the habits you have nurtured, developed and secured to your side over a lifetime and don't notice. The tone of your voice, its timbre, its decibels, highs and lows, and that's without your sentence constructions. Think about the way you butter bread, make tea, pour milk, discard the tea bag or scatter the leaves, blocking the sink or fouling the rubber plant. How do you eat food? Slurping soup, rustling sweets or popcorn in the cinema, chewing gum . . .?

'Why do you constantly listen to the radio's diatribe and talk all the way through? And at the same time magically believe you've absorbed everything ever broadcast on Radio Four, and suddenly you're the world expert on everything?' Thom had asked me.

'Does the way I bite my toenails irritate you too?' I wish I'd answered back, but our roles were set.

'And why don't you paint any more? You were a painter when I met you.'

'I don't have the time. I have to go out to work.' I hid my face with my hair in shame. Bad girl.

'Real painters find the time, they don't care about money. You're so materialistic.'

'But we have to pay the rent, Thom.'

'Oh, so it's my fault now, that you don't paint? I thought it would get back to me. Blame me! Everything you've sacrificed so that I can work my balls off.'

'No, Thom, I didn't mean it like that.'

'Have you ever thought that I might be the one who'd like to do the easy bit? Just get a job and not have to be bloody creative every day? I really don't think you realise what it takes to smear your soul on a piece of paper with cohesive sentences.'

The last part of the argument he used to move himself across the room, pick up his leather jacket and leave. He couldn't even be bothered to slam the door – another thing I had to do for him!

Annoying personal traits: for Thom I was knitted together with them. By the end, I could feel his shudder of dread as I entered our home, let alone when my skin touched his, or the weight of my hand was upon his shoulder.

I found our wedding album the other day. Daring myself to open it was like pulling the gummy gauze off a pusy, septic, scabbed wound – slow work, perilously slow and painful – *ouch!* on turning each page. The look on his face. Every frown caught by the intruding camera. He had thrown up outside the church moments before we made our pledges, his face strained with terror, white and grey with pain. How did I not see it on the day? Eaten up with my own numb mind-rush, marinating in a millennium jellied daydream; I even wore a medieval-style white dress. Maybe I did glimpse something, but quickly pulled the shades over my eyes. I grew blind so that I couldn't see anything but the wreath of smiles; I even missed my cousin puking up over the wedding cake. Yet I put it down to gastric flu doing the rounds. I'm sure that must have been a bad omen. My great-aunt Dottie had said that when I had joked about losing my engagement ring during my wedding speech.

'Not very funny,' she'd said to me later. 'Mark my words, girl, that's a bad omen good and proper!' Were her words the bad omen, or the lily-festooned hat she was wearing? Thom sat, frozen with a myxomatosis glaze, my husband the white rabbit, Thom the bunny. It was a carrot cake.

It wasn't even a shotgun wedding. There was no force. Is that true? Maybe not, maybe it was a bombardment of family mortar bombs going at us, with both of us supplying the shells.

That sorts out why I married. I thought I'd fallen in love, but what did I marry? What was Thom, what did he do? Thom was a writer.

Thom stayed home each day and wrote, as I went off to an office and typed to pay the rent. The idea being he'd get this great advance and we'd live happily ever after. Giving my time was a small investment for long-term happiness. Then, when the boat arrived, as it surely must, one day (each day we lived in greater expectation than the one before, until finally it tailed off altogether) I'd have babies and he'd metamorphose into Joseph Heller. By the time the kids had grown up and we were in our late forties, early fifties, there'd be time for the inevitable divorce, just like our parents. After all, why spoil a formula that worked for so many?

Each night I'd return to our domestic idyll with the shopping, and be greeted by the tippy-tip-tap of Thom's Apple Mac coming from the walk-in cupboard that was his work den.

'Darling? I'm home,' I'd say first of all, dropping my bags in the hall and rushing to fling my arms about his taut neck, and the noise would cease and passion would bounce off the walls and ceiling. Later I would say it to the fridge as I filled it, or to the table, still scattered with breakfast remains as I returned to what I'd left that morning. And that was what I came to expect. And then more. Extra mugs filled with a slow liquid decay, and crumb-littered plates from lunch scattered around the room.

Maybe once, he cleared the whole lot, washed, wiped, tidied and cleaned it all. I made such a fuss of 'you needn't haves' that he didn't bother again. Near the end there was less mess; he gave up even pretending to be there.

Why should he bother washing up, doing anything, when I was happy to have the new and unusual weight, a winter coat of extra responsibility in carrying him. Summer comes inevitably, and the stealthy burden of resentment creeps in and lays its eggs under the surface of your skin. Similar in many ways to cancer, it only appears visible when the conditions hothouse it to signal tiny bubbling impressions that raise the surface. I was not happy.

Discontent: restlessness, lack of contentment, dissatisfaction.

The breeding of discontent: when expectations no longer mirror the reality. Go for surgery and you might catch it early enough. Delay the build-up, but often, as in my case, it was malignant. It had roots wiring through me like a three-year-old verruca that had intentions to breed and nest – it would laugh in the face of freezing or laser treatment. It was in for the duration.

Realistic: regarding things as they are, based on facts rather than ideals.

My reality: a matter of perception.

Either I had begun to perceive myself or the facts differently, or I had projected myself into *Indecent Proposal*, a film I had once seen, starring Demi Moore and Robert Redford. When I should have chosen, if any, *The Palm Beach Story* with Gary Cooper and Claudette Colbert. Both the husbands played the part of creative but poor geniuses – architects! Both women went after money for their husbands' brilliant projects. The difference: one was a comedy directed by Preston Sturgis, the other I can't remember.

Sturgis's 1933 heroine placed in the nineties would have had the career herself. Not that she was completely without one. Her career was as wife, her main project, her husband, her income, his. There are still women like this, politicians' wives, my mother; career wives. The wind behind a man's sails, the bow to his violin, indispensable creatures. Crocodiles need them too, purveyors of natural harmony. But I am not a Plover bird. And if I was, I'd want a bloody big settlement too for continually laying all that oil on troubled waters, buttoning my emotional lip, carrying Dr Bach's Rescue Remedy at all times and remembering to spike his food with essence of marigolds (for constancy and faithfulness).

Could I ever do that?

Could I be an apple-pie mum? Could I?

No. If I was going to be anything, I suspect it would be closer to a tin of Heinz Treacle Pudding, but the custard would be home-made. I'd make sure he knew how to do that.

Maybe the next advert should read: 'Custard-making husband wanted. Bird's worker need not apply.' Would you answer it? And why haven't I ever dated an Italian, gay or straight? They know about food.

Mum's advice is be more simple; the solution will arrive. But meanwhile, the solution might not even call me back. Lomax.

Lomax is really the one stealing about my heart. He makes me thin with longing, while Ed, sweet Ed, makes me fat with dinners and squeezes my breast like a judge of fresh loaves or ripe pineapples. For that, I won't permit him to taste the flesh (I imagine him with his fingers like tweezers buried down inside my vagina, a brisk doctor doing a vaginal smear), no matter how many times he orders asparagus and another bottle of wine. I'll simply eat more lettuce to stave off the effects. Lettuce was used to cure drunkenness during the Roman Bacchanalian feasts, but in England it was used to promote fertility in young girls. Luckily, as I'm over thirty, if I was ever taken with baby into hospital I'd already qualify as geriatric. There is a bit in *When Harry Met Sally* when Meg Ryan cries out to Billy Crystal (forget the orgasm scene) in misery, '. . . And I'm going to be forty!'

'You're going to be forty?'

'One day, I will.'

Or something like that. And I'll look back on my life and what will I find? A few paintings, a few good friends, likewise shags and a husband. The fact that once I got married, no matter what the circumstances, it will be the crowning glory in my obituary, even though a few years later I don't even have his phone number, just like my real father. I can't even blame my hapless marriage on the craziness of youth.

'You could always go and get pregnant, have a baby. That would be nice.'

My mum's answer. Marking time like the rings on an oak, filling a life with meaningful landmarks. Is that why we get married, have children and start to measure our progress by theirs? Blink and your life is over, live in a state of rigmarole, standing up in order to lie down. Die down. If you're lucky, you might get your name on a blue plaque, or even a biography; entering politics is the easiest way. You can pay to have your name, along with thirty thousand others, put on a CD that is to be deposited on Mars, but do Martians have CD players? If not, only your children will carry your name into posterity – nobody else will bother in the marking of the passage of time. The majority of painters lie buried, forgotten.

My answer to my mum's baby prompt is, 'I'm much too young for that.'

'Gloria's daughter, you know, the Greenhams at The Beeches, is twenty-four and she's just had her second.'

'That's very clever of her. Can I see her work in the Tate?'

My mother doesn't even bother answering this dismal childishness, and a murmured 'sorry' escapes

my lips in the place the sneer was meant to go. I
know the comment is unworthy of me and not even
funny, but then, so are some of my mother's, such as,
'Are you sure you need another helping?'

Duh! Is President Clinton gay? Of course not, but
maybe I do need another helping (Casanova complex
taken into account).

That last night in the comfort of the spare room,
with the spare portable TV and me the spare daughter, I think and plan. I will go back to London
tomorrow and I will stay home, unplug the phone
and paint and paint, producing masterpieces more
lasting, more fun than any man ever could be. Why
the hell had I done this thing? Was my life too happy,
was I so bored, desperate, discontent? I thought of
Oscar Wilde, who maintained that he never sought
happiness in his life; he was more interested in
seeking pleasure the pain-wrought variety. Maybe my
seeking laughter was the same thing: the higher you
go, as low you'll fall. Of course, I'm not quite at
Marilyn Monroe's level, but I can work at it. I sipped
my camomile and started reading the spare old book
on the bedside table, *Folklore of the Northern Counties of
England and the Borders* by William Henderson. Nice
and modern: 1879.

If I ever wanted to get married again, I would bake
a cake – nicely and technically known as a Dumb

Cake – with a friend. It is made of flour, water, eggs and salt, mixed and baked, and when it's cooked we'd divide it up equally and walk upstairs backwards while eating it. Or wait until midnight on the dot to eat the cake downstairs, remove all the pins and fastenings from our dresses so that apparitions of our future husbands could appear and snatch off our clothes before we dived into bed and the visions would vanish. Remember to leave the door open during the whole procedure; if you don't, how can he be expected to enter? During the night I will dream of my future mate.

And this time I won't dream of Flipper the dolphin, or any colour/breed of rabbit! I'm off animals. Only the human variety is good enough for me.

Chapter 11

SOMETHING TO DO WITH MY HANDS

My body woke me this morning, tingling like a thousand little alarm bells ringing, shaking my cells and shouting, 'Get up, you lazy bint!'

There was no light coming through the curtains, so I turned to look at my radio alarm clock. It digitally shrieked back 5.25 a.m.

I couldn't get up! I couldn't get up at five-thirty in the morning, my mind told me, calculating that I must have slept for only five hours. 'You can't get up after only five hours' sleep, you'll be exhausted by the afternoon,' my mind nagged on. 'Get back to sleep, Ms Knott!'

I tried, God knows I tried. First I counted sheep, then dissected a mental pyramid and anagrammed

EastEnders. Nothing doing. Anxiety keeps you awake. Mustn't be anxious, mustn't get up and admit I'm awake, I repeated to myself like a mantra.

I settled into an erotic fantasy and drifted happily into Sleep Zone 5000. His arms curled around me, the warm breath from his lips soft upon my neck, his legs crossing mine, slumberous caressing, mmm . . .

How long can you delay sex, when bodies are screaming at each other in silent demand in public places, equally powerful, their ecstatic agony prolonged? How long can you keep your clothes on when, each night, separate and alone, you dream heavily scented mirages of his naked skin beneath yours? Am I to join the New Modesty brigade? Am I doing it so that he'll respect me instead of seeing me as raw meat? I don't think so. If I was, would I be lying, like so many who follow some set of rules just to get married, changing their behaviour into wedding snares? Then, disappointed, even surprised when their marriage lasts only seventeen months. The surprise is that it lasts longer than two weeks. And as I've said, I don't want to get married! I don't need to mark my life any more. If you think I'm protesting too much, I don't care. The right time will come. Meanwhile I'm painting beautiful, wonderful internal landscapes with coal-red suns and whipped blue night skies. It's got to end soon.

I've heard terrible tales of unrequited lovers who yearned through fifty years of a badly matched marriage, just waiting for the other to die so that freedom could beckon them to their true love. Masochistic misery if you ask me; convention wrapped in its pink satin bow; beastly belief. Untie the ribbons and change the story.

Of course, I could jump into bed with Lomax straight away if I truly wanted to, but I've always taken the easy option. There is much to be thankful for, but when it comes to relationships and sex, I've spat in the eye of modest convention and often acted exactly as I wanted to, sometimes unwisely.

The trouble with that is that you often find once you've had it, you no longer want it, that you end up accepting sex more readily than love, or worse, accepting love when all you wanted was sex. They're an uneasy exchange. I've also discovered the grazes. Erosions that appear from treating myself unkindly; it's like rollerblading down a gravel hill on your knees. You think it'll be fun, the bits that you want, like a large box of chocolates that you stuff down your gullet like a starving man, only to be surprised and disappointed to find that your eyes were bigger than your soul.

Heigh ho. I don't wish to appear glum about this subject, but in the end it is the lightness of being that colours all your perspectives. I eventually started to wonder what was the point of performing the act of intimate exercise with someone you wouldn't want to discuss the weather with, unless a pretty face to decorate your pillow in the morning is all you require; my pillows are pretty enough.

Why bother with joined-up sex, if you're unwilling to link the letters? Sex produces an extraordinary energy that either debilitates one or lifts one to the clouds, and it can sing you to a heaven in a unity of ecstasy unknown to mortal consciousness. The Hindus practise tantric magic, almost a religion in itself, but I don't want to cast spells; now I want to live within one, shared with Lomax. What am I saying, that I want to *live* with *Lomax*? No! I mean, *be* with him. That's better! Sometimes it's hard to clean out all the fairy tales.

I haven't, and I'm not going to put any evil-eye stuff about. Is that why I'm trying the unusual and exciting arrangement of sweating through the night and, once awake, feeling like my central nervous system is being shot through with caffeine?

I've become the kind of bore that can only be appeased with decaf: coffee, tea, Coke, chocolate. Sad but true; I never thought I'd see the day I'd grow up to admit to being a decaf freak. I can't even drink my vanilla coffee, it doesn't come minus the caffeine. I can't take the chance. I'm a high-wire queen about to topple. I'm a deep-sea diver with only just enough oxygen to make it to the top; a buddy would ruin me. It only takes a little push.

Lomax! Hold me in your strong arms and put your mouth to mine. Now! Now *kiss*. He holds me so close sometimes that I can feel the straining of his muscles as he tries to enter me – down, boy, down! I have to pull away sharply, however reluctantly.

And it is reluctant. My head is in confusion as my heart reels from one indecision to the next. The virtuous virgin game is a heady power trip.

What made me do that? I think. My heart's been interfering again; I'd never normally buy a purple dress. I'd never normally— As if I know what's normal! I'm starting to get confused, starting to forget how to separate; shadows merge on a concrete pavement and I think it's us. I want for him what I want for me, and at night I find myself saying prayers for him. How is it that I've come to be so cheap, suddenly? A throwaway identity, a takeaway soul – buy the dinner, get the girl, spirit and all.

Now is the time to start deep-breathing exercises, meditation and lots of dollops of healthy, good for you *ummmmm*-ing.

Dear God, please help me to reclaim myself. Let me

be the whole truth and nothing but. I'm not the salt to sprinkle upon somebody else's meal, I'm a feast alone, as you have made me, and I am blessed.

I got thrown out of the church choir when I was thirteen for discussing sex words in choir practice and giggling through the sermons, but that doesn't mean I have to give up my relationship with a God that can cement together the bits others cannot reach in me. I am a feast enough in myself, I find myself saying to the changing-cubicle mirror, but buy the purple dress anyway. It's nice to have a bit of damask keeping the flies off the ripe succulence beneath. Purple is a most spiritual colour, is how I justify the price. Damask doesn't come cheap these days, and neither do I! Not to myself, anyway.

The will-power, strength and courage I am exerting is enormous, and at times I wonder what for, what the hell for. Do I want marriage or diamonds, holidays or fish and chips, to have his babies or mend his socks, or just Lomax?

I just want Lomax. But nobody can own another person; slavery is outlawed in this country. *I want never gets*.

Today I will not think of Lomax once. But I have already broken my promise by starting the day with his name. I jump into the shower and sing, 'I'm going to wash that man right out of my hair, I'm going to wash that man right out of my hair,' *South Pacific*-style, with a Mitzi Gaynor twang.

The water pummels needle jets over my skin and falls hot to my toes until I turn the dial to full blue, and tense my skin in anticipation. The shock of the cold forces a little shriek from my lungs as my skin ripples over with goose-pimples like the longest row of dominoes ever to topple, or the largest plucked turkey. I bounce a purgatory dance upon my toes for the full minute, even flushing my scalp under the Icelandic stream, until I turn the damn thing off and wait for the afterglow. I enjoy the chattering of my teeth and wrap myself in a big towel like a pink sausage in a croissant. Why do it? I could say it's to get my circulation going, but really for the moment it stops me thinking about Lomax, stops me obsessing for that minute when I am overwhelmed by a physical other. Is that why people get into self-mutilation, distracting themselves with pain from the chaos of their mind? I should take up smoking to stub cigarettes out over my flesh; a nice, decorative pattern of pain tattoos; or piercing, that kind of thing. I'm consumed. Lomax is big. So big, he's climbed into my skin with me. Strong: so strong, I'm losing the battle and can't wait for the bliss of defeat, Daz-washing all my white handkerchiefs in anticipation.

363

Lomax stands dark and shadows my soul as well as my skin. Some days I look in the mirror and think I'm turning black, or have been broiling overnight on a sunbed. Well, Michael Jackson did it, changed his skin colour. Except maybe it's worse than that, because outside I still look the same. It's inside that's the problem, for if I was to have an internal, if I was to say, suddenly die, and a coroner had to open me up, that is where the disfigurement would have occurred. Nobody would be looking at the state of my clean or otherwise knickers when they were faced with a stomach full of marble intestines, incapable of doing their job.

I fill my nights with thoughts like these. My REM (Rapid Eye Movement) isn't doing its job. I plummet into a sleep of blow-tortured darkness. The pins-and-needles effect is my wake-up call, that and the strangulation of my sheets at grey dawns, or the spreading yellow light that glares through the curtains.

God, where am I? I have awoken again. The harridan hounds of hell enter my ears, *wakey-wakey!* Radio One's finest, Zoë Ball, screams from my radio until a record takes over and the relief sloshes me into a more relaxed, sloth-like dream state. Someone singing the inanely true, 'there's nothing like me and you', pukey, pukey.

There is always that split second on waking where

there is no possibility of remembering what has happened in either real or dreamtime for the last seven hours. Most mornings I'd be hard pushed to remember my name, let alone any pseudonyms I might have. It's like arriving at the same point of oblivion as being born, dragged through from one passage of reality to another. I suppose that was God's intention, the purpose of sleep. That every day, we have the chance to be reborn, a daily baptism into life, the shock of the new. Our chance to begin our lives again, forgetting the day's past judgements over breakfast; wipe the slate clean. And if, with that new day, you fuck up again? There's always another day, eh? Try this one, see if it fits? What can you do with today?

Problems begin when there's still a yolk's dribble of dream staining the white's new day. When bad dreams that drag you into the past, dirtying the bright, fluffy reality you'd hoped would turn into meringue. Dreams that could be glorious reinventions. I thought the whole point about dreams was you could have it like it was? Make up new good bits, get the job, the man, the rise, the joy – otherwise where does the jibe girls retort to salacious men come from? *Only in your dreams, sucker!*

This is my dream.

I am sitting on the expensive red carpet of a huge

winding staircase, talking to a girl I've never met before. We are inside a very large, grand house, the kind of house that is called a country seat, the type of house that holds all the pomposity of its own importance. It is only a different way of arranging bricks, in one style or another, I'm thinking, determinedly unfazed by the grandiose. This girl and I are talking about the owner of the house in a new, friendly way, cling-filmed with slight suspicion, both of us feeling our way, that we are two on the side. I know from the way this dream is shot with a wide-angled lens, the way I am both behind the camera and the woman on the stairs that the owner, quite clearly called Henry, is listening from the staircase above. I can see the side-parted fringe of his hair, as he anxiously leans over the stairwell to be sure to catch all our words. He is blond Nordic, English public school, more Harrow than Eton, his hair flopping lazily to one side.

'He likes being beaten,' the girl is telling me, as if she were describing someone's breakfast cereal preferences. Instantly my reaction is to recoil in disgust, yet there is a part of me that is interested in hitting this despicable, weak man, with his snobbishness, petty interests and big house.

I reply, 'Yes, I saw the whip and crop up in the cupboard. How hard are we allowed to beat him?' I want to know at what point this man will die, do you listen to his shrieks of, *stop!*

'Oh, as hard as you like, whenever you feel like it. He just laps it up.'

I look up the stairwell at Henry's eager expression on hearing talk of deviant, abusive behaviour; being passed from one girl to another. As I watch his face I think, You'd like that, wouldn't you? Wouldn't you, sad git! And for that reason, in the same way that you are so confident of your inherited wealth, I'm not going to do it! Think of it like death tax, a necessary yet tender pain.

Or am I?

I wake, shocked.

Lomax isn't like that, is he? No; there's no question. Lomax is special and delicious, with eyes you could dive into, skin to glide over, muscles to lean against and a brain to make you laugh.

It's not about Lomax, this dream. It's about me, it's from me, it's mine. My fear. My fear of myself. I rush to the bookshelf and consult my dream manual.

I know that dreaming about sex means you're desperate, you want some, you haven't got it, you dream about it. Simple. In the index I look up sex, all five pages of it, two entries sub-indexed under 'perversion'. I suppose whacking someone to death with a riding crop comes off as perversion? Apparently it is an attempt of the unconscious to come to terms with the dreaded LOVE word, with all its expectations and disappointments.

I was not in this for LOVE. I didn't advertise to fall in love, to marry. This was a girl who loves to laugh in bed: *Benny Hill, Morecambe and Wise, South Park, Ren and Stimpy*. I wanted a stand-up, funny man who did lying down too. Instead I get dreams to compensate for an unbalanced waking life. Either I am behaving too timidly, or I am trying for self-preservation, according to this worthy tome.

Self-preservation.

Perhaps I am trying to preserve myself from myself, like a lemon.

To preserve lemons:

> Choose ripe, washed, unblemished fruit. (Me?) Cut a vertical cross almost through the fruit and sprinkle into the flesh about 2 oz of salt per pound of lemons. Jam the lemons tightly together in a sterilised jar and squeeze enough fresh lemon juice over them to cover. The salt will draw out the juices and soften the peel. It is the rinsed peel you use, after four weeks. Discard the flesh.

Before I married I always did the flesh dump-and-runs. *I* chose *them*. I never took no for an answer, and once they had yielded to my dynamic demands and were thinking, Wow, I want this, I didn't realise I did, but I do now, I'd find the nearest skip in which to discard their ungainly desires (home/kitchen/kids), and run very fast in the opposite direction, changing my address on the way. This isn't being an armadillo; these aren't tank tactics; no, I wouldn't say that. I would say the opposite. In the past I felt so raw it was as though I was surviving third-degree burns; you can't get close to anyone that naked, but you could keep them near with cotton-wool wrapping until the scalding had healed, changing their aloe vera dressings until they were better. That's if you could be bothered.

Would I be bothered with someone like that, a little bird that required iodine-dropper feeding every hour? Only if I could take out an insurance policy that the bird would definitely live. Isn't that true for most people, or have I now become granite in my old age? I used always to choose the kitten in the corner with the bad paw, the social outcast that no one else would take home, let alone pay all their pocket money for. I discovered, after years of studying these types, one thing pets and people, people as pets, all have in common: they never acknowledge your part in their care, their part in your downfall – so don't do it for acknowledgement.

Outcasts always remain chippy, so don't imagine that with your care they'll become happy, successful, clean. Happy has to be worked on alone.

Another thing partners and pets have in common is that they always die – some sooner than others. We all die, so no surprises there, but who wants to get left with the burial arrangements?

Lomax isn't like that, I don't think, and neither am I any longer. Once I thought I held some reins, a saddle beneath my seat. I suddenly discovered that all that leather had been taken away, and that if I was to stay upon this stallion earth I had to learn to cling with my weak inner thigh muscles around its huffing back and belly, and entangle my fingers in its mane. Occasionally I may fall off, but isn't that part of life? Learning to climb back on quick, before you contemplate the bruising, before you acknowledge the pain, you're suddenly laughing again, and you don't even know what the hell about.

I am not looking for my other half, I am not looking for my other half . . . All I want is a whole that I like spending time with, flat-packed or upright, Never Eat Shredded Wheat. *North, East, South or West, be with someone you like best.*

Except with Lomax. I do things with Lomax I'd never do with anyone else, for anyone else. I start to say yes, and have to pull myself back, yanking at my own hair, kicking myself in the shin to stop myself cooking him soup or doing the washing-up. When I'm with him I say the word 'love' too much. Apparently there's not much I don't love these days, if you listen to me! I will slice my own throat if I start to go on to *adore*! *Fabulous! Divine!* Or *gorgeous-ing* about the place.

Where the hell has Hope May, or whatever I'm called these days, gone to? That's what I want to know. I feel like a sherpa who's climbed Everest too quickly, and has to wait for her soul to catch up; or maybe it's the other way round with me. Whatever: something's got to catch up with her/me. She's certainly not at home at night, because the girl who's pacing the boards tying her hands behind her back, (trying not to call Lomax) is not identifiably me. I would never behave like that, never! Tomorrow, I'll tell her to move out; I'm not having behaviour like that going on around me! I refuse, it's inhumane. Bugger off! God, I look dreadful.

'Hope? It's me, Lomax. Calling Hope! Are you receiving me?'

How can I pretend to be an answerphone message, now that my heart is throbbing through my eyes like a Warner Brothers cartoon character?

'Hello!' I hear my voice, alternating between girlish excitement and warm jelly sliding through the receiver as I pick up the phone, all in one word. Very clever, not many people can do that, huh?

'Fancy going to the seaside?'

'But it's Monday.'

'Yes, and tomorrow's Tuesday, and after that come the familiar Wednesday, Thursday, Friday and, of course, not forgetting good old Sunday. That was yesterday,' he explains helpfully. 'But what am I saying? You probably learned all this stuff in school.'

'Only ever in Latin, so it's great to have it translated. I'm sure it'll be useful.'

'So, what about it? Hastings, I thought, or Dungeness.'

'Not Brighton?'

'Definitely not.'

'But I like Brighton,' I say churlishly.

'We all like Brighton! But it's one thing to like a place, and quite another as to whether it will do us any good going there!'

'Has anyone told you that you speak like Jerome K. Jerome?'

'No. But I did ghost *Idle Thoughts of an Idle Fellow*.'

'But he wrote that.'

'Too damned idle; someone had to do it for him.'

'I see. I think the sea air will do you good. Hastings has an excellent fish and chip shop.'

'So we should go to Dungeness?'

'We can decide when you get here and you've checked which way the wind's blowing. I don't want to end up like Homer Simpson, or my hair looking like Marge's.'

'I don't know, you and Marge . . . I'm picking modom up, am I?'

'Well, that's what I thought this call was, a pick-up. Have I got it wrong?'

'What are you wearing?' He says this in a seductive and sexy tone, as though he has reached a hand through the receiver to open the buttons on my shirt and is slipping his fingers into my cleavage.

'Not an anorak!' I say.

He slams the phone down, and I have enough time (though not enough space) to do a cartwheel across my studio before the phone rings again. He spits three words out in a heavy Algerian accent before replacing the receiver: 'Pack an anorak!'

I go and pack my stuff. Plenty of mental games. I have no anorak.

He arrives looking like, well, to me, how all movie stars should look, but disappointingly don't. He is dressed like a fifties matinée idol going for a spin; a young Cary Grant in *To Catch a Thief*. Naturally, I bear a strong resemblance to Grace Kelly. You can't see it? You must be wearing the wrong glasses. I, however, have the right glasses from my dressing-up box, some nice kitten-heel sling-backs, some handy Capri pants with an open-fronted skirt attached. My shirt was tied under my bra, the first of the tummy tops, and a basket with a pair of plimsolls (for when my Capris turn into clam diggers), straw hat, cardigan, lipstick and the three C's – keys, condoms, cash. What else could I require? Neither of us recognises the other as I come out of my apartment door and he lounges by his new car that he never told me he'd bought. It is a bright red VW Carmen Ghia soft top. It is a baby of a car.

I walk towards him, and maybe it is the size of my glasses or the scarf wound about my head that disguises me; maybe he doesn't want to believe that he knows me? I sidle up to him and say with great delight, 'Nice red penis; how fast is it?'

'Hope!'

'That fast? Wow!'

'Would you like to . . . feel it, stroke it, maybe ride it?' He grabs me in a supremely delicious lipstick-ruining hug-snog.

'I have two choices,' I say into his mouth. 'Either you escort me upstairs and I have to rape you without anaesthetic, or we have to go right away.'

For the first time I display to him that I am a bubbling cauldron, capable of exploding.

'I think we have no choice but to do the operation. I am in your hands as a willing patient for this experiment.' His eyes gleam with excitement. 'Why hold out any longer? You know this is what we both want, Dr Clooney.'

'*Errrgh.*'

'OK, I'll call you George. Your place, eh?'

'No, I can't do it. I can't cheapen you this way. I want you to know that you're no ordinary doxy, trollop or hussy to me. I couldn't bear to see you so debased.' I say this while placing my hand upon his cock.

'Like you did to my big brother?'

'Yes, like I did to your brother. He didn't tell you that I did *that* with him, did he?'

'No, but you just have. You should know that my brother is the sweetest, discreetest boy ever to walk the earth. Except when he's with Eve.'

'Is your ear very dry?'

'Why yes, now you mention it.'

'My tongue's very wet.' I place it inside his ear.

'Unseasonably! *Arghhh!*'

My tongue and teeth nibble his ear, seducing him on the pavement against his car, and I start to whisper, very slowly and softly, 'Fish 'n' chips, fish 'n' chips, fish 'n' . . .'

'Greedy, greedy, greedy girl!' and he picks me up and dumps me unceremoniously into the front of the car. Luckily the roof is down.

We drive through the mug of early-morning traffic until we get to the A2, *West Side Story* blaring from the tape machine combating the lorry groans.

'Oh my God, I've forgotten something.'

'Now you tell me. Do you want to go back, poor little sweetie? What was it?'

'My swimsuit.'

'Buy a bikini when we get there. What's it for?'

'To go swimming in.'

'But it's March!'

'Almost April. And a Monday!'

We look at each other and laugh, and he squeezes my hand. I lean over to him and kiss his cheek. We leave the M25 and start into Kent, past Sevenoaks and through to Sissinghurst and all the trees, lacy with green, lean together, badly roofing the road, holes of sunlight raining upon our heads. Sussex, and the roads get smaller and the farm-shop signs appear, and you want to believe it's all their own produce growing organically and being sold fresh out of the pure dark earth. We don't stop; we're too busy talking and singing. Singing-along-a-Bacharach.

Hastings is a complicated town. It half works, and half of it's a postcard, and the bits that are working are the parts that they put on the postcards, and then there are the malls and arcades, the sad, wet seaside pier promenades full of fishermen, not promenaders.

Through the arcades weave day-tripping foreign students, smoking and laughing and slurping at lurid-coloured Slush Puppies.

'It's like *That'll be the Day* – Hastings, but different,' I explained, from my childhood memories of Gran and Grandpa's beach hut at St Leonards when I was six. 'You know, with David Essex and Ringo Starr.'

'Hold me close don't let me go, oh, no . . .'

'What about *Godspell*? He autographed my programme and gave me a glass of cider on the stage when I was five.'

'I bet you was a lovely little girl at six. Wanna lolly?' he said, licking his lips and putting on an eerily pervy accent.

'No, I wasn't!' I returned, dead straight. 'I'm not going to encourage pervy behaviour.'

'Sorry. So I bet you were a petulant little brat?'

'Hedging your bets rather, one extreme to the other, hot or cold, black or white? Yes, I was, my brothers always told me so; it was a self-fulfilling prophecy. I made their lives hellish.'

'Ish is a wonderful word. No sentence is quite complete without that tag. It holds all the promise of . . . nothing.'

'Ish? Swedish? Yes-ish?'

'I predict that -ish will be the word for the next

millennium, when commitment will be so far out of the line of reason, nobody will even do it in conversation.'

'I have a friend who is so afraid of being tied down that he will never say yes to an invitation until two hours before he goes out.'

'So does he ever get any party invitations?'

'Exactly. He did it on the instructions of his shrink, to make him more impetuous, instinctive.'

'And has it?'

'No; now he broods for hours afterwards about how he came to miss the party he was brooding about for hours beforehand. An excellent fellow.'

'Shrinks can be a dangerous thing.'

'Even the word.'

'I know a girl who went to see a shrink every day, and then went to be ordained so that she could have the sanctity of a dog collar when she shouted abuse at men.'

'How very Christian! Don't get me on to religion, otherwise I'll begin turning into Lucretia Borgia.'

'And we wouldn't want that . . .?' Lomax asked, sadly.

'You know that Pope Paul II apparently died while being sodomised by a page-boy? Apparently, in the tenth century it was all the rage to end your term as Pope in a sexual act.'

'Are you telling me I have to become Pope before we actually get to do it?'

'It? What's this "it" word?'

'Oh, just something I've had lying around since my pre-pubescent years.'

'Handy.'

'Pamela (H)and(y)-erson and her five sisters. They're all in there.'

'Please stop alluding to sex!' I said, visibly squirming in my seat. There is nothing worse than when your pot is about to boil and someone puts the heat up.

'You don't do it and you don't want to talk about it either, is that it? Prudish, there's that ish-word again.'

'I *do* want to do it! If you want to know the truth, I'm wetting my pants with expectation. I just hope you can live up to the fantasy!'

'Er, I really don't like doing it with the incontinent, sorry. I mean, maybe if you took the rubber knickers off, but I can't guarantee anything.'

At which point I had no other choice but to place my hand firmly over his knee and camel-bite it. I began to, then I reconsidered. He was still driving, and I was enjoying it.

'That must be the lamest, sweetest, itsy-bitsy camel bite ever. Are you very weak, little one?' he asked patronisingly.

'I didn't want us to crash. I couldn't die without having fucked you first, otherwise I'd become one of those frustrated ghosts wailing around corridors scaring little children.'

'Shall I pull over down that mud track?'

'No, let's go to a hotel and have sex on purple bri-nylon sheets,' I suggested.

'That sounds disgusting.'

'I know.'

'Pervert! I'm turning off here.'

We were nearing the sea, but the road turned into the built-up shame of south-coast suburbia, and we were lost among the rows of bungalows that soon became the terraces of a town with a rolling park and sign posts to 'Town Centre', 'Shopping Mall' and 'The Sea'. Civic Pride and the White Rock Pavilion presents Easter Specials, A Soul Extravaganza, Tavares, The Emotions, Alvin Stardust (*Won't You Be My Kookachoo?*). It's like looking at an old ad campaign for Starbursts (formerly known as Opal Fruits) – a rush of saliva hits the front of my tongue. All of those acts I was too young to see originally I could devour, but would Lomax want to? Would he tolerate sitting in the front row of the amateur dramatics rendition of *Forty-second Street*, with a box of Maltesers? We hadn't even had sex, and I was thinking like a couple. This wouldn't do at all.

'Lomax, have you ever had a yearning to—'

'Yes, up the pier.'

'I was going to say, see Tavares in concert.'

'My mind was still on a place to—'

'Get your end away.'

'We're like an old married couple, finishing sentences for each other.'

'Revolting, isn't it?' We both said at once, and laughed.

We found the car park at the end of the promenade, past the funfair, the rows of fruit machines, video games and penny dupes. And the Scandinavian brown net huts, just like in Beatrix Potter's *Tales of Pig Robinson*, the fishing boats lopsided, fading and waiting for their next outing. Endless gulls swooped for the chip-shop and cockle-stand remains.

We'd put the hood up for the last half of the journey when the clouds had started to screen the sun and the wind blew a cool March chill. I was wishing I'd brought my coat when we got out of the car, so I made do with doing up my cardigan. The glamour of my Capri-pants outfit looked suddenly out of place; Hastings was not the Monte Carlo of Great Britain, there were no Grand hotels serving cocktails, not even to Diana Dors standard; the streets weren't paved for kitten mules. I changed my shoes for my pumps, so much more practical! But then I had to take off the skirt attachment, and I stopped looking anything like anyone in *Rear Window*, except the nurse, or maybe the murdered wife. I knew that if I wasn't careful I'd end up as Miss Lonely Hearts, having fictitious dinners alone with an invisible friend. I put the skirt back on and did it up over the Capris, and looked just about normal, but the glamorous sex appeal had disappeared with the sun.

Lomax stood and waited, watching, with amazed intrigue playing between his brow and eyes, what I did with my costume, make-up and bag. He didn't say a thing. Finally, I said I was ready and he held out his arm. We walked along the promenade, through the kiddies' funfair and past the American candyfloss and donut stall with its sign of stars and stripes. The sea rose and fell like a tired working girl on to the discomfort of the pebble beach, her foam more grey than white, a mass of green-blue sludge that occasionally winked a glassy reflection.

The wind pulled at everything, pretending to be an impatient teenager in a dress shop. My hair whipped my face and Lomax's when he turned to talk to me, but otherwise we could barely hear each other's words for the wind snatching them away from our mouths. At least we could still lip-read.

The pier was half falling into the sea. Its white paint was peeling and blasted from the wood, its glass blown from the frames, but the metal turnstile was still in place, with a man sitting with his flask in the attached cupboard, collecting the thirty-pence entrance charge in an old cardboard KitKat box. One arcade was full of ancient machines called Mystery of the East, What the Butler Saw and Your Fortune Read. We went in and exchanged fifty pence for twenty old coins, much larger than the grasp of my small child's hand remembered parting with for sweets, reaching up to the counter to pay the nice lady at the corner shop, pre decimalisation. I put one in a machine that promised the erotic exotic and wound the metal handle, watching an innocent flicker of postcard immorality circa 1920.

'Lomax, look at this. It's so sweet,' I said.

'It's a stripping class! Hope, how can you call that sweet?'

'Anything that isn't legs-open pornography qualifies as sweet, these days.' I moved on to the fortune-telling machine that spat out a battered paper card.

'That's what we've got to do.'

'Absolutely,' Lomax said, still glued to the stripping machine.

'Have our fortunes read. This one's rubbish,' I said, scrumpling up the card and putting it in my pocket. It read, *You're platonic.* I wanted the passion card to show to Lomax. I didn't want the picture of the cold fish that mine was showing. 'Let's go to the palmist, up at the beginning of the pier.'

'What does it say? Are you superstitious?'

'No, but it might be warm in there.'

'I'll make you warm!' And he chased me past the pool hall and the empty pub tables, over the wooden slats that balanced on the corroding metal that held the beast wading into the sea.

Down at the end of the pier, the wind blew more aggressively and the last line fisherman was packing up his maggots while his sandwiches blew through the balustrade and into the hungry water.

I held on to the railings and pretended to be Kate Winslet in *Titanic*. I was obviously doing a fairly good impression, because Lomax came and stood behind me, Leo-fashion. But his hands went over my breasts and his mouth curved into my neck, and a peekaboo pressure pushed from his trousers into the back of my skirt, and the only witness seemed to be the naked, cheering sea.

Sensible Lomax had put on his anorak, a large pac-a-mac version that he shielded around me, protecting me from the spray. Behind me I felt something else happening, a hand inching my skirt up, and then my zip sliding down my bum. Now I held the front of the anorak with anticipation as both of his hands pulled down my trews and his hand slipped between my legs, his wet lips at my ear. 'Would you mind if I slipped something cold inside you?' he mumbled.

'As long as you put something on it to keep it dry, I'll make it warm.' I laughed back. A hand disappeared out of my bra and dived into the anorak's open pocket. I excitedly stared out to a sea that was beginning to clear from its swell and spray into a deep bottle green under the buffed blue sky. Lomax pulled aside my pants and pushed himself up and eased into me; a small gasp of expelling air rushed out of my mouth as he pressed me into the railings that bit into my hip.

'Ow!'

'Sorry, am I a bit big?'

'No, it's the railings.'

'Sorry,' he replied, manoeuvring me a little to the right.

'It's not your fault. Bloody Victorians.' I gasped as he hit a button inside me and rubbed warmly against it until my knees were collapsing.

'It's not their fault. I blame my parents for not making me to fit the Trojan size.'

'What? Stop it, please.' I laughed and panted simultaneously, needing the talking to stop if I was going to catch this next wave ashore in the rhythm of our bodies' push and pull. His body went rigid. 'Not you, the talking!'

'Oh, you mean I can keep on doing this?' He held on to my body and clapped me against his hips until I swallowed my shrieks and his head shuddered to a halt.

'Oi, you two. What do you think you're playing at?' said a voice from behind. 'I'll call the police if . . .'

I stepped out from behind the anorak and my skirt fell down to cover my undone bits, almost normal.

'Just playing at *Titanic*,' I said, smiling rather too exuberantly at an old man in a baseball cap with a cragged-up face and sellotaped spectacles.

'Just as long as there's no hanky-panky. This is a family pier,' he declared and walked away.

'Oh? Not, a family-making pier?' said Lomax turning to me, sniggering on my shoulder. 'We must have misread the sign.'

'Thank God for the anorak, and at least I looked normal,' I said, collapsing back into his arms and tripping on my trousers, that were now down around my ankles.

'Well, almost.' We both laughed.

'Time for a nice bri-nylon hotel?'

'We don't need one now, do we?' he said seriously, and looked at his watch. 'Look, I've got to get on and do some work.'

'Thanks, so do I, but I was willing to give up a day.

So we drove all that way for a shag against some railings? We could have done that in Hyde Park.'

'No, I was going to buy you some oysters at the cockle stall, but it seems to be closed. Maybe I can find you some crabs.'

'As long as you haven't already given them to me!' I snapped back.

How sweet; our first row.

Arsehole, I whispered to myself. He put his arm around me. 'Don't be like that,' he soothed. 'I thought you enjoyed it.'

'Like what, arsehole?' I smiled back politely. 'And if you're asking, no. I didn't come. Girls usually don't in weird positions with metal sticking into their guts. It's a man's fantasy, I think you'll find.'

I walked away from him, worrying that I didn't have my train fare back home, not until the cheque cleared from Lady Royston's spaniel. I thought about the last time I'd hitch-hiked. I wondered how long it would take me to walk back to London – seven, eight, eleven hours? Good job I like walking and that I'm a long-distance girl. By the time I got to the car – I had to get my stuff – I was quite looking forward to the walking adventure. Anger was a good motivator. Bloody Lomax! All that bloody time wasted thinking about him, bloody poof, anal retentive, and obsessive! I thought about scratching his car with my brooch pin. That's how grown-up I can get when pushed.

'So, are you ready to go?'

It was Lomax, talking as though nothing had happened!

'Do you think we should travel together? I could take the train. It might be less awkward, but I'd need to borrow some money.'

'I think it would be more awkward; we'd arrive at different times. The hotel wouldn't believe that we were newly-weds, they'd give the suite away to someone else. Do you fancy a chip? They're from the Dolphin.' And he pointed to where I had said the best chippie was. 'I didn't realise you were charging. How much money do you want, or will you take it in chips?'

He shoved the steaming, vinegary paper towards me and my saliva ducts opened. I might have found Lomax resistible but I couldn't refuse those fat, squodgy, lightly golden dreamboats. There is something about chips. I took one as though I was stealing it.

'What are you talking about? I thought you were going back to London to work. That's what you said.'

'No, what I said was, read my lips, I have to go and work. I want to do some research around Rye. It's where the murder happens in the book, and I want to get the details right. Then I've booked a nice hotel, to celebrate the will money and my next publisher's cheque. Actually I've spent that already on the car, but anyway, you get the idea. Or don't you?' He started laughing like a schoolboy and tickling me.

'Don't think you can get around me that easily. You're still an arsehole. Why do you need to trick me all the time? Where's the thrill?'

'The surprise. In making up, you understand now?' He smooched towards me. 'Will you forgive me if I pay to have our hands read? Let's go to the palmist over there. You'll see our destiny lies entwined together.'

All I saw or understood was that the money I had spent on therapy work obviously hadn't soothed the ghosts of my inner child's past. Any time anyone said they had to go – not me, I could leave any time I bloody well liked – I assumed they were leaving me, not the place or the thing we were doing. It was Daddy leaving little girl May all over again, for something better. Somewhere inside I still wasn't good enough to keep someone. Damn and blast! I thought I'd turned the corner on that. It felt like I was getting the Return to Go Monopoly card just as I was heading towards Mayfair, with the whole of Pentonville Road to Piccadilly standing before me covered in hotels. Do not collect £200.

Of *course* Lomax wasn't going to leave me in the middle of Hastings to the mercy of south-coast crims and inappropriate walking shoes! Woman, are you mad? Obviously. Only you would do that to yourself, I thought.

We entered the garden hut that was covered in mystic paintings of palms and butterflies and perched on the corner of the pier and the esplanade. It was a bit like seeing a Chinese restaurant in the middle of a village in the Rhondda; predictable yet strange.

Eileen McCutch was not dressed up like Gypsy Rose Lee; she looked like anyone's granny in her slippers and cardi, huddling towards three blaring bars of red electricity. She'd be going home with scorches on her legs if she wasn't careful, and her nylons melted on permanently.

'You first.' I nudged Lomax.

'Ladies first,' he replied.

I slipped my hand over the counter that was cut out from the weatherboarded division and varnished like a sauna's interior. On the walls were blown-up photocopies of hands with titles like The Adventurer. Pencil markings and scribbles pointed out obvious personality traits to the ignorantly uninformed like me. Between the hands fluttered more butterflies. 'I'll pay for the two of us,' Lomax said to her.

'Right you are,' she said, putting on her specs. And barely looking at me, she didn't hold my hand or gaze into my eyes or at a crystal ball. I don't know what I expected; a bit of chat I suppose, but all she did was scribble away with a pen on a piece of paper as though she was busy doing a multiple choice. When she was finished, she slipped it over to me and said, 'That'll be two pounds and fifty pence, thanks.'

'He's paying. Lomax, go on.'

'All right, miss bossy. What's it like?'

'Ssh! I'm reading!'

The Hand-reading Chart,
For your Guidance, Entertainment and Instruction.
Read only where the card is marked.
Your Virtues: Good brain, quick mind, plenty of courage, capable of leadership, amicably good-humoured, warm-hearted, sympathetic and a very independent spirit.

The bits that weren't marked proved there was no sign of creative imagination or attention to detail (handy for an artist!). Self-confidence, optimism and reliability remained unmentioned.

Your Future Holds: Travel overseas with new company soon. Changes in your social life – a lot of fun ahead. Health good. Length of life – over eighty (*so Nostradamus wasn't coming true this millennium!*). Money: large self-made gains after this year.

'So what does yours say?' Lomax interrupted, his head already over my shoulder and annoyingly reading a bit I hadn't reached.

' "Your Failings: Stubborn – very. Can be bossy." I should say,' he said teasingly. ' "And restless and impatient under moods." Is there nothing good about you?'

'No, moods are erratic,' I said, pointing it out. 'Now you've seen all my failings in one go, there'll be nothing to look forward to. Let's look at yours.'

'As in, I'll show you mine, if you show me yours?' We walked out and down towards the car park again, and swapped pieces of vital paper information. This takes trust, or foolhardiness.

'Hey, how come you got eloquence and I didn't? And reliability and passion? And an even temper,' I said crossly. 'Ah, but you're also jealous and conceited. Are you sure you and Toby had the same father?'

'Now, now, erratic! At least I have something to be conceited about. And between you and me, I think I know who fathered Toby, and quite frankly I wouldn't want to know that Mike Reid was my father, so don't tell him, hon, please,' he said, stroking my back.

'Ah, poor Toby, nothing to inherit but pure talent. But Lomax, what's it like knowing Chris Tarrant is *your* dad?'

'You know, her lack of authentic characterisation led me to believe she might be accurate, but since she's put down that you have both a quick brain and a long life, I can't believe that any of it's true.' Lomax's hands reached around my neck as if to strangle me, but he did it so softly it was more of a stroke. 'Except that it does say for your romance that you have a very happy phase ahead – ahh!'

I smiled at him and winked impetuously. 'If you're lucky.'

He was holding my hand, and used it to pull me close and kiss me. 'Sweetheart.'

I kissed him back. 'Right back atcha.'

Then there was one of the gazing moments, eye-to-eye contact, when the rest of the world disappears. Even if it ended, would it really matter . . . one of those. The sun even came out and the wind stilled, or was that something I imagined? One of us started smiling first and then the other, so of course we had to start giggling, and then our laughter had turned to hysteria and tears by the time we got to the car.

Later, as we drove towards Rye I asked, 'But what

was it with all those butterflies? Palmist and butter-flies, I don't get it.'

'She was probably a close friend of Vladimir Nabokov, or ran his fan club. He was a lepidopterist.'

'Whatever you call it, he was a bloody dirty old man with that *Lolita*.'

'He was a butterfly collector.'

'The Burmese call butterflies the soul-butterflies. They believe that when you sleep, all the souls of animals and humans meet up, and that if you wake too suddenly, your soul won't have a chance to creep back inside your body and you'll die.'

'Who told you that, the next-door neighbour? Or have you just made it up?'

'No, my Lancashire grandpa told me. He's dead now, but he was stationed in Burma during the war. Maybe he only told me to keep me quiet in the mornings when I woke up too early.'

'I'm sure it's true. I like to think of Nabokov as a soul collector.'

'Why is it posher than rent or records?'

'My great-uncle Walter said that the first butterfly seen in a year should be killed, otherwise you wouldn't be able to crush your enemies.'

'Did you have an uncle Mitty in your family too?'

'Yes, and an uncle Billy. All of us were struck with fervently creative imaginations. Now, do you want to check into the hotel first and have a lie-down after today's exertions, you poor dear? Or do you want to tramp around the town in search of the ghost of E. F. Benson? Your choice.'

'You mean, after the exhaustion of being shagged against the railings on Hastings pier?' I retorted loudly as we got out of the car for the benefit of any passers-by.

'But Hope, I did try to get the sheep off.'

'Ha, ha. I'm coming with you. Where's the hotel? Help, I haven't got my toothbrush or cleanser with me.'

'Toothbrush? Cleanser? What about condoms? I've forgotten those ribbed ticklers you like so much.'

'Well you can't expect me to sleep with you then, unless you get a penis extension.'

The hotel was a folly standing in the backstreets of ye olde cobbled Rye, near to the church. We checked in and Lomax insisted on seeing the room, but I wasn't allowed. 'I think you should have got "can be extremely bossy" written on your hand chart,' I said as I sat down to wait.

'No, this comes under romance – very.'

'I believe you.'

The whole of Rye looked like an American tourist's dream, and a modern developer's nightmare.

'This town's so cobbly-cute,' I said later as we walked around the pretty toy town.

'Just like you, honey! Actually the BBC pays to have it stay this way so that they can always shoot historical dramas here, and the odd comedy. They've got a few "towns", actually; one in Dorset, one in the East End.'

'And they are filled full of actors just like in *The Truman Show*, right? And you're Jim Carrey?' We made it to the side of the church, and I was reading the headstones. 'If I had some hemp seed and it was Hallowe'en, I could throw it over my shoulder and see my future husband scything it up behind me. Apparently.'

'Yes, or watch yourself being arrested. Is that why they call hemp seed marriage-banana?' He laughed at his own joke.

'There is something else you have to know about me,' I said seriously.

'Apart from the fact that your family came from Bedlam and that you advertise sexual favours in magazines? What can be worse than that?' Lomax said to me, face-to-face. Behind his head I watched the sun go down, and the church bells echoed over us and the dead buried beneath us didn't do anything.

'I'm never going to get married, and I'm never going to live in the country.'

'Hefty! I wasn't going to get married either, not until I was really old, and it was going to be to a seventeen-year-old, who I'd leave everything to. The family would get nothing. What do ya reckon?'

'Nice. And, I can't have children. It said so on my hand-reading; no crinkles on the side of my hand.' I stretched my hand out wide for him to see.

'It's fine,' he said nonchalantly. Was there nothing I could throw at this guy? But then I saw a little worry cross the flecks of his pupils. 'Linda Grant in *Sun Signs* says that Leos hardly ever have children. Plus, they're noisy and smelly and you have to spend all your money on education and nappies. Who needs them!'

'But I'm not a Leo,' I said.

'No, but I am.'

'Actually, I *do* have them. Look, I'll show you. This is how you hold your hand to count them,' and I showed him properly. We both had the same number of lines, but neither of us mentioned it.

'So that's your sick idea of a joke?'

'I had to do something for this afternoon. Only a little revenge, but I had you,' I said, grinning triumphantly.

'Right back atcha. I'm a Sagittarius; we're renowned breeders.'

At that moment I knew. This one was going to run and run, but I couldn't guess in which direction.

'Romantic. In fact, let's go back to the hotel. I have an idea. Can I whisper it into your mouth?' I didn't wait for his answer before I began kissing him.

'Wow, some whisper that turned out to be. I can do the rest of this stuff tomorrow, can't I?' He smooched up to my cheek. 'Goddess, let's go and do some serious laughing in bed.'

And we did.

Epilogue

THE HAPPY ENDING

In these past months of adventure I feel like I have met every name in a male baby directory. Of course I haven't, but there have been a few. I feel almost like Frank Sinatra singing, 'My Way' – maybe too few to mention. Those I haven't mentioned have been too dull, though not dull enough, to gain an entry. If I'd put them in, it would only have brought the tone down. There was the manic-depressive book dealer; the detective (not at all Chandleresque or Sweeney-like, more John Thaw – any series – my mother would have liked him); the rejected novelist; a rock guitarist; the businessman who dealt in ships and lived with his mother; an actor. As I put it down, they start to sound rather fascinating, but the reality, or my perception of it, made them rather shabby.

What was the point, I try to remind myself?

A bomb to blast me out of my usual habits. A chance to get fed. An opportunity to examine my behaviour in fast motion. No, it was the mating game. I hadn't got to the point of snatching babies, but I was on the way, with snatching husbands – it wouldn't have been long.

The expectations of love's young dream. But I'm not so young that I don't know that love is a dream. A dream that you wake from with insomnia and walk the earth with, trying to find the draught to knock you back out. I recommend very strong camomile tea. Excitement. Heart flutters. Raw nerve endings are no real ingredients to make anything permanent with. But what's permanent? A marking pen for school uniforms? No economy in the world is, and we aren't either.

Things change: people, places, myself, I know. Nothing ever stays as it is, or will be as it was. I am a sober, drug-free zone, sometimes, but faith has to be played with, chances cajoled, courage grasped and run at. At least throw the bloody ball up in the air and see if you can catch it. Don't just hold it always in your hand and refuse to budge. If you try to pretend that things are otherwise, that they don't change, that, to my mind, is contravening the laws of nature, Newton and the rest of the universe. So what if you don't catch it, and it drops on the floor? Nothing is any big deal in the end, you'll probably find a gold coin when you go and pick it up, or a different, bigger, better ball. See? Everything that happens is for the best.

How did I start this, what did I want? A husband, a boyfriend, some fun, a few dates, relief from the monotony of my one-brush life?

Where was I? Stuck somewhere in the confusion of men vs. boys, with not a goal in sight. I was brought up with two examples of men, my role models for partners; my mother's husbands.

First, my father, real, glamorous, treacherous, absent, maybe even gay, multi-married. The odd expensive jewelled bauble would arrive. Nothing for my brothers. I was the princess to his kingdom, the two of us were more alike than the rest of the family. He made sure I knew that, in the five short years before he left. He never had a real job, my mother told me. He was a dilettante. I could trace him if I wanted to. What does he do now? He's a nightclub designer in Miami.

Then there's my dad, my stepfather, Geoffrey. A good man, a kind man, a family man with no interest in conversation. Solid, dependable, dull, each day trotting to his City job, commuting the money back and forth to bring up another man's children; to care for my mother.

Which was the man of these two? Perhaps they were both boys. One only doing as he thought he should, the other only ever listening to his wants, and when things didn't work, he'd hop on a plane, do another geographical. Man or boy? Why didn't they have it tattooed on their foreheads? Girl or woman? Why can you not tell them from the colour of their eyes? There – I have been scattering judgements, kicking out in resentment. When what I wanted was to hear those ordinary words repeated to me me me meeee – only. This girl needs to hear it.

I love you.

Is that all I ever wanted? I could have said them to a mirror, but would I? NO. Somebody else was going to have to say them, because I sure as hell wasn't going to. Anyway, if I had said them, what would they have been worth? If you, boy/man, say them, you in all your glory, beauty and magnificence, why, I shall string myself to your boots and employ Superman's hearing device (at vast expense), just in case you should ever whisper them again and again and again. For once is never enough to the greedy child. What did you say? I didn't quite catch it.

I love you.

Say it too often and I won't believe you, you're a lying door-to-door hawker, giving me false hope and a sticker value I'll never achieve. Slap me hard, and there's proof of care to someone who likes their love undercooked to raw; in fact, to live in an open wound.

Now, I can say all this as I breezily return I-love-you volleys with, 'I know.'

Why wouldn't I, for goodness' sake?

A million to one – dates to goddess. I'll take them all, for I am them. We are all children, men, girls, women, boys, and the differences we choose to see are the divisions we place to separate us from each other. Dull, but true.

Lomax says the most perfect things. He rings me up and says, 'I've been thinking about you all day, I miss you.' And I reply crap stuff.

'I'm not surprised, the sun was shining!'

I do want to whisper and giggle like Meg Ryan, Goldie Hawn, Julie Christie, sweet, innocent young girlies. I don't, I can't.

I know what I should do if this affair is to stand a chance. I should tell Lomax that I have to go away to look after my sick, elderly godmother. I was never christened, but it sounds plausible, doesn't it? LIAR!

I could then go and stare at the sky for two weeks,

straight into the centre of the sun, until it melts the indecision from me.

What I mean is, maybe I could track down my real father. Find out for myself that the man I got to care for me was better than any absent reality that became a Superman in my head; the comic-book hero that appeared any time my mum blasphemed back at my taunts of Dad's perfection to her battle of strictures.

Poor Mum. I try to forget the cries of her frustrations against my cloven-hoofed, mule face. I was the hangover of their two-tier passion that probably turned to boredom and swift indifference over nappies, teething and my brothers. Us kids were the fallout which made them cling on for five more years. I know Mum could easily have got a bastard replacement, but she didn't. Instead at the Notting Hill Exchange she sacrificed excitement for reliable, predictable and for the bills to be paid. The family made, she tied herself to a kitchen sink's responsibilities. 'I'm not saying I didn't choose this life, obviously I did . . .' she once hinted to me before a distraction felled the end of the sentence and her hinting at other options. We sat down again after my stepfather had gone on up to bed, and we looked into the fire with our cups of tea. 'There were times when other things were possible, but this is what I chose and there is nothing to be gained in looking at it in any other way. "It makes for happiness to be what

you can, when you cannot be what you would,"
Girolamo Cardano said. You understand that, May.'

And she said it as if to imprint me with a wisdom it
is easier to say than understand.

So you see, I can't make any concessions, my
mother made them all for me, so there is no point
really in looking for my dad; I might as well get out
the American version of *La Cage aux Folles*.

Which brings me back to the whole damned
responsibility of choice, and the knowledge that the
more joy I am capable of feeling, the further I have to
fall when I drop, if you believe Newton. I suppose I
owe it to my mother and the solid pain of my birth to
go the whole hog, and not just look at the Grand
National on the telly.

Oh, Lomax, I don't know if I will ever be able to tell
you how hard it has been to let go of the ledge and
dive helmetless into the white-water roar of your
arms. Whatever I have said, whatever I say, what
would you say?

'It's a little purple, isn't it, May? But that is what I
love about you. Why choose one word when fifteen
will do?' And he would end with his upbeat, gurgling
laugh, which would give me the excuse to wrestle him
to the ground in open-armed, rib-tickling combat.

If nothing more is made from our union apart
from laughter, I will still have achieved my goals. I

never advertised for a husband, and I have made some fun friends. Sometimes it's hard to differentiate friendship from the other. Toby is now a friend, perhaps Steve; DB always was. Maybe everyone was a friend, and I might never get married or be monogamous, or I might be walking down the aisle in the next six months and be a faithful spouse for ever to Lomax, amen.

I might be with Lomax this week, this month, this decade, the rest of the millennium. I don't know. Really I don't want to know. I am not irresponsible, I could have his babies, but I am not so naïve to think that that could hold anything together. And that's fine. As long as we laugh together and not at each other (very important differentiation here) and want to be seen in public, it works. When he starts to hate my paintings and me his books, and his custard curdles and he turns to Bird's for help and a quickie, there is nothing to be done about it.

Meanwhile . . . the future. Would we ever live together? Yes, no, maybe, but in two separate houses. The way he brushes his teeth might start to annoy me; the extra knot he always ties in his laces. Let's not begin with what might annoy him – remember Thom?

It doesn't matter – you see, the major contract I've already made, the deal signed with a flourish, to Hope with love always, Hope the Goddess. This was the point, what the exploration of my heart of darkness alone procured. This is the happy ending. I've found it inside myself, content until the next adventure.

Which one is that?

The walk across the Kalahari Desert with a camel, six months living with the IK tribe in Africa, the swim across the Channel on a dolphin, the affair with Donald Trump – no, don't be ridiculous. But one thing I've always wanted to do is . . .

Oh, my! My exciting life.

Rosie Meadows regrets . . .

Catherine Alliott

Well, what could I say? If he was smitten then I could be too, and I sank back into the whole cosy relationship with a monumental sigh of relief. I didn't have to try too hard, didn't have to be too witty, too amusing, too beautiful . . . It was like landing on a feather mattress after all those years of being Out There.

Three years down the line, however, Rosie's beginning to think that 'cosy' isn't all it's cracked up to be. Bridge parties have never really been her thing, and it would be nice to feel beautiful just once in a while. Enough is enough. It's time to get her life back.

'Alliott's *joie de vivre* is irresistible' *Daily Mail*

'Hilarious and full of surprises' *Daily Telegraph*

'A joy . . . you're in for a treat' *Express*

0 7472 5786 8

HEADLINE

Suddenly Single

Sheila O'Flanagan

What do you do when you find yourself suddenly single?

Go suddenly suicidal?

Suddenly sex-crazed?

Or simply collapse in self-pity?

Alix Callaghan, who thought she was in control of her work-packed life, feels like doing all three when her long-term boyfriend insists on settling down to a sensible existence – complete with children, proper meals and early nights – but without her.

Though motherhood is the last thing on her mind, losing Paul hurts more than Alix will ever admit – especially to herself.

Now, with the men at the office eyeing up her job, not to mention the discovery of her first grey hair, she's beginning to wonder if being single again is all it's cracked up to be . . .

'Sparkling and inspiring . . . a must for the contemporary woman' *Ireland on Sunday*

'Fabulous . . . thoroughly enjoyable' *RTÉ*

'A rattling good read' *U Magazine*

0 7472 6236 5

HEADLINE

If you enjoyed this book here is a selection of other bestselling titles from Headline